ALSO BY TAYLOR BROWN

Wingwalkers

Pride of Eden

Gods of Howl Mountain

The River of Kings

Fallen Land

In the Season of Blood and Gold

REDNECKS

REDNECKS

TAYLOR BROWN

ST. MARTIN'S PRESS
NEW YORK

First published in the United States by St. Martin's Press, an imprint of St. Martin's Publishing Group

REDNECKS. Copyright © 2024 by Taylor Brown. All rights reserved. Printed in the United States of America. For information, address St. Martin's Publishing Group, 120 Broadway, New York, NY 10271.

www.stmartins.com

Map by Taylor Brown

Design by Jonathan Bennett

The Library of Congress Cataloging-in-Publication Data is available upon request.

ISBN 978-1-250-32933-2 (hardcover)
ISBN 978-1-250-32934-9 (ebook)

Our books may be purchased in bulk for promotional, educational, or business use. Please contact your local bookseller or the Macmillan Corporate and Premium Sales Department at 1-800-221-7945, extension 5442, or by email at MacmillanSpecialMarkets@macmillan.com.

First Edition: 2024

10 9 8 7 6 5 4 3 2 1

DEDICATION

To Jason Frye, son of Logan County, West Virginia, who asked the fateful question: "Do you know where the term 'redneck' really comes from?"

Thank you for bringing me the stories of Blair Mountain, and so much more.

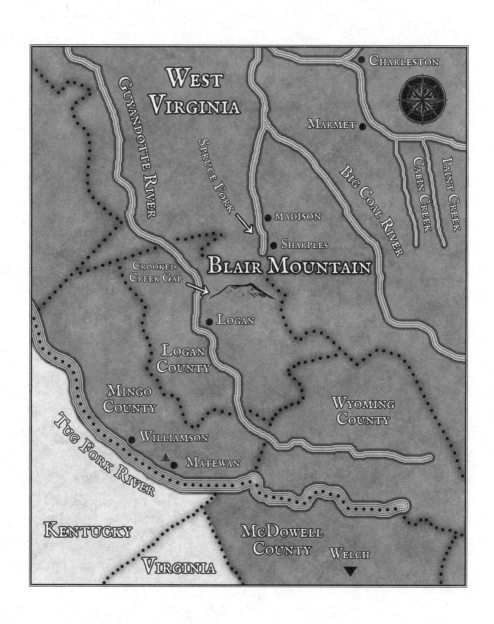

I'm not a humanitarian, I'm a hell-raiser.
—Mother Jones

—

I reckon you thought I had horns.
—Sid Hatfield

PROLOGUE

THEY WORK BENEATH THE pale flames of carbide headlamps. Some swing picks into the face, hewing the coal straight from the seam, while others shovel the black rubble into iron carts. All crouch like boxers in this shoulder-high chamber, which they call a room. They work dark to dark in this mine, descending before daylight touches the deep, coal-camp hollers where they live and surfacing ten hours later, soot-faced as chimney sweeps, the last glow of dusk to greet them.

The mine cars are drawn to the surface by mules born underground, animals who only know darkness, like some cave species, pulling their trains of coal through swinging trapdoors attended by ten-year-old boys who curse and sweet-talk them in turn. Boys they kick into the wall when they like. All breathe a black dust, explosive, which swirls through the cramped, yellowy light. The pickers and shovelers work with red bandannas knotted over their faces, the cotton black-fogged over their noses and mouths.

Perhaps it's an inadvertent spark from a miner's pick, striking an unseen shard of flint. Perhaps a pocket of methane has just been exhaled from the strata, freed after eons. The mountain erupts. A train of fire bores through the tunnels and shafts and rooms. Men are burned alive, boys buried underground. A great plume of ash blows from the mouth of the mine and rolls skyward, seen for miles.

The morning papers will read 21 KILLED IN MINE BLAST. The country will hardly register the news. Such headlines are frequent, far removed from the reading public, like earthquakes or eruptions on far sides of the world.

Outside the drift mouth, two miners lie on their bellies, heaving, their hands atop their heads. They look at each other. Red-eyed, dizzied, ears a-whine. The world blows around them, dust and smoke and red meteors of coal. Everything clad in a pale of ash, thick and wooly. Tonight the coal camp will wail with death.

One raises his head. "Told you she'd blow, ain't I? This wouldn't never happen at no Union mine. We'd have them vent shafts we asked for."

The other miner looks over his shoulder, eyes wild, as if the Devil might be standing behind them, marking their words. He hisses through his teeth: "Hush with that talk, man. You're like to get us kilt."

BOOK I
SHOOT-OUT

CHAPTER ONE

DOC MOO WAS UP at the coal camp above town, checking on an elderly patient of his, when the Baldwins came rattling up the road in a pair of tin lizzies, their rifles and shotguns prickling from the windows like hackles and spines. The doctor touched the small, three-barred Maronite cross at his throat.

"*Al'aama*," he whispered. Blindness. The same curse he used to hear his father utter in the back of their barn, swearing over a busted plow harness or olive rake on their farm in Mount Lebanon. Doctor Domit Muhanna hadn't seen his father since he set sail for America thirty years ago, at the age of fourteen, landing at the Port of New Orleans and traveling upriver on a Mississippi riverboat full of Kaintucks with long knives and short tempers—boatmen traveling home after blowing their pay in the taverns and flophouses of the French Quarter. Muhanna was headed for the University of Kentucky—a brilliant student, his family's great hope to carve a life for future generations in America.

He feared he wouldn't survive the Kaintucks and their beloved bowie knives until one of them slashed another over a galley card game and he managed to sew up the wound with catgut from one of their fiddles—suturing a skill he'd learned as a goatherd, not in any clinic, but the boatmen were well-pleased, slapping his back and pouring rotgut whiskey down his throat.

"Ought to bring ye to ever poker match so the hangman don't string us up!"

Muhanna graduated medical school and opened a practice in the feud-hot borderlands of Kentucky and West Virginia, earning a high place in the esteem of the community despite his tobacco skin. A man willing to mount his great white horse at any hour and barrel through the country darkness to attend to childbirths and hemorrhages and hysterias on both sides of the

Tug Fork River, fevers and gunshot wounds and the black-bloody lungs that came with years in the mines, sucking coal dust underground. Some people said he'd saved more Hatfields and McCoys than Jesus Christ—others said that wasn't but poorly few.

Now his patient, Miss Beulah, patted his arm. She didn't know Arabic, but she could tell a swear when she heard one. "Don't cuss 'em just yet, Doctor Moo." She cut her eyes at the Baldwins getting out of their cars. "Best wait till the thugs can hear you do it."

Miss Beulah had been born in Georgia sometime around 1850. She didn't know her exact age, but she'd got her blood the same year the War Between the States blew the country wide open and a whole bunch of men and women and children with it. People thought the Mason and Dixon line was some kind of sharp divide, like it was made with a captain-man's saber, but there wasn't a thing sharp and clean about it. It was more like somebody had blown them free with dynamite. Sherman had come through and burned their cabins to the ground alongside the big house and the gin house and the cotton cribs, and soon enough it was the whitecaps and Ku Kluxers night-riding through the land on their white-hooded horses, slinging their ropes and fire like hell on parade.

She and her husband came up to West Virginny in 1880 for him to work in the coal mines opening on the backs of the railroads carved through these mountains. Hellish work down there in the mines and these shabby company towns with their paper-thin houses and tin-scrip money and black dust that got everywhere, all the time—up your nostrils and between your toes. Every man jack of the miners, no matter his skin, came home looking dark as those ancestors of hers when they first stepped off the slaver's boat. Her husband had died of the miner's asthma in 1900 and she spent her days now on this little porch of her grandboy's cabin doing sitting-work, darning socks and quilting blankets, her feet swole up like pink-brown piglets beneath her rocker. The dropsy, what it was. The nice Doctor Moo came to give them a draining once every week.

Her eyes had been clouding these last few years, but she knew Baldwins when she saw them. They weren't but thugs, petting their oil-slick rifles like skinny little girls. Her grandboy Big Frank had gone to the Great War himself carrying such a gun. People said it was safer to serve Uncle Sam over there than King Coal back home. A statistical fact, that. Now she leaned and rang the spittoon beside her, gripping her rocker's arms hard enough the old chair crackled beneath her.

"Strength, Jesus," she said. "Strength for this ole tongue."

The gun thugs came strutting stiff-legged up to her house first. She figured they would. Their fine town shoes squelching in the muck. Above them, above the sooty roofs of the coal cabins and the steep dark sides of the holler, so steep the trees grew nearly lying down, big clouds of mist held sway. *Rain soon,* she thought. The head thug snapped his fingers like she was a dog. She knew who it was. One of the three Felts brothers who lawed for P. J. Smith who ran the Stone Mountain Mine that owned the houses and the store and the church and thought it owned them.

"Beulah Hugham," he said, reading from a list in his hand. "That you?"

"Miss Beulah to you. I seen that mug of your'n up here not a month back."

"I'm Special Agent Albert Felts of the Baldwin-Felts Detective Agency. The lessee of this house, Mr. Frank Hugham, has been terminated from his employ in consequence of joining the United Mine Workers of America labor organization. We're here to carry out the eviction."

Behind him, agents were already going to other houses, knocking on doors, using skeleton keys if no one was home. They were coming out with chairs and pictures and folded quilts, stacking them on the side of the street.

"Hell you is," said Miss Beulah.

"Excuse me?"

"Special agent, hell. You ain't got a lick of authority outside that gun on your belt. I ain't coming off this porch without some real law making me."

Felts took a step closer. "We'll see about that."

Doc Moo held up his hand. "Now hold on here, Agent Felts. Mr. Frank Hugham has already vacated. He moved to the Union camp up on Lick Creek last month. But Miss Beulah here is in no condition to be living up there in one of those canvas tents, all but out of doors. I already cleared this exception with Mr. Smith, the mine superintendent."

Since the start of the year, many of the county's miners had joined the United Mine Workers of America labor union. The coal companies had responded with mass firings and evictions. For weeks, the ousted families had been living in tents outside town. Men, women, children, pets, livestock. A few refused to leave home, too old, sick, or stubborn to budge.

The chubby-cheeked agent next to Felts shook his head. "Smells like bull to me, Boss."

Felts looked around, sniffed. "What doesn't?" Then to Doc Moo: "There will be no more exceptions starting today, Doctor, by order of the Baldwin-Felts."

Felts jerked his head to the other men, who palmed their belted pistols and started for the porch. Doctor Muhanna stepped in front of them, his heart firing rapidly in his chest. "This woman is a patient of mine, and this eviction is illegal. I want to see a court order."

In a flash, the blue-black gleam of a pistol in Felts's hand. "Here you go, Doc. See it here? Now, if you want a special dispensation for the old lady, you can ride your tan ass on up to the mine office and get yourself one. Till then, you stay out of our way lest you want to see how well you can stitch up holes in your own belly."

Moo gritted his teeth and knelt down beside the old woman. "I'll be back quick as I can, Miss B."

Miss Beulah patted his arm and leaned to his ear, her voice hot in his ear. "Nothing but thugs. Got-damned thugs, the lot of them. Don't strain nothing for them."

"Yes, ma'am."

Doc Moo was halfway to the mine office, hiking the rough road in his riding boots, when he heard shrieks and curses behind him. He looked back in time to see the agents lifting Miss Beulah from her porch in her rocking chair, hoisting her high on their shoulders like a queen or lady of renown, then setting her down in the middle of the muddy street, where she cursed and swung her gnarled fists at them.

"*Allah Yakhidkoun*," he hissed.

God take your souls.

CHAPTER TWO

SMILIN' SID HATFIELD, KIN to Devil Anse, stood on the plank porch of the hardware store, his palms set casual over the curved handles of his double-action revolvers. He was the tenth child of twelve. One of nine who survived. The badge over his heart read MATEWAN POLICE, with the number "1" stamped between an eagle's wings.

Chief.

His head was shaved high over his ears, his hair grown spiky from the crown of his skull. His tie was wide and flat and short, decorated with paisleys. People called him "Smilin' Sid" on account of the gold caps on his teeth, which flashed whenever he smiled, which was all the time. A gold metal smile, loved and feared. Folks said he was cut from the same stump as old Devil Anse himself, patriarch of the Hatfield clan, who lived in a bulletproof log fort not ten miles from Matewan, his beard grown long and gray as a wizard's.

Sid cocked his head. Thirteen men stood in the street before him. Men from the Baldwin-Felts Detective Agency. Mine guards. Gun thugs. Hard-faced men in city-cut suits, who thought they were the law here in the Tug Valley, where the railroads had come boring through the mountains at the turn of the century and coal became king.

Here, four of five towns were coal camps, company towns that smoked from the hillsides, and miners worked ten hours per day, six and one-half days per week, paid forty cents for each long ton of coal they blew, picked, and shoveled out of the sunless dark of the mines, where collapse and explosion and sickness lurked. A land where any attempt to organize, to join a union for better pay or safer conditions, was met with these men in the street.

The Baldwin-Felts, hired guns of King Coal.

Some of them cradled self-loading rifles disguised in butcher paper, like cruel bouquets. Others held their gun-hands inside their coats like upstart

Napoleons, thumbing the hammers of their pistols. They pushed their bellies with pride against their belts.

Sid smiled back at them, showing them the raw blade of his teeth.

They'd built themselves an ironclad automobile for use in the silver mines out west, using it to machine-gun striking miners as they huddled in trenches dug beneath the duckboard floors of their canvas tents. The *Death Special*, they called it. A girl was shot in the face, a boy shot nine times in one leg. For West Virginia, they'd built the *Bull Moose Special*, an armored locomotive that steamed past a strikers' tent colony up on Paint Creek in '13 with machine guns ablaze, blasting the brains of a well-loved miner across the walls of his frame house.

Now they'd come to Matewan.

Mingo County, West Virginia.

Sid's town.

That morning, they'd gone up to the coal camp above town and thrown out the families of every miner who'd joined the Union. While the men were at work underground, they'd forced out the wives and children at gunpoint, piled their belongings in the road, and barred the doors behind them. Quilts and kettles and hobbyhorses were hurled out into the rain, cane chairs and hanging mirrors and old war uniforms—anything the company didn't own.

Now they'd come for Sid.

Days back, their leader, Albert Felts, had offered him one thousand dollars to mount machine guns on the town rooftops—enough cash-money to buy three Ford motorcars fresh off the lot. Sid had smiled at Felts and told him what he could do with his machine guns, where he ought to insert them. The man didn't seem to understand that you could buy a whole valley, but not the people who lived in it.

Now Felts stepped forward from his bunch, holding out a writ. "We got us a warrant here for your arrest, Hatfield. You're gonna have to come back to Bluefield on the train with us."

Sid kept smiling. "Say I am, Albert?"

Past the man, not one hundred yards from where they stood, ran the heavy green water of the Tug Fork River, which divided West Virginia from Kentucky. In this borderland, Sid's ancestors had warred with the McCoy clan for thirty years before his birth. Hatfields had splashed back and forth across the Tug Fork in midnight posses and raiding parties, revolvers thumping against their thighs, shotguns slung across their backs on strings and ropes. Men of his blood had tied McCoys to pawpaw bushes and shot them to pieces. They'd set fire to McCoy cabins in dead of winter so that McCoy children went barefoot in the snow.

Sid had come up on a tenant farm just across the river. As a teen, he'd wielded a pickax and blasting powder in the mines, back-bent in those squarish caverns of rock eons beneath the earth where blackdamp could choke a man to death and firedamp blow him to kingdom come. Friends of his had been killed in roof falls and blasting accidents; he'd seen boys not ten years from their mamas' bellies with their fingers sheared off in coal conveyors— one squashed dead beneath the wheels of a mine car. A sight you never unsaw.

His hands were black-seamed from the mines, cuts and blisters healed with coal dust under the skin, as if tattooed. He'd worked as a smithy's striker, too, swinging a sledgehammer onto an anvil again and again, pounding shapes from that glowing iron, dousing red-hot horseshoes and plow blades in bubbling cauldrons of quench water. Policing was the first trade in which his face wasn't blacked with dirt or coal or soot, only his eyes and teeth to show.

"That's right," said Felts, cocking his head, his dozen thugs spread widelegged behind him. "We're taking you back to Bluefield in cuffs."

A warmth at Sid's hips. His shooting irons turning hot in their holsters, same as always before a fracas, as if they recalled the hell in which they'd been born. The red iron, liquid, hammered into the die. He looked from man to man of the Baldwin bunch. They were beginning to shift their weight from foot to foot before him, twitching their noses and tapping their fingers, wondering why he was still smiling.

Sid had dug the black veins of West Virginia coal that made the companies rich that hired these men. Money that could buy mansions on the shores of cold clear lakes and twelve-cylinder Italian automobiles and murder in muddy streets behind the gleaming badges of private detective agencies. Coal money, God-strong in Mingo County. Sid smiled because he was risen from the mud of this place, born to meet such men in the street.

The mayor, standing beside him, squinted at the warrant the Baldwin-Felts had produced. A misty rain was falling now, slanted and feathery, tickling the shoulders of the agents' suits. Tiny bright pearls in the wool. Sid knew these men had warred for their country in trenched hells of mud, killing Krauts with machine guns and hand grenades and trench knives. He also knew they were aliens in this place, in these jagged dark shadows between the hills of his birth. He stepped slightly back into the door frame, feeling the darkness drip down his face.

He could be happy-go-lucky Sid, devil-may-care Sid, the Sid who didn't but shoot pool and play poker and run around with the other young men, chasing bucks and gobblers and big brownie bass. But these Baldwins, they just wouldn't learn. They had to come here and throw his people out their homes without the due process of law. They had to hurl their family heirlooms and hard-bought belongings in the muck like a bunch of trash.

They had to put an old woman out in the rain.

There was the law of the courts, Sid knew, and the law that was older, deeper, which even the littlest trapper boy in the mines knew in his born heart. Which even that boy's greatest granddaddies had known ten generations back, in whatever highland or desert or forest raised them. There were some people these days who'd chosen to forget that older law, but only because they could. Because somebody had done away with their Baldwins for them, put them in prison cells or pinewood overcoats.

Not a month ago, this same bunch had been arrested for this same crime. Albert Felts had leered at the arresting deputy over a mine office desk covered in guns of every caliber and description. Large-frame revolvers and sleek automatics, bull-nosed shotguns and high-powered rifles with telescopic sights—the latest in handheld firepower. "Know this, I'll break the unions of the Tug Valley if I have to send one hundred more men to hell."

Here he was again, still cock-lording about, no matter his late arrest. A man irreformable, it seemed. The Baldwins had the coal operators on their side, which meant the judges, the politicians, and half the high sheriffs of the state. But Sid knew that wasn't the root of the problem, the real reason they kept coming back. The reason they could. It wasn't something they had on their side. It was something they lacked.

Fear.

They didn't know this county had been called Bloody Mingo long before the companies came to unbury the coal kept deep in the guts of the hills and send it forth in mile-long trains of dark rubble to light the boilers of ships and trains, steel factories and power plants. A land of fracture and feud, where men of the same family fought on different sides of uncivil wars and bands of marauders roved the hills since the days of scrape-fires and cap-shooters and a man had to be willing to kill and die to earn any single inch of respect.

They didn't know where they were. In whose valley they walked.

It wasn't a thing that could be told.

Someone had to show them.

Sid never took the wearing of the badge lightly. It made the whole town his family, his kin. Here in the Tug, lawing meant swinging fists and wrestling down drunks, raising ax handles and sometimes a gun. It meant sacrifice. A lot of people thought dying for something was the biggest sacrifice of all. Like Christ. But Sid knew there was something more than that. Something he'd learned from Devil Anse himself. They all had. A man didn't just have to be willing to die for his kin, but to burn in Hell.

To damn himself.

In the distance, the whistle of the 5:15 train, carrying the promise of arrest warrants for the Baldwins from the county seat. Mayor Cabell looked up from the writ. "You got to be shitting me, Felts. This arrest warrant is bogus."

Sid knew it would be. He leaned back farther into the shadow of the hardware store, feeling the darkness paint his cheeks, run down his neck. The butts of his pistols glowed like skillet handles beneath his palms.

"You'd better wrote that warr'nt on a ginger snap," said a listening miner, spitting in the road. "So ye could eat it."

The detectives in the street smiled, hard-faced, like it was all a joke. Then Albert Felts reached into his coat—or so Sid would tell the jury later. Albert Felts, who'd boasted he would break the unions of West Virginia if he had to send a hundred more men to Hell.

He would go first.

Sid's pistols leapt from his belt. He shot Albert Felts in the head, a halo of spray. The other agents dropped to shooting positions, drawing their guns to return fire, but the rifles of hidden miners cracked from trees and bushes and windows like a dam breaking. Like Sid knew they would. The Baldwins were sent tumbling and screaming, dying in the street. They turned tail and fled, and Sid stepped down from the porch and walked after them, his pistols barking again and again at the ends of his hands, like the barking mouths of dogs.

CHAPTER THREE

DOC MOO WAS HELPING load the mule-cart with the last of Miss Beulah's belongings, lashing them in place for the rough journey up to the Lick Creek tent colony above town. Her grandson Frank had brought the borrowed cart down from the camp, where the Union kept it handy to assist with evictions. He was a burly man, a coal hewer known for his strength in the mines, slinging a sharpened pick into the raw belly of a coalface hundreds of times each day, tearing the black guts from the earth. Not tall but wide, built like a fireplug. His muscles bucked beneath his loose cotton shirt.

"You ain't got to stay, Doc. I got this."

His wife, Evie, had been the teacher at the coal camp's colored school, well-respected in the local community. But she'd contracted the flu during the Great Influenza of 1918, during the deadly second wave of the epidemic late that year, and Doc Moo had been all but helpless as the secondary lung infection—pneumonia—starved her body of oxygen, as it had so many millions that year. A pair of dark blotches appeared on her cheekbones and then crept into her fingers, toes, nose, ears—*heliotrope cyanosis*, the purplish-blue coloration of dying tissue. Frank and Doc Moo had been sitting on either side of her bed the night she'd died.

Now the doctor shook his head, tightening a knot. "Least I can do. I just wish I could've stopped them. I shouldn't have left to go up to the super's office."

Miss Beulah looked down at the doctor. "Don't you go double-guessing what you done, Doctor Moo. No way them thugs was going to let me alone, no matter what you said."

She was sitting up on the wagon seat, her swollen feet propped on the footboard, her rocking chair lashed upside down on top of some packing crates in the bed. Up the dirt street, other families were loading their possessions onto carts or wagons, errant towers of chairs and tables and cookpots, candleholders and milk crates and rumpled bedding. A woman was weeping in Italian, trying to pick seeds from the mud—heirloom parsley and beans from the Old Country, which the Baldwins had cast out.

Miss Beulah jutted her chin at the mule standing patiently in the traces, sucking her teeth. "Fact is, we ain't but brutes to them, Doctor. There's the crux of it. No more'n beasts of burden for King Coal. My husband was working a drift mine in Pike County back in niney-nine and the foreman had him put iron helmets on the driving mules cause he was afraid of a collapse. Husband asked why the miners didn't get helmets, too. Foreman said, 'Kill a man and we can hire another. But you got to buy the mule.'" She shook her head. "If that's how the foreman thinks, imagine the gun thugs. They was on a mission to turn us out today and not a thing in this world was like to stop them. Not you nor me nor they own mamas if they was there. Onliest thing them thugs seem to understand is the pointy end of a gun."

Frank nodded from the other side of the cart, his big arms snapping tight a knot. "Maybe that's how we ought to be talking to them, then."

Miss Beulah snapped her head around at him. "The hell we ought, boy. I don't want to hear none of that talk, specially not in front of the doctor. A healing man."

Frank held up his hands like the old woman was pointing a gun at him. "Sorry, Mama-B. Not every day a man's got to swallow his grandmama getting throwed out in the rain."

Miss Beulah clucked. "Try being the grandmama."

Now she opened the large sack of wares on her lap, rummaging with one hand. "Here now, Doctor, I almost forgot I had something for you today. For that boy of your'n. Them thugs 'bout made me forget." She unfolded a patchwork bag with a single thick shoulder strap. "What we have here's a possibles bag, Doctor. Just like the frontiersmen used to carry slung over one shoulder. You said your boy got some ridge runner in him, would rather traipse about them woods than sit in a schoolhouse. Well, there's worse things, in my experience. But when he goes a-traipsing he better have a bag to hold his possibles, whatever he might need if these hills try and catch him out. Fire-striker and tinderbox, compass and cup and fishing hooks, candle stump and edibles and punkie dope. All he might need. Kept in one bag so it's always there."

Doc Moo took the bag from her, spreading it between his hands. It was perfect for his son, Musa, whose heroes were woodsmen like Davy Crockett and Daniel Boone and Kit Carson—deadeye scouts and rangers who'd worn animal skins and slept under the stars most nights, or so the dime novels told it.

"Miss Beulah, you didn't have to do this. Musa will love it."

"Least an old woman can do. Got to pay you some way for coming up here out your way. Now it might be patchwork, but she's double-stitched with denim gussets. Like to see somebody less than John Henry rip it sunder."

Doc Moo slung the bag over his own shoulder, trying it on. There was even a buckle to adjust the length of the strap. "His mother and I will feel better knowing he's got what he needs when he heads off in the woods."

Miss Beulah nodded. "I might not have growed up in these hills, but I learnt enough in my day to know you best respect them. They got everything you need to survive and double what you don't, specially these days. Used to be you just had your cold air, your rattler snakes, your panther cats. Now you got your Baldwins and blockaders crawling around ever damn street and crick." She sucked her teeth, squinting at the steep green sides of the holler, the heavy mist. "Rather have them old she-bears and catamounts still around stead of these damn thugs think they own the place."

"Amen," said Frank, coming around the cart to Doc Moo. "We best be getting on, free up the cart for the next family." He never blamed the doctor for the death of his wife, but there'd been a heaviness between them ever since. A mountain of trauma, unspoken.

Now he held out his hand, looking Doc Moo in the eye. "Thank you again, Doc."

"You're welcome."

The big man climbed up next to Miss Beulah and slapped the reins. Doc Moo waved to them as the cart went rumbling up the rough dirt street, passing between the close rows of coal-camp houses. Frank's mother had died in childbirth, he knew, and Miss Beulah had raised the boy after his father—her son—had disappeared, some said at the hands of Baldwin thugs, though no body was ever found. Now they sat side by side on the wagon seat. Big man and little lady, but with something of the same shape to them, the rake of their shoulders.

They'd just passed into the mists above the camp, becoming hardly more than shadows, vanishing, when Doc heard the first pop from the direction of town—a single pistol shot, like the first rivet or button popping from a seam, and then the rest of them broke loose from the valley floor, busting like a hundred sutures from a wound.

He swung into the saddle and steered his horse for town, heeling him for speed.

CHAPTER FOUR

MEN LAY DEAD IN the street, slathered in mud. Sid looked at them. No longer men. Bodies and rags, the ghosts blown from their flesh. Their limbs flung helter-skelter, their brains dark as mine shafts. The wet heavens pelted them without regard. Same as the quilts and crockery they'd hurled into the muddy streets earlier that day. The broken chairs and cracked mirrors and patchwork coats, the ridey-horses and play-pretties and dolly-rags. Meanwhile, several more men quivered or moaned or shrieked from their wounds. Snakes of blood spooling out of them, coiling red-bright under the gray sky, slithering among the discarded guns and hats and bags.

Sid's pistols were still hot, smoking slightly, like smithy's irons just quenched in the tank. His hat had been shot from his head, lifted light as a bird—a finger-size hole in the crown. He'd chased down one of the detectives and shot him dead in the post office. A fourteen-year-old bystander lay by the railroad tracks, gun-killed. Tot, his name. Several of the detectives had escaped, possibly wounded. Shots in the distance.

Sid replaced his hat and took a step back, looking toward the swinging bridge over the Tug Fork River, which crossed the state line into Kentucky. A border his people had crossed so many times over the years, wading or swimming or fording the river on horseback, midnight errands of love or fun or vengeance. A border they still crossed daily for work or well-water or whiskey from the Blue Goose saloon on the Kentucky side. Some of the miners were shooting down into the water, trying to hit the last of the Baldwins swimming toward the far shore.

Sid set his guns back in their leathers and stood over the body of Albert Felts as the street puddles quivered with the arrival of the 5:15 train out of the county seat. Felts was staring up at the drizzling gray sky, flecks of moisture beading over his still-open eyes. He was the only one of the bunch with any legal authority. A deputy's commission from an antiunion county—the kind handed out like penny candy in certain jurisdictions. A worm of blood had crawled out of the hole in his forehead and rolled down his nose, sliding beneath his right eye like a tear. A ragged crown of blood and brain matter seeped from the back of his skull.

Sid squatted down beside him, resting his metal teeth on his bottom lip. He glanced down. "Got ye a lot of brains for a fool, Albert."

Around him, miners were venturing forth from doorways and alleys, climbing down from roofs and tiptoeing onto Mate Street. Their backs hunched, their rifles still tucked to their shoulders. Behind them, dazed townsfolk stared at the bodies or touched the bullet holes in brick storefronts or shop windows. A woman screamed. Sid followed the sound around a corner. Bloody handprints on the wall and the mayor lying bull-necked in his bowtie, holding his bleeding abdomen.

He looked up at Sid. "They shot me, Sid. I think I'm dying."

"The hell you are, Cabell." Sid knelt down in the mud and latched his hands on top of the wound, applying pressure. The mayor was a friend of his, a chunk of a man married to the sweetest, prettiest woman in all the Tug Valley, Jessie Maynard, who had bold dark eyes and always called him *Sidney*.

The blood was pulsing from the wound, coming up dark between Sid's fingers. He raised his head. "Somebody get Doc Moo!"

He'd hardly said it when he heard hooves and looked up to see the doctor galloping down the street. The man leapt down from his horse and handed off the reins. "I heard the shots from the mine and came as quickly as I could." He dropped to his knees beside the mayor and tore off his white cotton shirt, popping the buttons, folding it sleeve over sleeve to stanch the wound.

Cabell's blood had begun pumping blackish from his belly, pulsing like Texas crude. Sid and Doc Moo looked at each other. Liver-shot, they knew. Moo gave a grim shake of the head.

No chance.

Sid blinked, his eyes deep-set in his skull. A wet sting in those dark coves, strange to him. He blinked it back and looked down at Cabell.

The man's mouth was open. "They shot me, Sid. How come they shot me?" His pupils were wide as wells, the light spilling out. Sid placed his free hand on Cabell's head, awkward-like. Like he was checking the temperature of a schoolboy. "Because they're sons of bitches, Cabell. But they're in Hell now. Burning this minute. Sent down as many as we could."

"Will I go down with them?"

"Hell, no, Cabell. You got a big kingdom waiting on you. Ain't one thug in the whole damn place."

They loaded the mayor onto the No. 16 train bound for Welch and the state hospital there—the same train the Baldwins had planned to take. Jessie and several others accompanied the dying man. She looked to Sid as she boarded the train, her dress bloodied in the fading light. She nodded to him, as if to say he'd done right putting those Baldwins down, no matter the cost.

Her dark eyes bored into him, same as they did during their long twilight walks along the Tug when the mayor had to be out of town on business and trusted Sid as his close friend and chief of police to keep his wife company. Evenings when the swells of her flesh moved beneath the thin cotton of her dress and a silver sheen of perspiration shone in the well of her throat and the dark green river burned like madness beneath the rising moon. Even now, Sid could feel his blood roving toward her, rising like a pistol.

One of the miners stood beside him as the mayor's train chuffed out of town. "That poor wife of his. Girl-bride to gun-widow. She'll be lonesome now."

Sid said nothing. He was still thinking of her, the dark sparking of her eyes in the dusk. Maybe the prettiest thing he ever saw.

CHAPTER FIVE

NIGHTFALL. MATEWAN WAS HAUNTED, the streets heavy with dread. Fear floated in the very atmosphere—Doc Moo could almost taste it, like bile on the back of his tongue. He'd overseen the laying out of the bodies on spare doors from the hardware store, readying them for the No. 7 train bound for the county seat. Their hands folded across their chests, their hats set over their faces. He'd had to chase away some of the town's little runarounds who dared one another to run up and spit on the corpses or steal their hats.

Seven detectives lay dead, including two of the three Felts brothers, along with two miners, one a teenager. The mayor would die before the night was out. At least ten killed. If Doc Moo wasn't mistaken, that made Matewan the bloodiest shoot-out in American history to date, even bloodier than the gunfight at the O.K. Corral or any of the others he'd read about in *Wild West Weekly*—one of his son's magazine subscriptions, which Moo read at the kitchen table when he couldn't sleep.

Worse, more violence might be boring toward them. Rumor had another gang of enforcers en route from the Baldwin-Felts headquarters. A kill squad. Whispers came floating down the dark streets, jumping from mouth to mouth:

It's another bunch comin' on the night train, armed with submachine guns.
Tom Felts himself leading them, brung the coldest mothers he's got.
He's like to be in a revenging mood, his two brothers laid out.

Doc Moo stood on the platform as the westbound train chugged out of town, carrying off the corpses. He was in his undershirt, with blood dried crusty along his arms and Musa's possibles bag looped over his shoulder.

Some people thought of doctors as prim men in offices who hardly touched people except with palpating fingertips and stethoscopes. But his own father had fought in a Christian cavalry unit during the 1860 civil war in Mount Lebanon and the Beqaa Valley, when the Maronite peasantry rose up against the Druze lords, and he'd seen the work of the battle surgeons firsthand—men who sawed through the bones of shrieking soldiers and dropped their gangrenous limbs in bloody buckets, just as their comrades were doing in America at the very same time.

His father had gone to war carrying a double-barreled shotgun with rabbit-ear triggers, long as a broadsword, and a fat scimitar on his belt, riding out from the mountain village of Hadath al-Jebbeh, where the family had roots going back to the 1100s. It overlooked the Qadisha Valley—the valley of the saints—a land of steep stone cliffs and mountain caves, which had sheltered Christian mystics and monasteries for centuries.

As a boy, Doc Moo had stared for hours at the ancient daguerreotype of his father as a high-chinned young horseman, posing between two other men with broad black mustaches and crossed bandoliers, their billowy pantaloons tucked into knee-high riding boots. Later, the man had been tasked an assistant in the medical corps due to the crude veterinary skills he'd learned on the farm.

"Physicians are respected in every country and culture of the world," he'd told his son. "Because of their learning and the lives they save, yes, but also the blood, disease, and death they daily face."

So, even as a boy, Doc Moo had known the dark valleys into which the path of medicine might lead him. It already had. He'd come to the Tug Valley at the invitation of a distant relative, Mr. Youssef Khoury, an early peddler who'd walked the backroads selling wares and sharpening knives, then opened a dry goods store in Williamson around 1900. Wheeling, in the north of the state, had a Maronite population of three hundred and a Maronite Catholic church—one of the only such churches in the country. Khoury hoped to build a similar community.

Doc Moo, as a young physician, had found as brutal a world as he could imagine, a land torn bloody on the backs of the railroads and coal mines. Injuries of incredible violence, horrific as battle wounds, and a feudist mindset that hadn't quite vanished with the end of the Hatfield-McCoy War. Though Khoury passed away not long after Moo's arrival, the man's reputation paved his entry into the community. Many of the miners distrusted the company doctors, who seemed more interested in the health of the company than the worker—so Moo was busy from the start, and the blood never ceased, running like the Tug itself.

Now he looked out at the ridges above town, high and bluish in the night, hissing with cicadas. The town of Matewan seemed so small in comparison, a cluster of brick and clapboard buildings crouched along the river.

On nights like these, Moo could squint his eyes and imagine the surrounding hills as the enormous swells of a great dark sea, the town floating like a raft amid those angry waters, and he thought of the night his New Orleans–bound steamer had run into a storm off Cuba. The hull of the ship groaned and thundered, the decks heaving, and he pulled himself green-faced to a porthole to find lightning flickering across vast mountains of seawater, their peaks risen white-capped, threatening to roll and smash the vessel.

"Doc?"

Moo started, turning to find Sid beside him. The young police chief thumbed up the brim of his bullet-shot hat. "Ain't meant to sneak up on ye, Doc. Not the night for it, I don't reckon." Sid squinted up at the ridges above town. "I just wished to thank you for what you done for Cabell today."

Doc Moo nodded. "I only wish there was more I could do. At least the morphine will have eased his final hours some."

Sid shook his head. "Gutshot." His teeth flashed in grimace. "You seen a worser way for a man to go down?"

Doc Moo thought of the breech births he'd attended, women shrieking in one-room cabins, hemorrhaging, bleeding to death while six or eight or ten children huddled in the barn or corn crib.

"Not for a man," he said.

Sid's temples flickered and he looked up the dark railroad tracks. He was quiet for a time, his jaw muscles working. "Might could be a second fracas coming down the line. Got it on good authority Tom Felts boarded the train in Bluefield with a whole gang of thugs." He turned to the doctor. "Think you could stick around case we get any more wounded?"

Doc Moo nodded. "Already planning on it."

Sid patted his arm and looked back up the tracks. "Thank ye, Doc."

Doc Moo left the chief at the station and walked back down Mate Street, hailing one of the town's young barefoots. He paid the boy a dime to run the news home that he wouldn't be back till dawn. "Don't tell them what's happened down here," he said. "I don't want them worrying all night over it."

"Yes, sir," said the boy. He looked down at his bare feet a moment. "But it was a lot of shooting, Doctor Moo. They might could of heard it even up there at your place. What if Missus Moo asks me 'bout it?"

"Tell her the truth if she asks. But leave out the part about this new squad coming in on the night train." He looked to the spot where the corpses had been laid out. "Just tell her we have grievous injuries down here."

"Grievous," said the boy, nodding, committing the word. "Grievous, yes, sir."

Buddeea, his wife, wouldn't be pleased to be kept out of the loop, but he'd rather endure her anger than give her another sleepless night—God knew she'd had plenty given his trade. She was tough—tougher than he was, probably. Tough enough to defy her strict Maronite father when he threatened to send her back to the Beqaa Valley if she tried to marry the young doctor she'd met at his tailor shop in Louisville—despite the fact that the young man was, by blood and confirmation both, a good Maronite. A member of the same Eastern Catholic church, in full communion with the Holy See. He said she wasn't ready to marry yet.

At seventeen years old, in a country still foreign to her, Buddeea had climbed out of her bedroom window, descended to the street by a rope, and eloped on horseback with that young doctor. She'd worked as his nurse before their first child was born, becoming no stranger to blood. Still, Moo would rather she saved her strength for what could be headed their way.

He unhitched his white gelding, Altair—"flying eagle" in Arabic—and led him down Mate Street, stabling him safely at the town livery. The horse was his one extravagance—a lordly charger, sixteen hands tall, ever ready to ford rivers and thunder through the night.

"You'll be safe here," he told the horse, filling a sack of oats.

Altair snorted, unhappy to be left out of the action.

When Moo got back, Sid and a local sheriff were standing side by side at the edge of the tracks, deputizing a long line of miners and townsmen, each holding his hat in his hands as he took the oath. Meanwhile, Ed Chambers from Chambers' Hardware handed out rifles and the ladies from the Dew Drop Inn ladled supper out of a big pot.

Moo stopped in at his office, where he cleaned the dried blood from his hands and arms, watching the liver-dark threads of the mayor's wound crawl down the drain. Then he changed into a clean shirt and looked at the shoulder bag on his desk.

"Possibles," he said, packing it with trauma supplies—extra [bandages], morphine ampoules, and tourniquets. Then he climbed to the [roof of the] building, where men were already posted with rifles. A heavy quiet [hung.] The station lights hovered in amber orbs of mist and the rails shone slick [as gun] barrels.

Muhanna rolled himself a cigarette—a rare indulgence—then lay flat [on his] back on the dirty cinder of the rooftop despite his clean shirt, pillowing [his] head on his black medicine bag, his hands crossed over his chest. He watched the smoke swirl upward out of his throat, climbing like prayers into the [sky.] He closed his eyes, feeling the tickle of misting rain on his cheeks.

He woke to a distant whistle. One of the miners squatted at his shoulder, rousing him. "Doctor Moo? She's roundin' the bends now."

Muhanna duckwalked to the edge of the roof and lay prone beside the miner, setting his medicine bag at his elbow. The pale eye of the midnight train came burning toward them, smoking like a meteor, the firebox roaring and the black chimney of the engine blowing fat blooms of coal-smoke between the ridges.

Miners crouched in second-story windows, behind cords of ricked fire-wood, in the forked branches of trees on the far side of the tracks. They huddled behind rooftop parapets and bulwarks of feed sacks, waiting, their hearts hammering like the single giant piston of the coming engine. Doc Moo knew they were imagining the *Bull Moose Special* with guns ablaze, wondering if some new death-bringer could be hurtling toward them, ready to tear apart their town like a team of steam-hammers. Brick dust and broken glass, blood pooling in the streets.

Sid was standing before the stationhouse, pale and lean, his face lined hard despite his scant years. He'd be first to meet the train. His palms rested on the curved butts of his pistols, patting them lightly, as if they were hot to the touch. Some folks said he could toss a potato high against the sun and split its belly with a bullet. Some said he could do it with either hand. That his fists were quick as a prizefighter's, and they shot fire.

The miner beside Doc Moo stared doe-eyed at the young police chief. He licked his lips and spoke softly, as if reciting some prayer of faith. "Let them sons of bitches come."

The midnight engine came hooting around the bend, huffing and smoking, roaring into town. Rifle barrels swung from alleys and windows and rooftops like steely antennae, following the cars, but the train never slowed, highballing

past the station at full speed. A flash of hard faces and dark hats through the windows of the passenger coach. Sid held down his hat with one hand as the train blew past. His mouth open, his metal teeth catching the station light.

"Smilin' Sid," whispered the miner. "Terror of the Tug."

The Baldwins had thought better of stopping in Matewan tonight, it seemed—or the engineer had refused. But Doc Moo feared they'd be back, and soon. Blood came of blood, and he was but one man to stanch it.

CHAPTER SIX

DOC MOO RODE HOME in the gathering dusk. Tomorrow was the first of June, just over ten days since the shoot-out, and the hills were explosive with life, sizzling with katydids and cicadas. The bats were out, wheeling and darting against the violet sky, catching insects on the wing. Moo rode loose in the saddle, weary, hardly touching the reins. Altair knew the way.

He'd been all over the county since dawn. He'd treated an aged farmer who'd cut himself sharpening a plow blade, been down to his office in Matewan for appointments with two regular patients, then came a call from a mine on the Kentucky side of the river. A twelve-year-old trapper boy had been knocked unconscious by a heavy swinging door he was tending. A boy his son's age, so concussed he couldn't remember his own name. Doc Moo expected him to recover, but he never got used to seeing boy-miners with their fingernails worked down to the bleeding quicks, their faces knotted early against the world.

He looked up into the dusk. The first silver pricks of stars. As always, the Tug Valley had been full of rumor and chatter. Word was, Sid Hatfield and Jessie Maynard, the mayor's widow, had been arrested in a Huntington hotel on charges of "improper relations"—based on a tip from Thomas Felts, who'd had his agents tail the pair.

"Improper relations!" roared the aged farmer as Doc Moo bandaged his plow-cut hand. "Done caught ole Sid with his drawers down, they did. Naked as Christ on Christmas. All he had on him was Albert Felts's pistol. A dark gun."

It was the word people used for a blued pistol as opposed to a nickeled one.

"Is that illegal?" asked Moo.

The farmer grit his teeth hard a moment, then sniggered. "Legal, Doc, I don't know. But I do know what ole Sid told them."

"What?"

"'Albert ain't asked for it back.'"

The man laughed and wheezed and laughed again. Moo often wondered how people on such isolated homesteads, high on the hillsides or deep in the hollers, always had the latest news, the stories cast mouth to mouth as if along telephone lines. His family was no different. They lived in a farmhouse above town, but there was the mail carrier, the book women, the tinkers, the pack peddlers, the neighbors—even the birds seemed to sing the news.

The farmer went on, ignoring the stitches Doc Moo was sewing into his hand. "Police hauled them off to the jailhouse, kept them there all night. Next morning, they go before the judge. Well, ole Sid, he smiles and pulls out a marriage license dated the previous day. Says they got it yesterday but couldn't find no pastor nor justice of the peace before close of business. Jessie tells the judge it was the mayor's last and final wish she marry Sid if he didn't make it. Which he did not. She asks that judge if he don't happen to know nobody willing to tie the marital knot for them? Yes, sir, that's how they come to hitch, Doctor Moo. Made things nice and proper, Sid and Jessie did, before they left that courthouse."

Moo thought of his and Buddeea's wedding. After she'd climbed out the window above her father's tailor shop, they'd ridden double through the night, leaving Louisville under cover of darkness and meeting a young Roman Catholic priest in a chapel along the Ohio River—a man Moo had enlisted into their cause, willing to marry the young Maronite lovers. One from the village of Hadath al-Jebbeh in Mount Lebanon, the other from Deir al-Ahmar in the Beqaa—come together in the New World.

They wed at dawn, as the light illuminated the mist-swathed river, and Moo had thought he could die right then, happy, with such a dark wonder of a soul bound to his. Already, at that age, Buddeea was formidable, a young woman of fierce will and spirit who seemed to whip back stronger whenever the world knocked the family sideways—and the Tug Valley could throw punches like the great John L. Sullivan, king of the pugilists. It had and it would.

Now, as Moo crested the last rise, the farmhouse came into view, the windows yellow-lit against the bluing earth. He could see Buddeea waiting for him on the porch. She was barefoot, her feet curled one on top of the other, as she watched the girls run pale-smocked around the yard, chasing fireflies. His heart swelled, his belly warmed. Those bare feet were a sign.

An unspoken language between them. Moo would not be going straight to sleep this night.

The girls—Adele, Corine, and Amelia—came running as he rode up to the house, hugging him as he descended from the saddle. Buddeea awaited her own long embrace on the porch. She stood up on her toes, burying her head in his chest.

"My Moo," she whispered.

Muhanna could smell dinner on the stove, wafting through the cracked windows of the house. After a moment, he lifted his head, looked around. "Musa?"

"Due home at dark."

They both looked west, where the last deep blue glow backlit the hills. They often joked that twelve-year-old Musa, youngest of the bunch, was their feral child. He'd strip off his school clothes as soon as he got home every afternoon and disappear into the woods in his frayed overalls—their "Little Wolf."

At school, though, he had a hard time fitting in. He was quiet, intense. It didn't help that he was darker-skinned than his sisters. The other boys teased him at times. They called him names. *Tan-assed, spawn of the Phoenician curse.* He'd bloodied their noses for such taunts, though he was more often the one who came home with bloody twists of paper rammed up his nostrils. But in the woods he was home, as natural a woodsman as any Mingo brave.

"Papa?"

Moo and Buddeea nearly jumped, whirling to find their boy standing at the other corner of the porch, barefoot, his possibles bag looped across his shoulder.

"Did you hear, Papa?"

"What?"

"The miners are gonna strike tomorrow."

Moo had heard plenty of talk of a strike coming, but tomorrow was news.

"Where did you hear that?"

The boy scratched the top of one foot with the other, biting his lip. "Come up on a copper pot off Lightning Branch. A couple of miners were talking loud, saying they told their crews not to pack no lunches for tomorrow. They'd be home by noon."

"*Musa*," said Buddeea. "I've told you to avoid those pots. Men get the devil in them on that likker."

"They didn't see me. I promise."

Moo felt his ire rising. "Of course they didn't," he said, "or you mightn't have made it back here, God forbid. Let those who want to remain unseen, unseen. Let those who want to remain unheard, unheard."

"They was talking pretty loud not to be heard, Papa."

"Supper in your room," said Moo, pointing upstairs.

Musa frowned and scampered into the house.

"Poor Musa," whispered Adele.

"Always in trouble," said Amelia.

"Serves him right," said Corine.

Doc Moo listened to his son's bare feet pounding up the steps to the second floor, feeling a small sorrow, but the boy had to learn to stay away from such trouble. These hills were crawling with danger, too much of it two-legged.

A strike. Moo shook his head. It seemed a peaceful action, a simple work stoppage. A laying down of tools, not a taking up of arms. But he'd been in coal country long enough to know better. The operators would fight tooth and nail to break the strike, bringing in scab labor from out of state to keep the coal running and an army of Baldwins and mine guards to stamp out resistance. The miners would fight back. Protests, picket lines, intimidation, sabotage. One side had power and influence; the other was willing to die. One of the oldest, bloodiest stories in a very old book—old as civilization itself.

At noon the next day, just as Musa said they would, the miners put down their shovels and picks and walked out of the mines, emerging into the harsh light of an alien sun.

They struck.

CHAPTER SEVEN

BIG FRANK HUGHAM, MISS Beulah's grandson, stood among the strikers who'd walked, ridden, and hitched to the county seat to hear Mother Jones speak. Mary Harris "Mother" Jones, once called "The Most Dangerous Woman in America," who waded the creeks when the mining companies controlled the roads. Mother Jones, black-clad like Death's own grandmother, who once held the bloody trench coat of a Baldwin-Felts agent before a crowd of miners: *The first time I ever saw a God-damned mine guard's coat decorated to suit me.*

So the rumors said.

"I hear she's more than ninety now," whispered one of the miners. "Still walking these same hills since 1899, where angels feared to tread."

"She come out of Ireland in Black '47," said another. "Same year as my great-gran, and her and her ten siblings ten years dead afore Mother Jones even stepped foot in this state."

In West Virginia, the old woman had found shoddy company-built villages where the rain fell black with coal dust and gaunt men white and brown and Black worked ten hours a day in the three-foot-high rooms of the mines. Men like Big Frank and his comrades, who undercut the coalfaces with their picks, drilled holes with hand augurs, and inserted black-powder cartridges, lighting squibs of waxed paper as they yelled "Fire in the hole!" and scrambled for cover at the nearest crosscut, shoveling the black wreckage of the blast into mine cars.

Sometimes they loaded ten tons per day, back-bent three hundred feet underground. They were killed in droves, by roof falls and explosions and years of coal dust in their lungs. *Wage slaves*, Mother called them, and their bosses she compared to the Russian czars.

Big Frank and his comrades were waiting before the county courthouse for the woman to appear. The strike was on and the crack of gunfire could be heard echoing along the Tug—quick, bloody skirmishes between strikers and Baldwin mine guards. Rifle slugs sparked against coal carts and hoppers. Sniper rounds pocked the automobiles of mine bosses; bullets punctured miners' shacks or spat up dirt at the feet of scabs. Now and then a mine guard or striker or scab staggered and fell, clutching himself, some part of him blown red in the dirt. Only in Matewan, where Sid walked the streets, did the gun thugs fear to tread.

Miss Beulah hadn't wanted Frank to chance the journey to the county seat. "Listen to it out there, Grandboy. It's death zipping through the air every second, looking to feed the worms. You asking for trouble, you go out there today."

But Frank had to get out of the sour-smelling canvas tent, out of the fly-ridden encampment where they spent their days. He was not a man built for idling. The chunks of muscle that encased his bones needed work, sweat, exertion—or else a sort of acid built up inside him, a bodily distemper worse to him than heat or cold, hunger or fear.

"I'm-a go crazy I don't get out this camp, Mama-B. Besides, it's Mother Jones we talking about. The Miners' Angel. How many chances might I get to hear her speak?"

It was more than that. Mother Jones had been a hero of Evie's. His wife had followed the fiery Irishwoman's speeches and exploits. He couldn't bear to miss her.

Now the crowd of miners fell silent as the old woman climbed onto the bed of a truck parked in front of the county courthouse. Her stage. She had white hair and wide hips and a black dress, frilly and handspun, a little black hat pinned on top of her curls. She looked like someone's prim grandmother, heavy-bodied, making her way to church or market. Then she cleared her throat, like jacking a shell into the chamber of a gun, and her Irish brogue boomed over the crowd.

"Boys, I am here to tell ye that we stand at the dawn of a new civilized state. Two thousand years since the Roman lords nailed Christ to that rugged old cross, the condition of wage slavery, worker exploitation, and child labor is sounding its death rattle, dying into history, and a new dawn shines before us."

Hurrah! cried the miners. *A new dawn!*

"That's right," said Mother. "We stand in the last bastion of nonunion mines in coal country. The other coalfields have been organized. Miners have leverage there, they have rights. No longer can they be bullied to work under loose tops, in gassy rooms. No longer can they be forced to toil fourteen hours each day, only to have their loads nitpicked by a company shill. Here we face the same enemy we faced in those other fields. Mine guards. Gun thugs. God-damned Baldwin bloodhounds. I say damn them all, by Jesus Christ."

Down with dogs! cried the miners. *God damn them!*

"I tell ye, boys, they don't scare me. Been facing them for nigh on twenty years, I have. A troop of them came into the New River fields back in '02, wearing their new suttler-cut uniforms and gray hats and big dragoon pistols, repeater rifles propped on their knees. Looked like the cavalry of some nation their own. Like hell they were. I came into a strikers' camp after a posse of Baldwins raided the place and heard the keening and the sobbing. I pushed open the door of a bullet-riddled cabin to find a miner with his brains blown across his bed, killed while he slept, and his wife wailing like a banshee, holding her husband's broken head in her lap."

No! cried the miners. *The poor woman!*

"So I was none pleased when I faced down that same Baldwin gang myself. On my way to Red Warrior to speak, I was, riding up a creekbed in a mule-cart with a forty-man escort of miners when I heard shots from the railbed above us. I crawled up that slope to find the Baldwins pushing a flatcar fortified with sandbags and a machine gun. I walked up to that car and set my hand over the muzzle of the gun. 'Ain't nobody dying today,' I said."

Mother's voice was a crackling Irish storm, thundering across the crowd.

"And you know who it was behind that machine gun? Albert Felts himself, it was. 'You God-damned hellcat,' he says to me, 'it'll be you gets killed you don't take your hand off my gun.'

"'Your gun?' I says to him. 'It's my boys bring up the ore makes this gun. My boys melt it in furnaces and roll it into steel. It's my boys dig the coal that fuels those furnaces. Hell, this gun is *mine*.'

"'Well, it's my finger on the trigger,' says he.

"'These men, they ain't at war with you,' I said. 'They're battling them that pay you, rich men in high houses never touched a trigger in their whole coddled lives. Coal barons whose fortunes come from even higher places, old men in boiled shirts in London and New York City, plump-fed on the stolen wages of a thousand thousand men who sweat when they work.'"

Damn right, said the miners. *There's the truth.*

Mother shook her head. "'We'll kill them all and you, too, you God-damned hellcat,' he says to me. I took off my black pot hat. I says to him, I said, 'Son, you touch a single white thread of hair on this here head of mine and that creek there will run red with blood, and it will be yours that crimsons it. I am leading a band of five hundred men up to my meeting at Red Warrior, every man jack of them armed with a rifle-gun. They're taking the high route along the ridge, and they've heard your shooting, they have. Their sharpshooters have got you dead to rights. You may start the shooting, but my boys will end it.'

"Well, I watched those Baldwins lift their eyes up the steep side of the ridge, where the vegetation grew thick enough to hide whole battalions. I watched them hunker behind their sandbags. 'You see,' I said, 'I hauled my tired bones up out of that there creek to save *your* lives. I don't want killing today. I got a meeting to hold.'"

What happened? asked the miners. *What did he say?*

"Didn't say a damn word, did he? Though I thought he might bust for fury. He let my boys cross the tracks to safety, he did, but I kept my hand on that gun. Didn't trust him no farther than I could throw him."

The crowd of miners looked at one another, eyes wide. They'd heard the story of Mother Jones and the machine gun before, but never from her own mouth. Her voice cracked and growled with power, coarsened by long, hard years spent on the road, facing down thugs and crooked lawmen who didn't kill her simply because she was an old woman. Who still might.

Mother wiped the lather of sweat from her brow and squinted into the crowd, rocking on her overburdened feet. "But the Baldwins ain't the only enemy we face, you know that. It's the men that hire them. The coal operators. *King Coal*. They like to call me an agitator. Hell, wasn't Washington? Weren't the pilgrims on the *Mayflower*? They like to ask me if I have a permit to speak. Sure, I got one. Patrick Henry gave it to me one hundred and forty-four years ago. Him and Jefferson, Adams, and Washington. And I damn well intend to use it.

"Now you men who fought in the Great War, you were told it was a war for democracy, were you not? A war to end all wars. You went Over There, you took down the Kaiser and the German Reich. You saved the world from oppression and came home and found what? More oppression. More autocracy. A new bunch of American kaisers, men who made their fortunes on the war, on coal and steel, arms and machinery, on the blood and muscle of American fighting men, only to abuse those same men back here at home, exploiting them in their mines and mills, factories and stockyards and killing floors. Robber barons and coal czars who use gun thugs and murderers to keep you in subjection, bent-kneed before them, your voices unheard. Same as the kings of the Old World.

"But these American kings, they know their time is coming, boys. They do. They know a great storm's upon them, ready to knock them from their high and mighty thrones. Oh, they'll fight, they will, but they don't know who they're fighting with. No, my boys. Some call me a humanitarian. The hell I am. I'm a God-damned hell-raiser, that's what, and we are going to clean up West Virginia. Not with any guns, no, but with the American flag. We are going to make West Virginia the leading state of *Americanism*. We're going to take that flag bought from British tyranny with seven long years of American blood, rip it from the hands of King Coal and his thugs, and plant it hard in the ground here. We are going to live beneath it. That flag is our banner, and no rotten robbers or gun thugs can take it from us, because I will just raise hell on them!"

Hurrah for America! Hurrah for the Union! Hurrah for Mother Jones!

Frank didn't cheer with his comrades, but the old woman's words had moved him deeply. A wind through a high forest, lifting his branches. His lungs felt wide and full, his bones double-strong. Around him, the miners began to sing the Union anthem, sung to the same tune as "John Brown's Body" and "The Battle Hymn of the Republic."

> *It is we who plowed the prairies, built the cities where they trade,*
> *Dug the mines and built the workshops, endless miles of railroad laid,*
> *Now we stand outcast and starving midst the wonders we have made,*
> *But the Union makes us strong.*
> *Solidarity forever, solidarity forever,*
> *Solidarity forever, for the Union makes us strong . . .*

Big Frank raised his own heavy bass—what a teacher during his short stint of coal-camp schooling had called a *basso profundo*—a rare voice, rich and rolling, which he let fly with the others. He rocked back on his heels, singing, imagining their voices weaving and meshing like hundreds of songbirds, even as the hills cracked and echoed with guns.

CHAPTER EIGHT

MOTHER JONES BATTLED HER way through the backstage crowd, her handbag dangling from one arm. She was beset by Union officials who wanted to meet her, who'd tell her how great she was and beg her to visit their districts. She kept moving, paying them no mind. She was making for a jug-eared young man standing alone at the edge of the swarm, hat in hand. His teeth flashed in his gaunt face.

"Sidney Hatfield," she said, taking his hand. "A God-damned pleasure." She clasped his hand in both of her own and held it against her heavy bosom, staring him deep in the eyes. "It's a long time I been praying for a boy like you, one who ain't afraid of the Devil. One who can show these boys how to stand up like men."

The young police chief rocked back and forth slightly, as if unsure what to say. He just smiled, showing his pink gums and capped teeth. "Yes, ma'am," he said.

Other men were pushing forward, pressing for her attention. Mother ignored them, keeping his hand clutched tight against her chest, squeezing it, searching him out with her eyes. She was making him uncomfortable but didn't care. She had to know. Had to know if this boy had the steel in him she hoped, the mettle to stand up to what was coming down the pike.

Plenty of people could be brave once, even several times over their lifetimes, but it took rare nerve to keep it up for weeks, months, years, while the kings of state and industry tried to grind you down in their gears and machinations. While the gun thugs haunted your waking hours and the bloodhounds crept to your door at night. While the reporters scandalized you in their papers and the spies wormed their way into your brain and bank account.

They'd been after her for decades, they had, the coal kings and steel barons, siccing their thugs and underlings on her, but they hadn't cracked her, not yet. Though, lying in her bed at night, she sometimes wondered how much longer she could hold up. Every day another fight.

It took the faith of a true believer to survive it, someone who loved their cause and people enough to die—or, rarer still, a born rebel, hard as Christ and mean as the Devil, who'd die before they broke. A fly on the back of an iron bull—someone who didn't know but to fight. Mother didn't sense a lick of quit in this boy, in his deep-set eyes and metal mouth. He seemed like the kind who didn't crack when you hammered into him, just turned harder, denser, meaner.

Blood would tell.

She squeezed his hand a last time, lowering her voice. "Give them hell, boy."

Later they were lined up for a photograph, a row of unionists staring straight-backed at the camera, as if before a firing squad. In the ashy grain of the image, Sid's head was cocked slightly over his stiff white collar and dark suit. His face cut hard and sharp, his cheeks dark, his killer's eyes aimed far over the photographer's shoulder, as if on a distant ridgeline. Smilin' Sid did not smile. He'd turned the dead mayor's jewelry store into a gun shop.

On the train home, Mother watched the high ridges chug past, so high and steep they seemed the eroded ramparts of some fallen castle. She dabbed her face with a handkerchief and wound the damp linen around her hands. She was feeling her age, she was. These speeches seemed to sap more of her strength every time.

By her own reckoning, she was more than ninety now. Naught but a child when she'd left the crag and heath of Ireland, huddled in the lightless hold of a merchant ship. She'd died several times since then, or thought she had. Memphis, 1867, when she'd washed the bodies of her four little ones for burying and then her husband's, too, as yellow fever raged through the workers' districts of the city and death carts trundled through the streets. Then Chicago, 1871, when her dress shop burned in the Great Chicago Fire, the flames roaring from ten thousand windows while people ran screaming through the streets, the sky black as night. The new life she'd worked so hard to create—incinerated.

After the fire, in a black-scorched building where the Knights of Labor met, Mother found yet another life—what would become her home for the rest of her years: *Wherever there's a fight.*

She was there for the early labor battles in Chicago, when the forces of industry decried the eight-hour workday as the work of foreign devils, agitators, anarchists. The early strikes were met with Pinkertons—the same breed of thug as the Baldwin-Felts. The skulls of factory workers were crushed beneath hooves and clubs, blown apart by pistols and riot guns.

In Chicago, Mother learned how the game was played. Then she took to the road. She'd walked these hills for twenty years in her black dress and spectacles, organizing, taking the Union into the deepest counties of thug rule. She'd waded up creeks to avoid patrols and led strings of miners' wives over mountains in dead of night, protesting, banging their skillets like war drums. She'd clapped her hand over the barrel of more than one angry mine guard's gun and stared him back to his runthood—God's truth, she had—and stood in front of the state capitol calling Governor Glasscock a *Crystal Peter* and *God-damned dirty coward* to the hurrahs of the hardest men on this earth or below it.

Her boys.

Oh, but the past year had taken a chunk of her. She'd been all over the country, speaking to steelers and shoemakers, iron workers and cigar makers. She felt heartsore, thin-boned and fleshy, in need of rest, a firm floor beneath her feet—and she a woman famous for calling her shoes her home. But her old battleground was calling her back. She had to come.

Men were taking to the hills, she knew. Striking miners who refused to sign the yellow-dog contracts of the coal companies, which forbade them to unionize. They painted their faces with ash and carried hunting rifles, patrolling the ridges and folds of the hills, watching mine operations from hidden perches. They were watching the scabs imported to work in their stead. Meanwhile, mine guards stood high on the coal tipples, as upon castle parapets, armed with high-powered rifles and telescopic sights.

War, building like methane in the chamber of a mine. Any day could come the spark.

CHAPTER NINE

MISS BEULAH SAT IN her rocker, trying to knit, but the needles wouldn't do right. Her mind wasn't in it. Neither her heart. She was worried, is what it was. Frank had gone to see Evie's people for Independence Day all the way over in Bluefield, a hundred miles away. He'd been due back on the evening train, but it had come and gone hours ago, the engine gnashing along the river.

No Frank.

An eruption of curses filled the night—tongues she didn't understand but could tell the meanings well enough. Somebody's daughter or husband, did this or didn't do that. Somebody's pig or dog or chicken, ate up this or trampled that. Sometimes you didn't need to know the words, even the tongue. There was a rhythm to the life of a lot of people living right on top of one another, even the fights.

Here in the tent colony, folks tended to cluster by language, but loosely. People speaking Italian, Spanish, Polish, Russian, even Hungarian. There were tensions that went back a thousand years, and those from just last week. People said there were tenement buildings in New York City that had a hundred different languages spoken inside their walls. Well, they had close to that here in the hollers of the Tug Valley, and naught but sheets of canvas separating them. Often, if you listened late at night, when most of the camp was asleep, you'd hear there was even less than that. Nothing but skin and sweat and breath.

But she minded a darker streak of late. People were raw, angry. Rumors kept coming through the camp, stories of beatings and disappearances. The work of the Baldwins, trying their hardest to break the strike. One of the stories came from McDowell County, where Frank had to change trains on his way home. Her neighbor Mrs. Louella told her while they were canning corn and beans, working on top of a washtub turned upside down on a packing crate, shooing the chickens that came pecking around their feet.

"This brakeman name of Collins over there, he started a new local going. The very next day, not one, not ten, but thirty-one Baldwins step off the train and call him out into the street. 'You the secretary of this new local?' they ask.

"'Seck-r-tary?' he says. 'I'm the Got-damned president!'

"Well, the head Baldwin, he walks and up bashes the man's face with the butt of his pistol-gun, knocks his teeth right out in the street. Says, 'You God-damned son of a bitch, you get out this county by tonight!'

"He did, too. Lit out afore the sun was even down, ain't been seen since."

Now Miss Beulah shook her head, thumbing the sharp tips of her knitting needles. If they'd do a white man that way in broad daylight, what might they do to her boy caught out after dark?

FRANK HEARD THE HARD click of bootheels coming down the hall. He sat up from the cot. The walls of the cell were etched with the names of past inmates and skinny rats scurried along the floors, ribs visible. It must be after midnight, but there was no window to tell the hour.

That afternoon, he'd been on the station platform in Welch, switching cars for the last leg of his journey home, when someone clapped a hand on his arm. He whirled to find three lawmen standing behind him. Two of them had the flaps of their holsters unbuttoned, their hands on their pistols. Deputies. Between them, holding Frank's arm, was the sheriff himself.

"Frank Hugham of Mingo County?" he asked.

Frank withheld the urge to rip his arm from the man's grip. "Yes, sir."

"You're under arrest."

Frank looked around. The platform swarmed with passengers. Any one of them could be a Baldwin undercover—someone who'd recognized him from the Mother Jones speech. After all, this was the town of Welch, seat of Mc-Dowell County—a stronghold of the Baldwin-Felts.

"On what charge?" he asked the sheriff.

"I'll be asking the questions, boy."

The deputies put him in handcuffs and herded him to the county jail, knee-ing and yanking him down the street like an animal, though he didn't fight them. When they took him to the back door of the jailhouse, a basement door, he went cold.

No one booked him.

They slung him into a windowless cell and clanged home the door. He looked out through the bars. "I'd like to send word to my grandmother where I'm at."

The sheriff sniffed. "Only message you're sending out will be to God."

Frank lay in darkness for hours, realizing he'd fallen inside one of the stories they were always hearing in the mines and coal camps. The way order was kept. Whenever the miners started to rise, weaving their spirits together like the blood and muscle of a single strong creature, the operators came down with beatings and disappearances, wedges of fear that broke the movement's back sure as mauls and ax blades. When he was just a boy, his own father had gone missing this way. Left the mine to walk home and never turned up, as if he'd been raptured, sucked straight to heaven.

Baldwins, people whispered. *Too much union talk.*

Frank shook his head. As he'd waited these long hours in the cell, fear and anger had grown into twin mountains on his shoulders, high and dark and heavy, but he was determined to keep to the sweet narrow valley between them: faith. Mama-B had always taught him that faith was the greatest weapon they had.

Faith can cut you free of fear. Tell me, what sword or gun can do that?

Besides, he was no stranger to cramped walls and darkness and whole mountains squatting on his back. He'd made his bread in such places, his name. Lightless chambers where nothing breathed but mules and men, where the fossilized ghost-shapes of weird prehistoric beasts swam flame-flickering through the walls. He'd sweat and bled in such cells six days a week since he was a boy.

The lone lightbulb sizzled to life in the corridor and the sheriff appeared with several white men in plain clothes. Thick wrists and fistlike faces. Baldwins, plain enough. The sheriff unlocked the door and the men filed in, crowding the cell. They were so close Frank could smell the likker and aftershave. He looked at their hands. Fingers already curled, almost fists.

"Time to take your statement," said the sheriff. "Down the road apiece."

Frank was sitting on the very edge of the cot. His legs wide, his hands held cuffed between his thighs. He knew what *down the road apiece* meant—the same it had for decades. Out in the woods or down by the river, where there were no witnesses. He breathed in, out.

Faith.

"If it's all right with you, Sheriff, I'd prefer to make my statement right here."

The lawman cocked his head, squinted. "If that's how you want it."

Frank never saw the blackjack. One of the Baldwins must have had it hidden up his sleeve, the lead-filled head cupped in his fingers. A crack at the back of his head, then darkness.

He woke dizzied and sick, retching on himself, trapped in the trunk of a car. The chassis squeaked and banged beneath him. A logging road deep in the woods, he thought, better for mules than automobiles. His head pounded, as if someone were beating on the base of his skull with a ball-peen hammer.

The car squeaked to a halt. He felt the chassis springs unweight as the men stepped out of the car. Someone opened the trunk and he saw six of them silhouetted above him, their faces slightly doubled from the blow to his head. No sheriff now. The reek of whiskey was coming off them like an atmosphere. Corn likker, strong enough to dull their sympathies, to make it harder to remember what they might do to an unarmed man in the woods.

Two of them reached in and pulled him out of the trunk.

"Shitfire, if he ain't the heaviest son-bitch I ever had to tote."

Another one squatted down before him, a pale scar between his eyes. He was holding a pipe wrench. "Bet you wish you ain't joined the Union now, nor listened to a single word of that whore-bitch Mother Jones."

They began drawing their implements from the car, gripping and regripping drain pipes and ax handles, testing their balance and heft like ballplayers.

Frank held up his bound hands before them, his palms steepled together.

A couple of the men softened slightly, like they might relent.

The squatting man swung the wrench.

It caught Frank across the temple and his vision redoubled, pitting him against twelve interwoven ghosts. He went wild, fighting them with the sledge of his interlaced fists, but the blows were coming from all sides now, breaking against his arms and thighs, smashing into his soft places. Expert strikes to ribs and kidneys and the backs of his knees. Flesh ripped and bones cracked and tendons screamed. Then he was on the ground, curling his head under his arms, protecting the one thing that might never heal.

They beat him until he could feel his ribs and shoulder blades breaking apart, caving like the rafters of a house. His consciousness grew smaller, retreating to a far corner of himself, a last place of light. His mind went to his wife, Evie—to her lying dark-bruised in her last days, dying in their shared bed, and to his grandmother waiting tonight in her rocker, not knowing what happened to him. The same way she'd waited when his father disappeared.

Something cracked open inside him. His spirit broke from his flesh, flying out to them, flashing through channels unknown, leaving the pipes and ax handles behind, the bootheels and curses. He was a bird wheeling high over the hills, held between heaven and earth. His flesh dead weight five hundred feet below.

The men slackened, breathing hard.

"He dead?" asked one.

Another man toed at Frank's heel. "Reckon so. Ain't made a peep. Nobody takes a beating like that without screaming for Jesus or they mama."

"Check his breathing," said the one with the wrench, holding out a pocket mirror he carried for the purpose. "If you can still find his mouth."

One of the others knelt down, holding the mirror to the wrecked lips. He looked back over his shoulder, shaking his head.

The man with the wrench grunted. "Let's go."

They'd cranked up the Ford and thunked the car into gear before Frank exhaled. He'd been holding his breath for years, he thought. Now his own lungs sounded strange to him, wheezing beneath the broken timber of his body.

He'd been lying there for what seemed hours when a passing train made the ground rumble, shaking him awake. He began to crawl in the direction of the sound. Every inch brought stabs and hammers of pain. No matter. What they'd hit him with were feathers compared with the wrecking ball of Evie's death. Somehow, here on the verge, he felt her close. Her warmth and love. *Evie, Evie, give me strength . . .*

At first light, he awoke at a coaling station beside the railroad tracks. He didn't remember arriving there in the night. The first lances of dawn glowed on his face and he spread his fingers through the gravel of the railbed. Shore for a drowning man. He closed his eyes. Later, the hiss and chuff of a slowing engine, the sound of boots dropping onto the gravel. He cracked open a swollen eye to find two white men bent over him, a driver and brakeman, both wearing the buttonhole pins of the railroad brotherhood—the trainmen's union.

"Jaysus wept," said the brakeman. His accent Irish. "Who did this to ye?"

"Baldwins," croaked Frank.

"Bloody fooking savages," said the driver, kneeling beside him. "Not to worry, lad, the brotherhood has got ye now."

They spirited him out of McDowell County inside the engine's cab, wrapped in a woolen blanket. He was shivering despite the season. They whispered to switchmen and yardmasters, transferring him between two different trains. He was ferried in crew compartments, guarded from snooping rail police and sheriff's deputies. Late that morning, a coal train made an unscheduled stop at Matewan, where two trainmen helped him onto the platform.

Sid was already there, chatting with the stationmaster. When he saw Frank, the golden smile vanished from his face. A bone-white mask, gaunt and irregular. His eyes seemed to retreat back into his head, twin black hollows.

He turned to a pair of the town boys standing nearby, wide-eyed at the gruesome sight. "Get Doc Moo," he snapped. "Now!"

CHAPTER TEN

DOC MOO TRANSFORMED HIS small office into a makeshift clinic, setting up a folding field hospital bed. The big coal hewer had a list of injuries that would have killed most men. Fractures, contusions, lacerations, concussion, possible internal bleeding. He had blood in his urine and stool; Moo feared a damaged spleen. He'd lost multiple teeth, and two of his lower incisors had been kicked through his bottom lip.

Usually, Moo could separate himself from his patient, keeping his emotions checked behind a wall of professional focus. A worried, angry, or grief-stricken physician was no good to anyone. But now, for the first time in years, he felt the stones of that well-constructed wall quivering, the mortar eroded. A man beaten with less mercy than a rabid dog.

That afternoon, two men rode down from the tent colony to visit Frank and bring back news. They were twin brothers, Bonney and Lacey, coal shovelers known as the Hellfighter twins for their service in the Great War. Doc Moo let them see Frank alone. When they came out of the room, their faces were stony, eyes hooded, but he could feel the fury radiating from them, as if gasoline ran in their veins. When they swung onto their borrowed mules, he saw the imprints of pistols beneath their loose cotton shirts. He couldn't help but think of his father riding in that Maronite militia, farmers and schoolteachers going to war.

They spoke to Sid down the street, then rode off, back into the mountains.

At the end of the first day, while Frank was sleeping, sedated on morphine, Doc went up to the roof for one of his rare cigarettes. Sid soon appeared, his hands resting on the curled butts of his revolvers, his watch chain dangling from his vest. He'd kept deputies posted outside the building since Frank's arrival, never straying far himself. "How is he, Doc?"

"Stable for now. My biggest fear now is internal injuries. I've set and splinted his fractures, but I'd like to get him under a radiograph."

"Who's got one?"

"State hospital in Welch."

Sid shook his head. "Death sentence to send him back there. He might go in that hospital alive, but he'll come out a corpse. That town's crawling with Baldwins. I can't protect him there."

Moo nodded. "I feared the same thing," he said. "And the next nearest radiograph is too far. Maybe once he's strong enough to travel." He shook his head. "Big Frank, out of everyone. As if he hasn't had hell enough."

Sid nodded. "Reckon that's why they chose him, Doc. They're trying to send us a message."

Doc Moo pulled hard on the cigarette, taking the smoke deep into his lungs. He knew it was bad for him, but didn't care. Sometimes you just had to hurt something—better yourself than someone else. He blew out the smoke, looking at their little town along the river. "What are we going to do, Sid?"

Sid's face went hard, like Moo had rarely witnessed. No smile in sight. "They sent us a message. Reckon we'll send one back."

Moo swallowed. "What kind of message?"

Sid looked downriver. "One loud enough they ain't apt to mishear it."

CHAPTER ELEVEN

THE MINERS MET IN the restaurant below the Union office in Matewan.

Big Frank, you seen what they done to him?

On the Fourth of July, too.

It can't stand.

The restaurant owner was new in town, sympathetic to their cause. "The Mohawk's runnin' too much coal," he said, going from table to table, pouring coffee from one hand, tea from another. "Slap in the face, what it is."

Mohawk Coal and Coke. The operation cascaded down the mountainside like a patchwork fortress of wood siding and corrugated tin, arrayed with catwalks and coal elevators and chimney stacks. The headhouse ran conveyors down the slope to the tipple, which straddled the rail lines, washing, sorting, and dumping coal into the beds of fifty-ton gondolas. Mohawk had never quit production, no matter the strike. The chimneys kept chuffing; the conveyors didn't stop. Laden hoppers rattled down the rails. It smoked right at the edge of strike country.

A giant, burning fuse.

The restaurant owner lifted his eyes to the ceiling. "I hear they got a new crate of Winchesters upstairs . . ."

As soon as the miners had sneaked out the back door with the rifles, the restaurant owner was at the telephone. He cranked the magneto and set the black horn of the receiver to his ear. Some company spies worked side by side with the men in the mines; others poured their coffee.

He spoke cryptically into the receiver. "The cows are in the pasture. I repeat, the cows are in the pasture."

A tinny voice came back through the line. "The wolves are waiting."

THE MINERS CLIMBED THE back side of the ridge, trudging single-file along game trails and pushing through laurel slicks, slapping at the flies that frenzied about their heads. Damp-dark patches of sweat hung from their collars and armpits. They had their rifles cradled across their chests or slung from makeshift slings. A few carried neat parcels of sticks wrapped in wax paper.

Dynamite.

Now and again, they squatted on their haunches to rest, leaning against tree trunks to roll cigarettes and smoke pipes, passing a jug of corn likker hand to hand.

I hear Sid's got a .38 Special, Smith & Wesson.

Got him a S&W all right, but it's a .44. Seen it up close one time.

When you get to Hell, ask Albert Felts. He's seen it closer than any of us.

The sun descended as they climbed, the shadows growing longer, sharper, as if the world were growing claws. They reached the top of the mountain and slithered into position.

Below, inside the Mohawk tipple and headhouse, the Baldwin mine guards were alert, waiting behind a Browning heavy machine gun trucked in for the occasion. One of the guards glassed the hillside with his binoculars. The shadows were weaving and merging, turning the mountain dark as a slag pile.

Maybe the savages weren't coming. Maybe they'd turned chicken or stumbled past a liquor still and got themselves scuttered. He was about to lower his field glasses when he caught sight of something on the ridgeline, a tree with a strange burl grown from its trunk, like the carved face of a wood sprite or faery. Then he saw other such knots and burls, as if some carver had been at work, cutting an army out of the ridge. He saws trees with roots the size of men's arms, bolls like human thighs, a boulder that could be wearing a hat. A flitter of sparks, like the scrabble of a hobnail boot on stone.

"Jaysus wept."

He turned his head to tell the others what he'd seen, what army had grown from the forest, but the mountain spoke first.

CHAPTER TWELVE

THUNDER ROCKED THE VALLEY, rattling the windows in their frames. No, not thunder. Doc Moo stepped outside and found Sid at the little bench in front of his and Jessie's shop, where he kept a constant game of checkers going with Ed Chambers from the hardware store, his best friend.

They nodded politely at him. "Doc."

Before Moo could reply, the mountains thundered again, heavy enough to jostle a man's heart in his chest, to rattle the pistols at his sides. Sid and Ed barely looked up from the board.

"Tug boomer," said Ed.

Sid nodded. *Dynamite.*

The Mohawk tipple had been blown apart, the shattered planks and beams fluttering down like feathers and falling leaves. More mines were dynamited that week. *Messages.* In the tent colonies, the explosions were whooped and cheered, as if the roof-beams of heaven were cracking over droughted land. Men hooted and hollered from the hillsides; they yawped and trilled. They felt the weight of their debts lightening with the flying debris, as if the company ledgers had been blasted into oblivion, vaporized. Some had. Their hearts felt buoyant in their chests. They felt, for a moment, made of more than muscle and blood, skin and bone. More than strong backs and dirty hands for King Coal.

They'd gained the upper hand. They patrolled the streets of the company towns and occupied the ridges above them, smoking cigarettes and holding rifles in the crooks of their arms, each walking tall like Sid himself. Beneath their watch, the headhouses were dark-windowed, cold. The coal lay safe in the mountains. They could feel their leverage, their momentum, swelling like a tectonic force beneath their feet. Finally, the coal companies would have to reckon with their demands. An eight-hour workday, a joint commission to mediate labor disputes, the right to elect their own checkweighmen at each mine.

They walked taller. They felt lighter, as if the great thumb of King Coal weren't squashing them so hard into the ground. They were no longer beasts, bent-backed and voiceless, to be used up and spat in the dirt. They were men.

Sid and Ed kept up their game, their pieces scraping across the board.

CHAPTER THIRTEEN

The saddest day I had was in speaking at a number of points from Bluefield to Huntington, West Virginia. There had been a strike by mine workers and in the cold fall days, with a sprinkle of early snow, the miners and their wives and children had been evicted from company houses and were suffering. Worst of all, men in the Army uniform were being used by the mine owners under the pretense of "preserving order."

–Josephus Daniels, Secretary of the Navy, 1920.

A GROWL BETWEEN THE hills, distant at first but growing louder, nearer. Sentries hollered the news from mouth to mouth, down the creeks and across the ravines.

"The Army is coming! The Army is coming!"

A military convoy. It came crawling through the valley, slow and immense, a river rising between the hills, carrying supply trucks and motorcycles, mules and wagons and a wheeled artillery gun. The governor, at behest of the coal operators, had asked the War Department to intervene. Five hundred soldiers from an infantry regiment out of Camp Sherman, Ohio—the first federal troops to step foot in the Tug Valley since the Civil War. Their canvas tents bloomed overnight, their guns oiled bright beneath the sun.

No public assemblies would be permitted, no parades. No rallies or picket lines. The soldiers patrolled the roads with fixed bayonets. They greeted every train at the station, ensuring the influx of strikebreakers—scabs—wouldn't be harassed. They guarded every mine. Beneath their watch, men from out of state blasted and shoveled and hauled coal out of the deep bellies of the hills. The coke ovens fumed again from the hillsides, the conveyor belts rattled.

The tipples, crouched high astride the railroad tracks, dumped their coal into waiting hoppers.

Soon, long trains of dark rubble were winding along the Tug Fork, car after car after car, creaking out of the cold valley.

THE THIN SMOKE OF crooked tin stovepipes rose from the tent colony, smudging the white sky. Families huddled in the chow line, hands tucked under their arms, waiting for bulldog gravy and water sandwiches—lard-soaked bread. Their faces white and pink and brown, as if shaped and fired from varying admixtures of clay. A ragged tribe, clad in chin-knotted headscarves and tatty hats. The men clenched smokeless pipes in their jaws. Shaggy dogs roamed the encampment, hopeful of scraps.

Miss Beulah sucked her teeth. The hogs, soon for the knife, were lean in their pens. A sickness had reached West Virginia. A chestnut blight. For the first fall in the history of the land, a child couldn't hurl a stone at a tree and collect the fallen chestnuts for their mother to dry or roast or fatten the pigs.

She turned and hobbled through the flap-door of her tent. Inside, the sourish smell of people living close. Her grandboy Frank was lying on his cot, still swaddled in bandages from the knocking those thugs in McDowell had put on him.

Miss Beulah shook her head. Thought they'd killed him, they did. They didn't know what stuff Hughams were made from. Her boy was a hewer, after all, broad-built like John Henry who raced the steam-hammer, driving spikes until his hands turned cold blue and his heart blew like a bomb. But it wasn't just her grandboy's body that stood up to those thugs, it was his spirit, no matter how many clubs and pipes and bootheels they laid into him. It was his soul, big with faith.

He had some new knots and lumps where his cracked ribs and shoulder blades had knit themselves back together. Doc Moo said the bones would be stronger where they broke, like when the shop men welded back a cracked axletree or track rail. Still, the sight of him shirtless pained her, the big burls of muscle welted and scarred like a butcher's block. It made her think of her husband, the cat-o'-nine scars all ridged across his back like the very map of Hell. A world made in fury instead of love. Those scars had itched him all his life, and he'd liked her to keep her nails long so she could scratch him before bed. It helped him sleep.

"Mama-B?"

Her grandboy's voice broke her spell. More and more, she tended to get lost in her memories, in the company of the ones who'd passed before her. Not lost, maybe. Maybe just finding her way home.

She spooned some of the thin soup for him. He sat up in bed, wincing. "Mama-B, I'm thirty-damn years old. I can feed myself."

"Hush up, boy. Doctor Moo said good eating is the best thing for you. You got to eat not just for your belly but all the broke bone and meat of you. You ain't been putting it down like you should."

"Hell I ain't. Give it here."

Miss Beulah handed him the bowl and spoon, smiling to herself. She hadn't spent this long on earth without learning how to deal with the mule-headed men of her line. "I'm-a watch you eat it, though. Make sure you don't pour it out."

"I won't."

"I'll see you don't."

In the distance, the *crack-crack* of gunfire. Just when they got the strike to hold, a thousand combat boots had landed in the valley, heavy as blows. Ten soldiers at every mine.

The Regulars, people called them. The governor claimed it was to maintain law and order, but Miss Beulah knew that was a hot crock of bull. The coal operators had wanted them to come, even planned it. The Baldwins couldn't break the strike, but the Army?

Another stammer of rifle fire in the distance, echoing through the valley.

"Them high-pars been cracking all day," she said.

The Regulars were repelling attacks at the mines, shooting and moving through the trees, up the mountainsides and along the ridges, sending the strikers to flight. During the Great War, miners had been exempt from the draft. America needed all the coal she could get to fire the boilers of troop carriers and battleships, the forges of steel mills and gun factories. Still, tens of thousands of mining men volunteered, same as her grandboy had. West Virginia had more volunteers per person than any state in the union. Shooting at Baldwins was one thing—the miners weren't about to shoot at American troops.

"It's guerrilla war out there," said Frank. He was holding the spoon overhand, supping the soup between sentences. The battling seemed to stir his spirit, which both heartened and worried her.

Miss Beulah sucked her teeth. "Ain't no war if you can't shoot back."

"That's true." Frank scraped his spoon along the bottom of the bowl. "But the Army can't stay here forever."

Miss Beulah looked out through the narrow slit of the tent door, shaped like a cat's eye. Her rocker sat out there wearing a pale dust of snow, shivering slightly on the duckboards. She pulled her quilt tighter around her shoulders. She felt cold all the time now, bone-cold, like it was creeping into her marrows. A shiver went through her—her mama always said that was Death passing close.

Miss Beulah shook her head. "Neither can we, boy. Neither can we."

CHAPTER FOURTEEN

DOC MOO STOOD BELOW the Lick Creek tent colony, rubbing his hands together as he waited for the inspectors to arrive. Winter came fast to the Tug. Skeletal trees stretched from the snow-clad hills, clawing skyward, while colonists bent toward crude metal stoves, as if worshiping the meager warmth they emanated. They were long-jawed, angular with hunger. The tents were slopped with mud; some had collapsed. The camp could be traversed only on narrow duckboards laid helter-skelter across the mire. Dawn found the earth broken-mirrored, glazed hard with ice.

Doc Moo was waiting for the chief inspector of the state health department and a major of the Army Medical Corps. They were making an investigation into the hygiene conditions of the tent colonies inside the strike zone. He'd been writing letters to state health officials and politicians for weeks. He didn't know if one of his letters had triggered a response, but a survey had been ordered by the state health commissioner.

The inspectors arrived at the Lick Creek colony in a mud-splattered Ford sedan, standing dumb-faced on the running boards a moment before stepping down into the cold slop of the holler. The major wore a pair of heavy trench boots and canvas leggings, while the civilian inspector had donned a set of rubber waders like a fly fisherman might wear.

"Doctors," said Doc Moo, extending his hand. "I am Doctor Domit Muhanna. Welcome to Lick Creek."

"Muhammad?" asked the inspector.

"Muhanna."

The inspector and the major introduced themselves in turn, but their eyes remained on the frigid squalor of the camp before them. A pair of barefoot boys—one Black, one Spanish or Italian—chased each other between the tents, making gun noises with long sticks as they leapt across the half-frozen creek that squiggled through the middle of the colony—a rocky ditch riddled with trash and offal, chicken guts and tin cans and broken glass bottles.

The inspector's mouth hung agape. "Insanitary," he said. "Unsuitable for habitation."

"That's what I've been trying to express to the authorities," said Doc Moo.

The man said nothing, pulling a clipboard from his briefcase. He took off through the colony, shaking his head, holding the case in the crook of his arm as he scratched down notes. Doc Moo and the military doctor fell in behind him, watching the man mutter and scribble, jabbing the dots of exclamation points.

The Army physician crossed his arms behind his back, looking out at the place. "I was on the Western Front in the winter of '17. I used to think those conditions were poor."

"I've been trying to tell someone," said Doc Moo. "Sending letters every week. The few replies I've received have suggested the inhabitants simply vacate to more suitable premises." He looked around at the steep snowy hills in every direction. "But to where?"

The same pair of boys darted across their path again. They leapt the frosty creek and looped around the nearest tent, ducking their heads around the outer flap to look at the strange men. The state inspector stared at them a moment, then turned to Doc Moo and the major.

"People are going to die here," he said. "Women and children are going to die."

Before they could reply, the man turned on his heel and set back off through the camp, his head swiveling this way and that, his hand constantly scribbling, cataloguing the number of tents and residents, their ages and ethnicities, the multitude and depth of the sanitation issues.

"A perfect breeding ground for epidemics," he said. "Pyrexias. Bacterial, viral, parasitic. Typhoid, influenza, pneumonia." He turned to Doc Moo. "Where are the privies, Doctor?"

"There's a trench latrine dug behind those tents."

The inspector shook his head, making more notes. "Diarrhea, helminthiasis, hookworm, roundworm." He looked at Doc Moo. "Doctor Muhammad, why didn't you report these conditions to the authorities earlier?"

Doc Moo felt his nostrils flare wide. He inhaled slowly, trying to control the Old Country blood firing beneath his skin, curling his hands into fists.

The Muhannas couldn't trace their bloodline in an unbroken line back to the twelfth century without some pride in their name and the weight of their word.

The major stepped forward. "I believe it's Doctor *Muhanna*," he said. "And the doctor was just telling me he *has* been reporting it."

"Well, this is the first I have heard of it."

Ahead, Doc Moo saw Miss Beulah sitting in front of her tent in her rocking chair, her shoulders wrapped in a large quilt as she worked with a pair of knitting needles. She looked up as they approached, smiling.

"Good afternoon, Doctor," she said. "I see we got some company today."

The inspector stopped in front of her. "What is your age?"

Miss Beulah stopped knitting. She was still smiling, but her eyes had narrowed, creased like firing slits. Doc Moo had seen the same look on Sid's face, staring at Baldwins or company men. "Been a few years since a man asked me that." She raised an eyebrow toward Doc Moo, curling it like a question mark.

"This is Doctor Taylor with the state health department," Moo told her. "And Major Drake. They're making an assessment of the health conditions in the tent colonies. They're here to help."

"Your age, ma'am?" asked the inspector again.

"Hmm," said Miss Beulah. She sniffed. "My best guess is seventy-two."

"Your best guess?"

"That's right."

"What year were you born?"

"Long about eighteen and forty-seven. If I knew for sure, I wouldn't be needing to guess how old I was, would I?"

"You really should not be sitting outside given the air temperature, not at your age."

Miss Beulah kept smiling, a vicious little light in her eyes. "You want to come in my tent and warm me up?"

Doc Moo coughed into his fist, tears in his eyes. The inspector stood slack-mouthed, his pen paused for the first time since they'd entered the camp. Finally the major stepped forward and thumped him on the back. "We better keep it moving, Doctor. Lot of ground to cover today. Don't want you losing your waders before noon." He winked at Miss Beulah and ushered the inspector down the road.

Doc Moo shook his head. "You are bad, Miss B."

"Bad is what I'd do to that there inspection man. Break him in half, I would. They don't make menfolk like they used to." She scraped her knitting needles together like knives. "Do they look the same on the inside as they used to, Doctor Moo?"

Moo started to say that human physiology evolved much more slowly than the world around them, but he could hear a train crawling along the river and cinder from the engine's stack had begun falling around them, floating down like hellish snowflakes, crackling on the tents and top of his hat. Around them, the hills looked heaped with ash instead of snow—smoke-stained by the coke ovens and collieries. He thought of how Miss Beulah's husband had died, his lungs clogged with black dust, and the lungs of the people in the mills and factory towns.

"I'm not so sure they do look the same," he said. "On the inside. Speaking of menfolk, how's Big Frank mending? Hadn't seen him in the last couple weeks."

Miss Beulah sucked her teeth. "Sometimes I think you done fixed him up too good, Doctor. I might should of let you cap him just a little. Keep some of that plaster on him."

"Why's that?"

"He's out at all hours, seems like."

"Whiskey?"

Miss Beulah rolled her lips inside her mouth a moment. "No, sir, not whiskey, nor women neither. You know how you said a man's broke bones, they heal stronger at the breaks? Well, I fear his spirit might of done the same."

"Is that such a bad thing?"

Miss Beulah squinted out at the ashen hills. "Just seems that anything with too much spirit in this valley has a way of ending up in a pine box."

CHAPTER FIFTEEN

SID SHOVELED SNOW FROM the front of the store each morning, white cheeks blown hard and red over a dark wool coat and muffler. Soldiers in heavy Mackinaws stood on rooftops and water towers, breath smoking against the cold gray sky. Patrol horses clopped through the streets. The Regulars stood guard at the mines and train depots; they patrolled both sides of the river. Trainloads of scabs arrived daily, taking over the houses in the coal camps and company towns.

Sid's trial loomed. He and twenty-some townsmen and miners were up on murder charges for the Matewan shoot-out. Rumors came drifting down the street like smoke.

You hear? The judge's resigned, joined the prosecution instead.

This new judge, word is he don't allow no women nor Negroes on his juries.

They're gunning for us, Sid. High-hat thugs in hundred-dollar suits.

Sid said nothing, flashing his teeth at the news.

Meanwhile, at least two witnesses wouldn't be taking the stand. One, a state trooper, had been killed in what was said to be a drunken pistol-fight with some local bootleggers. Two miners came to tell Sid and Ed the news as they sat huddled at their checkerboard.

"Word is, this state police tried to skin some likker boys out their Hi-Po, thought his badge meant he ain't have to pay for it."

The second miner sniffed. "Reckon he did pay at the end."

"Course," said the first, "recall that rifle-kilt innkeeper, sniped off his front porch a few weeks back? Heard he aimed to testify, too, same as that trooper."

The other miner shrugged. "A shut mouth swallows no lead."

MOTHER JONES RODE SHOTGUN in one of the Union relief trucks, a be-ribboned stack of presents in her lap. The road was a mess, a steep slog of mud and snow that threatened to beach the one-ton chassis on its undercarriage. Again and again, the convoy halted for the drivers to rock one of the vehicles out of the muck and mire. They jammed duckboards beneath the wheels for traction and secured heavy tow chains to bumpers and axles. Their breath smoked from their mouths as they worked, pale in the chill air, while the coke ovens fumed from the hillsides.

It was Christmas Eve.

Mother watched them work to dislodge a truck full of country hams. Far below them, down the sheer slope of the ridge, a mine tipple stood over the railroad tracks, smoking beside a dark green bend of the Tug Fork River. She could see the scabs down there, small as ants, climbing the catwalks and working the conveyors, while the Regulars stood guard with their rifles, ensuring the coal kept running.

Mother shook her head and looked back to the road, where the drivers and relief workers were standing in knee-deep muck, rocking one of the trucks on its axles. There was a time when she would've hiked her skirts and rolled up her dress sleeves and worked right alongside them, helping to unstick the mired rigs, but she was past those days. It wasn't that she was getting old; she'd *been* old for twenty years and more. Most women her age weren't but skulls and bones coffin-nailed six feet underground, or else a million grains of ash spread to the four winds or jammed in a mantel urn. She reckoned God just kept her around to raise hell on the coal kings and robber barons, and that's what kept her going.

Still, the holidays seemed bleaker of late, bluer. She kept going back to her Memphis days, golden days—a fire burning in the hearth and babes on every side of her, fine-haired, glowing like peeled potatoes. Her husband, George Jones, home from the ironworks, where he forged parts to repair steam engines and sawmills. A man well respected in his trade, who carried the thick swell of the work in his arms and shoulders. A real man, he was. They had a small freestanding house and went to Mass in a little converted schoolhouse where the priest was Irish and the light of Sunday mornings was a thing to behold—enough to lift the sorest heart.

But they lived near Bayou Gayoso, a swampy offshoot of the Mississippi where wild Kaintucks moored their flatboats and floating shanties packed the marshy banks—a place the high-class Memphians didn't visit. When the yellow fever came, it hit the poorer neighborhoods hardest. People called it the "strangers' disease" since Yankees and immigrants had no immunity to the mosquito-borne plague. The city burned barrels of tar in the streets and the infected were made to wear yellow jackets and Mother watched her four little ones die one by one, jaundiced and gum-bleeding, spitting up the black blood of the disease in their final throes, and she could do nothing. Then it took big George himself.

The banshee shrieks sounded ceaselessly from the other homes along her street, and for a time Mother became one of them—a spirit of uttermost woe, wrapped alone in her cloak, wailing without end. Even now, more than fifty years later, she could hardly turn her mind's eye upon that time, like the haunted or accursed room in an old manse—a door best kept shut.

George's union local had held a service in his honor, and then Mother had gone north to Chicago. Thirty years old, she'd lost four children and a husband. But she'd gain another family in the years to come—a whole people, hardworking and poor, worked to the bone and spat out in the dirt. A people who swung picks and molded iron and rolled steel, who kept the lights on and boilers burning.

The door latch clicked, breaking her reverie, and the driver hauled himself back into the cab. When he removed his flatcap, the balding dome of his head steamed in the small cab; his galoshes were mud-caked to the knees. "Now I know why old Saint Nick had him a sleigh," he said, wiping the fogged-over windshield with a red bandanna from his back pocket. "And a team of them flying reindeer."

Mother looked down at the mine tipple straddling the railroad tracks far below them. The hopper cars were moving slowly beneath the chutes, each receiving its fifty tons of lump coal. Up Lick Creek, the strikers were shivering in their canvas tents, their belts cinched down like nooses, while the coal operators kicked up their stockinged feet at home, smoking one-dollar cigars and drinking brandy before the roaring fires of stone hearths.

"Give me old Donner and Blitzen, and there are some sons of bitches I'd like to dump a load of coal in their stockings this Christmas, that's for damn sure."

"Maybe light it on fire, too," said the driver.

Mother grinned. "Aye, they never seen a Missus Claus like me."

THEY DISTRIBUTED THE CHRISTMAS hams and gifts beneath the cold gray light of afternoon. The children danced and shrieked with glee over the marbles and building blocks and checkerboards. Mother had bought most of the presents with pocket money the Union gave her, along with donations from supporters who'd read of the conditions of the tent cities in the *United Mine Workers Journal*.

It was no day for speechifying; Mother sat back and watched the people enjoy themselves. The menfolk were erecting a spindly Christmas tree in the middle of the camp, heaving like synchronized sailors on an array of thick hemp hawsers secured to the upper trunk, chanting as they worked. *Heave, ho. Heave, ho.* A hunk of a man worked one of the ropes all by himself. Not tall but broad, stout as a bull, and working with a wide-legged ferocity, a near violence. He coiled the rope around his forearms, doing the work of two men at once.

The Union driver knelt down beside her. "That's the man them McDowell thugs kidnapped and beat down," he said. "Big Frank Hugham, strongest hewer in the Tug."

Meanwhile, some of the children were building a mine tipple, erecting it out of wooden blocks and tin cans and mismatched pieces of metal erector sets. Barefoot children, Black and white and brown, working side by side, tonguing their cheeks with concentration—Mother wondered where else in the country you might see such a sight on Christmas Eve. Even in the company coal camps, there was segregation. The men were all paid the same—so many cents per ton, no matter their skin—but some companies gave better houses to white families, and the schoolhouses were often separate, sometimes the churches.

Here in the tent colony, left to their own devices, the people seemed well mingled, unified in common cause. Clusters of Italians, Spanish, Slavs, Blacks, and whites. Mother worried over the day when the operators and Baldwins would find a way to drive wedges between the workers, to divide them color from color, tongue from tongue—to crack the solidarity that gave them strength. Black versus white, native versus foreign, Protestant versus Catholic. But that day was not today.

A cry rose and Mother looked up to see the ax-sharpened base of the Christmas tree slide down into the posthole they'd dug, the evergreen fronds shivering into place, dumping powdery ledges of snow. The colonists clapped and cheered and whistled between their fingers. The children skipped and ran circles around the tree.

Later the big miner came up to her. He took off his cap, rolling it between his hands. "Mrs. Jones?"

"I am," she said. "You're the one they call Big Frank, are you?"

"Yes, ma'am," he said.

"The one those thugs took to the woods?"

"Yes, ma'am."

"I'm sorry for what you went through, son. I reckon they wanted to make an example of you. Find the strongest man they could and knock him down."

The big man nodded, his wide jaw muscles flickering.

Mother took his hand. "You gave them one, too, a powerful example. You, son, you showed those thugs it's a damn sight harder to put a coal miner in the ground if he don't want to go."

The big man blinked, his eyes wet. "I never thought of it like that, ma'am."

Mother squeezed his hand. "Do," she said. "Do think of it like that."

The relief workers were loading the trucks to go when Mother noticed a little girl off on her own, hunched over an exposed rock a little distance from the other children. Mother ambled over, holding her skirts in her fists. "And what are you building here, my girl?"

The girl leaned back and Mother saw a wooden blockhouse, windowless but for slits where straight little twigs stuck out. "It's a fort here like what old Devil Anse lives in," she said. "It's to keep us safe from the gun thugs."

"You don't feel safe up here, my dear?"

The girl looked up. She had enormous blue eyes and a pointed chin. "They're gonna hang Smilin' Sid from the neck till he's dead. Then who'll protect us?"

CHAPTER SIXTEEN

SID AND JESSIE RODE the train into Williamson, the county seat, disembarking at a station fortified with sandbags and concertina wire. They trudged down the snow-scraped sidewalks of town, heading toward the courthouse, passing soldiers posted on rooftops and Baldwins who glared from doorways and street corners. Sid walked with his hands in his front pockets, gripping a brace of pistols, smiling as he went.

The courtroom was brimming with spectators, the galleries flocked with miners and townsfolk come to watch Sid face down the legal artillery of King Coal. Everyone turned to watch them enter. Sid and Jessie smiled, walking down the aisle arm in arm. They hadn't had a church ceremony and the spectacle seemed part wedding, part prizefight.

He leaned to her ear. "You the prettiest thang in here. Like always."

Sid had on a sharp new suit, chocolate brown, and Jessie wore her finest dress, bedecked with rings and pearls. She was savvy about such things. "We can't let them make us out like a bunch of crude folk," she'd told him. "The operators want us to look like a bunch of murdering savages, same as the feud days, so the rest of the country won't give a damn what happens here."

On Jessie's instruction, the other defendants had ironed their denim coveralls or donned tweed or corduroy jackets for the occasion—some slightly ill-fitting, borrowed from friends or neighbors or the late mayor's wardrobe. They sat on the hard benches and looked out the broad courtroom windows, which gave onto the Tug Fork River and the brown rise of a hill on the Kentucky side, wooly with bare-branched trees. The presiding judge sat high at the bench, a thickset man with red hair and blue eyes.

No sooner had they sat down than a well-dressed gentleman rose from the gallery, buttoned his double-breasted coat, and approached the prosecution's table. Sid followed him with slit eyes. Thomas Felts, founding partner of the

Baldwin-Felts, sole survivor of the three Felts brothers. He was in his fifties, clean-cut in a dark suit and wire spectacles, his pouty mouth and chin starting to sag over his double-starched collar. He lived in a big brick house in Bluefield alongside the coal operators and politicians he served. He went to their churches and country clubs. He was their hard man, the muscle behind their law.

Sid smiled, wondering what it might be like to have him in a dark room. Just the two of them and naught but something sharp or heavy in their hands. Picks or shovels or hammers. He wondered how long Felts would last with him in the black chamber of a mine. The hot squirt and crunch of the man in that dark place, how he would squeak or moan or gurgle before he ceased, his spirit sinking down through the layers of coal and slate to meet his brothers in torment.

Felts bent at his waist and whispered to the prosecutors, cocking his head in Sid's direction. The attorneys set their hands on the table and looked back and forth at one another, their rumps wiggling like they had tails. They asked to approach the bench. The judge's face reddened at what they told him—a fiery bluster that matched his scalloped hair. He raised the gavel high beside his temple and hammered the sounding block.

"It has come to my attention that persons in the gallery have brought side-arms into my courtroom. Let it here be known clearly, no firearms will be allowed in my courtroom but those of my deputies. None, no matter what carry permits you have. Deputies will search all persons at the door for the duration of this trial."

Tom Felts was looking directly at Sid now, smirking like a pastor with an eye for sin—for the pair of pistols bulging the pockets of his coat. Sid shone his gold teeth back at the detective, cocking his head toward Jessie. "Won't he look pretty with a hole in his head?"

THE TRIAL SEEMED ENDLESS, a drone of procedure that reminded Sid of his worst schoolhouse days, when the trees waved outside the windows and the river ran high through the valley and he was supposed to pay attention to the scratch of strange formulas on a chalkboard that had scant to do with the limited sunshine he could soak up before his life ran straight down into the black depths of the mines, sure as a tunnel on the railroad tracks.

When the sun dipped behind the western ridge, they still hadn't gotten to the part where they entered their pleas. Everyone was tired—defendants and attorneys, families and reporters alike—ready to go home to their hotel rooms or boardinghouses or apartments. Ready for a drink, a hot supper, a tumble in the bedsheets. The judge gaveled and cleared his throat. "A last matter to attend. The bonds of all defendants are hereby revoked."

A roar ripped through the courtroom, hisses and boos and shouts. The judge slammed down his gavel again and again. "Order, I said order in the court. All defendants will be held in the Mingo County Jail for the duration of the trial."

The roars redoubled.

Can he do that?

You got to be kidding.

Who's paying this son of a bitch?

The men looked to Sid. He rose, buttoned his coat, and held out his arm for Jessie. They led the other defendants up the aisle, toward the deputies who'd escort them across the courthouse lawn to the county jail. Sid smiled wide at Felts as he walked past, as if he and Jessie were headed out on a sweet Sunday stroll, their cares no heavier than songbirds in the trees.

As a teenager, he'd had a habit of scowling all the time, not wanting people to see his rotten teeth. The dentist told him it was too much chew at too early an age that did them in. Not twenty and a head full of dead teeth. He was getting in trouble, too, hair-triggered to fight—especially after a couple snorts of corn likker. So he quit drinking and saved his money, building up a sheaf of bills in an old shoebox.

He thought he was buying gold, but it was more than that. His caps taught him smiling was the way. Everyone reckoned you smiled or frowned on account of your spirits, high or low, but he'd learned it worked the other way around, too. If you scowled all the time, the world was likely to scowl right back at you, heaping trouble in your lap with both hands, frowning on you at every opportunity. But if you kept a smile on your face, things had a way of working out. They really did. And if they didn't, if the world insisted on putting sons of bitches in your path, serving them up on you again and again, you might as well smile wide while you stuck your pistols in their bellies and blew their guts to the wind.

All these legal wigs, they didn't scare him much. They had their leather briefcases and thick-lens spectacles, their hard-starched collars made as if from diploma parchments, but they'd not risen from the mud of the Tug Valley. They'd not ridden a coal car deep into the roots of the earth or worked all day on their knees in the damp and dark, swinging a pick into a coalface or shoveling coal into a mine cart. They'd not resisted the thousand-dollar bribes of the Baldwins for mounting machine guns in their towns or stood smiling before the most feared and hated gun thugs in the history of the state and shot them dead in the street. If a jury of his fellow Mingo residents wanted to hang him for that, so be it.

He'd stand smiling at the noose.

"WE GOT TO DO something," said Frank. He and a group of other miners were standing around a barrel fire in an alley near the courthouse, rubbing their cold-chapped hands together and passing around thinly rolled cigarettes, sharing to make the scarce tobacco last. News of the trial proceedings had come to them by-and-by throughout the day.

"Judge done took their guns from them, might as well strip them naked for the Baldwins crawling round this place. Now he's got them locked up for the whole trial."

"Like he done made his decision already," said Bonney, one of the Hellfighter twins.

"Ain't his decision to make," said Frank. "It's the jury's. Guilty or not ain't his say. That's the law in America."

"Least it's harder for somebody to ambush them on the way to court every day," said Lacey, the other twin. "They'd have to do it on the courthouse lawn, and not even the Baldwins got the gall for that."

As they talked, a pair of state troopers turned their horses up the alley, the hooves and tack ringing loud in the narrow space, jangling, coming right toward them. Frank side-eyed them. Ever since the beating, men in uniform made his blood jumpy.

He lowered his voice. "Don't count on it. Baldwins ain't the least afraid of the law. They got the law fixed so it serves them, not us."

The troopers rode with their left hands on the reins, their rights spread wide on their thighs—close to their guns. They could tell Frank and the others they needed burn permits in town. They could order them to vacate the area. They could arrest them if they resisted.

"So what can we do?" asked one of the other miners.

Frank sniffed. "They ain't afraid of the law, we got to make them afraid of us."

"How? We don't got permits to carry guns inside the city limit."

Frank looked at them. "If there's enough of us, we won't have to."

CHAPTER SEVENTEEN

SOMETHING STRANGE WAS AFOOT at the Mingo County courthouse. Men began to turn up in the streets of the county seat. Unfamiliar faces. Men from out of town. No one knew where they came from, who'd sent or summoned them. They dismounted from trains or arrived in automobiles. Some appeared overnight, as if they'd walked down out of the hills or risen from chambers underground. They spoke little. They smoked cigarettes or chewed toothpicks. They were every color of man, every size. They spoke in various accents and tongues. They had thick knuckles and callused hands, broad backs and brutal forearms—the muscle of working men.

They accumulated in the streets, as if called to this place. They wore small white badges of solidarity pinned to their chests. They were watching the courthouse, all of them, from every side and street. From every corner and sidewalk and storefront. They were watching, waiting.

Union men.

The jurors became fidgety in their hard wooden chairs, glancing again and again toward the doors and windows of the courtroom. The judge called the counsel to the bench, demanding to know what was the meaning of the men gathered in the streets. "I will not be intimidated, nor have my courthouse besieged." He stabbed his finger down on the bench. "The rule of law will prevail in West Virginia."

One of the defense attorneys spread his arms wide, as if to show the judge the size of a very large fish. "Perhaps they want to ensure the safety of the defendants in case of an acquittal, Your Honor. After all, this town is swarming with Baldwin-Felts agents who won't be happy to see Sid Hatfield go free."

"It is the duty of the *state* to protect the defendants," said the judge. "Anything else is vigilantism."

The last of the Army Regulars had withdrawn two weeks ago, loading up their canvas-topped trucks and wagons and rumbling out of coal country, so the burden of maintaining order fell back to the state police. At the judge's order, the troopers turned the county courthouse into a citadel, a mountain fortress.

They hauled in sandbags and established shooting emplacements, mounting a belt-fed heavy machine gun on the front steps to deter the men milling in the streets. Men who dug coal and welded ships and swung sledges in stockyards, crushing the skulls of cows whose meat was ground into the hamburger that sizzled on griddles across the country. Men like Big Frank and the Hellfighter twins, who stood and watched, unarmed, staring unconcerned at the guns aimed in their direction, waiting as the jurors retired for their deliberations.

CHAPTER EIGHTEEN

SID WATCHED THE JURY foreman rise to read the verdict. He was an old mountaineer who'd ridden his mule into town when the ridges were still snow-heaped and brown, naked of leaves. Now the hills were full and green outside the courtroom windows, bursting with life. A trial of forty-some days and nights. More than two hundred witnesses. Enough lies and truths, testimonies and cross-examinations, facts and speculations to fill up the onionskin pages of a Holy Bible.

The bailiffs had wheeled out a scale model of Matewan, a detailed miniature of town complete with the railroad tracks, the train depot, the main street of downtown, and the models of the various buildings: the Old Matewan National Bank, Chambers' Hardware, Nenni's Department Store, the Urias Hotel.

Sid had watched the attorneys poke at the tiny town with wooden pointers like schoolmarms, opining on the locations of shooters, victims, witnesses, hiding places, escape routes, even the direction of the sun, the way the shadows had been flung across the scene. They were each trying to tell their own story of how the fracas had unfolded, who'd drawn what gun first and whose fault it was and who was acting in self-defense—overlaying their own kind of map on the place.

Even Sid was less sure what had happened that afternoon on Mate Street. Every successive witness offered a new story, a different angle. A unique window or doorway or gunsight. Each new testimony—sometimes twenty a day—called up a different truth, a new cinema picture in his mind, each vision a little different from the memories already in place. Each one elbowing for territory in his mind.

He reckoned that was all part and parcel of the legal strategy. These attorneys, they picked apart a thing until there was so little left they could put whatever story they liked in its place. There was the thin coal seam of the truth buried deep under the mountain and they sent a whole town armed with steam-hammers and dynamite to find it. Little surprise all they found was a bunch of rubble, just dust and ash blowing in the wind. They might as well have dropped a bomb in the middle of the Tug Valley for whatever truth they thought they were going to find. They might as well as have blown the top off the mountain.

He didn't let himself get too attached to any of it, to all the lies and slights swirling around his head. If he did, he might turn dark and cold, carrying it like a bone between his teeth he could never bury or crack. The same bone so many of his ancestors had carried to the grave, feudists long before Devil Anse himself who held their grudges tight as gods or lovers or kin, and died for them. Better to smile and keep in mind Baldwins were Grade A sons of bitches, and if putting them horizontal was a sin, it was also a public service. He'd known that when he took the badge, known what the people wanted. Someone who wasn't just willing to die, but to kill.

His smile disappeared but once during the proceedings, when the lead prosecutor turned a hooked finger on Jessie, as if he would pull down the top of her dress, and accused her of *improper relations*—that term again. Sid's smile vanished, sunk down some dark mine shaft inside him. His face turned cold and ugly, hard as the limestone hillsides dynamited to build the roads to the mines. His hair stiff as the naked timber of a ridge. His temples flickered beneath his hairline, as if hot magma swam inside his skull, his eyes crazed bright enough to split a man open, to spill a heap of guts on the floor.

The prosecutor's tongue turned thick in his mouth, as if he'd been snake-bit.

In the gallery, miners leaned to one another.

If he can kill ye smilin', what happens if you make him angry?

Now the jury foreman coughed into his fist. His chin was bladed clean, his overalls ironed board-stiff. His hands were shaking, making the verdict flutter. It was obvious he had a fear of public speaking—either that, or he was afraid of the words he was about to read. What they might mean for his family and homeplace. Whether he'd have to look over his shoulder for the rest of his days, fearing the crack of a rifle that could drop him neatly from his mule, his brains puffed pink into the breeze.

The old mountaineer licked his chapped lips and cleared his throat again. He read the verdict with his head bowed to the paper.

"We, the jury, unanimously find the defendants not guilty."

A roar exploded in the courtroom. Everyone leapt from their seats and cheered, flinging their hats to the ceiling as they shook hands and slapped backs and embraced. Sid and Jessie clasped in the aisle and kissed long on the mouth, like at a wedding, her nails clawing through his coat, and the flung volley of hats and caps and bonnets seemed to float on the very breath of the cheers, trembling high among the rafters before they came tumbling back down. Someone ran to the window and shouted the news to the crowd outside, and the cheers redoubled, thundering outside the courthouse walls even as the judge hammered away at the gavel, trying to call the place to order.

Sid and Jessie rode home to Matewan on a special train, finding the once-bloody streets crowded with well-wishers—miners and organizers come down out of the camps and colonies to give Smilin' Sid a hero's welcome. Every last man wanted to shake the hand that held the bright gun that shot down the most dreaded thug in the whole history of the state. Sid and Jessie lived just two hundred feet from the station—a distance it would take them two hours to cover, cheered and congratulated at every step, from every angle.

Sid's smile flashed gold in the sun, but his eyes were narrow, slit dark as those of a gunfighter in a Hollywood western, *Riders of the Purple Sage* or *The Last Outlaw*. He was watching every hand for a weapon. A knife or pistol or sawed-off shotgun—a retaliatory strike.

He knew the war had just begun.

BOOK II
ASSASSINATION

Injunctions and guns, like morphia, produce a temporary quiet. Then the pain, agonizing and more severe, comes again. So it is with West Virginia.

—Mother Jones

CHAPTER NINETEEN

THEY HATCHED IN THE predawn glow, miners creeping forth from pale canvas tents and ascending into the hills. Strings of men with patchwork coats and bolt-action rifles, pushing through laurel slicks and crawling over fallen trees, man after man after man. A chatter of rain through the trees and their boots slipping in the muck. Their quiet, muttered curses.

Mierda. Cazzo. Gówno. Shit.

They climbed high enough to look down on the company-owned towns sleeping along the river, the square little roofs and whispering stovepipes and duckboard streets arrayed like the neat, miniaturized world of a model train-man.

A world once theirs.

Those roofs had once sheltered their own families, who now lived in mud-plashed tents that skirled and flailed with every weather. Those black-bellied stoves had cast the aural warmth of marriage nights and Christmas mornings. Their own stockings had hung from those mantels. Their babes had been conceived in those beds; their wives had sung old ballads and hymns from those small stoops.

Now other men slept in those same beds, in the shelter of those hard roofs and milled plank walls. *Scabs.* Men from out of state, whose labor kept the mines smoking on the hillsides, the coal carts and conveyors trundling toward daylight. The company ledgers in the black. Kept the Union miners sleeping in canvas tents, their demands unmet. Their wives dull-eyed with hunger, their feet dark-slopped with mud. Their children's faces gaunt, so they could see their little skulls pressing through the skin, creeping toward the surface. Their grandmothers shivering, hacking in the damp air of the tents.

Below them, the dawn light crashed down through the valley, striking along ridgelines and searing down railroad tracks, making the muddy streets of the mine towns glisten like the trails of garden slugs, their nightly goings left bright and new on the dawning world. The Tug Fork River shone like a giant thunderbolt between the blue hills, rippling beneath glowing banners of mist.

A sight so pretty it hurt.

The miners swiped the rain from their eyes and propped the barrels of their rifles on mossy logs. They sighted on the tarpaper roofs far below, waiting while the telegraph lines were cut and the blowers wet the tips of their cow horns. It had been nearly a year since Smilin' Sid faced down the gun thugs in Matewan. Nearly a year since they'd been evicted, their possessions hurled into the muddy streets, their families forced to live in stinking canvas tents, in the slop and cold.

Long enough.

The wail of the first horn pierced the dawn, high and eerie, like the call of some ghost or beast of myth, and the Tug Valley erupted.

CHAPTER TWENTY

BULLETS SNAPPED ACROSS THE river and came hissing through the woods, slapping bark from trees. Doc Moo moved on all fours, head low, his pants dark-kneed with dirt. His white shirt soaked with sweat, nearly translucent against his olive skin, his eyeglasses perched foggy on the tip of his nose. His graying temples oozed with exertion, fear. He cursed beneath his breath, in his mother tongue.

"*Al'aama.*"

The Battle of the Tug—so the papers were calling it. A battle of snipers and sharpshooters. Striking miners exchanged fire with Baldwins, scabs, and state police. Small bands of fighters stalked the ridges, hunting one another. Small communities like Rawl and Sprigg and Blackberry City, perched high along the riverbanks, looked abandoned. People were afraid to go outside; the air was full of death. They'd taken to sleeping in cellars or under beds, their children curled in bathtubs. At night, any light could draw a shot.

Now Moo was in the very thick of it. That morning, he'd found the new commander of the state police waiting outside his office. Captain Brockus. The town fathers of Williamson had made much of the man's pedigree. He'd served his entire life in uniform, commanding infantry forces in the Philippines, Mexico, and the Great War. He was not from West Virginia, but Tennessee. A thirty-second degree Mason, a member of the American Legion, a Shriner.

"The meanest old son-bitch ever shat behind a pair of shoes," said one of his troopers during a routine visit to Doc Moo's office.

Brockus had been appointed for his abilities to restore law and order—to keep the miners in line. Moo knew most of his fellow professionals supported that mission, especially in the bigger towns. Physicians, bankers, attorneys, businessmen, and clergy.

"Somebody's got to put them back in the ground," a local druggist told Moo. "Mines or graves, their choice."

Captain Brockus enlisted only overseas men into the new state constabulary—combat veterans with experience in foreign wars. Doc Moo had passed their patrols while making his rounds. Troopers with campaign hats rammed low on their heads, cutting their faces with shadow. Hooded stirrups, horse pistols, carbines in saddle scabbards. This morning, he'd found Brockus and a squad of them sitting on their horses in the street outside his office, waiting for him.

"Doctor Domit Muhanna?"

He'd brought Musa to the office today—the only way to ensure the boy wouldn't run off to the woods, becoming the target of a sniper's bullet. The boy stared wide-eyed at the captain's giant chestnut gelding—a horse trained to perform the cakewalk, the quick-step, the Virginia reel for the crowds. Doc Moo pushed his son slightly behind him. "Yes, Captain. That's me. Is there some trouble?"

Around them, the distant crack and carom of rifle fire. The din of gunfire had been nearly constant for three days. The antiunion forces had been driven to the Kentucky side of the Tug Fork, so the river itself became a battle line.

"No, Doctor, not beyond the obvious. Fact is, we're here to ask for your help."

"Mine?"

The captain swung down expertly from his horse, his spurs ringing. He wore a big revolver at his hip with a curved white handle, ivory or pearl. His bearing was stiff, militant, his chin shaved clean despite the battle around them.

"Doctor, I have it on good authority that you're a man respected by miners and coal company men alike, as well as the local townspeople and professionals. A man willing to ride to either side of the river day or night, treating people in medical duress no matter their color, creed, or political bent. That's earned you the respect of both parties in this affair."

"It's simply the oath I took, Captain."

The captain nodded and looked out at the hills. "Doctor, this valley is imperiled, and every man, woman, and child has now become a kind of patient of yours. Their conditions are dire. They need you."

"I don't understand."

"We need someone to arrange a truce." He paused. "Someone to cross the river."

DOC MOO WAS PREPARING his medical kit when Musa tugged on his sleeve. He looked down to see the boy holding up his most prized possession, his possibles bag. His brow was set like a little soldier's. "So you'll have your hands free for climbing."

Doc Moo's heart squeezed like a fist in his chest, making it hard to speak. "Thank you, son," he managed, taking the bag from him. "I'll take good care of it."

He packed the bag with gauze, tourniquets, iodine, morphine, forceps—everything he might need to treat a gunshot wound—his own or someone else's.

In the street, the troopers tied a white flag with a crudely painted red cross to a thin whip of hickory and ran it down the back of his shirt, securing it beneath his belt, while Doc Moo knotted a length of borrowed shoestring to the temples of his eyeglasses so he wouldn't lose them while dashing across the river.

Captain Brockus held out a small derringer on the flat of his palm, a tiny two-shot pocket pistol. "A final instrument for your kit, Doctor."

Moo looked down at the gun. Too often he'd had to clean up the mess such an instrument made of someone's insides—too often he'd failed.

"No, thank you, Captain."

"There's mad blood stirring in these hills, Doctor." He glanced toward Musa, lowering his voice. "This item might be the only thing between you and a rabid *dog*. The kind for which there's but one *cure*."

Doc Moo touched the small Maronite cross hidden beneath his shirt, a gift from his father before he left home. "With respect, Captain, it won't be the only thing."

He crossed the footbridge at a sprint, drawing fire despite the emblem whipping over his head, the bullets smacking the water around him, and then he was starting the long climb through the trees, the red cross rattling over his head like some terrible joke, an invitation to shoot.

He rested in the crater of a wind-felled blight tree, again touching the three-barred Maronite cross, which resembled a Lebanese cedar—a tree whose timber Solomon had used to build the Temple of Jerusalem, whose bark Moses had used to treat the lepers. Saint Maron himself had been a mystic, a priest who left the great Christian city of Antioch to live high in the mountains, where he converted an old temple into a monastery and prayed for long hours exposed to wind and rain, snow and hail—a man who could free himself from physical suffering, it was said, achieving a mystic union with God and nature. Doc Moo wondered what the old black-robed saint would think of these mountains, their slopes slashed and dynamited and drilled into a scarred landscape, their trees blighted, fuming with gun smoke.

Rarely did the doctor resort to the tongue of his childhood, but the old language seemed made for prayer, the words rising in incantatory strings, curling like smoke, like they might just touch the ear of God.

"Aydan idha sirtu fee waadi . . ."

Yea, though I walk through the valley . . .

A round whizzed overhead and struck a tree behind him, tearing a wound in the trunk, the thunder-crack echoing beneath the canopy. The doctor touched his forehead to the earth, unable to remember the prayer. He'd been struck dumb, the thoughts knocked from his skull. He lay a long moment heaving, gathering himself, finding his way back to the beginning of the psalm, letting the words come again.

"Aydan idha sirtu fee waadi . . ."

He raised himself from the dirt, the crushed green ferns uncurling beneath him, as if drawn by his body's gravity, and then he was scrambling up the slope again, his hands grasping clods of dirt and mossy stones and raw weeds—whatever gave purchase. Praying despite his ragged breath and blowing lungs, praying and climbing, grasping the words of the psalm as he said them, gripping them like handholds, while death shrieked through the air.

Nearing the top of the ridge, he paused and looked back over his shoulder. The Tug had become a green curve far beneath him. Doc Moo placed the three-barred gold cross between his teeth, then took it inside his mouth like a host. Like the blessed flesh of Christ, whose blood dripped outward into the bulbed needles of the tree of life. Like a Lebanese cedar, whose rich hearth-smoke he would give so much to smell again, floating through the souk of his home village. To scent it in the collars of his parents when he embraced them. To smell it, one day, in the hair of his wife and children, burying his nose in the crowns of their heads.

A shot ripped through the branches overhead, shattering the bottle-green leaves. Doc Moo climbed over the top of the ridge and pulled the thin hickory flagstaff from the sheath of his shirt, raising it aloft like some slim weapon of peace.

CHAPTER TWENTY-ONE

SID WALKED DOWN MATE Street under a high sun, gold teeth aflash despite the gunfire. Friends in dark hats flanked him on either side, armed with repeaters, while the hills crackled and popped around them.

This sudden bout of violence had been waiting in the springtime air. Everyone felt it. The atmosphere over the river had turned sulfurous, yellowy—a hot-tempered haze too thick to breathe. Tree pollen and wet spring heat, blighted chestnuts and ten thousand minds bending toward rupture. Only the hatching mayflies seemed unaware of the coming violence, swirling dumbly between the riverbanks, drawing trout to the surface.

Sid could hear the sharp crack of high-powered rifles and the lesser pop of pistols. Now and again, the *tat-tat-tat* of the state police machine gun. Word was, the troopers had been churning and sliding down the muddy roads in their automobiles, snow-chains on their rear tires, trying to sweep up miners for arrest.

Matewan was a ghost town. All the businesses were closed, the doors barred. Chambers' Hardware, Dr. Witt's Dentistry, Leckie's Drug Store, even the post office. Many of the scabs had fled, their company-built houses pocked full of holes, their windows shot dark. Rainwater dripping through their roofs. People were living in root cellars and basements and bathtubs. They rode the trains lying flat between the aisles, praying they wouldn't catch a sniper's bullet.

Sid's hat lay far aback his head, haloing his face. Now and again, a round spanked the dirt in his vicinity. He didn't flinch, didn't frown. In the crook of his arm, he cradled a Winchester repeater—a lever-action .30–30 from a crate delivered on the train from Cincinnati, the oiled rifles packed like skinny sardines, destined for his and Jessie's gun shop. The receiver was machined from solid steel billet; the blued octagonal barrel glistened with a light coating of Cosmoline. A handsome piece, carried like an instrument of civil commerce.

He was headed for the Matewan rail depot—the long, red-roofed station where a train had just made an unscheduled stop, the dark engine ticking alongside the platform like an overheated machine gun. Closer, he saw P. J. Smith, mine super of Stone Mountain Coal—the man who'd had the Matewan families evicted last year.

Smith, dressed in a light suit and straw hat, was overseeing the unloading of a boxcar—a shipment of long wooden crates, which his men were transferring to a teamster's wagon. He turned around when he heard Sid's boots on the platform and set his hands on his hips, elbows thrust wide, as if to make a larger silhouette.

Sid stood before him and cocked one ear to the hills, revealing his dark gums and gold teeth. The air was a constant, muted thunder. "Ain't it some strange weather we been havin', Mr. Smith?"

Smith lifted inside his toes, tapping the planks. "What do you want, Hatfield?"

Sid squinted out over the surrounding hills. "Almost sounds like Indypendence Day, don't it? Except it ain't no celebration for them in these hills. No, sir, reckon they still fighting for their freedom."

"I got business to tend to, Hatfield. They can go back where they came from, they don't like it here."

Now Sid leaned to one side, looking past the man's shoulder. The blinkered draft horses stamped the dirt, ready to return to the stabled darkness of the livery, their hay beds and sacks of oats. "What you got in them crates, Mr. Smith?"

"Secure yourself a warrant and I'll be happy to show you the waybill, *constable*."

Sid had lost his position as police chief due to the shoot-out, but the people had elected him constable of the county's largest district. He sucked on one golden tooth. "You ask me, Mr. Smith, them crates look sized just about right for some rifles."

Smith clapped his toes on the platform again. "Well, you sure would know, Hatfield."

Sid's eyes flicked back to the man before him. "Say I would?"

Smith's cheeks had colored, his heat rising clear as red mercury in a gauge. An ire he could not fully control. He leaned forward at the hips. "I do. I say the mayor gets gut-shot and you feast on his leavings, turning his store into a gun shop. Convenient, that."

Smith's men had slowed their loading, watching over their shoulders. Sid licked the edges of his teeth. The name of Jessie, his wife, lingered unsaid in the air, so close.

"*Leavings*, Mr. Smith?"

Smith didn't notice how the smile had left Hatfield's face. The rarity of this event. No, Smith's blood was up, his neck bulling out from his open collar. He'd had no one to vent to but his wife at the dinner table.

"Arming these fucking animals. They'll believe anything that senile old bitch Mother Jones and the rest of those agitators tell them. 'Case you ain't noticed, this country runs on coal. Coal is King. And some poor son-bitch has to dig that coal up out the ground so the rest of this country can have their lights on at night and their radiators running. The job ain't pretty, never has been, never will be. Dark, dangerous work. But it don't take a fucking genius, now does it? And it's equal work, equal pay. Forty cents a ton, no matter if you're white, black, brown, red, or blue. Tell me where else you can get that in this country.

"Those operators up north, they're closer to market. Down here, we got hairline margins, everything against us. We got to dig deeper and ship farther. We put picks and shovels in the hands of men and pay them for honest work. But the Union tells 'em that ain't good enough, has 'em throw down their picks and take up arms. Now we got a bunch of unhappy Blacks, wops, Polacks, and hillbillies with guns. What a world, Hatfield. What a fucking world." Smith leaned farther forward, his hands on his hips. He couldn't seem to help himself. "And you're just riding high on the hog, ain't you, boy? Sucking at the *teat* of it all."

Sid had been watching the man with a kind of violent fixation, as if he must memorize every last crease and pore and cleft of his face. As if this were a face he would like to paint or sculpt one day—a face he must fix clearly in his mind, at this moment, in case he never saw it again this way.

"What you saying, Mr. Smith?"

Smith leaned farther forward, his torso near parallel to the wooden planks. He enunciated his words clearly, loudly, as if speaking to a fool. "Suck-ing-at-the-*TEAT*-of-it—"

The blow came so fast that witnesses would never agree how it happened. Whether Sid's fist, as he maintained, or the steel butt of his Winchester had struck the blow that landed P. J. Smith in the hospital for nine days. There was no wind-up, no telegraphing the strike. There was a flash and a crack and the superintendent of Stone Mountain Coal lay curled on the platform, wailing, his arms covering his head, as if to hide what had become of his face. His blood rilled toward Sid's boots, seeping between the planks.

Above them, from the hills, a roar like applause.

CHAPTER TWENTY-TWO

DOC MOO SAT ON the floor of a bullet-sieved cabin, a cigarette trembling between his fingers. Adrenaline was still coursing through his blood. Thin lances of light floated around him, beamed through coin-size holes in the walls. Before him sat the masked leaders of the antiunion forces, a party of Baldwins and company men assembled in a hillside village where the crude cabins and outbuildings hung perched from the steep face of the slope. They'd set woodstoves and upended tables and sacks of oats beneath the windows, rising now and again to shoot.

Their commander wore a dark muffler to hide the lower half of his face, but Doc Moo thought he recognized a small scar between his eyes.

"What brings you to our lovely hamlet today, Doctor?"

Doc Moo stared at the man's scar. If it was the man he thought, he knew him by reputation alone, a war hero and veteran mine guard who'd been a captain of the guard during the Paint Creek Mine War. Some said he'd run one of the machine guns on the *Bull Moose Special*. The miners called him "Bad Tony."

Doc Moo composed himself. "The strikers have agreed to quit shooting if you promise to do the same. Captain Brockus got word yesterday."

Bad Tony, if that's who it was, was sitting with his back against a pie safe full of feed sacks, his hands folded atop his binoculars, his rifle leaning against the wall. Above him, the kitchen window. Spidery cracks radiated from a neat, dime-sized hole in the single remaining pane. Around him, men whittled at the floor with their knives or watched the smoke curl from their pipes.

"Them boys running short on ammunition, that it, Doc? Used up all the cartridges the Union handed out?"

Moo sucked on the cigarette, hearing the wind whistle through the scatter-shot walls. "Given the way both sides have been going at it, I'm surprised there's a single round left in either West Virginia or Kentucky."

"Shame more of ours ain't struck home," said one of the mine guards.

"I'm sure they feel the same way across the river," said Doc Moo.

"Hell, they're just living off the teat of the Union over there," said the man. "Rather fight than work."

Bad Tony nodded in agreement. "That's right, Doc. They opened fire on men just trying to do an honest day's labor."

"I'm not here to take sides," said Doc Moo. "I'm here to arrange a truce."

"How do we know the Union didn't send you here themselves? Maybe there's a squad of Lick Creek boys laying in wait down there, ready to shoot every one of us the second we come out from behind cover."

Doc Moo felt his chest swell. That old Muhanna blood stoked again. He pulled his feet into his hips and sat cross-legged, looking at the men around him through a veil of smoke. "I don't know any of you men behind your masks, but many of you know me. I've treated you when you were ill or injured, your wives, your children, your neighbors. You've knocked on my door in the middle of the night and I've come. I didn't ask your political party, church, or employer. My vocation is to heal, not to divide. I'm here because this valley is wounded, hurting. Bleeding. *Our* valley. The Battle of the Tug must end. It's time to call a truce."

"The Regulars ain't coming to help?" asked one of the men.

"No, the President refuses to send troops again."

"And the state police want this ceasefire?" asked Bad Tony.

"Captain Brockus himself sent me."

The man looked around at the others, who nodded or shrugged or shifted their eyes to the floor. Then back to Doc Moo. The pale scar gleamed between his eyes. "Truce," he said. "But you best keep something in mind, Doc. You might not always have the privilege of treating both sides."

THE MINGO COUNTY COURTHOUSE brimmed with irate merchants and business owners, men in high white collars and double-breasted coats, their pink cheeks puffed with indignation. More than two hundred of them, sitting in the gallery and the jury box and the balcony. They twisted in their benches and spoke over their shoulders, their voices thundering beneath the same ceiling where Sid Hatfield—*that murdering blackguard*—had been acquitted.

You heard about the super down at Matewan? Man ain't out the hospital yet.

They had to wire his jaw shut, he's sucking his suppers through a straw.
Hatfield's the reason for this mess, stirring the miners to fight.

Tomorrow was Matewan Day, the first anniversary of the massacre that pitched their county into turmoil, unrest, insurrection. The day that dried up business, left dust gathering on the shelves of their dry goods stores and draft horses languishing in their liveries, the wagons and carriages unhitched. The day that Sid Hatfield shot down those Baldwin detectives in the street and coal production slowed to a rattling cough. After all, this black rock, born from thin seams of primeval wetlands compressed beneath the earth's surface and lumped into the stockings of wicked children on Christmas Eve, was the dark heart of every business in this county. The lifeblood of commerce. It was the very ink that kept their ledgers in the black. But it was combustible, too, ready to burst into flame.

The latest bout of violence ended three days ago with a truce, but they feared what new trouble Matewan Day might bring, what new disorder to threaten their livelihoods. They were sick of the strikers and agitators in their county, the filthy tent colonies pitched in the hollers, and the constant eruptions of violence in the coal camps. They were loud men, afraid of the riot reaching their own doorsteps—a marrow-deep fear that made their bones feel bendy, their hands clammy and soft.

We can't have these people just living in the hills.
The shooting could reach town, what then?
Law and order must be restored. Else we're doomed.

They hushed as the doors creaked open and Captain Brockus of the state police entered the courtroom. The man's boot-spurs rang down the center aisle, echoing across the stone floors. Captain Brockus, his face pale and stern as a marble bust. The mouths of the gathered men parted at his passage. Brockus carried his campaign hat beneath one arm and the white dome of his forehead sloped back to a last vestige of hair cropped close to his skull. His badge gleamed hard and bright. Surely, here was a man who could put these agitators to ground.

Brockus stood with his back to the judge's bench and squinted across the gathered crowd, as if searching for a certain steel in the men's eyes. His thighs looked huge, encased in the flared hips of his riding breeches, and the heels of his riding boots were set close enough to touch. He cleared his throat, hard and crisp.

"I applaud you men for coming here tonight, for answering the call of duty.

You men gathered here, you've been summoned because you are the *better people* of Mingo County. The kind of men who stand for law, order, and American patriotism."

The crowd nodded, whispering among themselves.

Here, here.

Yes, we are.

The better people, damn right.

"What we have here is a state of war, insurrection, and riot. Mingo is crawling with agitators, outlaws, and malcontents, ready to plunge this county into complete and total anarchy."

Damn agitators.

Poisoning the county.

Enough is enough.

Brockus looked across the crowd, meeting the eyes of this man, that man. They sat taller as they met his gaze, surer. Brockus held up his free hand, gesturing with his thumb, as if holding a holy writ before them.

"Now it's up to you to determine the fate of your county. It's for you men to decide whether disorder, violence, and agitation will carry the day, pitching Mingo into lasting darkness, or will you stand against the rising tide of lawlessness?"

Damn right we will.

It's our patriotic duty, is what it is.

Sure as kicking the Krauts out of France.

Brockus reached into his pocket, pulling out a folded paper. "I have here a warrant to vest *posse comitatus* power in a force of able-bodied townsmen, deputizing this citizens' militia to aid in the capture, arrest, and detainment of any person suspected of inciting riot or insurrection in Mingo County."

The townsmen sat erect in their seats now, holding the handrails.

Somebody's got to do it.

Give me a rifle, I'll learn to shoot.

We'll string up Hatfield and watch him dance.

"You will become the county's Vigilance Committee, issued rifles and armbands, and asked to remain at the ready, casting aside all pursuits should you hear the call to arms. Four blasts on the town fire siren, repeated three times. I warn you, unless you are willing to take up a rifle, this county is all but doomed."

The men were rocking in their seats now, their collars strained, their bowlers and top hats rumbling atop their heads. Brockus set his campaign hat on high, a slight rake of shadow across his face. His clear eyes shot across the courtroom. "Now, those of you willing to shoulder a gun for law and order, please rise."

In a single movement, more than two hundred men shoved upright from their seats, thrusting their right arms high and straight as rifle barrels.

Doc Moo, standing in the shadows at the back of the courtroom, let himself out the door.

CHAPTER TWENTY-THREE

SID PARTED THE BLINDS of their apartment above Mate Street, bending in his striped silk pajamas to look down on the street where the shoot-out had taken place exactly one year ago today. Where the gun thugs had been laid out before him, their blood spooling into the muck, and the mayor moaned with a bullet buried in his gut.

In the early light, Sid could see strange bodies hovering upright all over town. He wiped his eyes. Not ghosts but men, their pressed trousers and three-piece suits looped with leather cartridge belts, their military-issue rifles fresh from the crate, the blued barrels glazed with packing grease. They wore white armbands on their sleeves—an army birthed overnight from the county courthouse.

Jessie came to the window beside him. "What is it, baby?"

"God-damned Vigilance Committee, already out."

"Vigilance?"

"Vigilantes. Puffy spoon-suckers don't know they pricks from gun barrels."

"*Sidney.*"

Sid knew their kind. Men who considered themselves rare and fine, turning up their noses at the people of the hollers and mines. They'd never descended into the black gut of a mountain before dawn and worked till night, missing the day's short leap of sun from ridge to ridge. Never seen their kin hungry, truly hungry. Men who could afford for the world to stay the way it was. Who'd fight to keep it that way. They stood high-chinned at street corners, holy with duty, each armed with a rifle and eighty rounds of ammunition.

Sid rubbed his chin with the back of his hand. "Like to see how cock-tall they walk after a week in the Stone Mountain Number Nine."

Sid thought of them staggering into the light after twelve hours underground, six days in a row. A miner's week. Their faces blacked with coal, their fingernails. Their armpits rancid, their spines crooked, their shoulders like balls of carbolic acid. Their palms ripped bloody from the hickory haft of a pick. Humble and sorry-eyed, like they'd look at the point of his bright gun.

When he didn't move from the window, Jessie slipped her hand inside the fly of his silk pajamas. "Speaking of cock-tall." Her breath tickled his earlobe. "I need that pistol of yours more than them this morning."

Sid remained bent at the window, his nose thrust to the glass. An attitude of furious fixation, like a bird dog aimed at the street below. His temples rippled; his breath whistled through clenched teeth. His eyes zeroed on this corner and that.

Jessie's hand found hold, coaxing and tugging him, drawing his attention back into the room. Her teeth found his earlobe, her breath tickling him, humming into his ear canal. She knew how to steer him from fixation. To loosen the bone clenched between his teeth. The one he and his ancestors could carry to the grave. She pressed her belly against his hip, her damp, scratchy heat against his thigh.

"Please, Sidney."

Sid yielded and straightened from the window, letting the blinds fall back into place.

A MUFFLED RHYTHM OF raps on the door downstairs—the Union's secret knock. Sid uncoupled himself from Jessie, his skinny thighs smacked rosy. Still in his pajamas, he took his bright gun from the side table and descended the stairs in his bare feet, skipping the steps that groaned. He held the pistol close to his belly, pointed at the door. Through the peephole, he saw one of the Union's organizers, Lavinder. The man was looking over his shoulder, chewing his bottom lip.

They spoke in the dark of the stairwell, voices just above a whisper. Spies could be listening, their ears pressed to drilled holes in the wall or resonating pipes. The organizer's face was sharp, a flinty mask of angular facets and creases. A man accustomed to living on a knife's edge. He once told Mother Jones he couldn't carry her across the creeks any longer—the Felts brothers had thrown him from a moving train, putting a permanent crook in his spine.

"Governor's thrown down martial law again, Sid. President refuses to send the Regulars, but the governor's got the state police and eight hundred men from the new Vigilance Committee all under command of Major Davis, the Bulldog."

"That jowled son-bitch from the old Paint Creek days?"

"That's him, Sid. Union-buster to the bone. It's different this time."

Sid wiped his nose with the back of his hand, still holding the lustrous pistol. "Say it is?"

"Governor's set strictures in the martial law." He passed a paper to Sid. "Nine in all. No right of public assembly, no right to bear arms. Holds a pillow over the press's face. Not so much as a Union handbill allowed. Unconstitutional is what it is. They got us by the short and curlies, Sid."

Sid didn't look at the paper. The striped silk pajamas hung reckless from his bony shoulders, flowy as a robe. The bright gun glowed in his hand. He leaned to one side and stared over the man's shoulder, at the door, as if he might walk out in his nightclothes and start shooting occupiers in the streets. His metal teeth gilded the darkness.

"We'll see."

CHAPTER TWENTY-FOUR

"DON'T YOU *THINK* OF going into town," said Miss Beulah, leaning nearly out of her rocker.

Frank put both hands out, palms forward, as if to push her gently back into her seat. "I'll be careful, Mama-B. But somebody's got to get the new journals out."

Behind him, hidden beneath an old coat, sat a stack of the latest copies of the *United Mine Workers Journal*, hot off a UMW truck.

"You ain't no paperboy," she said. "Let one of them Union people do it."

Frank crossed his arms. They were sized like country hams, but the left one was slightly smaller now than the right, welted with scars from that beating the thugs had given him last summer. His forearm had received a direct blow from a tire iron. If he hadn't spent years with a pick and shovel in hand, said Doc Moo, the bone would've split clean in two.

"I've told you, Mama-B, I *am* one of them Union people."

The old woman huffed through her remaining teeth. "You're Hugham first, that's what."

"And you taught me Hughams don't kneel to no masters but our own."

"You seem awful close to kneeling to the Union."

"I ain't kneeling to it, Mama-B. I'm standing up."

"Tell me one thing. You fought in that Battle of the Tug earlier this month?"

"I did."

"You shot anybody?"

"I shot, but never aimed at nobody. We been stuck up here in these tents for a year now. We just trying to strike some fear in those scabs and mine guards. Make sure they know we're still here and we ain't going nowhere till something changes. We can't. Got nowhere to go and no money to get there. You're the one once said the only things them thugs listen to are gunshots. Course, some people let things get out of hand."

"Well, ain't that always the way of a shooting match, boy."

"I wish it ain't come to that, Mama-B. I hope it don't again. But it's been twice now in the short life of this country that a bunch of shooting was the only way people got their freedom. Once for independence, once for emancipation."

Miss Beulah set her hands on her knees. Just a night ago, they'd had a bonfire in the middle of camp, and she'd sat back in her rocker and watched the embers racing toward the stars, heaven bound like hundreds of souls. Thousands. Tens of thousands. She'd taken her grandboy's hand and held it in both of her own, her thumbs working over his calluses and lumpy knuckles. She'd thanked God for bringing him home to her. Now she had to fear losing him again.

"I believe in the Union, son. I do. Solidarity forever, there's a slogan to stand behind. I just don't want it to be my boy's blood spilt for it."

Frank nodded. "Hell, Mama-B, that makes two of us."

Miss Beulah nodded at the stack of papers. "Go on, then. But if you let something happen to you, I'm-a hold my breath till I die and come find you. You won't hear the end of it for all damn eternity. Heaven will be some kind of hell. You keep that in mind."

Frank nodded, hefting the papers under his arm. "I ain't apt to forget it."

"One more thing, boy."

"Ma'am?"

"I love you."

CHAPTER TWENTY-FIVE

THE MUHANNAS RODE THE train up to Williamson, the county seat, to attend mass. The small Catholic church was built high on a hillside over town, where snakes, bobcats, and even the priest's pet rooster had all found their way into the service on occasion. After mass, they walked down the steep streets into town, the three pigtailed girls nearly skipping, so excited were they for hot fudge sundaes from the ice cream parlor at the River View Hotel—a Sunday tradition.

Doc Moo and family sat at the long marble counter of the ice cream parlor, relishing their post-church hot fudge sundaes. The girls swung their knee socks and patent leather shoes beneath their stools, chattering away, while Musa read his latest copy of *Wild West Weekly*, his cowlick standing up from the crown of his head like a little black feather. Adele, the oldest, kept licking her finger and trying to smooth it down. Meanwhile, Moo and Buddeea were sharing a banana split, slowly deconstructing the domes of ice cream with long spoons.

There was only one other patron in the place—a hard-faced man in a worn suit who sat slightly crooked at the counter. Since the start of martial law, miners had been arrested for consorting in groups of three or more—*bunching*—or being in possession of labor journals. Anything deemed *agitating* could bring out the cuffs. The prisoners were brought to the county jail in chain gangs, herded like cattle into overcrowded cells where they pissed in corners and shat in buckets—such were the stories Moo heard during his rounds.

Now Musa leaned over and tugged on his father's sleeve. "Papa, look."

Moo and Buddeea turned to see the great chestnut gelding of Captain Brockus pass before the front window of the place, big as a dreadnought, the captain's striped green trousers and hooded stirrups flooding through the glass. The rest of his patrol followed, their horses smaller, their spurs and tack clinking as they passed before the hotel.

"The captain," said Adele.

"Such a beautiful horse," said Amelia.

"Sure is proud of himself on it," said Corine.

The bell jingled and Captain Brockus strode into the place, three troopers in his wake. He strode straight to the lone man at the counter, his boots ringing on the parquet floor.

The hard-faced man looked up from his ice cream. "Good day, Captain. You and the boys come for banana splits?"

The police commander's face was shaved clean, humorless as a bust. A powerful scent of aftershave filled the parlor. "A. D. Lavinder, we have it on good authority you're in possession of a sidearm."

Lavinder. Moo had heard the name. A Union organizer.

The man continued to eat his sundae. "I got a state-issued permit to carry a sidearm on my person, Captain."

Captain Brockus bent toward him—brisk, exact. "I am the state, Lavinder, and your carry permit is null and void under martial law."

Lavinder spooned another bite from his sundae. "And what a *state* it is."

The troopers unbuttoned the flaps of their holsters. The bow-tied servers wiped down the bar and retreated through the swinging doors to the kitchen. Moo and Buddeea hustled Musa and the girls from their stools, leaving their ice creams unfinished.

Captain Brockus ignored them, his attention focused on the man at the counter. "Surrender your weapon and we'll take you in peaceful. Major Davis wants to see you."

"The Bulldog wants to see me, does he?" Lavinder took another heaping bite of his sundae, sucked the spoon clean, and held it upright before his face, examining his reflection. He looked wistful almost, like he was seeing something he might not see again. Then he set the spoon down on the counter. "Well, you go tell the Bulldog, if he wants to see me so bad, he can come by my office at Union headquarters."

Moo was herding the family toward the door as fast as he could. Captain Brockus looked up sharply at them, his eyes saying: *Git out.*

The Muhanna clan had just stepped outside when they heard a sickening smack, like a side of beef slapped down on a butcher's block, and a single high animal shriek.

Moo pushed the family along, arms wide, trying to shield them. Their faces were white; the girls were holding their mouths, beginning to cry. No one would forget that sound, the violence of it. They were nearly to the corner when Moo looked back over his shoulder. The troopers were dragging the man toward a waiting car. His body hung limp between them, the toes of his shoes scrawling dark lines across the cinder.

FRANK CROUCHED IN A corner of the kitchen, his heart galloping in his chest. One of the servers eased open the back door and ducked his head into the alley.

"Clear," he said.

Frank took up the satchel of UMW journals he'd been ordered to hand off to Lavinder for distribution in town. The man's beating had sent his blood running crazy, spiking under his skin. Now he had to calm himself and walk out of here like he hadn't more worry than a woodlark.

As he stepped toward the door, the server put a hand to his chest. "Just leave the bag, man. There's too much heat out there. We'll burn 'em in the furnace downstairs."

Frank shook his head. "These are all we got for this town. No more's being printed. I'll get them back to my contact and they'll work out a different plan."

"Them tire irons ain't taught you nothing, I reckon."

Frank slung the satchel over his shoulder, securing it beneath his once-fractured arm. "Just the opposite, boss."

He peeked out the door himself, made sure the alley was still clear, and then stepped out. A pair of cats looked up from their meal of dead rat. Faces scar-flecked, ears nocked. Frank looked to the river. It was close, flowing green and dark past town. The safest escape would be to cross the Tug and take to the hills on the Kentucky side, but the journals would be ruined—the water was too high this time of year to wade. In the other direction, he had to cross at least four city blocks before he'd make it to heavy woods where he could disappear.

He thought of Mama-B up there at the holler, sucking her teeth at his predicament. *I done told you.* He turned from the river and gripped the satchel strap at his shoulder, heading up the alley toward town.

The two cats paused to watch him pass, jaws bloody. Williamson always seemed a strange town to him. So wide and clean in the avenues, so dank and dark in the shadows. Maybe that was all towns.

He emerged onto Second Avenue, where the state police were loading the limp man into a car in front of the hotel, surrounded by a throng of onlookers. Everyone distracted. He turned and headed up the sidewalk in the opposite direction, trying to walk like a man who knew just where he was going, who wasn't carrying a satchel of red-hot contraband. A prize for any of the state troopers or vigilance men posted around the place.

He crossed the street and kept heading south, his boots clicking on the cinder. Most people were headed in the opposite direction, flocking toward the spectacle. He turned up the next alley, a narrow brick ravine of fire escapes and cigarette butts. There was a tavern and pool hall on the next avenue, and the railroad tracks ran through the center of town another block past that.

Frank was just to the end of the alley when a pair of state troopers turned the corner on foot. One of them held an unlit cigarette between two fingers.

"Officers," said Frank, bowing his head slightly.

They didn't move for him to pass, a wall of green wool and brown leather. They wore knee-high riding boots and thick gun belts with crossed shoulder straps to support the weight of their pistols. Their wide campaign hats were slightly cocked, shading their faces. In the distance, Frank heard the hoot of a train.

The first trooper lit his cigarette—Captain Brockus didn't allow his men to smoke on duty, but the captain was otherwise disposed at the moment, handling the situation in front of the River View Hotel. The trooper blew smoke from beneath his wide hat. "Where you think this boy's going in such a hurry, Trooper Gibb?"

The second trooper shrugged. "I wouldn't want to hazard a guess, Trooper Biggs, not without seeing what he's got in that satchel of his."

The first one drew on his cigarette. "Boy, what you got in that there satchel?"

Frank heard the train engine again in the distance, sounding from the edge of town. The words came quickly to him, almost without thought. "Library books."

"*Lie*-berry books," said Trooper Biggs, laughing through his teeth. "You hear that, Trooper Gibb? I don't recall there being no library in this town, fine a place as it may be. You?"

"No, Trooper Biggs, I surely do not."

Frank looked back slowly over his shoulder, stretching his neck. He could feel a strange sensation in his limbs, a kind of power. His thighs hung heavy as field guns, loaded. His chest and shoulders broad as a breastplate. His arms had ripped the guts from mountains, had absorbed the iron hate of men.

He nodded back the way he'd come. "The library's in city hall," he said. "Just a little closet of a place." He looked at the men, sniffed. "You got to be a Mingo County resident to get a card."

The first trooper flicked his cigarette away. "Set the bag on the ground, face the wall, and spread your legs."

Frank thought of Mama-B high up there in her rocker, waiting for him. He thought of Lavinder, just now, and his own beating not a year ago—a body left for dead. He thought of how puny these men were without their shields or pistols or batons. What he could do to them with his bare hands.

He began to comply, squatting as if to set the satchel at their feet. The troopers had their palms resting on their revolvers, casual. Men so sure of themselves, their rank and power. Frank let the satchel touch the ground just a moment, as if to surrender it for their inspection, only to snap it back hard to his chest and explode from his crouch, bull-rushing them, driving between the two troopers like a siege ram. They were thrown back stumbling and falling against the brick walls and he was already halfway across Third Avenue, cutting diagonal to intercept the coal train.

He had the satchel clenched in the crook of his arm, his boots cracking across the asphalt. A roadster hooted its horn and Frank flew across the hood hardly breaking stride, hearing the shouts of the troopers behind him. He sprinted past a line of storefronts and cut toward the train.

The coal hoppers were unladen, headed downriver into the coalfields, the engine picking up speed as it cleared the edge of town. He hit the crushed stone of the railbed at full speed, lungs searing and breath tearing from his chest, driving all his strength into his feet. The train seemed to get faster with every chug of the engine, ratcheting away from him, the iron cars retreating from his grasp, and he heard shots behind him, bullets hissing and sparking. He gave up his spirit, same as he had beneath the falling clubs of the Baldwin thugs, he gave it up to Evie, to God, to whatever may come. Then his hand found the iron rung of a coal hopper's ladder and he was hanging from the car, throwing the bag into the empty hull and hurling himself over the side as shots ricocheted off the iron.

He lay in the bed of the coal hopper heaving, clutching the satchel against his chest with both arms. Above him, a flurry of daylight stars.

CHAPTER TWENTY-SIX

THE SEVEN MEN MOVED slowly along the ridge above Matewan, their lanterns swinging red in the darkness, the glass globes tied with bandannas to mute their glow. They spoke little, their boots moving through bloodied pools of light, stepping over deadfalls and mossy rocks. Big Frank and six others, all of them Lick Creekers who'd served in the Great War.

The Bad Seven.

For months, the seven veterans had served as the tent colony's sentries, perching at points around the holler to watch for gun thugs or police posses or vigilante townsmen. Two of them, Bonney and Lacey, the Hellfighter twins, had served with the 369th Infantry, the famed Harlem Hellfighters—a Black regiment that spent more time in frontline trenches than any other American unit. Four months in some of the most hellish conditions ever known, when the earth was soaked with blood and men lived among rats and lice and human corpses.

On a moonless night in 1918, they were in an observation post on the edge of no-man's-land when they heard the sound of cable-cutters clipping barbwire. They fired an illumination round, alerting their lines to an attack just as the Germans charged. Between them, the brothers killed six enemy soldiers who came over the parapet into their post, fighting with spiked trench knives and the club ends of their French Lebel rifles, turning back the twenty-four-man assault.

They were narrow-shouldered and wiry, fast and tireless as coal shovelers, and crack shots. Their upper arms bore matching tattoos of coiled rattlesnakes—the 369th's insignia.

After Frank's narrow escape, the brothers were furious.

Man shouldn't have to run for his life just for carrying the wrong paper.

It can't stand. This is America, we got rights.

Not no longer. Our rights end at the point of their guns.

Then, three days later, the final straw. Their man Sid Hatfield was called to court for assaulting P. J. Smith, the mine super who'd thrown them out of their homes a year ago. As his train rolled into town, he found a gang of state troopers and armed vigilance men waiting for him at the station, ready to give him a dose like Lavinder's at the ice cream parlor—or worse.

Sid narrowly escaped, jumping off the far side of the train as it slowed and then disappearing among the coal cars, only to reappear on the "Great White Way"—the wide concrete avenue laid through the heart of town—walking with his fists buried in his coat pockets, clutching a pair of Colt pocket pistols as he passed through the steep canyon of storefronts and office buildings. By the time he turned onto Logan Street, where the courthouse stood high and solemn beside the river, pale as the stone ghost of a building, he'd become the head of a small parade, a throng of supporters who filled the sidewalk and spilled over into the street.

"Ye done good," said a woman. "Put that God-damned mine boss in his place."

"That's right," said another. "Down at ye feet, bleeding like a stuck hog."

"Amen," said a man. "How many families he's put out in the cold?"

Sid's eyes flashed to the clock tower on top of the courthouse, squinting as if to read the time or discern what shadows might linger beneath the white face of the clock. Baldwin sharpshooters or bomb throwers, the long arms of King Coal.

Nothing.

Finally he stood before the front steps of the courthouse, the pale marble of the building thrust from the dark earth of the bottomland like the jagged tip of an iceberg, like the building might spread in ever-widening floors and chambers beneath the ground, too deep to fathom. He was about to climb the steps when a deputy leaned toward him from the shadows.

"Pistols, Sid."

Sid sniffed and turned over his guns. Before climbing the steps, he looked down at his hands, which had been squeezing the baby automatics buried in his front pockets, their checkered grips emblazoned with rampant Colt medallions.

People whispered what he'd seen: *A twin pair of colts, red-stamped on his palms.*

BONNEY AND LACEY CALLED a meeting of the sentries.

"Enough is enough. They got to know we ain't to be bullied no more."

"We been on defense too long. Time we take the fight to them."

"King Coal ain't the only law in these hills."

"What you say, Big Frank?"

Frank looked down at his hands, black-creased with coal seams that would never wash out—the dust tattooed beneath the skin. No blood on them, not yet. Slowly, as if it weighed a great deal, he got out his clasp knife and unfolded the blade. He pushed the point into the cup of his palm, drawing up a red seam of ooze, the ore of men. Then he held out his open hands. The knife in one palm, a welt of blood in the other.

The seven men made a blood pact, nicking their palms and clasping hands. They were the Bad Seven, scourge of King Coal, bane of the Baldwin-Felts. Besides Frank and the twins, there were the Zielinski boys, veterans of the Blue Army on the Western Front, and the Provos—Provenzano cousins, who'd served in an Alpini regiment. There were several white sentries from the camp, native-born Mountaineers they knew and respected, but those men might assume they were in charge by skin or birthright—not of this crew.

Now the Bad Seven were heading south along the ridge that ran down toward Matewan. The moon was clouded out; the weaving red glow of their lanterns was the only light. The midnight train had come and gone some time ago.

Frank moved in a kind of trance, his feet sorting the dark trail almost on their own, rarely stumbling or slipping. He felt the same way sometimes in the dark room of a mine, when his body seemed to do all the work without him and it seemed he could feel his fingertips in the very point of his pick, taking a coalface apart in half the swings it would take another hewer.

His own Black regiment, though combat-trained, was mainly used for stevedore work during the war, unloading ships at the docks in France. One time, when a Royal Navy submarine moored nearby to receive supplies, the British sailors let Frank and the men tour the underwater boat. Frank's comrades snickered and joshed him before they climbed down the narrow hatch.

Hell, Big Frank ain't fitting down there.

Quick now, who brought the axle grease?

Should of saved some bacon fat from breakfast.

Inside, a series of cramped iron chambers that could dive two hundred feet below the surface, into depths where little light reached, and the crew working in near silence, reading gauges and twisting valves while the screws rumbled through the metal skin. Even there at shore, unsubmerged, some of the others began to panic inside the dim confines of the vessel, unable to imagine being trapped in the dark belly of this whale beneath ten tons of ocean. But it didn't bother Frank, who was accustomed to working shoulder to shoulder with men who blew black powder charges with whole mountains sitting just inches above their heads. The submarine seemed cozy almost—the kind of place he could imagine himself working, were he allowed to man such vessels.

Frank had something of the same sensation tonight on the ridge, he and the other six men moving inside a dim tunnel of lantern light, bound in common toil. A dark world surrounding them on every side, binding them close. When they came upon their destination, it was near what Mama-B would call the witching hour. Three or four o'clock in the morning. A time when the haints came out, when the rest of the world was asleep. Their red-glowing lanterns assembled like spook lights on a rocky thrust of the ridge.

Below, the dark outlines of a mine, tipples and conveyors and headhouse surrounded in barbwire, like some remote military outpost. One by one, the dim red lanterns were extinguished, like souls winking out. Seven darkened forms began filtering down the steep face of the ridge.

CHAPTER TWENTY-SEVEN

DOC MOO SMELLED SMOKE. He'd spent the night on the cot in his office after being called to town to treat an older miner who was coughing up blood—miner's asthma. Now he rose in his skivvies and went to the window. A strange, reddish dawn, as if a storm were coming. He cracked the window and the smell grew stronger.

He headed to the roof for a better look. There, he saw a dark weed of smoke sprung from the ridge above town, twisting and curling, growing leaves, spreading wild across the sky. Soon a whole tree, holding the red-rising sun like an angry star in its branches, while dawn light rifled across town like tracer fire. A bad omen. Moo went to the corner of the roof and looked down to the street. Sid was sitting on the bench in front of the store, straight-backed, his morning coffee steaming on the side table.

After his recent court appearance, Sid had been forced to sneak back out of Williamson, hopping a train from the switchyard south of the station. In the coach, a local newspaper reporter recognized him.

"How come you came to town alone?" the man asked, licking a pencil nub.

Sid showed his teeth. "When I aim to go someplace, I aim to go it alone. They got in the habit of blaming me for every last thing that happens down at Matewan."

The reporter scribbled down his words in shorthand, then perched his pencil above the pad. "And what do you make of today's verdict?"

"Verdict?"

"You haven't heard? The six surviving Baldwin-Felts agents from the Battle of Matewan were acquitted today, found not guilty on charges of murdering the mayor and a fourteen-year-old bystander."

The Baldwins had been tried one hundred miles away, in friendly territory.

"Care to comment?" asked the reporter.

"No."

Soon the verdict hit the papers, the hollers, the camps. Doc Moo had known there would be a reaction. There had to be, sure as physics. Next day, he was walking down Mate Street when a mine downriver exploded. Moo felt the detonation in his bootsoles, an underground thunderclap like the joinery of the earth had blown a rivet or busted a seam. Like something evil was down there, breaking loose. Around him, townsfolk stood dumbstruck, staring down at the street mud like it might start squirming. He looked over to see that Sid and Ed's checkers pieces had been thrown clear off the board, strewn helter-skelter beneath the table.

Now the red dawn light slanted down on the Tug Valley, burning the mist from the hills, as if the whole valley were smoldering, and the tree of smoke spread wicked across the sky, like the very spirit of hell let slip from the earth. A fine rain of ash had begun to fall, peppering Moo's bare shoulders. He leaned over the edge of the roof, calling down to Sid. "Is that the Stone Mountain burning?"

Sid's teeth shone like red copper in the dawn. "Reckon somebody ain't too happy with ole P. J. Smith. That mine of his got up in smoke."

NOON THAT DAY, A pounding on Doc Moo's office door. He descended the narrow flight of stairs and opened the door to find Captain Brockus and a trio of state troopers. When Brockus had come to see him during the Battle of the Tug, he'd held his campaign hat under his arm, his hands clasped like a man at church. This time, he kept the round hat rammed low on his head, the brim flecked with ash. He hooked his thumbs in his thick leather gun belt.

"Doctor Muhanna," he said.

"What can I do for you, Captain?"

"We've come to ask you a few questions."

No room for the men in the narrow stairwell, so Doc Moo pulled the door closed behind him and stepped onto the sidewalk. "I'm with a patient," he said. "So we must be quick."

"It's come to our attention that you are the primary physician of a Mr. Frank Hugham, formerly of the employ of the Stone Mountain Mine. Currently a resident of the Lick Creek encampment?"

"I've been the longtime physician of his grandmother, Miss Beulah Hugham. I treated Mr. Hugham for the wounds he received after his arrest in Welch."

Brockus raised his chin. "We have no record of any arrest of Mr. Hugham in McDowell County."

Moo ground his teeth. *Of course you don't.* "He was arrested on the rail platform last July, held without charge in the county jail, then taken out into the woods in the middle of the night and beaten very nearly to death."

Captain Brockus made a grim line with his mouth, as if skeptical of the claim. "And when was the last time you treated Mr. Hugham?"

"I'm sorry, Captain, but I'm afraid such a disclosure would be a breach of doctor-patient confidentiality."

"There's no such law in West Virginia."

"It's part of the Hippocratic Oath, Captain, which I swore to uphold when I became a medical doctor. I'm sure you take your own oath very seriously. May I ask what this is about?"

Brockus sniffed. "Mr. Hugham is wanted for questioning on a variety of topics, including an assault on two of my troopers in Williamson."

"Assault?"

"That's right," said the captain. He cocked his head to eye the smoke still drifting over town. "Among other things. He seems to be a hard man to locate these days."

"Well, I'm sorry I can't be of more help, Captain." He put his hand on the doorknob. "Now, really, I must be getting back to my current patient."

Brockus pulled his riding gloves from his belt and snapped them against his thigh. "You know, Doctor Muhanna, we seem to find you in a lot of suspicious positions. Up at the tent colony, in the very same ice cream parlor as the agitator Lavinder, and now we hear you weren't home last night."

Doc Moo felt his blood rising. This rod-spined son of a bitch out of Tennessee, with his prancing horse and white-handled pistol, who'd beaten a man unconscious in the town ice cream parlor in front of his family, his wife and girls. As if his badge gave him that right. Moo breathed in through his nose, out through his mouth, thinking what Buddeea would say: *He just wants to rile you, Moo. That's exactly what he means to do. Don't let him succeed.*

"I have multiple witnesses who can confirm my whereabouts last night, but I'm sure you know that already. Now, I'm afraid I've kept my patient waiting long enough. You can make an appointment to talk further, if you like. Thank you, Captain, and good day."

Doc Moo closed the door and climbed back up the stairs, his blood pounding like a drum inside his head, hammering at his temples. He entered his office and locked the door behind him and leaned back against it, his chest heaving. Then he stepped into the examination room, where his patient sat waiting on the edge of the padded leather exam table, holding a flame-scorched forearm in his lap.

Big Frank.

"You ain't have to do that, Doc. Captain learns you lied to him, there'll be hell to pay."

Moo had been cleaning the burn when the pounding came at the door downstairs. Now he sat on his stool and laid a sterile dressing over the blistered skin. "I am oathbound to do no harm. And handing you over to that son of a bitch would be harmful indeed."

"You got to think about the harm to you and yours, Doc. You got youngins at home."

Moo began to wrap a roll of gauze around the dressing, careful to make the turns regular, firm but not tight enough to impede circulation. "I am thinking about it, Frank. All the time. But the man I choose to be will have a great influence on who my children become. I have to remember that, too."

He cut off the end of the gauze with a pair of stainless shears and reached for the bandaging tape. Big Frank touched his elbow, looking him in the eye. "I want to thank you, Doc. For what you done for me, for Mama-B." The big man paused; his chest swelled. "For what you done for Evie. I know you done all you could for her."

A sting behind Moo's eyes. "I wish I could've done more."

"If something happens to me—"

Moo put a hand on the man's shoulder. "You know I will, Frank. Look after her."

Miss B.

Moo furnished the man with fresh dressings and instructions to keep the burn clean. Then Frank crouched at the window, watching for a signal from the woods across the railroad tracks. When it came, he descended the stairs and slipped out the door. Doc Moo watched him sprint across the tracks and vanish into the trees just as a coal train came howling past, cutting off anyone who might try to pursue him.

CHAPTER TWENTY-EIGHT

FRANK'S EYES SNAPPED OPEN. He'd heard someone scream, in the dark of his dreams or outside his head. It sounded like Evie. His heart was hammering and he was already sitting up in bed, throwing off his covers, his bare feet slapping the duckboard floor. He went to the tent door in his long johns to find Bonney and Lacey already there, breathing hard.

"Another raiding party," said Bonney. "Coming at speed."

"Troopers?"

"A whole carload."

Brockus and his men had arrested more than thirty miners from Lick Creek after the Stone Mountain burned. A reprisal. But they'd narrowly missed the Bad Seven, who were on their way home from Doc Moo's office in Matewan at the time. Frank's forearm was still in bandages, seared when a silo of slack coal went up like a torch, sending out flaming debris.

Now Bonney reached under his shirt and held out a pistol, butt first. "We get arrested, ain't no getting out, not for us. They'll make sure of that."

The twins knew Frank kept his rifle hidden in a hollow log high up on the ridge, far out of range of Mama-B, who would raise hell on him if she knew he had a rifle-gun. Too far to grab it in time. Frank took the pistol.

"Godspeed," said Bonney, squeezing his shoulder. Then the brothers were gone, sprinting off to their own posts. They expected he'd do the same.

Frank looked over his shoulder. The old woman was still asleep, wound up like a corpse in her quilt, breathing through her mouth. Frank looked down at the pistol. It was an old cap-and-ball Colt, a Civil War–era revolver modified to fire cartridges. Something Devil Anse might have carried back in the feud days. Frank thumbed the release and checked the cylinder. Only half the six chambers were loaded.

"Hell."

A hiss behind him: *"The Devil's right hand."*

He wheeled to see Mama-B sitting upright in bed, pointing one long crooked finger at the pistol in his hands. She was wild-eyed, her hair crazed from sleep, her remaining teeth bared. "Hell you doing with a pistol-gun in my house?"

"It's another raiding party coming, Mama-B. Almost here."

Her face changed and she threw off her quilt. "Run now, boy. You got to run!"

Outside, Frank could hear the roar and splash of automobiles coming, shouts and barks and the ringing pans of the camp's makeshift alarms. He shook his head. Mama-B slung her swollen, twisted feet onto the floor but Frank went to her instead, cupping the back of her neck with his free hand, kissing her on the forehead.

"Run, baby," she said, pushing on his chest with both hands. "Please, baby, run!"

He shook his head again. "I'm tired of running, Mama-B. It ain't like you taught me."

"I done *taught* you to stay away from pistols. Ain't the same as no rifle-gun. Please, baby. Give it here."

He kissed her on top of the head, keeping the pistol out of her reach. "I love you, Mama-B. Whatever happens, remember that."

"You're just angry, son. Leave it."

"Maybe that's what the world needs, this anger I got."

She was screaming behind him, wailing as he stepped out onto the small duckboard porch. The motorcar had come to a halt fifty feet short of the tent, parked slightly crosswise in the muddy street, and the state troopers were just stepping down in their dark green uniforms, holding Thompson submachine guns high in the crooks of their arms. Their roving eyes would find him soon.

Frank felt the pistol hanging low beside his leg, heavy with power, the single long finger of the barrel. *The Devil's right hand.* The woman had always taught him that. He looked at the screaming camp, the blighted ridges and ashen sky.

He raised the pistol.

CHAPTER TWENTY-NINE

THE FIRE SIREN SOUNDED over the roofs of the county seat. Salvo after salvo, sounding through the walls of law offices and drugstores and funeral homes, breaking into boardrooms and bank vaults. They blasted into the church sacristy where Doc Moo sat with Father Rossi, checking the old priest's blood pressure. Moo's mouth went dry; he knew what those four-blast salvos meant.

The call to arms.

Father Rossi, a wizened Sardinian with bright eyes, put his free hand on Doc Moo's shoulder, smiled, and nodded toward the inflated cuff on his arm. Doc Moo looked down and nearly jumped, realizing he'd kept pumping the rubberized air bulb long beyond the normal point. The cuff was squeezing the old man's arm like an iron claw, surely bruising him, while the fire siren continued to wail.

Doc Moo thumbed the valve, letting out the pressure with a hiss. *"Ita paenitet, Pater."*

I'm sorry.

The two of them spoke Latin when they were alone—a language they'd both been taught as boys, on different sides of the Mediterranean, and which had followed them into their professional lives. The old priest waved his hand, dismissing the apology. *"Est nihil, Doctor."*

It's nothing.

Father Rossi had not come to this small parish church in West Virginia for rest. A lot of Italian, Spanish, and Polish miners lived in these hills, mostly Catholic, and a pastor had been needed. After the parishioners' needs proved too much for a less experienced priest, the Church had asked Father Rossi to come—a veteran of Italian Harlem, known for his steel in the face of La Cosa Nostra. He liked to call Doc Moo his "Son of the East"—a reference to Moo

hailing from the Levant, a region whose name came from the Italian *levante*—
"rising"—as in the rising of the sun in the east.

Now the old priest nodded toward the small sacristy window, outside of
which the firehouse siren sounded a final salvo. "*Sanguis exspectem,*" he said.

My blood can wait.

"*Es certus?*"

Father Rossi nodded, switching to English. "You refused to join the Vigilance Committee, no?"

Doc Moo nodded. "That's right, Father."

The Sardinian gripped his arm. "Of this I am glad. But perhaps, Doctor, God
placed you here today to hear these sirens, no? Someone who is *not* a member
of the committee." His hand tightened on Doc Moo's arm—surprising strength
from the small man. "Someone to stanch the spill of blood."

Doc Moo nodded and began to pack his medical bag. The priest followed
him out to his horse. Below, they could see men hurrying from all directions
heading to the firehouse with their rifles. The old man stepped down and
touched Altair, the white swell of his great chest. Then he looked away from
town, toward the tent colony.

"*Alis aquile,*" he said.

On eagle's wings.

IN TOWN, THE MEN of the Vigilance Committee felt their hearts strung
high in their throats, as if they'd driven too fast over a sharp spine of railroad
tracks and been launched weightless from their seats. They leapt from desks
and counters and barber's chairs, lifted on the very blasts of the siren. They
tucked their ties between their shirt buttons and took up their rifles, slinging
cartridge bandoliers over their suit jackets and dress shirts and work blouses.
They kissed their wives and saluted their secretaries and ran outside, holding
their hats down, making for the firehouse.

They'd heard story after story of the striking miners, tales of violence born
in the tent colonies coughed up in the hollers and hanging from the hillsides.
The hacked slopes were blistered with shoddy canvas tents, peopled with
gaunt figures risen of every color and coast. Potshots had struck the cars of
mine bosses and state police; bullets had perforated boxcars and passenger
coaches that passed beneath the road.

Now the news came leaping down the streets, jumping ear to ear.

"You hear? Raiding party went up Lick Creek this morning, almost didn't come back."

"I heard the miners were banging damn pots and pans like sirens."

"That's right. Then this big Black one stepped out in his underclothes and threw down on them with a horse pistol."

"He didn't."

"He did. Blasted a piece of brightwork right off the car."

"They shoot him down?"

"They'd liked to. But the ridges opened up on them, snipers on both sides, shots smacking all around the car. The pistoleer vanished among the tents and the Bulldog stepped down from the car. Just stood there unfazed, what I heard, like he had on an ironclad slicker. Ordered his troopers to open up with those new Thompson guns they got."

"Trench brooms?"

"That's right. Strafed the hillsides till they went silent."

"Then what?"

"Then they hightailed it back to town for reinforcements. Us."

NOW THE WHOLE VIGILANCE Committee was riding in a convoy of Fords and Studebakers and Packards, wedged three abreast in the back seats with rifles propped upright between their knees, the barrels swaying like reeds in a stream. The twenty-some automobiles clattered and bounced, engines racing, their thin tires slurring and bumping up a rocky creek road that paralleled the Lick Creek tent colony.

In the back of one of the cars, an insurance broker sat jammed between a store clerk and a druggist. The latter two hadn't stopped talking since they loaded into the Studebaker. The clerk shook his head. "Shiftless, what they are. Would rather whine and strike than earn a fair day's wages."

"Simple genetics," said the druggist. "Violence and sloth, it's in the blood of these hillbillies, handed down for generations. Then you got the Blacks from down South, don't know how to work without a whip at their backs. Poles and Wops fresh off the boat, thinking this country owes them something. Far as I'm concerned, they don't like it here they can go home."

The clerk nodded and wiped his mouth. "We've let it go on long enough. It's time they learned some law and order. We'll put them in jail or back underground. Walking upright or laid flat in boxes, their choice."

"Amen."

The insurance broker lowered his head between them to pray. He asked God to give him courage and judgment, to help him act rightly in the face of whatever may come. To honor himself, his family name, and the people of his town. The car bounced hard through a rut and his brow pressed firmly, surely, against the barrel of his rifle. He pulled back to feel a thumb-size print of gun oil glistening in the middle of his forehead. As if he'd been anointed, given a blessing of some kind. A touch of holy oil.

He started to swipe it clean but didn't, thinking of the conniption his wife would have if he stained another shirt. He touched his ribs. He'd left his handkerchief in his coat. He didn't want to use his hand—he needed his fingers clean and dry, grippy on the gun. He thought of cowboys rubbing sand or dirt or clay between their hands before a fight. Now he understood.

So the mark was still there half an hour later when they stepped down from the cars at the top of the road and formed a skirmish line along the ridge, each rolling the heavy bolt of his rifle to chamber a round. Still there as they entered the woods on foot, in unison, state troopers strung throughout the line like infantry officers. They would come down on the tent colony from above, flushing the strikers into the open where they could be arrested or else.

The insurance man was handy with a rifle. There was a wood-paneled room in his home where the white skulls of stags hung from the walls, the thorny crowns of their antlers curling sharp and wild from their bony bosses—animals he and his forefathers had felled. But it had been years since his rifle put a trophy on the wall or food on the table. Now his family ate store-bought meat seven days a week—beef from the great Midwestern stockyards, inland seas of flesh where men in gum-rubber aprons swung sledges on killing floors awash in blood, crushing the skulls of tag-eared beeves. Now his belly pushed plump against his belt and his hands would blister from carrying this rifle for a single long afternoon.

Still, the thumb of Cosmoline gleamed over his brow like a benediction as he moved with the line of vigilantes descending the slope. He'd been too old for the Great War, but West Virginia simmered with insurrection. Law and order had to be maintained. He'd do his duty to protect his family from the violence festering on the edge of town, threatening to run wild through the streets.

They leapt across a small creek and passed through a grove of blighted chestnut trees, the trunks swollen and misshapen like the gangrenous limbs of a giant. Now the pale, pointed tents of the Lick Creek colony appeared in the narrow holler below them, pitched like the tattered wigwams of some heathen tribe. The thin spires of their many cookfires and stovepipes and burning trash coalesced into a ghostly cathedral of smoke, weightless over the encampment.

CHAPTER THIRTY

FRANK AND THE REST of the Bad Seven lay still, moving only to swipe the sweat from their eyes. They were crouched in the camp's overwatch post, a high grove of trees toward the back of the holler from which they could observe the entrance to the colony. The vantage gave them a clear line of sight at the reaction force sure to come roaring up the road into the camp.

Frank still couldn't quite believe what he'd done that morning. A strange sense of wonder had filled him as he stood barefoot on the duckboard porch of the tent and raised the heavy revolver from his side, watching as if in a dream as he held it unshaking at the end of his once-broken arm and thumbed back the hammer and pulled the trigger, the big gun bucking in his hand, blasting a brass mirror from the side of the car and the troopers seeming to levitate before him, wide-eyed, unable to believe what they were seeing.

Never had Frank felt himself so much a man in full, spitting in the face of these men, their overarching power, deciding his fate for himself. Then the hills seemed to respond, unleashing fire on the raiding party, the rounds of the Bad Seven and other shooters roaring down on them, ripping up the ground at the troopers' feet. As if he were not one man but many. A whole army hidden in the trees. He was gone by the time the Bulldog could step down from the car to take control of the situation, ordering his officers to strafe the ridgeline before retreating for reinforcements, red-faced with rage.

Next to Frank, Bonney adjusted his rifle and winced. A bullet from one of the Thompsons had gone right up the sleeve of his shirt, torn a furrow inside his forearm, and punched out through the denim patch at the elbow.

He kept his eyes on the entry road, speaking to Frank through his teeth. "They keep calling it a state of war and insurrection round here, right? As if we missed that fat son of a bitch down there thirty times from this range. As if we couldn't have shaved his fucking mustache with the first shot." Bonney shook his head. "As if we wouldn't have put a bullet in his head, this was a real war."

Frank nodded, lying prone, squinting through an old set of binoculars. "You ever think all this could come to that, a second Civil War?"

Bonney looked at him. "You don't?"

Before Frank could answer, he saw a bloom of dust. "Movement on the road."

"What is it?"

Frank worked the thumbwheel, trying to bring the twin spheres of vision into focus. The binoculars were nearly antiques, the lenses foggy, the sight picture never quite clear. "Somebody on horseback," he said.

"How many?"

"Just one so far."

"Scout?"

"Doubtful. They wouldn't want to give us no warning."

The rider had come around the bend at a fast trot and now pushed the horse into a full gallop, thundering down the road, crashing through puddles and slop. No rifle slung across his back. No bandolier. A white horse.

"It's Doc Moo," he said. Frank rolled over and waved to one of the other shooters, a man perched high in the crux of a white oak with a telescoped rifle. He signaled him not to shoot. When Frank looked again through the binoculars, the doctor had entered the camp but remained on horseback, riding fast through the tents, scattering chickens and dogs, coming finally to where Mama-B sat on her rocker on the same duckboard porch where Frank had made his stand that morning. He knew there was no moving that woman from her porch short of hauling her off it, like the Baldwins had done.

Through the foggy world of the glasses, Frank watched Doc Moo jump down from his horse and crouch beside Mama-B, talking hurriedly. She twisted in her chair and cast her hand in their direction. The doctor nodded and stood in the middle of the road, where he would be visible, and began to wave his hands.

"The hell's he doing?" asked Bonney.

"I ain't for sure," said Frank. "Trying to signal us, I think."

"Signal us what, they coming?"

Frank wiped the lenses of the binoculars on his shirttail and looked again. Doc Moo had quit waving his hands wildly and now had only one arm raised, high and straight, pointing to the ridge above them to the north.

Frank wheeled to look. "Oh, Jesus."

A ratcheting bark of automatic fire.

THE INSURANCE MAN HAD watched one of the state troopers freeze midstep, rigid as a dog on point, staring down on a small copse of trees, a woody island lying between them and the tents. *Movement.* The trooper stayed that way a long moment, only his chest moving, the black knot of his tie rising and falling on top of his green uniform blouse and his campaign hat raked forward like a drill sergeant's, his chin dripping sweat. Then he raised his Thompson, thumbed off the safety, and fired.

A man seemed to detach bodily from one of the trees, thrust from the upper limbs, becoming visible as he tumbled down through the branches, his rifle clattering after him. He smacked the ground and wadded into a ball. The whole copse exploded with return fire, the colony's sharpshooters sending rounds streaking through the woods, ripping through laurel slicks and cracking off tree trunks.

The insurance man stood dumbfounded a moment, unable to comprehend the death shrieking through the woods around him. Then he was down in the underbrush, crawling on all fours for the carcass of a blight tree, throwing his rifle over the top and aiming down on the copse. The big .30–40 Krag kicked hard against his shoulder, his right hand rolling the bolt up and back and forward and down, chambering another round, the woods around him cracking and screaming with gunfire.

Nearby, he saw a trooper rise and turn and shriek, seeming to hurl his submachine gun toward the branches overhead, a ragged wing of muscle and blood erupting from his shoulder blade. He fell wailing and writhing, his boots heeling the dirt in crazed gouges, as if someone had put pepper sauce down his pants. Men rushed to give aid and the insurance man turned back to see the miners breaking from the trees, sprinting wild-armed across the meadow.

Without thought, his mind fired with blood, he threw down on one of the runners and led him through the open sights like a flushed dove and pulled the trigger, feeling the buck of the rifle against his shoulder and watching with strange glee as the man slapped his rump as if stung. He staggered, reeling and stumbling, nearly falling but not, skipping and hobbling lame-legged into the trees.

Then the whole force of troopers and Baldwins and vigilantes was rushing down into the colony, a line of them thundering high-kneed behind Captain Brockus, who led the charge with his pistol drawn upright beside his head, a silver whistle shrieking between his teeth. The insurance broker, sprinting down on the camp, could almost imagine they were coming down on a party of Comanches or Filipinos or Johnny Rebs, same as his ancestors had done.

The mining families scattered before them, scrambling from the cat-eye flaps of their tents and fleeing toward the river, their dirty heels thumping down the duckboards and the babies screaming in their arms and men scooping up children, throwing them over their shoulders, others kicking open the doors of jakes and tripping on their own drawers, some veering and crashing into tents that imploded on top of them.

The vigilantes flooded through the colony with knives bared, slashing the pale tents and screaming the people out of them, kicking over stools and coffee cans and corn crates of household belongings, cutting open sacks of grits and flour and beans from the supply tents, ringing themselves in fodder, shooting at stray dogs.

A trooper handed the insurance man a can of kerosene and pointed to the spilled foodstuffs. The broker began pouring the fuming liquid onto the carpet of grits and beans, tipping the can here and there like it was his wife's watering pot.

"Do those," said the trooper, pointing.

A line of ten-gallon metal milk jugs, standing like artillery shells beneath the canvas fly of a supply tent. The insurance man lifted off the lids and looked down into the bluish pools of buttermilk quivering in the cans. Here was the pap and manna of the camp, shipped in on Union relief trucks, as instrumental to insurrection as gunpowder or dynamite. He tipped the can and spiked each jug with a slug of kerosene.

When the can was empty, he walked out of the tent and found himself alone. The miners had fled, harried down toward the road at the bottom of the hill. Others were being driven out of the creek, their laundry spinning downstream, and still more were climbing from beneath the shadow of the little stream bridge with their hands over their heads. The townsman stood at the edge of the camp with the rifle slung across his back and the can dangling at his side, emptied. The earth fumed around him, soaked with kerosene.

He didn't move. Below, the troopers were sifting the males from the roundup and lining them up along the railroad tracks, chaining them into a long gang of prisoners, wrists shackled, ready to march them down the tracks to the county jail. A motley band of rebels, some fifty of them, their faces black and brown and white beneath shabby caps and fedoras, some with bandannas knotted at their throats, wearing stained overalls or ragged vests or torn shirts.

The insurance broker stood amid the wrecked camp, crowned in a glory of fumes, looking down on this parade of clinking chains and iron manacles, the men's shoulders bowed, their hands cuffed at their waists. His chest swelled with pride.

For the first time in weeks, he was not afraid.

Behind him, the colony was a mess of toppled canvas, nearly every tent flattened or lurching or flapping like a sail, sliced to its interior. Amid the fuming wreckage, a single ancient Black woman sat in a rocking chair. She seemed to be signaling him. The insurance man squinted.

She was giving him the finger.

CHAPTER THIRTY-ONE

AFTER THE RAID, DOC Moo decided to bring Musa to help him fix up Miss Beulah's tent and treat any wounded. He'd tried to keep the boy protected from the violence, but it proved impossible.

The day of the raid, Musa had come home with his shirt collar torn open and dirt pushed down into one ear, his knuckles swollen from contact with the nose of a schoolmate.

Buddeea set her hands on her hips. "What happened this time, Musa?"

The boy sniffed. "One of them Smith boys said Papa was a coward for not joining the Vigilance Committee. A tan-assed coward."

He and the girls went to the school in Matewan, not Williamson, or it would have been much worse. Matewan was Sid's town, after all. Still, the boy saw only one side of things at school, in town, even at church. He was the son of a physician—a certain vantage. Moo decided it was time for him to see how the people lived in the tent colonies. How fortunate he was. What conditions existed on the other side of the tracks—in the back of the hollers where few townsfolk ever went.

Buddeea was wary at first. "Are you sure, Moo? It's a lot for a boy his age."

"I know, Booty. But it's getting tougher for him at school, and it might get worse before it gets better. For all of us. We're becoming outsiders like we never were before. If, God forbid, the troopers or Baldwins or vigilantes try to run us out of the valley, or something happens to me, I need him to know why, to see the other side. The girls understand. I'm not sure Musa does."

Buddeea nodded. "Don't underestimate him, Moo. He might understand more than you think. But take him with you. Not just to see, but to help." They embraced and she leaned close, her lips almost touching his ear. "And remember something, *habibi*."

Moo raised his eyes. "Yes, my love?"

"If any of those sons of bitches touch you, I will burn their houses down."

Moo couldn't help but grin. There was fire in the woman's blood. Her ancestors had been shepherds, farmers, and warriors for a thousand years, surviving beneath the heels of Byzantine emperors, Mamluk soldieries, and Druze lords. He kissed her. "*Ya albi.*" My heart. "I know you will. But let us keep the matches in the box for now."

They rode up to Lick Creek in the afternoon, Musa on the pony mare he shared with the girls. The boy rode with his possibles bag looped over his shoulder and his worn plug hat rammed low on his head. Moo thought he'd be forced to make his son don his riding boots and saddle the pony, as Musa much preferred to ride bareback and barefoot like a little brave of the Plains. But the boy seemed to understand the weight of this journey and didn't argue, showing up with boots on and tack in hand, a determined look on his face.

When they arrived, the camp seemed worse than Moo had left it. A vast wreck of trampled tents and knifed foodstuffs and gunshot livestock. Pigs, chickens, even the camp's milk cow lay dead. Mud-caked figures stooped low over the ground, hunting for household belongings, poking sticks into the muck. Someone wailed over a dead dog. Flies were everywhere, dizzy with opportunity.

Musa's face knotted up. Doc Moo thought for a moment the boy would cry.

"Who done this, Papa?"

Doc Moo thought a moment. It was a complicated question, in fact. The coal operators, the politicians, the state police, the county vigilantes. Money became influence, influence became policy, policy became force. And the miners were no saints, meeting violence with violence.

He sighed. "Men did this, son."

"Bad men?"

"Some."

"Will they go to hell?"

"I don't know."

The boy's knuckles grew white on the reins. "I hope Smilin' Sid sends them down."

"Musa!"

They spent the rest of daylight raising tents and treating minor wounds. As dusk fell, Moo told his son to head home for supper. "Tell your mother I'll be home late."

"I can stay, too."

"No, you have school tomorrow."

"I know why you're staying, Papa."

"Why is that?"

"For the ones got away. Case any of them is hurt."

Buddeea had been right, as usual—the boy understood far more than Moo realized. *Saw* more, grasped it. So he'd also understand such men were fugitives now, wanted men, and his father could be committing a crime in helping them.

"That is our secret, my son. Understand? For your mother's ears only."

The boy straightened and nodded, a soldier receiving orders. "Yes, Papa."

NEAR MIDNIGHT, A SPECTER came lurching down out of the trees, bloodied and hobbling, one leg locked straight at the knee. His overalls hung tattered from his shoulders, a strap dangling at his side.

Miss Beulah took Doc Moo's hand. "Thank you, Jesus."

Big Frank. He'd been shot in the buttocks of all places. An oblique angle, but the bullet had buried itself deep in the soft tissue and would require extraction. With Miss Beulah acting as his nurse, Doc Moo had the man lie face down on the bed and gave him a morphine syrette, then set about cleaning the wound with antiseptic, the gauze clamped in a pair of forceps.

"You're lucky. Without so much muscle tissue, the bullet might have penetrated all the way into the rectal cavity."

Miss Beulah leaned over her grandson. "Hear that, boy? That big-ole butt of your'n done saved you."

The big coal hewer turned his head toward her. "I should thank you, Mama-B, where I got it from."

She slapped him on the arm. "Your granddaddy liked it."

"Jesus help me."

Once the wound was clean, Doc Moo gave Frank a knotted bandanna for his teeth and set to extracting the bullet. Despite the morphine, the man's body quaked and shuddered with pain; what little sound he made came guttering through his teeth. The pain threshold of miners always impressed him. He thought their constant exposure to discomfort must inure them, like the saints and monks who taught themselves to endure extreme pain and cold.

Once he'd removed the bullet, he gave Frank a second sedative to help him rest and left alcohol, swabs, dressings, and written instructions for frequent cleaning of the wound. Frank had to return to the hills as soon as possible— the troopers could return at any time—so the cleaning would have to be done in the field.

Outside, Doc Moo went over the procedure with Miss Beulah. "Make sure he knows how important it is. If he misses even a single day at first, it could infect and I'll have to admit him into a hospital."

"Which he won't never walk out a free man."

"I'm afraid not. Also, I'll need to check the wound once a week for the next month. We can do it on the same day we do your checkup." He looked back through the tent flap, glimpsing the bloodied sheet that lay over the man's buttocks. "I'm sorry, Miss B. I know that was harrowing to witness."

Miss Beulah nodded. "I seen things in my years, Doctor, but it hits different when it's your own boy." She shook her head. "Frank don't know it, but time was I marched with Mother Jones myself in one of her mop-and-broom brigades. Twenty, twenty-five years ago now. After my husband died of the miner's asthma."

"You marched?"

The old woman sucked her teeth. "Damn right I did. Just us womenfolk together, raisin' hell on scabs and gun thugs, banging pots and pans, giving them cowards a hundred earfuls at once. Didn't have no guns, mind you, but we sure had them pointed back at us. Thought they might use them, too."

She shook her head. "Dying wasn't nothing to me back then, I was so mad. Then Frank come into my care and I had to let the anger go, couldn't raise a boy right with that fury inside me." A wetness rose up in her eyes. "Reckon that boy saved me."

"We'll make sure he heals up good, Miss B."

Miss Beulah squeezed his arm. "Thank you, Doctor."

CHAPTER THIRTY-TWO

SID STOOD BEFORE THE United States Capitol, the slave-built facade of quarried Virginia stone dancing slightly over the vast green lawn, undulant in the sweltering heat of a D.C. summer. A great bastion, white and proud, broad-shouldered in the very center of the federal city. How often he seemed to find himself standing before such structures—buildings designed and constructed to appear stern and just and strong in paintings and photographs and the eyes of those who entered them.

Sid leaned and spat in the grass. Now, as he'd felt in the past, he sensed the deep and wide roots of the place, as if the basements and foundations spread miles wide beneath the earth, in vast hidden chambers, connecting at some black and utter depth to the courthouses whose own proud facades broke through the coal-rich earth of West Virginia like chiseled-down mountains. Every one of them trying to stare him down.

Sid straightened his jacket lapels and swaggered forth to testify before the Senate committee on the mine violence in West Virginia.

Hearing Before the Committee on Education and Labor
UNITED STATES SENATE
July 14, 1921

COAL COMPANY LAWYER: Mr. Hatfield, you spoke about Mr. Felts shooting the mayor. How many shots did Albert Felts fire?

MR. HATFIELD: Well, I didn't have time to count them.

COAL COMPANY LAWYER: How many shots did Albert Felts fire?

MR. HATFIELD: I didn't have time to count them. If you had been there I don't think you could have counted them.

COAL COMPANY LAWYER: You say he shot more than once?

MR. HATFIELD: I couldn't say how many shots he shot.

COAL COMPANY LAWYER: When you were tried you were defended by the attorneys for the United Mine Workers of America, were you not?

MR. HATFIELD: Mr. Houston and Mr. Burkinshaw.

COAL COMPANY LAWYER: The United Mine Workers paid all of the expense of your defense, did they not?

MR. HATFIELD: I suppose they did.

COAL COMPANY LAWYER: Wasn't it your defense that Albert Felts fired two shots, and wasn't that the defense made by your lawyer, that he pulled out his pistol and shot Mayor Testerman, and then turned over his shoulder and shot at you? Wasn't that the defense?

MR. HATFIELD: I believe that was the testimony of some of the witnesses.
[. . .]

COAL COMPANY LAWYER: Mr. Hatfield, did you not within less than two weeks after Mayor Testerman was killed, marry his widow?

MR. HATFIELD: I did.

COAL COMPANY LAWYER: And are you not now running his place of business?

MR. HATFIELD: I am.

COAL COMPANY LAWYER: Don't you know, Mr. Hatfield, that a number of witnesses who testified before the grand jury, one of whom also testified against you in the last trial, have been assassinated?

MR. HATFIELD: I do not know that.
[. . .]

COAL COMPANY LAWYER: Are you not under indictment in McDowell County, an indictment returning this week, charging you with a conspiracy, in connection with others, to blow up the coal tipple at Mohawk?

MR. HATFIELD: That is the first I heard of it.
[. . .]

COAL COMPANY LAWYER: Are you not under indictment for knocking down Mr. P. J. Smith with a rifle, the man who now sits back of you?

MR. HATFIELD: Not as I know of.

COAL COMPANY LAWYER: You were arrested, were you not?

MR. HATFIELD: No, sir, I was not.

COAL COMPANY LAWYER: You did have a rifle with you, did you not?

MR. HATFIELD: Yes, sir.

COAL COMPANY LAWYER: And you got into a controversy with him?

MR. HATFIELD: I slapped him down.

COAL COMPANY LAWYER: And you hit him with a rifle, didn't you?

MR. HATFIELD: No. I hit him, but not with no rifle.
[. . .]

COAL COMPANY LAWYER: Have you not been instrumental in bringing a number of rifles into Matewan?

MR. HATFIELD: Yes, I sell rifles.

COAL COMPANY LAWYER: Where did you get them?

MR. HATFIELD: From Cincinnati.

COAL COMPANY LAWYER: How many did you bring in?

UNION LAWYER: I am going to object to this line of testimony.

COMMITTEE CHAIRMAN: All right. He does not have to answer.

COAL COMPANY LAWYER: I will ask you if you have not brought in and distributed through your place several hundred rifles since this trouble started?

UNION LAWYER: We object.

COMMITTEE CHAIRMAN: You need not answer.

COAL COMPANY LAWYER: That is not a violation of the law, Mr. Chairman.

COMMITTEE CHAIRMAN: We are not going to insist on his answering.

COAL COMPANY LAWYER: All right. A short time ago, since the establishment of military law, did not the military authorities seize from the Norfolk & Western Railway ten cases of rifles and ammunition that had been consigned to you?

UNION LAWYER: We object to that.

MR. HATFIELD: They did not.

COAL COMPANY LAWYER: At Bluefield?

MR. HATFIELD: They did not.
[. . .]

SENATOR: I want to ask you, before this killing, how long had you been chief of police of this town?

MR. HATFIELD: Going on to two years.

SENATOR: Had you ever been in other difficulties or shootings of any sort? I do not want to embarrass you, and if you do not want to answer the question, you need not.

MR. HATFIELD: Well, one time I had a little shooting match with a fellow by the name of Wilson, the mine foreman for Mr. Lindon.

SENATOR: How long ago has that been?

MR. HATFIELD: Why, something like five or six years ago.

SENATOR: Something like five or six years ago?

MR. HATFIELD: Yes, sir.

SENATOR: And from that time on you did not have any trouble?

MR. HATFIELD: No, sir.

SENATOR: Were you arrested for this shooting that took place several years ago?

MR. HATFIELD: I was not arrested, but I went and give up and was tried and found clear.

SENATOR: You were tried and come clear of that?

MR. HATFIELD: Yes, sir.

SENATOR: And that is the only previous difficulty you had had for which you have been tried?

MR. HATFIELD: It is all I had anywhere.

SENATOR: And you said that you had been marshal about six months?

MR. HATFIELD: No, going on two years.
[. . .]

COMMITTEE CHAIRMAN: What is your age?

MR. HATFIELD: Twenty-eight years old the 15th day of last May.

MOHAWK. SID LOOKED OUT the window of his room at the Hotel Harrington, just half a block from Pennsylvania Avenue. His temples throbbed. God-damned *Mohawk*. That indictment was the one surprise of the day's proceedings. He knew the high-talking lawyers of the coal operators would try to stick him however they could. A lot of talk is what it was. They didn't seem to understand that you needed a rope to hang a man or a gun to shoot him. That you couldn't talk him to death, even if you could make him wish to die for want of silence.

But Mohawk stuck in his craw. Apparently, it was true. He'd been indicted on charges of attacking Mohawk Coal and Coke. The place had been shot up good last summer, left punctured and smoking on the hillside, the tipple dynamited—a response to the attempted murder of Big Frank Hugham. Sid welcomed the attack, but he'd been miles away at the time, at home in Matewan playing checkers with Ed. The indictment had come out of McDowell County, the same county where Frank had been attacked. It was a frame job, plain as day. A maneuver to draw him into enemy territory. Enemy streets, spies, courts—penning him like an animal.

That night, flat in his bed in the nation's capital, Sid dreamed of fording the Tug Fork on horseback like so many Hatfields before him, bloody-minded on dawn raids, the green river coiling cool around his knees and the hard barrel of the animal wide as a dreadnought beneath him. His guns blazing white-hot at his hips, as if newly forged. He and the horse rose smoking from the far side of the river like a single beast and entered the gates of the enemy stronghold, the guards pulling back their rifles and setting them spear-straight at their heels to allow his passage, their eyes gone wide and strange, their mouths slack, as if witnessing the rise of a centaur or other beast of mystery from the storied waters of the Tug Fork.

Sid clopped down the paved streets in the dawn, heading for the courthouse, whose square bright turret stood against a backdrop of dark hills still shrouded in mist. The light came slantwise through town and Sid's shadow, lean and black, skated across the brick and clapboard facades on the far side of the street. He was bare-chested, his pale torso zigzagged with blood or war paint like some savage come newly blooded from the wilderness. The town was full of shadows that darted at the edges of his vision, slipping from alleyways or attic windows just before he could catch them.

As he passed through the streets, he began to feel a heat building in his hands, pulsing through his palms. Hotter, hotter, throbbing in time with his heartbeat, quickening as he neared the courthouse at the center of town. A searing white pain, cracking into his bones, as if his marrow might burst through his flesh like tree sap in a wildfire. Finally he released the grips of his pistols and looked down at his hands. His palms were blistered and red, stamped as if with a branding iron, bearing the angry red shapes of running ponies.

When he looked up again, the town was gone. He was riding upon a vast prairie of stone, dead flat for miles, where no green thing grew. In the far, far distance, he saw hills standing black as night, hunched beneath the dark bellies of flickering storm clouds.

Toward these he rode, his scorched palms held smoking at his sides.

CHAPTER THIRTY-THREE

DOC MOO AND MISS Beulah sat side by side in the darkening holler, watching the fireflies spark heavenward from the grass. It was August 1, nearly a month since the raid on the camp. The arrested miners were still imprisoned, packed into the county jail without bail. Many of the toppled tents had been propped back up, their knife-wounds stitched, but the place appeared more squalid than ever.

Doc Moo shook his head. He was already worried about the coming fall. Three children had died last year of pneumonia. "If conditions don't improve by first frost, we're going to have a heavy toll on our hands."

Miss Beulah nodded. "Hell, I'm surprised I done lasted up here this long."

"Now, now, Miss B. You're stout as a horse."

"I ain't scared of what's to come, Doctor Moo. I believed in the Glory since I was a child. I look forward to finding out, either way. It's the rest of these folks I worry over. They ain't had all the years I had on this earth."

Frank appeared at the edge of the holler, walking toward them. Fireflies flashed around him as distant thunder throbbed through the sky. He and the other Lick Creek fugitives, still wanted, had an outlaw camp somewhere up in the Mingo hills, hidden with the help of a valley moonshiner and said to be guarded and booby-trapped.

Frank's wound was healing well, but he'd developed a slight limp. It hurt Doc Moo to see how much punishment the man's body had taken, nearly every inch of him lumped or scarred. The mines could break down a man physically before he was even forty; the human anatomy simply wasn't designed for it. Moo had seen it again and again. But this wasn't the mines—it was everything the man had endured in the past year. Beaten, burned, shot, chased. Still, he seemed to carry a certain pride that wasn't there before. He swaggered through the holler dark, his forearms curled like old war clubs.

"He's mending," whispered Miss Beulah, watching him. "Though I do worry, Doctor, what wounds he's got on the inside still to heal."

Doc Moo nodded. Truly, he'd noticed the man seemed quieter in the weeks since the raid, harder. Something he couldn't diagnose from any medical volume. A hooded steel in the man's eyes, a tension in the jaws. He remembered something his father used to say.

Careful, when you beat a dog, you don't awake the wolf.

Two men had followed Frank down the slope of the ridge. Bonney and Lacey, the Hellfighter twins. They hovered at the edge of the woods, their rifles cradled against their chests, watching for ambushes or raids. Frank carried only a large revolver strapped across the middle of his chest, holstered on a long leather belt, no shirt beneath his overalls.

He stopped just short of the lantern's glow, as if unwilling to step into the light. "Y'all heard about Sid?"

CHAPTER THIRTY-FOUR

THE MCDOWELL COUNTY COURTHOUSE stood like an ivy-clad fortress before Sid. Stone ramparts thrust from the coal-rich earth; rough walls covered in climbing ivies like the storied colleges of the North. The clock tower rose high among the surrounding hills, a four-cornered spear with white clock dials and a single small cross perched from the sharp slate point of its roof.

Sid squeezed his hands at his sides, then opened them. He was unarmed, his hands strangely light without the weight of shooting irons hooked across the palms, almost buoyant. Hands that could pat the heads of dogs or children, squeeze the neck of a loved wife or son. Hands that could do the gentler work of men, unburdened by the need to speak fire from each fist.

Back in Washington, he'd sought counsel from his friend Senator Montgomery, once the miners' great hope for governor: "My advice, Sid, submit peaceably to the Mohawk charges. Leave the guns at home. Act as a law-abiding citizen and you'll be treated as such. The rule of law will prevail. I have to believe that, even in McDowell County."

Sid had turned and squinted out the senator's office window. A short walk and a man could touch the white marble monuments of the young republic, cool despite the summer sun.

"All right."

Today, his lawyer would request a change of venue, a motion to move the trial out of this enemy stronghold where the coal operators had hands in every office and men on every street. Already their party had been tailed. On the train, at breakfast, outside their hotel. Baldwin thugs, sure as sugar was sweet.

Sid had smiled at them, then spat between his teeth.

Now, standing across the street from the courthouse, he squinted up at the shaggy green walls, the louvered chamber of the belfry. Jessie stood beside him, along with Sid's best friend and checkers adversary, Ed Chambers, and Ed's wife, Sallie. A young Mingo deputy, their bodyguard, trailed a few steps behind them, his thumbs hooked on his belt, one of Sid's big pistols hanging from his hip. Ford touring cars and runabouts were parked along the far curb, their ribbed convertible tops latched tight in case of rain, and Sallie carried an umbrella. Everyone seemed worried of showers today despite the present sun.

Beyond the automobiles stood an eight-foot stone retaining wall that kept the high green mount of the courthouse lawn from spilling over onto the sidewalk and street. The stone-built place looked proud of itself, standing tall and wooly-green on its little hill, the dormers studded with tiny crosses. The front steps rose to the shadowy alcove of the entrance, dark as the tunnel to the other side of a mountain.

Sid's hands were humming, so strangely light. He spread his fingers wide at his sides. So many things such hands could do but shovel and hammer and kill. The thought of flight drifted through his mind, that deftness of touch. He sensed even now that he was less a man than a vessel, a conduit hard and true enough for forces greater than himself, like hot magma shot through the pipe of a volcano. Like a gun.

"Well." He stepped into the street.

Sid and the others were at the first landing of the courthouse steps when they spotted a party of their fellow codefendants coming down the sidewalk, still some distance away. The sight whelmed Sid with warmth. Familiar faces, encountered far from home. His hand, freed of the strong gravity of a pistol, lifted high from his belt to hail them, his fingers open. His smile toothy and wide, like a boy's.

As if at his signal, the sky cracked open and the first round hit his chest like a hammer, driving white-hot into the meat of him, his deepest places. Then another and another, barked red-mouthed from that tunnel at the top of the courthouse steps, a sudden hayfork of lead that lifted him straight from his heels, weightless for a moment, angel-light, almost flying—then dropped him onto the landing below. The last of his heart was tumbling out of his shirt-front and rolling over his hands, pattering all across the naked stone. And he thought: *Rain.*

THE SCREAMING OUTSIDE OF Sid's dark-gone skull had not abated. Baldwin gunmen were everywhere. They'd come out of the shadows on every

side. The young bodyguard pulled Jessie shrieking from her husband's riddled body and hustled her down the street to the sheriff's office, where they
found a note pasted on the door stating that the McDowell County sheriff was
out of town on personal leave. The office closed, locked. Jessie kicked and
hammered at the door, howling, as if Sid might still be alive on the other side.

The young bodyguard held his face in his hands. He'd been tarrying at the
bottom of the steps, assuming his job was done, his charges delivered safely
to court, when he sensed the heat of Sid's dark gun on his hip, blue-black and
radiant, like he'd left it out in the sun. He was looking down at the piece when
he heard the shots.

Back on the landing, Sallie Chambers lay humped on top of her husband's
body, screaming, roaring through snotty threads stretched across the black
oval of her mouth. She was turning out the pockets of Ed's coat and pants,
coins and toothpicks and lint, showing how he'd been unarmed when one of
the Baldwins, after shooting Sid, had run down the courthouse steps, reached
across her chest, and fired straight into Ed's neck, then followed his somersaulting body down the steps. He'd knelt to place his pistol in Ed's ear, under-
hand, like a doctor taking a reading, and blasted his brains across the stone.

Now the man jabbed a finger at her. "Get her out of here."

Other agents, their biceps bunched hard under their coat sleeves, hooked
her under the shoulders and ripped her screeching and wailing from her husband, her face a wrenched fist of agony, as if they were tearing her guts out
on the landing.

Even as Sallie was being pulled from her husband, a cold and alien pistol,
full of empty shell casings, was being fit into Sid's still-warm hand. He no
longer smiled, his lungs coughed red over his golden teeth. As Sallie's hands
were ripped from the lapels of her husband's coat, she looked up to see one of
the gunmen, a man she recognized as one of the Baldwins who'd survived the
Battle of Matewan.

"We ain't come down here for this!" she screamed.

The man shrugged his heavy shoulders. "We ain't come up to Matewan for
this, neither."

"Yes, you did!" she screamed. "That's God-damned right what you come
for!"

CHAPTER THIRTY-FIVE

DOC MOO WATCHED THE coffins being carried across the green slate of the Tug Fork like the trophies of ants. Their sleek forms bobbed along the wood-and-wire footbridge on the bearers' shoulders as summer rain slanted feathery through the valley, pattering through the leaves and dimpling the surface of the river. The streets of Matewan were muddied, slogged and churned with the throng of two thousand mourners who trailed the caskets across the sagging belly of the bridge and climbed toward the graveyard on the far shore, the stones set on a steep green slope on the Kentucky side. A silent column of grievers, dead-eyed as they passed the militia patrols, their faces drawn down hard as masks. Their breath blew through their teeth as they climbed the steep hill to the cemetery.

They'd seen their darling, Smilin' Sid, made to frown inside a white casket, his hands crossed over his chest. Two-Gun Sid, hero of the mining man, shot three times in the heart on the steps of the most public building in all the land, in broad daylight, while his killers walked free. Known members of the Baldwin-Felts Detective Agency, who hadn't even worn masks.

Some of the mourners were adorned in the regalia of fraternal orders, their stoles or sashes emblazoned with mysterious insignia. Others wore what they had, black suits or overalls or their uniforms from the war. Most of the women were dressed in black, frowning trap-jawed over stiff collars, gripping their umbrellas with white knuckles. Doc Moo saw the vigilance men and troopers staring open-mouthed at these grim furies, as if they were in the presence of something holy or wicked. More than one of them took a step back, perhaps fearing one of the women might spear her umbrella through his eye.

What they did not see, he knew, were the men hidden in the hills around them. Men like Big Frank and his comrades, unable to show their faces to the authorities, who crouched in thickets and slicks, rifles in hand. Men who would risk prison to see their man honored. They were up there, Doc knew, rain streaming down their faces.

The eulogist was Senator Montgomery. A man, many said, who would've been governor if his votes hadn't all gone floating down the Tug, cast out of ballot boxes by Baldwins and bribed officials. He spread his arms wide against the gray sky, his shoulders sodden, his hair slicked jagged across his forehead. His eyes smoldered in his heavy face.

"We have gathered here today to perform the last sad rites for these two boys who fell victims to one of the most contemptible systems that has ever been known to exist in the history of the so-called civilized world. Deliberately shot down, murdered in cold blood, while entering a place that should have been a temple of justice. And by whom? Men who are taking their orders from coal operators who live in Cincinnati, Chicago, New York City, and Boston. Sleek, dignified, churchgoing gentlemen, who would rather pay fabulous sums to their hired gunmen to kill and slay men for joining a union than to pay like or less amounts to the men who delve into the subterranean depths of the earth and produce their wealth for them."

Amen.

"There can be no peace in West Virginia until the enforcement of the laws is removed from the hands of private detective agencies and deputy sheriffs who are paid, not by the state, but by the great corporations, most of them owned by non-residents who have no interest in West Virginia's tomorrow."

Amen.

He looked out across the two thousand mourners, the rain beating down on their shoulders, riffling the surface of the river. Few umbrellas before him. Few hats. The people stood bareheaded, the rain running down their faces.

"Is it any wonder that even the heavens weep?"

CHAPTER THIRTY-SIX

The New York Times

August 3, 1921

"The Primitive Mountaineer"

Hatfields and Mccoys are as famous in the West Virginia mountains as ever Armstrongs and Eliots were on the Scotch border. They carry on clan feuds in the ancient way. Sometimes they do a little outside shooting from habit or to keep their hand in. They are a curious survival, a sixteenth century fauna flourishing in the twentieth. They are of the days before the law. They wage private war. . . .

Sid, a pleasant young chap . . . sometime the spirited Matewan Chief of Police, perished in no tribal combat. . . . Sid and a companion were killed in front of the court house. Who fired the first shot, after a short parley, amicable at first, isn't made clear; but perhaps the private detective Lively acted his name. Surely, if Sid had got the "draw," an artist of his experience would have made full use of it. The good behavior of the crowd of mountaineers deserves a kind word. There was none of that neurotic excitement which would have blazed up in communities of ordinary heredity.

It was an orderly, quiet and successful shooting match. That it took place in the shadow of a court house needn't prompt us to any obvious moralizing or righteous indignation. These men are of an inheritance and habit apart. Only slow time can cure them. Meanwhile, time is not so slow in killing off their most active specimens.

* * *

THE NEWS OF SID'S killing whips and tumbles through the mining camps like a wind, spiraling in hearths and campfires and twisting the cap-lamp flames of men underground into new and furious shapes, horns and antlers of fire. All over the state, miners are coming down from the hills, rising up out of the ground. They gather in a holler fifty miles north of Matewan, summoned by whisper and ire. They have cut the telegraph lines around their encampment and set out armed patrols on the roads, carrying a motley assortment of weaponry. Sleek rifles, double-barreled family mantelpieces, and outsized revolvers from the previous century, exhumed from dusty bureau drawers or attic trunks.

They are men long accustomed to the flickering darkness of the mines, men who've learned the bravest of their kind can be shot dead in the street and no one will care. The greatest newspaper in the land will make light of his death. Will say he deserved it. And the public will hardly hear, deaf to their cause.

They are a hundred men at first, then two hundred. Five hundred. One thousand. An army of men rising from the earth, clad in blue-bib overalls. They hail from Italy and Poland, the Deep South and Appalachia. One in five is Black. They wear red bandannas knotted around their necks, as if their throats have already been cut.

People will call them primitives and hillbillies, anarchists and insurrectionists.

They will call them Rednecks.

BOOK III
THE MARCH

In our hands is placed a power
Greater than their hoarded gold,
Greater than the might of armies,
Multiplied a thousand-fold.
We can bring to birth a new world
From the ashes of the old
For the Union makes us strong.

—Ralph Chaplin, "Solidarity Forever"

CHAPTER THIRTY-SEVEN

MISS BEULAH SAT IN her rocker knitting, listening to the sounds of the holler. A band of coyotes yowled high up along the ridge, wailing like spirits through the night, and she could hear hushed voices coming from the other tents. Somewhere in the camp, a woman was sobbing, muffling her cries into a quilt or pillow.

Miss Beulah whispered a prayer for whoever was hurting so bad.

Lately, she'd been staying up as late as she could, awake in her rocker until her thoughts turned strange, mingling with dreams, and the weight of weariness carried her to bed. Otherwise, she couldn't hardly stomach the emptiness of the tent, the damp and smell of her own sour bed. When they'd lost Evie, the lonesomeness had been big as the world, bitter as every winter that ever was, and now she was starting to feel a woe like that again, pressing on her chest like an anvil, trying to sink its way in. It hurt sometimes just to breathe.

It was Sid, just buried, and it was Frank. It was knowing they could do her boy just like they'd done Hatfield. Hell, they'd tried already. It was knowing he could never come home, not for good. He'd be hounded always, wherever he went, same as whatever prey those coyotes were chasing.

Her chin dipped to her chest. Once, again.

Her eyes closed. In her dream, she saw a wolf trotting along the spine of the ridge, turning now and again to look over his shoulder, to listen for the cries of the hounds and coyotes always on his heels, haunting his tracks through the world. He was on the trail of something himself, scenting his way through the darkness. Soon he was descending the creek toward her, his broad shoulders burling over the stones. Then he was out of the trees, following the dark jag of creek into the narrow holler, the high banks hiding him as he stepped from stone to stone, leaving no tracks. A big wolf, big as a man. He rose up out of the creek on two legs and Miss Beulah started awake, knowing already who it was before she even lifted her head.

"Grandboy," she said.

Frank knelt down before her, bowing his head to her knees. Same as he'd done as a boy, when his daddy disappeared. Same as he'd done as a man, when Evie died.

They wept together.

"You come to say goodbye," she said.

"I got to," he said, his great chest throbbing against her shins.

She ran her long nails through his hair, scratching his scalp. Same as she'd done for his granddaddy. "I know," she said. "I know."

THE BAD SEVEN MADE their way toward the Redneck army under cover of darkness, hitching rides on freight cars and coal hoppers, walking wagon-roads where the grass grew tall between the wheel tracks. They cradled their rifles across their chests and took to the trees at the passing of horsemen and motorcars, wary of state troopers and vigilance patrols.

Soon they began to meet others marching in the same direction, wearing neckerchiefs and carrying rifles. They were streaming out of coal camps and tent colonies all over the state, heading for a certain dark fold of hills near the village of Marmet. The Redneck encampment.

From there, this miners' army would have to cross more than fifty miles of hard mountain country to reach the Tug Valley, where Smilin' Sid had been shot down in cold blood and hundreds of miners were still in jail, imprisoned for weeks without charge. A terrain made as if with God's claw hammer, stove with dark hollers and hatchet ridges and tooth-breaking roads. On the way, they'd have to march through the territory of Sheriff Don Chafin. "The Czar of Logan," as he was called—a bull-cheeked lawman known to receive a cent from the coal operators for every ton of coal that came out of Logan County.

A fortune.

Already, Chafin had stood wide-thighed before the newspaper reporters, his fancy fedora set dainty atop his head, his bowtie knotted hard at his heavy throat. "No armed *mob* will cross the Logan County line."

The Czar carried a pistol with twelve notches filed into the receiver, one for every man he'd killed—*enough to make a saw file*, men whispered—and maintained a small army of deputies and undercover agents who rode every train in and out of the county, hassling anyone suspected of Union business or sympathies. His men had pistol-whipped reverends for speaking well of labor unions, planted moonshine stills under the homes of Union miners, and fed prisoners plates of beans mixed with crushed glass, too fine to detect, so they writhed in torment for hours before they died.

Two years ago, these stories had whipped the state's miners into a frenzy. Five thousand of them had come together to cut down the Czar for once and all. Only the state's promise of a special commission to investigate the abuses of the coal operators had stopped them from marching into Logan to hang the man from the nearest tree branch or lamppost. Nothing had come of the investigation—the state had appointed the Bulldog to head it.

This time they wouldn't fall victim to more false promises, the slick words of politicians and state officials bought and paid for by King Coal. They squatted around hundreds of campfires, cradling their rifles like lean foundlings of steel and wood, their pipes and cigarettes pinched between gnarled fingers. Frank and the Bad Seven listened to them, hearing the words of these men like their own.

Constitution don't near touch these hills, seems like.

It's back to a monarchy, like Revolutionary times.

Time to march on King Coal, chop the legs out under his throne.

They spat hissing into the flames. This time, it would take an act of God to stop them.

CHAPTER THIRTY-EIGHT

MOTHER JONES STARED OUT at the landscape passing before her window, the blunt green hills knuckled beneath the sun. She could almost sense the fury they contained, the clenched fist of their power. An emanation, like fuming nitro. In these hills, her boys were rising, gathering, grieving bloody-minded for their murdered darling, and she was going to them, journeying to their encampment.

Mother looked down at the telegram in her lap, the message she'd come to deliver to her boys. She rubbed a finger along the top of the envelope. Her hands looked like those of an old crone, knobby-knuckled with twisted fingers, red-blue veins spidering beneath the translucent film of her skin. She was tired, she was. She'd just returned from speaking to striking factory workers in Mexico, where they called her "Madre Juanita" and doused her in blue violets and red carnations—a lift to her spirits, crushed flat by news of Sid's murder.

She shook her head, looking out the window. She'd seen so many boys cut down in these hills, losing a hand or foot or some better part of their mind. Families thrown out on the street with no compensation, sleeping along the roadsides like creatures not yet civilized. Their faces long-jawed with want, their cheeks soiled with every manner of filth. Little children among them— boys, she feared, who would bear the bitter seed of injustice into manhood, exploding with revenge in ages to come, trying to make even with the people who'd robbed their mothers and fathers of even the slightest splinter of pride or dignity.

Perhaps the first wave was now. Their darling, Smilin' Sid, shot down like a dog in a street. Mother shook her head. That boy had made an impression on her. A lean killer, born hard, willing to stand smiling before the hired gunmen of King Coal and send them home horizontal, laid out on spare doors from the hardware store. The hero they needed, who carried their hopes in his bones. To murder him, unarmed, was to stick a knife through the ribs of ten thousand men. To kill something that lived close to their hearts. And to do it barefaced in broad daylight—that could not be brooked. Now they were coming from all over the state, marching along the roads, riding on the tops of boxcars, hanging from the engines of commandeered passenger trains.

Mother had seen them out her window. They wore their uniforms from the Great War, where they'd seen their friends blasted into treetops or machine-gunned in tangles of barbwire, their bodies strung like scarecrows across no-man's-land; or else they wore the uniform of denim overalls and red bandannas knotted at their necks. Their faces didn't carry the penny-bright shine of those boys who went overseas in 1917, so sure of glory and triumph. Those myths were dead, gunned down in trenches, on courthouse steps.

No, here was an army of the hollow-eyed and grave—men who'd been fighting for years, suffering under the thumb of King Coal—men who'd just seen their smiling boy killed cold-blooded in the street, and the papers mock him, and the governor ignore their pleas.

Men ready to die.

Mother realized she was holding the telegram envelope against her chest, squeezing it hard under her thumbs, like a letter from a lover. She breathed in and out, trying to corral the wild loping of her heart.

She knew she was not as dangerous as she once was. Time was at her heels. Her mind wandered sometimes and her speeches could zag strangely or ramble on too long. The rheumatism could flare like wildfire in her joints and her feet bark like dogs at night. Fear, that little snake, could skate through the pigeonholes of her heart.

Most of all, she feared they were marching toward a battle they couldn't win.

She looked down at the telegram envelope. She prayed her boys had not lost faith in her. That they would believe the story she told. She prayed they would still listen to their mother.

CHAPTER THIRTY-NINE

SHERIFF CHAFIN—THE CZAR OF Logan—smiled to himself, thumbing a pea-size scar on his chest, kneading it beneath his fine cotton shirt. His men were digging trenches and felling trees, erecting breastworks along the northern border of Logan County. The latest rumors put the Rednecks in excess of ten thousand men—an army of miners who thought they were going to march into his county, hang him from a sour apple tree, and continue down to Mingo, springing their comrades from jail and running the Baldwins to ground.

The Czar sniffed. First, they'd have to get past Blair Mountain, the double-headed green monster where he was establishing his defensive front. To bolster his standing force of three hundred deputies, he was raising a regiment of special constables, mine guards, Baldwins, and other toughs called in from around the state. What's more, he'd formed a law-and-order committee like the one down in Mingo. Townsmen had turned out in droves, breathless to heed the call of duty. When the time came, they would muster at the sound of the Logan fire alarm and convoy to the front in a fleet of private automobiles.

Already, the gun racks at the hardware stores and pawn shops stood stripped of arms, every last rifle requisitioned for the county defense, and the stockpile of military-grade weaponry at the Logan arsenal had been distributed among his deputies. One thousand rifles, ten belt-fed heavy machine guns, and sixty-seven thousand rounds of ammunition. The machine guns were being positioned at strategic mountain passes and choke points to provide overlapping fields of fire.

He'd known this day might come; he'd been preparing, planning his defense. The governor was up in his office in the state capital filing formal requests for the federal government to send in troops, but Chafin couldn't count on those damned wrigglers in Washington to move their feet. Not soon enough. These miners had taken the killing of Sid Hatfield like the murder of a brother or son.

The Czar touched the little nipple of scar on his chest, four inches beneath his bowtie. Two years ago, he'd got deep into the rye during a trip to the state capital and the brown water had gone roaring through his head like a torrent, sending him to the Union's state office with his pistol out, ready to rile the scum bastards at gunpoint, prod them about like a bunch of fat heifers at auction. Maybe make them waltz or dance the polka. He'd received a .22 caliber bullet from a Union vice president during that incident. It failed to kill him but left a tiny third nipple, like a little kiss from God.

"Sumbitch should of used a bigger caliber," he liked to tell people.

Now he was standing at home plate of the county baseball field, thumbing that little scar. He'd instructed his deputies to go into the scab camps and conscript every last miner at the threat of losing his job. Objectors were to be thrown in the county jail, packed ten-deep if need be, their arms busting out through the bars. Let them piss in their shoes. He aimed to build a volunteer army of three thousand defenders and wall off the county like a mountain fortress. His men might be outnumbered, but they'd hold the high ground, entrenched along the ridges with high-powers and automatic weapons, ready to pour fire into the mountain passes and narrow roads leading into the county.

Now one of his deputies came hustling up. "We just got the news on the wire, sir. Mother Jones has been sighted on a train heading down the Kanawha River. She's on her way to meet the marchers."

The Czar felt a cold little twinge at the sound of the name. "Mother Fucking Jones," he muttered. The old bitch had called for his head more than once, urging the miners to string him up or knock him down. She was a force; he couldn't argue that. Still, looking out across the county ballfield, the Czar felt his smile coming back into his face, even wider than before.

The deputy held his hat in his hands. "What should we do, sir?"

The Czar nodded toward the squadron arrayed in the outfield. Flying ships built of canvas and wood and wire, wasp-light and deadly, their wooden propellers cocked slantwise. Secret weapons he'd been itching to loose. Dreaming of it.

He sniffed. "Let the old bitch come."

CHAPTER FORTY

MOTHER JONES STOOD BEFORE the motley ranks of the Redneck army, waving a roll of paper in her hand.

"You boys know what I have here, do you? A telegram from the President of the United States of America. Yes, I have. Sent straight to me. A promise, boys. A promise to rid this state of the gun thugs who haunt your homes and streets, who evict families and shoot strikers and break the backs of unions. Men like the Baldwin-Felts sons of bitches who machine-gun tent colonies with armored trains and beat miners to death and turn their wives and children penniless into the streets. Men who murdered our dear Sid in cold blood and broad daylight, in front of his wife, on the very steps of an American courthouse."

Mother Jones, in her black dress, looked back and forth over the crowd, looking into the faces of her boys. A hardscrabble lot, wide-eyed like nocturnal creatures, accustomed to toiling in the dark chambers of the mines. Hard men—no other kind survived this life. Their red bandannas looped their necks like those of wild bronco riders or a whole army of Billy the Kids. Mother's heart moved in her chest as they cried to her.

Read it!

Let's hear it!

Please, Mother!

Mother nodded and set her eyeglasses low on her nose and read aloud from the paper in her hands, quoting the President: "I request that you abandon your cause and return to your homes, and I assure you that my good offices will be used to forever eliminate the gunman system from the state of West Virginia."

Mother pushed her eyeglasses high on the bridge of her nose and squinted again into the crowd, staring her truth into them.

"Disband, boys. Go home to your warm wives and little babes. You have done enough already. You see what you boys have accomplished, do you?" Mother shook the telegram beside her cheek. "You've spoken into the ear of the President of the United States, and he's heard you for once, he has. Not only heard but responded, given his promise to run these God-damned gun thugs out of the state for once and all. Don't spoil that victory, boys. Don't spoil it by going to war."

Silence a moment, the men unsure how to receive such news. Presidents never heard their cries. Presidents heard the cries of senators and governors and congressmen, barons and magnates. Men who wore high hats and black tails, who had country houses and maids and tailors. It seemed too good to be true. They looked at one another. It had to be.

"Let's see the telegram," yelled someone from the crowd. Then others joined in—they wanted to see some evidence of the President's pledge.

Let us see it!

Could it be bogus?

Show us it's real!

A Union official stepped from the corner of the stage with his hand out, ready to inspect the telegram, but Mother snapped the paper to her chest. "Go to hell. It's none of your damn business. This is a private communication to *me*!"

She feared blood, certainly. This ragtag army was no match for the might of the United States Army, which could bring whole nations to their knees. Crack infantry divisions, complete with artillery and air support, could come weaving into these hills like a giant serpent of steel and fire. She feared the creeks would run red from Blair Mountain, where the Czar was building his defense.

Her boys might think she'd lost the fire and lightning in her own breast. Not hardly. But she was older than they were, wilier by half a century and more. Like an ancient she-bear, long accustomed to the various trickeries of men, Mother sensed a trap, a great set of iron jaws buried in the earth of these hills, waiting. So she'd done her best to turn them back—by whatever means necessary.

When she wouldn't turn over the telegram, her boys denounced her. Mother Jones was a fake, they said. A charlatan. A liar. Mother Jones, who once warned the governor that if he didn't rid this state of *these God-damned Baldwin-Felts mine guard thugs,* there would *be one hell of a bloodletting in these hills.* Mother Jones had lost her nerve.

So they said.

These men, who'd fought for their country in the trenches and killing fields of the Great War, where their chances of survival were higher than in the depths of the company mines. These men, they no longer heeded their mother. They marched past her, into the hills.

CHAPTER FORTY-ONE

DOC MOO RODE THROUGH the falling darkness, his horse stepping carefully on the rough road up to Lick Creek. The Tug lay two hundred feet down the steep slope, roving through the trees, and the bats were up, darting through the dusk. Altair seemed slightly nervous this evening, wary of the shadows crawling across the ground—unusual for the big gelding.

Doc Moo rubbed the animal's shoulder and smiled, thinking of Musa, who loved this hour most—the time between the dog and the wolf, when the shapes of the world shifted like smoke. The boy would be headed home now, racing barefoot through the woods, due at the dinner table just before the last sliver of sun slipped behind the western ridgeline.

That boy. He'd come from the womb more fully formed than most, more like some animal cub born with tough feet and a quick mind. Many a time, Doc Moo or Buddeea had panicked to find the boy's crib empty, only to discover he'd not only managed to climb out of the open-top cage and survive the long drop to the ground, but to crawl outside onto the porch or even into the yard, undetected by his mother, father, and three older sisters. Later, the family would joke that the house couldn't be haunted because Musa had scared all the ghosts away, sneaking up on them, and the boy seemed to have some deep connection with the hills of his birth. He knew the name of every weed, shrub, tree, insect, bird, and beast long before he knew the name of any President, and he could disappear for hours in the woods.

Lately, though, given the boy's age, Doc Moo had begun to wonder if there might be more than birds and bees drawing him afield. After all, a few of the surrounding farms did have daughters his age. Most of them were several miles away, but that was nothing for Musa . . .

Doc Moo heard an automobile coming up the road behind him and twisted in the saddle to look. It was being driven hard, the headlights jouncing over the rough road, flashing in and out of the trees. He could hear the motor racing. He steered Altair to the side of the road and waited, watching the open-top touring car come around the bend amid a pale plume of dust and skid to a halt just short of him, jacklighting horse and rider in the headlamps.

Moo held up his hand, shielding his eyes as he stepped Altair out of the glare. Three men got out of the car, the springs squeaking beneath them as they rose. They had khaki shirts and white armbands and hitched their trousers when they stood. Town men, well-bellied. A trio of rifles stood inside the car, propped upright between the seats.

"Mingo Vigilance Committee," said the driver. "State your business."

"I am Doctor Domit Muhanna, a known physician in this county."

"And your business?"

"The same as most members of my profession. Treating the sick."

"I know who he is," said one of the others. "He's the one doctors them folks up at Lick Creek." He spat. "Walked out the Vigilance Committee meetin' at the courthouse, he did."

"Is that right?" said the first. He whistled. "Too chicken to join the law-and-order brigade, that it?"

Despite himself, Doc Moo felt a flush coming into his cheeks, his blood rising. These son-of-a-bitching gasbags who thought they were tough. As if he hadn't seen more blood in a single hour than the three of them put together. He thought of what Buddeea would tell him to do. Count to ten before he replied.

Moo got to three before speaking through his teeth. "My business is healing people, not carrying a rifle. Now, if you'll excuse me, please, I have patients this evening to attend to."

One of the men took hold of Altair's bridle. "Afraid we can't let you do that, Doc."

"Excuse me?"

"Too dangerous up there at Lick Creek. No more'n a slum, breeding ground for disease and violence. Can't let nobody of your station up there, 'specially not after dark. Besides, you might be carrying contraband."

"Thank you for your concern," said Moo, "but I will travel freely inside my own county. Now please let go of my horse."

No one moved.

Moo could feel the wildness rising in him now. The old Muhanna blood churning, crackling beneath his skin. "I will ask you again, sir, to unhand my horse."

The man holding the bridle swallowed and looked at the other two. They said nothing.

Moo inhaled, his nostrils flaring. It was decided then. Slowly, deliberately, he rose from the saddle and began to dismount. He had not sailed seven thousand miles across the world, traveled up the Mississippi River on a riverboat full of knife-wielding Kaintucks, and graduated from the University of Kentucky College of Medicine with top marks, carving a position of respect for himself and his family out of the very flesh, blood, and bone of these hills to be bullied by a trio of chubby sons of bitches in khaki shirts and armbands.

He stepped to the ground before them and thumbed the three-barred cross at his throat, looking from man to man. His eyes were wide open, blazing like spot lamps. "*Allah maei,*" he said. God is with me.

The first man stepped forward, cocking his fist back. "The fuck you say?"

MISS BEULAH SAT IN her rocker, watching the sky. The bullbats were up, flurrying through the dusk. Dark came early in these narrow hollers, but that upper sky remained a long time aglow, flushed with a sun she couldn't see go down. The air seemed shifty tonight, full of haints or echoes, worlds past or yet to come. She felt it inside her, too. *Nervy*, her mama used to call it, like the veil between worlds had stretched out thin, and your own bones and tendons and nerves were raw, able to feel things you normally couldn't.

Doc Moo came walking up out of the falling dark, his brown canvas pants tucked into his riding boots. He looked harried, his shirt sweat-sodden, wrung slack at the collar. Breathing harder than usual, too. Heaving. Closer, she saw his bottom lip busted and a trickle of blood running from his nose.

"What got hold of you, Doctor?"

Doc Moo shook his head. "It's nothing."

Miss Beulah squinted. She'd never seen the good doctor angry, but there was a fury in him now, burning just under the surface. It was coming off him like a sweat or fever. She could almost smell it. "No offense, Doctor, but it looks a damn sight more than nothing."

The doctor smoothed his shirt. "I ran into a carload of vigilance men down the road. They tried to keep me from coming up here, as if they could tell me whom I can or cannot treat."

Miss Beulah nodded at the state of him. "Looks like you ain't listened to them."

The doctor sniffed, holding his black medicine bag stiff at his side. "They were lucky I was outnumbered."

"Mm-hmm," said Miss Beulah, fighting a grin. She'd known the good doctor had some grit in his veins—you couldn't do what he did without it. Still, she didn't know it went all the way down to his fists.

She shook her head, sucking her teeth. "It's blood in the air tonight, Doctor Moo. I can almost taste it." She thumped a heel on the duckboards. "Why don't you sit down and cool yours a spell."

The doctor turned over a milk crate and sat down next to her, placing his medicine bag between his boots. He wiped his nose on his handkerchief, blood on the white linen.

"Sometimes it seems worthless, Miss B. All this work and care to stitch people back together, to stanch wounds and set bones and battle infections, and every time I finish one, there are ten more, like holes busting loose in a dam, except it's blood instead of floodwater."

Miss Beulah put a hand on his arm. "Blood and time, those ain't battles you can win. All a body can do is keep up the good fight. And you fight harder and better in your way than most anybody in this whole valley." She squeezed his arm. "When the doubts come clouding, you remember that."

He nodded, and she squeezed his arm harder, making sure she had his attention. "Even when I'm gone, Doctor Moo, I want you remembering that. Like a little whisper in your ear. Like I'm haunting you. You hear me?"

He squeezed his eyes shut and cocked his head, as if listening to a distant sound. "I hear you, Miss B. I do. Thank you."

The doctor returned the bloody handkerchief to his coat pocket and took a deep breath to regain his composure. He dropped his voice. "Any sign of Frank yet?"

It was the night of his final checkup for the bullet wound he'd suffered in the Lick Creek raid. Miss Beulah shook her head. "He come by night before last, said he and his men was headed up to Marmet to meet the rest of them that's gathering for the march."

"I thought that might be the case."

Miss Beulah nodded. "I knew he would. Soon's I heard about Sid." The news had punched her square in the chest. She'd jerked back in her rocker and felt her arms stiffen at odd angles. She hadn't felt the same since. "I took it so hard cause I knew what it meant, I knew he'd go off to fight. And there ain't a damn thing in this world I could say to stop him."

Doc Moo leaned forward, setting his elbows on his knees. "Word is, Mother Jones tried to convince them to go home."

"I heard that, too, and I heard they ain't listened to her, neither."

The doctor nodded. "Well, sometimes it takes time for a mother's words to sink in."

Miss Beulah sniffed. "Ain't that the truth."

"Well, we can hope that's the case here."

"We can, Doctor, and we will. But the Devil's in these hills tonight, walking above ground. I can sense it. He don't stay long under the Lord's eye, no sir, but it don't take much to spark hell when you know just where to strike."

The doctor opened his mouth, but no words came.

CHAPTER FORTY-TWO

A COLUMN OF UNIFORMED men marched down a dark road between the hills. Three hundred troopers and lawmen advancing into the territory north of Blair Mountain, where the Rednecks were known to hold sway. Their heavy boots rose and fell within a pale cloud of road dust, their spurs ringing beneath the stars.

They were on a special mission for the Czar.

The men were nervous, their eyes flitting left and right. They'd been given a list of several miners to arrest—men suspected of clashing with state police weeks ago. But the hills were full of hundreds of armed miners now. Thousands. The road crunched like gunpowder beneath their boots and violence hovered around them like firedamp, awaiting a spark. Some traded sips from hip flasks or jelly jars, whispering between their teeth.

You ever feel like a goat on a string?

Damn sure. And with the wolves and panthers loose.

Just when Mother Jones is urging them home, too.

Before them walked a group of miners they'd already arrested during the advance. The prisoners shuffled down the road in the new-fallen darkness, their manacled hands clasped before them like men on a religious pilgrimage, heading for high temples or holy caverns in the hills.

Least if we get bushwhacked, those poor sons of bitches will be first to get it.

Now the prisoners looked back over their shoulders, seeing the hard face of Captain Brockus, stony and pale beneath his campaign hat. The man noticed nothing amiss, it seemed. No lights had ignited against the quick clawing of darkness over the land. No lanterns, no candles, no electric bulbs. The coal-camp cabins sat silent beside the road, dark-windowed despite the black wires strung roof to roof.

Too dark.

The holler grew narrower as the column proceeded, deeper. The skeletal fortress of a mine rose before them, darker than the surrounding night. The coal tipples and silos and headhouse made eerie silhouettes against the sky, like the remnants of an abandoned civilization. A tiny industrial outpost on the frontier, zigzagged with catwalks and conveyor belts. Their boots crunched toward the place, marching between the cheap, dark cabins spread before it.

They were nearly to the mine when the prisoners glanced toward a boardinghouse beside the road and then looked quickly away, too quickly, as if they'd seen something they shouldn't. Captain Brockus widened his eyes in the darkness to see a line of men on the porch of the house, the blued steel of their rifles just visible, like drawn swords. He raised his fist, halting the column in the road.

"Who goes there?"

A voice from the porch: "We that live here. State ye business."

Before Captain Brockus could reply, someone shouted from the back of the column. "We come for you, you God-damned Rednecks!"

The night shattered with gunshots, great roars of flame crisscrossing before the eyes of troopers and deputies and miners, slugs of lead goring bellies and ribs.

The electric lights of the mine exploded to life, blasting the road with light, and the human shield had worked. Manacled prisoners lay bloodied and screaming in the road, loud enough for all the hills to hear.

CHAPTER FORTY-THREE

THE NEWS CAME BURNING through the Redneck ranks, streaking along the ridges and down into the hollers, jumping creeks and rivers like a wildfire. Sid Hatfield's body barely cold in the ground, and now more of their comrades had been shot down in the street—while handcuffed. Just when they'd been sitting around their bivouac fires, staring into the coals, wondering whether Mother Jones did know best, whether they should go home to their wives and babes. Now that notion was gone, dead as those men in the road.

Shot them down same as Sid, unarmed. Un-American, what it is.

Only way we're getting our rights is at the end of a high-powered rifle.

Same's our forefathers done. Ain't a lick different.

Who'll do it but us?

THEY MARCHED ON BLAIR Mountain at dawn. Thousands of red-necked men filing along mountain paths, tromping down roads and railroad tracks, their ranks bristling with rifles. Frank and the Bad Seven crossed the Big Coal River and climbed a steep lookout above the roar of Drawdy Falls, seeking a vantage point.

They could see columns of armed men filling the roads and creekbeds in every direction, long rivers of them weaving along in mismatched uniforms and denim overalls, laden with weapons of every era and description. Single-shot scatterguns and black-powder rifles, horse pistols and trench guns and grenades smuggled home from France. Grim-faced, they raised hymns and ballads of their own making, songs of hanging the sheriff and whipping the company men, climbing the mountain and crossing the river.

O Mama, don't you weep, don't you mourn,
O Mama, don't you weep, don't you mourn,

Chafin's army gonna drown, O Mama, don't you weep.
When I get to Mingo gonna sing and shout,
Ain't nobody there gonna turn me out,
Chafin's army gonna drown, O Mama, don't you weep.

Reinforcements flooded in from out of state. Frank and his comrades met miners from the Ohio, Illinois, and Indiana coalfields. They came riding in on top of boxcars and passenger coaches, sitting on flatcars or hanging from the hoppers of coal trains. Their bodies festooned the cars, hands and boots and rifles hanging in the wind, the engines throbbing beneath their weight. The boldest among them crouched right on the cowcatchers, watching for ambushes.

The president of each local mobilized his men into a combat battalion. They raided company stores as they marched, walking out with shotguns and rifles and dynamite, even a Gatling gun—weapons the coal companies had stock-piled against just such a revolt. By afternoon, the Redneck army had amassed at the foot of Blair Mountain, a combined force nearly the size of the 1st Infantry Brigade. They practiced military drills in the hollers and small-unit tactics along the woody slopes.

Frank and the rest of the Bad Seven were tasked with teaching small groups of men how to fire and maneuver, how to flank machine-gun nests and assault fortified positions—tactics they'd learned in the service. They stood before rounds of miners and spoke of *individual initiative* and *rapidity of decision*, *resolute daring* and *driving power*—infantry principles from the Great War. Frank wore his overalls rolled down to the waist, the straps tied like a belt, the August sun flashing off his scar-flecked shoulders.

Late in the afternoon, he heard the Logan fire siren sounding on the far side of Blair Mountain, calling the defenders to their posts. He knew King Coal's whole army—Baldwins, deputies, constables, troopers, mine guards, and vigilance men—must be piling into automobiles and roaring up the steep and rocky roads to fill the vast array of trenches, sharpshooter's nests, and machine-gun emplacements strung along the mountain.

During the Civil War, guerrilla bands had crawled these hills, Frank knew. Snake Hunters and Moccasin Rangers stalked and bushwhacked one another, visiting atrocities, and the state militia had fought the Shawnee and Mingo tribes in these lands a century before that, hand-to-hand at times, both sides taking scalps in what would become West Virginia. Who knew what frays in ancient times, fought with sledges or sharpened flints.

Now, as darkness fell, two great armies were encamped in Appalachia, each on one side of Blair Mountain—a great knuckled fist risen against the impending night.

CHAPTER FORTY-FOUR

DOC MOO RETURNED FROM his evening rounds to find Buddeea standing on the porch, waiting for him.

"Father Rossi called," she said. "Several miners were killed north of Blair Mountain. Word is, they were unarmed, used as human shields by the police."

"*La sama Allah.*" God forbid.

Buddeea came down off the porch and hugged him close, talking into his collar. "There's no stopping it now."

Moo nodded. *War.*

Buddeea looked up at him. "What are you going to do?"

No question now. "I'm sworn to treat the sick and wounded. I have to go where they're sure to be."

Buddeea nodded. "Battle lines are being drawn, Moo. You know you can't be on both sides of this one."

"I know which side I'm on."

"Good." Buddeea took the back of his neck and set her forehead against his. "I packed your bag already. Clothes, sandwiches, coffee, dopp kit."

"Thank you, Booty." He paused. "You know this could make things tough for us in the future. The family. These hills have long memories. Some folks won't forget which side we helped."

Buddeea's dark eyes flashed up at his. "Let them remember. We are rock, Moo, till the stars fall and the seas dry up. They will *break* against us." She'd gripped his coat lapels in her fists and now she let them go, smoothing them. "Besides, I'll have my matches ready."

Moo smiled. "My sun." He held her forehead against his a long moment. "I better start tonight."

She raised up on her tiptoes and kissed his forehead. "I know."

Moo went inside to his home office and put together a trauma kit, taking all of the morphine ampoules, gauze, surgical dressings, alcohol, and catgut sutures he had on hand. He'd have to stop in town to raid his office cabinet. Medical supplies would be scarce in the field.

When he was ready, he backed the car out of the barn, set his kit in the back seat alongside the bag Buddeea had packed for him, and said his good-byes to the girls, bending down to hug each of them in turn. Adele, Corine, Amelia. He looked around for Musa.

"Took to the woods after supper," said Buddeea. "Soon as the call came from Father Rossi. Said he had a trotline to check on."

"More like a sweetheart," said Adele.

"Gross," said Corine.

Buddeea frowned. "I told him to be back in an hour. It's been two. He'll be getting the switch when he gets back."

"Poor thing," said Amelia.

Buddeea hugged him again at the car. "God protect you, Moo. I love you."

"I love you, Booty. Give Musa my love when he returns, along with his whipping."

"I will."

"*Ya 'amar,*" he said. My moon.

"*Ya rouhi,*" she said. My soul.

CHAPTER FORTY-FIVE

BIG FRANK WALKED THE camp with Bonney and Lacey as the fireflies sported about them. Men were oiling rifles and sharpening trench knives, sipping whiskey or scribbling letters to wives or mothers or sweethearts. A sound of hushed voices around the place, like purling water.

Near a schoolhouse at the edge of the holler, they heard a man preaching. A white man in his forties, long and lean, with jet-black hair combed high over a broad forehead, over crinkled cheeks and a crooked mouth. He stood on a high hickory stump, looking from man to man in the gathering dusk.

"Above ground, I serve our Lord and Savior Jesus Christ in the little white churches and revival tents of the hollers. Below ground, in the mines, I'm a slave to King Coal, sure as any damned dweller of Hell."

That's right.

A large clan of miners squatted before him in the falling darkness. The reverend looked across his gathered flock. He seemed to speak from the side of his face, his eyes aimed one way, his mouth another, as if someone had slapped him hard across the jaw and his face never righted.

"Bible says it's a season for all things under heaven. It's a time to weep, a time to dance. A time to be born, a time to die. A time for peace, and a time for war."

Amen, said his men.

"Boys, I been praying hard on this one, asking Our Father for a sign. And I received it, clear as day. We all done. Them boys shot down in the road. Our Father, he's told us what to do, he has. What we ought already to know. It's time to put down the Bible and take up the sword."

Damn right, said his men, thumping the butts of their rifles on the ground. The reverend squatted down on the stump before them, his knees cocked wide. He swung one eye from face to face. His voice came softly from the side of his mouth, in strange singsong: the challenge and password of the Redneck army.

"Where are you going?"

To Mingo.

"How are you coming?"

I come creeping.

"We're the tip of the sword, boys. Tomorrow we eat breakfast in Logan town, and march on Mingo after that."

Hurrah!

The reverend rose and started toward the twin crests of Blair Mountain, the miners filing along behind him, entering the woods. Frank and the twins watched them a moment.

"You think that man ought to be leading a party to the front?" asked Frank.

"Not without us," said Bonney. "Like to get somebody killed."

"What about the others?" The Bad Seven had been split apart to train different groups of miners; they hadn't rejoined the others yet.

Bonney looked around. The camp was swarming, a sea of men. "Ten thousand of us, we might search all night and never find them."

Lacey nodded. "Ain't but a scouting party. We'll be back before the main assault."

Frank nodded and slung his rifle over his back. "Let's go."

The long file wended upward through the twilight, passing through the long shadows of the forest, past flint-scarred boulders and shallow caves. The cankered trunks of blighted trees floated like witchy totems in the falling darkness. They knelt at creek sides to fill their upturned hats, the water dripping silvery from their chins. Little sound but for the click of their boots on the rocky trail, the huff of their common breath.

They camped fireless on a ridge a mile above the schoolhouse. The breastworks and trenches of the defenders were built into the mountain above them, manned by the allied forces of King Coal: Baldwins, deputies, constables, troopers, and civilians who'd raided their wardrobes for khaki attire and wide-brim hats, a makeshift uniform. The Coal Operators Association had financed these guns and munitions, and their army had tied white armbands around their sleeves for identification. *Whites,* they called themselves.

Frank could see the flicker of their cigarettes and cookfires along the defensive line, could even hear their voices cascading down the mountain and through the trees, an odd word caught here or there in the darkness like something on a hook. He and the others maintained light and noise discipline, eating thin sandwiches from wax-paper wrappers and cold cans of beans, bedding down on blankets and sprawled coats, their rifles cuddled like spindly lovers, their cheeks twitching beneath the tickling creep of insects.

CHAPTER FORTY-SIX

DOC MOO DROVE THROUGH the night, hunched at the wheel of the Ford, straining to see washouts and rockslides and fallen trees. He rarely drove the car, finding Altair a much better conveyance for the rough terrain of the mountains, the rutted roads and rocky trails, but the four-wheeled machine could serve as an ambulance in a pinch.

Nearer to Logan, he twice encountered blockades, men with rifles and red bandannas who stood behind mule-carts, letting him pass after a cursory search of the vehicle. As a medical doctor, he could cross more freely through the lines.

"Thank ye, Doc, though it's gonna be them Got-damned Whites in want of doctoring. No disrespect."

"None taken."

Moo had spent much of the night circling wide around Logan County, intending to come down on Blair Mountain from the north—the side held by the miners. Faintly, he thought he could make out the double hump of Blair Mountain in the distance, darker against the dark sky, though he couldn't be sure. He knew he must be close to the encampment, though he hadn't seen a soul in miles. The road was rocky, little more than a damp creekbed carved by spring freshets. He was just thanking God for his good luck—not a single blowout on the drive—when he rounded a bend to find a fallen tree blocking the road.

A chestnut. One of the old-growth giants that somehow escaped the saws and axes of the previous century's timbering interests, only to succumb to the blight. A cankered tower, fallen. Still, he couldn't rule out the possibility that it had been helped along, felled across the road for the purpose of ambush. He cut the engine, killed the lights. The darkness swarmed in, the hissing roar of katydids and cicada. There was a pressure in the atmosphere, a tension—he could feel it pressing against his chest. He sensed he was not alone.

Psychosomatic, he told himself. *Inner conflict projected into the physical body.*

He took the flashlight from the leather compartment hanging on the inside of the door, tested the lamp against his hand, and stepped down from the car. As a doctor, he'd always felt clothed in a cloak of protection—the high regard that humankind had held for his profession since ancient times. But that cloak had worn thin over these past months—especially after his run-in with the vigilance men at the foot of Lick Creek. Now, unarmed in the darkness, he felt naked.

He was out of Mingo. Here his face was not recognized and his name carried no weight. His heart was thumping in his chest; his respiration had doubled. Deliberately, he slowed his breathing, deepened it. He knew that psychosomatic phenomena worked both ways. Physical stillness could be projected back into the nerves, the mind. He made himself stand still for ten long breaths, then approached the tree.

Stories told of old-growth trees that took ten men to encircle their trunks, arms spread and hands clasped, and Doc Moo had taken his family to see the Mingo Oak at the Trace Fork of Pigeon Creek—a tree said to be the oldest, largest white oak in all the world. Almost two hundred feet tall and thirty feet in girth, towering limb-spread against the sky like the tree of another age, which it was.

The chestnut before him was pulpy and ruined; it reminded him of the great, gangrenous limb of a giant. Still, a smart bushwhacker would fell just such a tree to fool his quarry. He put his hand on the limb. The wood was soft, like flesh.

Doc Moo realized the car might fit beneath the slanted trunk if one of the main branches were cut away. He went to the storage bed mounted at the rear of the car and paused, listening to the mountain night. Then he began unbuttoning the leather boot stretched over the bed to retrieve his ax.

"Hello, Papa."

"*Ya eadra!*" Oh Virgin. Moo leapt backward with fright, his hands clutched over his heart as Musa sat upright from the storage box.

"What the hell are you doing here, son?"

The boy stepped down from the bed and adjusted the possibles bag slung from his shoulder. He looked hard-browed at their surroundings, then to the stars, then back to the road—establishing the cardinal directions, his father knew, something the boy could do at a glance, day or night. "I heard Mama get that telephone call from Father Rossi and knew you'd be coming here. I didn't want you coming alone."

"Me? You didn't want *me* coming alone?" Moo was irate, all but spitting with fury. "This is not a game, son. You hear me? Not one of your Westerns or pulp novels. Men have been killed already, and I fear it's just the start. This is no place for a boy. None." He set his hand to his belt. "I ought to lash the Devil from you."

Musa came forward, head down. "I know, Papa. I'm truly sorry. I am. I accept whatever punishment you see fit." He looked up, innocent-eyed. "Though a wise man once told me it's better to ask for forgiveness than permission."

"*Al'aama.*" He'd told the boy that not two months ago, when the pair of them had ventured across the property line on the eastern edge of their land to pick their game sacks full of ripe blackberries on a morning they'd gone hunting and the turkeys had stood them up—putting the doctor in a mood.

"I am taking you back at once. And you will be confined to the house until I see fit to unground you. No more of your barefoot, carefree days in the woods."

Musa winced. To him, a punishment worse than any whipping. "If that's your wish, Papa, I understand. Though if it helps, I did just ride several hours confined in the trunk of an automobile?"

"By your own volition, son. No, it doesn't help." Moo turned and looked back the way they'd come, the utter darkness of the road. He shook his head.

Musa spoke up again. "Since we're so close to the Redneck camp, perhaps it would be better to spend the night there and travel home in the morning?"

Doc Moo looked at his son. "How do you know we're close?"

The boy looked to the sky. "I believe those are the lights of Logan town to the south of us, on the other side of that ridgeline." He pointed to a subtle blush of light on the underside of the clouds. A yellowish glow, as from streetlamps and porchlights. "Perhaps the roads will be safer come morning."

Doc Moo growled. He couldn't argue with the boy's logic. It was a miracle they'd had no blowouts, breakdowns, or accidents on the way here given the poor state of the roads, the lack of visibility, and the patrols.

"First we have to get through this tree," he said. "Fetch the ax."

Musa straightened. "Yes, sir." He fished the large felling ax from the bed, slipped the leather sheath from the blade, and approached the chestnut. The pair of them were standing there, appraising the immensity of the task, when

Musa touched his father's arm and nodded back up the road. "Someone's coming, Papa."

Before Moo could ask how the boy could know such a thing, a band of shadows emerged from the darkness. A crew of miners, their dark overalls crisscrossed with bandoliers and rifle slings. Their leader had a long telescoped rifle cradled against his chest.

"I'm Pope," he said. "And these here are the Coal River Hellcats. You on your way to the Redneck camp?"

Doc Moo nodded. "I'm a physician."

The man named Pope clucked his tongue, squinting one eye at the big chestnut. "Well, let's see if we can't get this tree out your way then."

As if at his command, the miners parted and a pair of Black men came forward. One was old, stooped and bowlegged, and the other little more than Musa's age. A teenager. The older man eyed the tree, palming it here and there like a sick body. Then he began drilling holes in the trunk with an augur. Meanwhile, the boy rolled blasting powder into fused paper cartridges and inserted them with a ramrod, gently, as if priming an old muzzleloader.

At Pope's request, Doc Moo reversed the car to a safe distance and the rest of the Hellcats took cover behind trees or rocks or the car itself.

"Fire in the hole!"

The boy lit the fuses and dropped down into the roadside ditch as the lines crackled, the sparks disappearing into the trunk. A moment later, the charges blew in neat succession, blasting great chunks from the tree. When the air cleared, a notch wide enough for a car lay smoking in the road.

The Hellcats cleared the charred debris and stood aside, saluting Doc Moo and Musa as they drove through the gap and continued on toward Blair Mountain, the powder-smoke trailing them into the darkness.

CHAPTER FORTY-SEVEN

DAWN CAME CREEPING THROUGH the trees, slinking across the ground and crawling into the hollows of men's eyes. They cursed the light and pulled their cloaks and blankets over their shoulders for a moment's more rest. Frank shivered and pawed the earth for Evie, her warm belly, finding only the bony limb of a rifle. A cold hurt poured through him, even in sleep.

Then a pop, gun-loud, and he came fast awake.

The reverend was already up, skipping through the encampment in his hobnail boots, pulling together a detail of men to investigate the sound. He tapped Frank and the twins, his finger over his lips. They nodded and followed with several others, a small squad moving through the foggy woods, careful of every twig and dry leaf beneath their boots. They snaked through a tangled maze of thorn thickets and laurel slicks, creeping to the shoulder of an old ridge road.

A black Studebaker was parked bug-eyed in the lane with one wheel missing from the hub, the front axle perched on the thin arm of an iron screw jack. A blowout—the sound they'd heard.

Tools and rubber tubes littered the ground. A man sat behind the wooden hoop of the steering wheel, one foot propped on the running board as he sipped from a quart jar. A badge on his chest. He was watching two other men who knelt in the dust of the road, laboring with spanners and wrenches on the front wheel. A small local boy stood barefoot behind them, handing them tools like a surgeon's assistant.

The men's coats and rifles were piled in the back seat of the topless car, their shirts spread sweaty across their backs despite the early hour. The man behind the wheel sipped again from the jar and eyed the line of earthworks and machine-gun nests spread across the mountain above them.

He turned his head to the boy. "Tell you what, son, we gonna show these Redneck sons of bitches today. They'll be hightailing it for cover, begging for mercy." He sipped from the jar, breathing through his teeth. "If these two can ever fix this flat."

The reverend motioned for the squad to circle closer. They followed his lead, stepping lightly through the trees, willing the weight out of their feet, high into their heads, moving like wraiths in the dawn. The reverend led them with one ear cocked before him, as if receiving messages on some secret frequency.

By the time they circled back to the road, the Studebaker was off the jack, the tools stowed, and the boy sent home. The two deputies were cradling their rifles now, sweat-drenched, swiping their foreheads with the backs of their arms. The third man leaned on the car, a pair of heavy pistols slung low from his belt.

Frank, the twins, and the rest of the reverend's squad watched from the woods. One of them bent to his leader's ear. "Shoot 'em, Rev?"

The reverend shook his head, his eyes glassy. "Every man must be given his chance at salvation."

Then, unannounced, he stepped from the trees. Frank and the others fanned out behind him, rifles shouldered, the barrels ticking with their breath. The reverend held out one arm to the deputies in the road.

"Where are you going?" he asked, singsong, stepping closer.

The password.

The eyes of the trio widened as they took in the strange band—white and Black men armed together, materializing out of the woods.

They swallowed and licked their lips. "Say again?"

The reverend stepped closer. His eyes still glassy, his voice calm, like a man speaking to a panicked horse. "How are you coming?" he asked.

The two men looked to their leader, still holding his quart jar. The man's jaw hung open, locked in place. The reverend's demeanor shifted, his face crinkling like a fist. "The password, man!" he hissed. "The pass—"

The leader dropped the jar and went for his pistols as his comrades shouted "Amen!"—the Whites' password. Tongues of fire leapt forth in the road, cracking and smoking, knocking men backward as if mule-kicked.

Now silence, the reek of spent cordite. Frank saw Lacey holding his breast with one hand, looking stunned, and one of the Whites was still alive—the leader, his quart jar making a muddy stain between his boots.

"Gore," said one of the reverend's men. "Chafin's chief deputy. He used to be a Union man."

"Traitor," said another. He stepped over and placed the barrel of his rifle against the lawman's heart, as if pinning him in place. This day, this road, this story handed down. He waited a long moment, in case the reverend would speak otherwise, staying his hand.

Silence.

"For Sid," he said, unsmiling.

He pulled the trigger.

CHAPTER FORTY-EIGHT

DOC MOO HAD SLEPT fitfully inside the wooden heat of the schoolhouse, listening to mice scamper about the rafters. When the miners had learned he was a medical doctor, they'd insisted he and Musa spend the night under the only roof about the camp, as if they were dignitaries, even though Moo had made it clear they'd be leaving at dawn.

"We're planning to use this place as the infirmary," said the miners, ignoring his protests.

Musa, on the other hand, seemed to sleep perfectly well, his hands crossed over his chest as he lay flat aback the teacher's desk. Moo and Buddeea had many times caught the boy sleeping outside on the porch, seemingly immune to heat, cold, or insects. A hard little knot, he was. The toughest spot in the wood. Still, Moo didn't think the boy ready to see what the world might reveal of itself through this mountain. Better to have a few more years unhaunted. He'd take him home at first light.

Finally Moo felt the weight of sleep falling over him, pulling down his eyelids. His mind let go, cut adrift, and he floated into strange lands of dream. Mount Lebanon under a veil of night darkness, the full moon flying high over those rugged mountains whose great cedars had sheltered his people for centuries, and then he was down beneath them, floating in the saddle, riding in the same militia band as his father, Maronite riders with long shotguns held across their knees and their mountain ponies passing through the great pillar-like trunks of the Cedars of God, strange glimmerings of moon-shadow playing across their shoulders, and he knew his father was leading these horsemen and he wanted to reach him. A longing in his chest. He wanted so badly to see his father again, as a young man or old, and he urged his horse on, toward the shadowy figure leading the riders—

"Papa," whispered Musa, shaking him gently. Now louder: "*Papa.*"

Doc Moo jolted upright, the longing still in his chest. The schoolhouse windows had a pale glow and Musa was standing beside him.

"Something's happened, Papa."

"What do you mean?"

"Shots."

Doc Moo rose and went to the schoolhouse window. The miners were stirring in the dawn, gray-blue shadows rising from spread coats and dewy canvas tarpaulins, many of them turning their heads toward the slopes of Blair Mountain.

"From Blair?"

Musa nodded. "Yes, sir. I reckon a mile, mile and a half at most. Pistols and at least one high-power."

Doc Moo looked at his pocket watch. "We'll wait twenty minutes for casualties, and then I take you home."

Eighteen minutes later, two Black miners emerged from the woods, one of them carrying a wounded man across his shoulders. Doc Moo stood on the schoolhouse steps, watching them come. "Fetch my kit from the car," he told Musa. "Also, clean water and an empty bucket, wherever you can find them."

"Yes, sir."

Others from the camp were flocking to the miners, pointing them toward the schoolhouse. They were nearly there before Doc Moo realized it was Big Frank carrying the wounded man on his shoulders—and it was one of the Hellfighter twins. The other brother was escorting them, a rifle in his hands, carrying their extra bedrolls and long guns strapped across his back.

Sweat streamed from Frank's chin. "Where you want him, Doc?"

"Inside. On the teacher's desk."

Frank turned sideways to fit through the door and Doc Moo cleared the desk, making room to lay him out on top. The man had been shot in the chest and the round had exited through his shoulder blade. Blood in his mouth, coming down his chin. One of his lungs was likely punctured, filled with blood, and Doc Moo suspected extensive internal bleeding. He knew what he would have to do.

He began cutting away the man's shirt and overalls. A woman came up, a miner's wife. "I was a Red Cross nurse during the war."

Doc Moo nodded. "Thank you. There are dressings in my bag there. Let's get pressure on the wound."

"Yes, sir."

Doc Moo looked at Frank. He was covered in blood, breathing like a bel-lows. His eyes on the man he'd carried, the hole in his breast. Behind him, men were crowding the schoolhouse doors, some of them stepping inside to see the man struggling on the table.

"Frank, can you watch the door? We don't need an audience."

"Yes, sir, Doc." The big man moved toward the schoolhouse entrance, shoo-ing the onlookers outside.

Doc Moo took the wounded man's hand. His fingertips were bullet-hard, callused from shovels and picks. His torso tightly wired, hardly an ounce of fat to hide the marvel of tendons and muscle beneath the skin, the bloody hole in his chest. On his arm, a tattoo of a coiled snake on a shield.

"Can you tell me your name, son?"

"Lacey," he said. His eyes rolled back in his head like a drunk's, a pair of yellowish slivers. After a moment, they found the doctor again. "My brother?"

"I'm here." Bonney stepped forward to take his brother's hand.

"*Bonbon*," whispered Lacey. Then his eyes rolled back again and his hand went slack. His blood-slickened fingers slipped free.

Bonney looked up. "He dying, Doc?"

"Not if I can help it." While the nurse kept pressure on the wound, Moo unrolled his belt of instruments on the table, scrubbed his hands, and took the scalpel from the roll. He was sterilizing it when Musa entered through the back door with a canteen and empty bucket.

"Water there on the corner, bucket at my feet."

"Yes, sir."

"Now please wait outside."

"Yes, Father." He went back outside to wait on the rear stoop.

Doc Moo felt the soft spaces between the man's ribs. He could feel the in-ternal pressure between the bones, the blood distending the man's thoracic cavity. He talked to him as he prepared to cut, though he knew the man was past the point of hearing. It was something his father had always done, talking to the animals whenever he had to treat them, to stitch up a wound or swab out an infection.

"This is called a thoracotomy," he told the unconscious man. "It's to relieve the pressure on your organs. I'm doing it to help you."

Doc Moo cut between the third and fourth true ribs, a two-inch incision. A stream of blood came flowing from the man's side, curling down his ribs and off the edge of the desk, splattering into the tin bucket Musa had set on the floor.

As the blood drained, Doc Moo exhaled and looked up at the nurse. She had a square jaw and lined face, her eyes hard and clear. "Thought I'd left the war behind," she said. "Till the minute I got home."

"Amen."

Ten minutes later, Doc Moo walked out onto the schoolhouse stoop. He looked like a butcher, his once-white shirt slashed with blood. Hundreds of men were gathered, waiting to hear. They stood in their overalls and bandannas, holding their rifles, their mouths slightly parted. Their eyes on him. He worried at the power of his words, what fury they could ignite. Ten thousand men sweating kerosene, their lungs full of coal dust and blasting powder, and he held a match. He took his handkerchief from his back pocket and wiped his hands, bloodying the white linen, trying to find the words.

He looked out to the miners. "I'm sorry, boys. I did all I could. He's gone."

The men exploded with fury, bellowing and roaring, their rage rolling through the camp like thunder. Soon they were forming into columns and charging rifles, marching toward the slopes of Blair.

To Logan!

To Mingo!

Free our boys!

Let God take the rest!

Bonney had stayed beside his brother inside the schoolhouse. Now he emerged on the stoop next to Frank and Doc Moo. His face was stone beneath his tears. "You done what you could, Doc. Thank you. Now it's our turn."

They began to go, but Moo stayed Frank a moment, a hand on his arm. "You don't have to go. You hauled that boy down off the mountain. You've done enough."

The man's nostrils were flared, his chest a bloody bulwark. Doc Moo could sense the fury inside him, smoldering, as if magma might burst from his skin.

"With respect, Doctor Moo, I'm just getting started."

He walked down the schoolhouse steps after Bonney, joining a column of men already marching toward the mountain.

CHAPTER FORTY-NINE

FOR THE FIRST TIME in years, Mother Jones wept. The tears came churning out of her eyes in sorties, squadrons, battalions—swamping her. She was on the train out of coal country, her face a red sea. For hours, she'd been watching the army of miners headed in the opposite direction, a whole tide of them marching up the tracks with their knotted bandannas and slung rifles, some of them hanging from coal hoppers or riding on boxcars.

She twisted her handkerchief in her hands, hard. Her born sons were long dead, struck down as babes, and she'd made this whole nation of boys her own. She'd fought and cared for them as best she could, putting every ounce of herself into their futures. Oh, how she loved them. Now she feared they were marching to their deaths, and she could do nothing to stop them.

A steward knelt beside her in the aisle. "Are you okay, Mrs. Jones? Anything I can get for you?"

She wiped her nose with her handkerchief. "No, young man. It's just I fear these boys are marching to slaughter."

The man nodded. "Some of the railroad brothers gone to fight with them," he whispered. "That's the word on the line."

"They have the cold fury now, like I've not seen. It's no show. They are marching to work, they are. They mean to use those guns sure as shovels and picks."

The steward nodded. "Reckon there comes a point a person just don't care no longer. Rather get killed standing up for himself than cowering in fear."

Mother nodded. "I understand that. Well, I do. But I've been around a long time, son, nigh on ninety years. Long enough to smell a trap. I believe the coal operators and Baldwins *want* them to march. It'll force the Army to intervene again, in force this time." She shook her head. "I've preached a storm coming, I have. Backlash. Revolt. It's inevitable. Americans will only live so long without freedom. It's oxygen to them. The very lifeblood of the Great Experiment. But war? No, son. Not like this. Whole universes of pain and grief come of that, blasted across generations. That's got to be accounted for. I did my best to stop it. To talk them down. Desperate, I was."

She looked down at her hands, which had held the telegram. Phony it was, though she'd hardly admitted that even to herself. Perhaps she'd hoped if the whole world believed it, the President would have to make it true.

She shook her head. "I lost their trust."

The steward nodded. "If you done a bad thing, it was for a good reason. So you're even in my book, Mrs. Jones." He paused. "What are you going to do next?"

An attack of the rheumatism was coming on, she could feel it. It would spread through her body like a wildfire, seizing her up. Soon her joints would be gripped in searing fists and her feet would swell up, threatening to bust from their little black pumps. Nodules would break out on the backs of her hands, pale hives she'd scratch bloody if she didn't mind herself. She might even be bedbound. *The spirit is willing but the flesh* . . .

"I'll keep fighting, son. If I can't do it in on the ground, I'll see what sway I've got in the high offices." She looked out the window. They were slugging across the rolling fields and vast plantations of Virginia, heading for the nation's capital. She began opening and closing her fists, as if readying for a prizefight. "We'll see if I'm as dangerous as I used to be."

But by the time they rolled into Union Station, the rheumatism had its teeth in her. The steward helped her down from the train and a pair of old family friends met her on the platform—the Powderlys, her hosts in the federal city. The steward helped her all the way to their car. She climbed into the back seat, gritting her teeth against the pain.

"Give them hell, Mrs. Jones," said the young man.

She squeezed his upper arm.

"Born to," she said.

CHAPTER FIFTY

DOC MOO STOOD ON the schoolhouse steps. Aeroplanes were wheeling over Blair Mountain, their shadows shooting down through the trees. Biplanes with open cockpits, so close he could see the pilots in their goggles and leather flying caps, the white silk scarves snapping from their necks.

The Logan Air Force.

They were hunting for red bandannas, he knew, turning razor-edged on their wingtips to look down through the trees. First blood had been shed on the mountain this morning. One of the men killed was Sheriff Chafin's chief deputy, a man called Gore. A sworn officer of the law. Doc Moo could almost hear the voices on the defense line, the townsmen in khaki and armbands.

Anarchy is what it is.

Killing Gore? That ain't anarchy, it's an act of war.

If it's war they want, we'll give it till the creeks run red.

Meanwhile, miners were still swarming in from every point of the compass. Word had company stores raided of arms, men in overalls training in the clearings, and Black miners eating in Jim Crow restaurants right alongside their white comrades, rifles propped against their tables. Moo feared what the country might do to put such a movement back in the ground.

Moo loved America, he did. This country had attempted a "Great Experiment" for the promotion of human happiness—a written recognition that all men were created equal, endowed with certain inalienable rights, and the state existed to guarantee those liberties, not to impede them. In practice, those high ideals made it a nation of deep hypocrisy—a country ever on a knife's edge, ever failing to live up to its own principles. A nation ever in conflict with itself.

Here, he thought, on this mountain, they would see what happened when those rights and liberties had been taken from those to whom they were promised—taken for years and years, at the ends of fists and ax handles and guns.

Musa came running around the schoolhouse and grabbed his sleeve. "Papa, look." He pointed to a biplane circling just west of Blair Mountain, gyrating like a hawk over a field mouse. The boy ran inside to the map tacked to the wall, tracing his finger along the blue line of a watercourse, then came back out to the stoop. "It's flying over Crooked Creek."

Doc Moo had seen Big Frank's column march off in that direction. Now, as he and Musa watched, the biplane carved upward into the blind white eye of the sun, as if going to hide. Then, moments later, it came diving back toward the creek, as if lining up for a strafing run.

"*Ya Yasue.*" Oh Jesus.

A CURIOUS WHINE FROM the sun. Big Frank looked over his shoulder, squinting. While Bonney was out front scouting for the column, shaping his grief and fury into a spear, Frank had volunteered to help carry the column's Gatling gun—a prize piece stolen from a company store, slung from a long pole like a killed animal, and carried between his shoulder and that of a burly Marine Corps veteran called Crockett. The six-barreled contraption could fire nine hundred rounds per minute as the gunner cranked the firing handle, spinning the ring of octagonal barrels.

They were headed for Crooked Creek Gap. A smaller force than those marching on Blair itself but well organized, led by Great War veterans and a small stick of human dynamite named Bill Blizzard—a man well-named, people said, built of fury and blasting powder, with a square jaw and three-inch fuse.

Frank knew him by reputation. An Irishman out of Cabin Creek, eighteen years old when the *Bull Moose Special* rolled past his tent camp and machine-gunned the place. People said his mother, called Ma in honor of Mother Jones herself, went out in her nightgown and tore up the tracks with her own bare hands, her fingers bleeding, her arms veined with baby copperheads, so those gun trains couldn't come again. Such was the story told deep in the mineshafts, high on the shanty porches.

"We're going to give them such hell, we are, they'll think they died and already went," Blizzard had told them. "While the others hit them head-on, we're going to bust through the Gap and flank the sons of bitches."

Now Frank looked up again. Everyone did. The curious whine was becoming

a wail, a rising scream. A shadow leapt from the sun, streaking down on them like a predatory bird.

"Ground attack! Everybody down!"

Men scrambled for cover, diving behind rocks and trees and creekbanks, throwing their hands over their heads as the ship roared just over the treetops, shrieking with banshee wire and engine power. Miners squeezed themselves into tight little balls and Frank and the other gunbearer hunkered beside the Gatling gun itself. Then the ship was gone, droning off into the distance. Slowly, the miners uncovered their heads, looking up slack-jawed to find a blizzard fluttering down through the trees.

Leaflets. The papers alighted along the creek like a strange flock of birds. They stuck in branches and snagged in briars and pasted the creekbanks. Some caught in the reeds or went shooting and swirling down the creek itself, washing up on stones downstream. Some of the men cursed and squinted down the sights of their rifles, hoping to get off a shot at the departing biplane, while others reached out their free hands, trying to catch one of the papers still twist-turning toward the ground.

Frank raised his head to find one of the leaflets stuck upright between the ringed barrels of the Gatling gun. A breaker boy plucked up the paper and held it under his nose, frowning. The others crowded around him, waiting.

"Well?"

The boy licked his lips, squinting. "Ain't got my readin' glasses."

One of the other miners—an old graybeard with rosy cheeks—snapped up the handbill and held it beneath his wiry spectacles. He cleared his throat. "By the President of the United States of America," he read. "A Proclamation."

Then, as the man's eyes scanned down to the finer print, his face contorted like the young miner's had. He began to read slowly, haltingly, the words strange on his tongue. "*Whereas*, the governor of the State of West Virginia has represented that domestic violence exists in *said State*, which the authorities of *said State* are unable to repress, and *Whereas*, it is provided in the Constitution of the United States that the United States shall protect each state in this Union on application of the legislature or the executive when the legislature cannot be convened, against domestic violence . . ."

The man looked up from the paper, his mouth slack.

"The hell? T'ain't but a bunch of *whereas* and *thereof* and *aforesaid*, the whole damned thing. Like they want to read us to death."

The big Marine, Crockett, pulled a flask from the bib pocket of his overalls and sucked off a pull. He was a bear of a man, shirtless beneath his overalls, with a round grizzled face and the word TEUFELSHUND tattooed across his hairy chest in olden script. Devil Dog. A nickname the Marines had earned at the Battle of Belleau Wood, advancing again and again against German lines.

Crockett shook his head. "Sounds like legalese to me. Lawyer talk, like all them high-hat city folk fancies. Keeps 'em feeling high and mighty, lording us over."

The first man held out the paper. "Anybody know legalese?"

When no one spoke, Frank held out his hand. "My wife was a school-teacher," he said. "Give me a look."

He took the leaflet and scanned the lines. The others gathered close, looking over his shoulders. Frank looked up. "It's an ultimatum, near as I can tell. President says we're *insurgents* and we are to *retire peaceably to our abodes* by noon tomorrow."

The miners waited. "Or what?"

Crockett stoppered his flask and spat. "Or next time it won't be a bunch of papers they drop on our heads."

CHAPTER FIFTY-ONE

ON BLAIR MOUNTAIN, THE defenders were stuffing their ear canals with cotton balls and chewing aspirin tablets. The relentless gunfire was giving them headaches. Some had spit their fillings out. The whole mountain thundered and smoked, as if preparing to erupt, and thousands of spent shell casings littered the trenches, so that treasure-seeking boys would be digging up brass shells instead of arrowheads for decades to come.

Down on the shoulder of the mountain, on the defense line near Crooked Creek Gap, a local reporter was embedded with the defense forces—the same reporter who'd caught Sid on the train home from Williamson, delivering news of the acquittal of the Baldwin-Felts agents for the Battle of Matewan. Now he was holed up in a machine-gun nest alongside a grizzled major in the defense forces named Antoine "Bad Tony" Gaujot. A veteran of the coal wars, short but hard-made, with a pale scar between his eyes and the tattoo of a heart on one forearm that *thump-thump-thump*ed with the recoil of his Colt Model 1895 machine gun—an air-cooled, belt-fed, gas-operated monster mounted on a heavyweight tripod.

Earlier that day, before the shooting started, Bad Tony had wiped down the barrel and action with an oiled rag. "Used this same honey up on Paint Creek, nineteen and thirteen. She's a real slick piece."

The reporter held his pencil perched. "Paint Creek? You mean you were on the *Bull Moose Special*?"

"Don't write that down."

The reporter quickly retracted his pencil. Bad Tony had fought in Mexico, the Philippines, France, and the American mine wars. Rumor was, he'd been narrowly acquitted of murder while serving in the 2nd West Virginia Volunteer Infantry, having shot a private in the neck with a purloined captain's pistol during an arrest attempt. He went on to earn a Congressional Medal of

Honor during the Philippine Insurrection, swimming across a swollen river under heavy fire to steal an enemy canoe—a medal he wore as a fob on his watch chain.

For hours, he'd been running the gun like a jackhammer, expertly traversing it back and forth, the heart throbbing on his forearm as he sent fire downrange, the black tie of his uniform tucked between his shirt buttons. Now he called back over his shoulder, not taking his eyes from the iron sights.

"Reload!"

A runner came ducking up with a pair of wooden ammunition boxes, the caliber stenciled on the sides. He unlatched the top and presented the draped canvas belt of cartridges over his palms like an offering, sliding it carefully through the gun before Bad Tony jacked back the gas lever, recharging the weapon.

"Keep 'em coming, son."

As Tony brought the gun back online, jingling hot casings at their feet, the reporter rose to his knees and sighted over the edge of their log-built nest, raising his field glasses. Down the slope of the valley, he could see a cluster of buildings—a bullet-sieved farm where a large force of miners had holed up.

Twice already, they'd tried to mount a charge up the valley, a denim swarm of them scrambling over rocks and deadfalls, howling like Johnnies or Comanches. But the defense line had held strong, the fire of three hundred rifles and two machine guns cutting the legs from underneath them, sending them scurrying back with their wounded.

Tony was lighting a cigarette, talking with his teeth clenched. "They keep coming, they'll do the job for us. We can drive coffin nails all day."

The reporter, glassing the tree line diagonal to their position, landed on a bearded man, big as a bear, standing bare-shouldered in a pair of overalls and a rumpled brown hat. He appeared to be urinating on a tree. The reporter held the man in the converged spheres of the binoculars' focus, as if zeroing a rifle. A single word to Tony and the man would be dropped like a king buck or black bear or the great Sasquatch himself. Then the bearded man jiggled, replaced himself, and turned to squat beside a large Black miner—and the reporter saw a ring of six barrels aimed right at them.

"Gatling gun!"

He ducked as fire erupted from the tree line like sudden-shot lightning, hissing and cracking into the logs of their emplacement. Bad Tony cursed, dropped his head, then inched up to return fire. Through a sliver between logs, the reporter watched the miners break again from the shattered farmhouse, flooding upward beneath the suppressive fire of the Gatling gun. Soon Bad Tony was swiveling the barrel between the marchers and the wood line every few seconds, hammering off rounds, trying to stop two leaks with the same plug.

"God damn them, they don't know when to quit."

He spat out his cigarette and squinted behind the pop-up rear sight, working the elevation wheel to keep the gun on target. He was breathing hard and steady through his nose, his nostrils flaring. Spent shell casings rattled at their ankles, the gun hammering out empty cartridge belts like tickertape, running through one box of ammunition, then another. The reporter could see the heat radiating from the weapon, a gout of crackling, dangerous air.

The reporter chanced another look through the sliver—the flood of miners was closer than ever, weaving in and out of the trees and rocks, rising higher in the valley. Tony emptied another belt of cartridges and fed in the next, racking the bolt.

"Aim low!" he shouted down the line. "Aim at their feet, hit 'em in the chest!"

The deputies and civilian militiamen were popping from their trenches to fire and dropping down again, tucking their heads between their shoulders. Tony swiveled to run more rounds into the tree line. His chin was dripping sweat and the gun's muzzle had begun to glow red, inflamed.

Tony called over his shoulder to his ammo runner. "Start the truck."

"Yes, sir."

Tony cocked his chin toward the reporter. "Hey, Mister Newspaperman. You got a gun, little pocket pistol or something?"

"No, sir."

"Too bad. We get overrun, it might be the only thing standing between you and a cut throat."

The reporter got out his penknife—a tiny folding blade he used to sharpen his pencil nubs. He rammed his eye into the gap of the log-built emplacement again. An incoming round could zip right through the chink and hollow out his skull, but he couldn't help himself. He had to see what was coming.

His heart lurched—they were so close now, no more than a hundred yards, as if they'd leapt forward when he wasn't looking. Like banshees or ghost soldiers. Their brows were knit hard over the iron sights of their guns, their hands rolling bolts and working levers and shouldering rifles with relentless exactitude, again and again, as if swinging sledges or picks, burrowing through fire instead of earth, digging toward the defense line.

A jet of dirt and wood chips struck him in the face—a round that nearly slipped between the logs. He fell back, holding his eye with one hand. The bullish snout of the machine gun was glowing red above him, throbbing with every burst, the slugs scoring the rifling from the barrel. Rounds began popping off without Tony even touching the trigger, igniting in the overheated chamber. The man's face looked scalded, blistered, as if he'd stuck it in the hot door of a stove. He'd been running the gun for nearly three hours. The action jammed with a terminal *clack* and Bad Tony barreled his hands to his mouth, shouting down the line.

"Fall back, fall back! Join up at the next ridgeline!"

The runner and Bad Tony each lifted a leg of the tripod, carrying the machine gun like some biblical relic, red-glowing, and the reporter scrambled for the truck behind them, squinting his clogged eye, still gripping the penknife under his thumb.

At their backs rose a wail, high and bloody, like the damned let slip from Hell.

CHAPTER FIFTY-TWO

FRANK LEAPT TO HIS feet, sounding a great howl as the defenders fled for their lives. The spike of triumph was in his blood, singing like moonshine. He could've roared the top off the mountain. He could've climbed a tree and kissed the sky.

Crockett reached up and hauled him back down behind the gun. "Fuck's sake, you like to get ye head blowed off. They might of left a sniper for us."

The miners were overrunning the abandoned trenches, holding up prizes of left-behind guns and rations and cartridge boxes. Frank slapped Crockett on the arm. "You see them sons of bitches run, Crock, did you? Snipers, hell! They didn't have no time for that."

The tattooed Marine grunted. He'd been kneeling behind the Gatling gun like a lineman, one eye squinted, cranking the firing handle to send rounds right over the charging miners' heads, pouring fire into the enemy positions. Meanwhile, Frank had fed in clip after clip, handing back the empties for the ammo boys to reload. With six barrels, the gun would never overheat.

Every few seconds, the muzzle of the enemy machine gun would swing their way and the air would shriek around them, rounds crazing and swarming and cracking up the trees, trying to stamp them out same as the clubs and boots of the Baldwins except a single one of these slugs could punch a heart or brain or belly out. Then the enemy gun jammed and the defense lines broke before the charging miners.

Crockett spat a black string of tobacco between his teeth. "I seent 'em run, all right. And I know they about to squat their puckered asses down right on the next ridge and make us do it all over again."

Frank clapped his hands on the man's hairy shoulders and shook him. "Crock, you sweet-shooting son of a bitch. You're just a regular Davy Goddamn

Crockett, ain't you?" Frank rose again to his full height, barreling his hands to holler all through the valley. "We got us Davy Goddamighty Crockett down here!"

High on the line, the miners lifted their rifles and cheered.

THE FORD MODEL T truck rocked and slewed down the dirt road, the driver spinning the big wood-hooped steering wheel back and forth with both hands, working to keep the overloaded rig from careering into the trees. Bad Tony rode shotgun, giving directions, his head jammed forward like a bloodied hood ornament while deputies and militiamen clung to the slat-wood bedsides and running boards, swinging with the turns, ducking as low-hanging branches whipped past their heads. A convoy of delivery trucks and paddy wagons and roadsters followed in their wake, their thin tires cutting a fine billow of dust from the valley floor.

The defenders were breathing hard, their hearts charging in their chests, their mouths full of hot dust and the sulfurous tang of spent gunpowder. The driver slung the truck around a sharp bend and one of the militiamen was thrown from the side, grasping empty fistfuls of air as he slammed into the hard pack and rolled wild-limbed in the road. The men riding in the cargo bed beat on the roof of the cab, telling the driver to pull over, but Bad Tony reached over and seized the wheel, yanking it straight.

"No time for that."

The Rednecks had broken through the western end of the defense line, flooding into Logan County along the vein of Crooked Creek. Now Bad Tony and his men had to cut them off before they punched through the Gap itself and marched straight into town.

Tony directed the convoy to the base of a ridge overlooking the approach trail where the Rednecks were sure to soon emerge. The men dismounted, boots and loafers smacking down in the dust. They scrambled up the back side of the ridge, hunched and sweaty, clawing for handholds, grabbing stones and roots and small trees, ripping the feathery roots of weeds from the hillside. Along the sharp spine of the ridge, Tony stood small and angular beneath a film of blood and dust, like a man made with a hatchet. He pointed chop-handed, barking orders like he had in foreign wars.

"I want ten new emplacements along this line. Deputy, you form ten five-man details to cut trees and drag deadfall for new breastworks."

"Yes, sir."

"Trooper, you form ten five-man details to dig trenches for the emplacements."

"Yes, sir."

"Deputy, form three bucket brigades to unload the trucks and bring all that ammunition up the ridge. Whoever's left, send 'em on up to me, them and your best shooters."

"Yes, sir . . ."

CHAPTER FIFTY-THREE

FRANK AND CROCKETT WERE climbing a rocky path with the Gatling gun slung between them, sucking wind, their boots slipping on mossy stones and loose dirt. The air was thick with flies; the heat heavier with every step. The faster they marched, the better chance they had of punching through the Gap before the defenders could regroup and put up another line of resistance.

Frank's heart felt like a piston in his chest, driving the blood through him, pushing a sea of sweat up through his skin. He didn't mind the fry-oil crackling in his shoulders and thighs. He was all man now, putting his strength to work. The big Gat had become his swinging pick. With it, he would cut the guts from whatever stood in their way. Mud, man, or machine. He would cut a hole through the mountain if he had to. The spike of triumph had lingered with him. He wanted more of it. They all did. They weren't going to be stopped.

Aeroplanes droned in and out of hearing, tracking them, and barefoot boys ran along the higher paths, acting as scouts and messengers. The miners kept coming to slap Frank and Crockett on the shoulder or shake their hands, offering them prized cigarillos or nips of corn likker. Marching along, they began to piece together a rowdy ballad, their voices rising to the tune of "John Brown's Body."

> *Davy Crockett has arisen from the grave,*
> *Davy Crockett has a nation he must save,*
> *Davy Crockett has arisen from the grave,*
> *And he's got him a Gatling gun!*
> *Glory, glory, hallelujah! Glory, glory, hallelujah!*
> *Glory, glory, hallelujah! The Rednecks are march-ing on!*

A Devil Dog unleashed on the kings he once warred,
He's wield-ing the lightning of a terrible swift sword,
He will loose their souls before the fury of the Lord,
Davy's got him a Gatling gun!

Frank thought back to the songs of Lick Creek, those nights when they'd gathered round roaring fires and sung at the tops of their lungs, and it seemed the steep dark slopes of the holler projected their voices high into the night sky, racing starward with the embers. He thought of Mama-B back there in that camp all but emptied of menfolk, waiting for news from the march.

She'd been the only mother he ever had, and he knew the world had taken its picks and shovels and axes to her heart. The unspoken atrocities of her childhood, raised in bondage, and the ropes and night riders of Reconstruction. Her husband dying of dust in his lungs, her daughter-in-law—Frank's mother—in childbirth, and then her son—Frank's father—vanished, killed at the rumored hands of company men, his body never found. A life lived under the thumbs and heels of thugs.

Frank did not want to drive another nail into her heart. But he was standing against the same forces that had taken what she loved. No matter what happened, he hoped she'd be proud. Around him, the miners were throwing in a verse of the Union hymn, which went to the same tune—a song their voices had carried so many times at Lick Creek.

They have taken untold millions that they never toiled to earn,
But without our brain and muscle not a single wheel can turn.
We can break their haughty power, gain our freedom when we learn
That the Union makes us strong.
Solidarity forever, solidarity forever,
Solidarity forever, for the Union makes us strong.

Their voices carried up and down the creek, as powerful as a river, a changing tide, and Frank joined in the next chorus, feeling their power flood through the hills, toward those men standing on high before them, looking down their rifles. High as the stars over the mountains. They would reach those storied heights, he thought. They would pull them down to the earth, where the rest of them lived.

*   *   *

BAD TONY SLAPPED A mosquito from the base of his neck, then spat into the dirt of his freshly dug trench. Fat earthworms were still wriggling in the turned earth.

"Davy Crockett, huh?"

"Yes, sir," said the runner boy, relaying the latest rumors come bounding through the lines. "That's what the miners are calling him, that machine-gunner of theirs. The one running the Gatling gun. They say he's a overseas man. A Marine. Said he run a Vickers gun in the war, put a hundred Krauts in the ground at Belleau Wood. Got him a Navy Cross."

Tony squinted down the sights of his machine gun. He'd paid the boy a nickel for the latest news. "Did he now."

"That's the story going round," said the boy. "They say he's from the back of beyond, the far side of the mountains someplace. Name of Crockett. Say he's Davy reborn with six barrels instead of one. A Devil's Hound."

Tony sniffed. "*Teufelshund*," he said. "A Devil Dog." His own machine gun had cooled, the red glow gone from the muzzle. The barrel was gun-black again, glistening with fresh oil and a new belt of cartridges. He watched the approach trail, waiting, thumbing the medal on his watch chain.

The reporter was holed up beside him, his notepad out. He licked his lips. "Major Gaujot, is it true you and your brother are the only pair of brothers to receive the Congressional Medal of Honor in different wars?"

Tony's eyes flitted in the reporter's direction. "Sure, it's true. Jules, he got his for actions in 1911, just a couple months after they given me mine, said he'd bust if he didn't get one for himself. He was down in Arizona when the Mexican Revolution broke out. First Cavalry. There were some American POWs trapped on the other side of the border. Jules gets on Old Dick, his horse, rides down there under heavy fire, and arranges a surrender. Saved those prisoners' lives."

"And is it true he got into some hot water back during the Philippine Insurrection?"

Tony shrugged. "That was way back. It was the water cure is all."

"The water cure?"

Tony traversed the gun slowly along the approach trail, not looking up. "Only way to get them padres down there to talk. Force four, five gallons of water down their throats, till they look like they're expecting twins. Then

TAYLOR BROWN   194

kneel down hard on their bellies, pump it back out like a bubbling spring. Makes the truth come babbling out."

"Christ."

"They docked him a month's pay, three months' command suspension. Ten years later, he wins the Medal of Honor. Shows what they know."

The reporter was scratching furiously in his notepad, while the runner boy knelt there hang-jawed, awaiting orders. Bad Tony sighted along the approach trail, poking holes in the brush with his eyes. The Rednecks would appear any moment. He cleared his throat. "Tell me something, boy."

"Yes, sir."

"Old Davy Crockett never earned himself no Congressional Medal of Honor, did he now?"

Before the boy could reply, a flash of red bandannas along the trail.

Tony squeezed the trigger.

CHAPTER FIFTY-FOUR

ROUNDS CAME SHEARING AND cracking through the trees.

"Shitfire!" cried Crock, sticking the last leg of the tripod in the dirt. "They done tripped the trigger." The miners were supposed to wait to advance until the Gatling gun was in position, ready to provide covering fire. Crock flipped up the rear sight of the gun and squinted downrange, setting the windage with his thumb and forefinger.

"Load!"

Frank dropped the ammo bag off his shoulder, drew a long brass magazine, and thrust it into the top of the gun. One hundred rounds.

"Ready!"

Crock spat. "Git ye some, you sons of bitches."

He began to crank the shooting handle, sending rounds into the machine-gun nest at the top of the ridge. Beneath them, miners were pushing their way up the approach trail, moving from tree to tree, while others had taken to the creek itself, crouching as rounds chipped and scored the rocks, making them spark and fume.

"Reload!" cried Crockett.

Frank rose to pull out the empty magazine and swap in a new one, dropping down just as a hail of fire tore through the woods around them. He could feel the rounds hitting the fallen chestnut against which he crouched, the blighted wood shuddering like flesh. There was a small clearing beneath them full of tall grass and wildflowers. The site of an old homestead along the creek, just the fire-scarred stone chimney left of a small cabin that once stood there. The faint outline of the structure's foundation. Miners began sprinting across the clearing, arrowing through the belly-high grass, a pale cloud of dandelions rising in their wake.

A second wave took off and a slash of automatic fire ripped through them.

They struck wild poses, lurching and rampant, turning back the way they'd come. A young miner lay heaving in their wake, slumped at the base of the ancient chimney. He was holding his belly with both hands, his blood scattering through his fingers.

THE REPORTER COULDN'T LOOK away. The wounded miner's face was wrenched, his mouth gaped, his prayers or blasphemies inaudible, shattered by the crisscrossing hatchwork of gunfire.

Beside him, Bad Tony's machine gun bucked and thundered, belting out long chains of fire, splintering saplings and stitching tree trunks. A round cracked the chimney-stone just above the young miner's head and Tony sent a firm order down the line: "Nobody fire at the wounded miner."

The reporter lowered his binoculars, wondering at this unexpected mercy. Then a band of rescuers broke from cover and Tony grunted with satisfaction, waiting until they were in the open before he hammered into them, the heart tattoo thumping wildly on his forearm. Two of them fell and the rest turned tail, dragging their wounded back into the trees.

Tony turned to the pressman and grinned. The white blister of scar shone between his eyes. "Bait and wait. Works every time."

But as soon as the defenders eased up to survey the damage, a line of fire came streaking down from the opposing ridgeline. The Gatling gun. Precision bursts began tearing into the defense line, finding chinks and exposures. A round caromed through their nest and Tony yelped, finding a splinter driven straight through his cheek. He touched it gently. A look of wonder on his face.

"Davy Goddamn Crockett."

When the reporter looked back to the clearing, the wounded miner lay still. A bloody star in his chest, blown ragged for all to see. An execution. On the opposite slope, shadows were moving through the trees, gathering like a storm, hundreds of shades merging amid the red flicker of bandannas. He could almost sense the ire of that massing shadow, hearts pounding like fists, as if Sid Hatfield had been shot down again, right before their very eyes.

If they all charged through the Gap at once, nothing could stop them.

CHAPTER FIFTY-FIVE

SHERIFF CHAFIN STOOD AT home plate of the Logan ballfield, leaning cross-armed against a black Stutz motorcar. He was watching one of his biplanes sideslip the crosswind on final approach.

Behind him there was panic in the streets, as if barbarians had already breached the town gates. The fighting was audible, the incessant crack of highpowers sounding over the ridges, crackling through the atmosphere. Stray rounds punched through kitchen windows and barn stalls and car doors. People were fleeing, strapping grandfather clocks to the roofs of automobiles and throwing saddles on shuddering horses.

I hear the Rednecks are at Crooked Creek.

That ain't but four miles from here.

They'll pick us clean, take everything ain't nailed down.

Chafin stood at ease. His head, hat, and smile all cocked at the same angle, his bull neck pinched over his bowtie. An unworried man, thumbing the nipplelike scar beneath his shirt. Word was, the Union official who'd shot him had thrown out his little .22 pistol after the incident, disgusted. "That Goddamned son of a bitch is liable to get well. If I'd had my .44, he'd be gnashing his teeth in Hell."

Chafin always smiled at that, and he'd learned a lesson, too. Don't use a weapon fit for the task. Use the biggest piece of ordnance you've got.

The biplane cleared the trees and bounced down in centerfield, bird-light, as if the very ground were unsafe. Chafin made a chopping motion and the pilot cut the engine, the wood-and-wire wings drooping slightly as the propeller chucked to a stop. The airman hung his elbow over the side of the cockpit, keeping his gloves on. A local man, he'd been an Army flight instructor during the Great War.

"Line's holding strong at Blair itself, Sheriff, but it don't look good at

Crooked Creek Gap. Tony Gaujot's barely holding the line. The miners mount a full charge, they're liable to break right through the pass. There's plenty enough of them to do it."

"Not to worry, Captain." Chafin motioned the man from the cockpit. "We got an ace up our sleeve."

Reluctantly, the airman climbed down from his ship, not taking off his gloves or flying helmet. Obviously, he didn't like being on the ground under the present circumstances. Chafin led him to the back of the Stutz, a seven-passenger model with a large traveling trunk mounted to the rear bumper. He set his palms on the lid and kept them there, as if feeling the warmth or strength of a living thing. Gauging its power.

He looked at the pilot. "Got us a chemist up in Charleston. What you might call a patriotic man, respects law and order. He made up something real nice for us. Real nice." Chafin flipped up the brass latches on the trunk and raised the lid. "The Rednecks ain't listened to them Presidential leaflets we thrown down on them. Maybe they'll listen to these."

The pilot stepped back from the trunk, his face white. "I was hired on for reconnaissance, Sheriff. Not for that."

Chafin cocked his ear toward the storm of gunfire coming off Blair Mountain. "You hear that, Cap? It's a war on. At our very doorstep. Surely you ain't the kind of man who'd let these Reds march in here to loot, pillage, and plunder us—not when you could do something to stop them?"

Chafin put one large ringed hand on the pilot's shoulder, friendly-like, thumbing the rough twill of the man's flying suit. Not even the pastors of Logan County were safe from his reach. Everyone knew that. Not even the Devil. Chafin smiled, squeezing the pilot's shoulder. "A man such as that, Cap, I wonder how he could *live* in this town after that. Hell, not even *his people* would be safe."

CHAPTER FIFTY-SIX

DOC MOO STEPPED OUT onto the front stoop of the schoolhouse, looking for Musa. Blair Mountain loomed huge before him, a forested monster quaking with gunfire. All day, bloodied men had been coming down off its slopes, staggering or crawling out of the trees, palming their punctured bodies, the worst of them carried down on wool blankets or makeshift stretchers.

He'd turned the schoolhouse into a field infirmary. The teacher's desk had become his operating table, though it looked more like a butcher's block now. The wounded were laid out shoulder to shoulder on the rough plank floor, tended by wives and daughters who'd arrived in nurses' caps with U.M.W. lettered on them—United Mine Workers. Moo thanked the Holy Mother for their arrival. The bodies were placed beneath a shade tree outside the place, covered in quilts and sheets. An old rope-swing swayed over them, as if counting the dead. Doc Moo could see it through the crazed glass of one window.

With the patients stable for the moment, he'd come to find Musa. He'd been using the boy as his runner, sending him out into the camp and surrounding homesteads for supplies they needed—dressings, sponges, salt, even catgut and fiddle string for sutures. He had Musa deliver everything to the foot of the stoop and wait outside, so he wouldn't see the carnage inside the place. But they'd be out of floor space for the wounded soon and the new casualties would be laid outside on coats or quilts for all the world to see.

Doc Moo had sent the boy for a bucket of water from the pump; he should've been back by now. He worried Musa might have tried to sneak up the mountain, eager to see some of the action. He had a tendency to roam, after all. Buddeea sometimes joked the boy would walk to Texas and back if they'd let him.

"Probably come back better fed than he left us, too."

Doc Moo couldn't disagree. Musa was born to the woods, able to read, hear, and speak its varied languages in ways few could. They didn't know where

he got the knack, teasing that he'd caught the ghost of an old Kentucky fron-
tiersman or Mingo warrior—perhaps the great Chief Logan himself. But this
was not the time. In fact, as Doc Moo thought about it, he was displeased. He
picked a cigarette out of his shirt pocket. He had a neat little quiver of them in
the false bottom of his medicine bag, lined up like rifle cartridges.

Rightly displeased, he decided, lighting the cigarette, sucking the smoke
into his lungs. Those dime novels the boy read of the heroic exploits of Daniel Boone and Kit Carson and Buffalo Bill Cody made much of guns and glory,
saying nothing of the everyday violence of breech births and busted spleens,
hoof-cracked skulls and bladder tumors. Nothing of real gunshot wounds, what
they did to the insides of a person, their organs, or the evils of well-fed town
men in nice cars, drinking likker and carrying clubs. The violence that was all
around them, every day and night, and didn't need to be sought out.

Doc Moo realized he was holding his breath and blew the smoke hard out
of his nostrils, closing his eyes. A pleasant, tingling burn.

"Papa?"

Doc Moo fairly jumped, looking down at the boy. "Where have you been?"

Musa held up a wooden pail with a rope handle, the water sloshing down
around his bare feet. "Said you wanted clean water and the camp pump is drawing silt. So I went to the farmstead yonder and ask to draw from their well."

Doc Moo took the bucket from his son. "You should've told me before you
ventured that far." He rarely got irritated with his children, but guns were
cracking on the mountain and men groaning along the schoolroom walls and
bodies lay cold beneath the shade tree—things no boy should see. No child of
his. He should not have let it happen. He should've known.

"This is not a game, Musa. Do you understand me? Men are being killed
on that mountain. Today, in this very schoolhouse, men have died. And more
will yet. Do you understand?"

A wetness came into the boy's eyes. "I'm sorry, Papa."

Doc Moo poured the water into a tin pail waiting beside the door. He would
soften, but not yet. The boy had to know he was serious. He handed back the
bucket. "Fetch another. And this time, ask if they don't have a yoke so you
can carry two pails at once."

Musa straightened. "Yes, sir."

Then he was gone, his bare feet flashing as he scampered away, the empty
bucket swinging from his shoulder. Doc Moo looked at his cigarette. Nearly

gone, burned down to a cinder. He squeezed it in his fist and looked at the sky, angry with himself. His temper.

Another biplane was nearly upon the camp, its shadow stretching across the clearing. They'd been flying nonstop, running reconnaissance for the defense forces. He turned and stepped back into the schoolhouse, looking at the ragged forms along the walls, men maimed and lumped and stitched like the survivors of some terrible train wreck.

As his foot touched the floor, the boards bucked beneath him and the windows blew out, a crazy gust of glass. Moo found himself flat on his belly, ears whining and vision blurred. His hands went scrabbling for his eyeglasses. *There.* Then he was up and running, jumping off the stoop, into the smoke.

"Musa!"

CHAPTER FIFTY-SEVEN

FRANK AND CROCKETT UNCOVERED their heads and looked at each other. The explosion had jolted the mountain itself, sending a hard quiver through the ground. The sound was still echoing across the ridges, inside their own skulls. For the first time in hours, no shots could be heard. As if a truce had been called. Even the insects were quiet. Silence, like awe, filled the valleys.

"That wasn't no diney-mite," said Crock. They both knew the heavy *whump* of an underground blast—the kind so common in the mines. But this was something else. Sharper, unmuffled, and above ground. "Sounded like France, what it sounded like."

Frank looked up through the broken canopy. They were high on the spur of a ridge and the sun was starting to get low, the shadows growing long. He looked back at Crockett. "Artillery shell?"

"Didn't sound like no howitzer to me."

"Air bomb?"

The big Marine shook his head. He'd jested the leaflets could be just the start of what might befall them—but the reality was harder to fathom. "Cain't be. Bombs, on American soil?" He touched the TEUFELSHUND tattoo on his chest and jutted his chin toward the far side of the mountain. "They wouldn't dare, not even them sons of bitches. Hell, this is *America*."

He said the word with tenderness, like the name of a daughter or lover or wife. Someone he loved unconditionally. A land for which he'd killed and nearly died in the war—who knew how many times.

Frank looked down at the scars along his own arms, the marks of heels and wrenches and tire irons. Even easier to pull a trigger or release a bomb from hundreds of feet away, thousands.

He shook his head. "You ask me, Crock, there's different Americas. America if you got means or don't, if you work in a tie or neckerchief, up in the office or down on the killing floor. White or colored, man or woman. Native or not. I reckon there's Americas they'd drop a bomb on, and ones they wouldn't even think it."

"No," said Crock. He couldn't seem to swallow it. His face was twisted up.

Frank pointed over the man's shoulder. "Look."

A black plume was rising from the base of the mountain, rolling upward. Out of the smoke a biplane emerged, small as a flea, droning toward them.

The calm broke. Gunfire erupted from the mountainside, hundreds of miners trying to hit the machine. The pilot rolled and dived, cutting low across a ridge as high-powers cracked like whips from every side. Then the plane was banking, carving toward them at treetop level, coming straight up Crooked Creek with a second bomb.

Crockett's eyes widened and he turned toward the men on the steep slope behind them. "Git cover!"

Frank slid down into the crater of an overturned chestnut tree, deep as a foxhole, turning back to realize Crockett hadn't followed him. The big man was still up there on top of the ridge. He'd gone red with fury, almost purple, gathering up the Gatling gun in both arms and staggering to an exposed point on the spur. Now he was swinging the weapon around on its tripod, cranking the elevation screw, lifting the six barrels toward the airplane flying straight toward him.

Frank yelled at him but nothing came out of his mouth—as if he'd gone hoarse, lost his voice, the very air sucked out of his lungs. But it wasn't that. The machine was just too loud as it bore down on them.

CHAPTER FIFTY-EIGHT

DOC MOO RAN THROUGH the camp, tearing through a miasma of smoke and dust out of which men reared with bloody ears and clenched teeth, holding bloodied parts of themselves.

"Musa!" he yelled, barely able to hear his own voice. A high whistle filled his skull, whining between his ears. "Musa!"

A riderless horse galloped out of the fog, walleyed with panic, the empty stirrups swinging wide. Moo was nearly to the edge of the camp when he tripped on a rock and went tumbling, tasting dirt in his mouth. He was scrambling to his feet when someone grabbed his arm.

"Musa!" He squeezed the boy to his chest, then thrust him out to arm's length, making sure he was intact, unwounded. Then he squeezed him again, hard enough this time he could feel the young bones flexing beneath his arms.

Musa was pointing out something to his father. Doc Moo turned to look. The bomb had come down just at the edge of the clearing, in the trees. Their trunks were splayed outward from the crater, charred and smoking, the smoke seeming to boil up out of the earth. If the bomb had landed even two hundred yards deeper into the camp, they'd be surrounded by blasted bodies, shorn limbs strewn bloody through the grass.

Doc Moo took Musa's hand and led him toward the nearest cover, the shade tree with the bodies laid out beneath it. The blast had blown back some of the blankets, revealing the waxen faces of the dead, but he couldn't worry about that now. He knelt with Musa at the base of the tree, holding the boy's upper arms. "Can you hear me?"

Musa nodded. "I covered my ears and opened my mouth," he said, miming the actions.

Doc Moo wasn't surprised. The boy must have read the procedure in one of his books or magazines—how to survive shellings and bombardments.

"Good," he said, beginning to hear his own voice. "Good. Now I've got a mission for you, Musa. It's very important. If the miners are successful, this fighting could reach all the way to Mingo County, all the way home. I need you to get your mother, your sisters, and Miss Beulah over to the Kentucky side of the Tug, out of harm's way. These bombs could be the first of more to come. A real war. You'll need to travel down the western side of Guyandotte River, away from the fighting, until you're well south of Logan, then you can read the land from there. That's the better part of thirty miles. Do you think you can handle that?"

"I don't want to leave you, Papa."

Doc Moo nodded. "And I'd rather have you here with me, Musa. A father should never have to send his son on such a mission, but these are extraordinary circumstances. You are a *man* of the Muhanna household now. Sometimes we have to do things for our families we'd rather not. My father, he used to say character requires us to place what is right over what is easy. That's what we're doing now."

Musa looked at the smoking trees, the schoolhouse, the shattered sky— empty for now. Then back to his father. "What if they drop more bombs here, Papa?"

Doc Moo squeezed his son's arms. "Then our family will be all the more fortunate you're somewhere else."

The boy nodded. Tears in his eyes, but he wasn't crying. He had his possibles bag looped over one shoulder and his heavy leather belt held the sheath of his bowie knife, into whose hardwood handle he'd etched its nickname, TOOTHPICK. His belt buckle was cinched on the outside of an overlarge chambray shirt and he hadn't even brought a pair of shoes. A family joke that his hard brown feet could tolerate broken glass and hot coals but not a soft pair of loafers.

He stared down at those feet, then looked up again. "What about the O'Donovans, our neighbors the far side of Panther Creek? Their daddy died with the influenza last year."

"What about them?"

"Can I bring them with us?"

Doc Moo cocked his head. "Don't they have a daughter about your age?"

The boy straightened. "What's that got to do with it?"

So there *was* something else drawing the boy into the woods. "Nothing," said Moo. "Yes, you can bring them, too." He moved his hands from the boy's arms to the back of his neck.

"Listen, Musa. I know I'm hard at times, cross. But know this, I cannot imagine any other son I would entrust with such a task. If something were to happen to me, I could not be more proud of you to carry the Muhanna name. I thank God for you every day." Moo brought their foreheads together. "I love you, *Ibni*."

My son.

"I love you, Papa."

CHAPTER FIFTY-NINE

BY THE TIME THE biplane touched down at the Logan ballfield, it looked like a flying briar thicket. A mad tangle of leaves and branches and bird nests were snared all through the undercarriage and landing skids from the pilot's treetop escape. A long string of bullet holes had been stitched across the fuselage.

Sheriff Chafin waited, leaning on the long black hood of his Stutz. The pilot climbed down from the cockpit and removed his gloves. His hands were shaking.

"How many pounds of explosives did that chemist of yours pack into those damn things? First one near about blew me from the air."

Chafin chuckled, thumbing his chest. "I think the Devil's got dust shaking from his rafters." He lifted his eyebrows. "You think them Rednecks heard it?"

"Heard it? There's people in Peking with their eardrums bleeding. Ain't you afraid what the baby-kissers in D.C. are gonna think of you dropping bombs on Americans?"

Chafin waved his hand. "Americans, hell. Half of them was born to foreigners or slaves, the rest to granny women in shacks or dirt-floor cabins."

"Well, if they were born in this country—"

Chafin clamped a hand on the man's shoulder. "Nobody's going to make a fuss, Cap. I can assure you that. Now, you want to see people in an outrage, you let this bunch of Rednecks come marching into a civilized town like Logan. The papers won't get enough of it."

"I near about got killed. Some crazy son-bitch was on the spur above Crooked Creek with a Gatling gun, already cranking the firing wheel as I flew up the Gap. I dropped the second bomb there as ordered, but it was a dud, thank God. Don't know if I'd of survived the blast."

Chafin squeezed the man's shoulder. His fingernails were clean and neatly filed; fat rings shone about his knuckles. "You done the right thing, Cap. What you had to for law and order." He leaned closer. "For America."

The pilot opened his hands, closed them. "It don't feel like it."

"Hell, that wasn't nothing. Warning shots. Wait till the government planes get here."

"Government planes?"

"Sure, you ain't heard? General Billy Mitchell, chief of the Air Service, he's champing at the bit to show what his planes can do. He was just up in the state capital, done up in his ribbons and spurs, telling the papers how his air forces could snuff out this uprising in no time flat. These marchers don't stand down by noon tomorrow, we ain't gonna be the only ones dropping bombs. Far from. They got squadrons ready to scramble, loaded with gas and incendiaries."

Chafin looked out toward Blair Mountain. "Hell, these sons of bitches ought to thank us for giving them a taste of what's coming down the pike if they don't turn tail and run. Soon it's gonna be the whole world coming down on their heads." He shrugged. "We'll say we tried to warn them."

CHAPTER SIXTY

MOTHER JONES MARCHED THROUGH the staggering D.C. heat, heading toward the State, War, and Navy Building on Pennsylvania Avenue. She was wearing one of her black dresses, frilly and hand-sewn, her hair knotted snow-white beneath her black bonnet. Her handbag was pinned hard beneath her elbow, her heavy ankles grinding beneath the wide girdle of her hips.

She'd spent two days bedridden, sick as she'd ever been. The rheumatism. A severe attack. Pain pulsing through every inch of her, sheets soaked, cheeks scarlet, forehead shining with sweat. Never had she felt so old, so helpless. The fever stoked memories from dark corners of her past, raising them up like ghosts. The forgotten faces of gun thugs and corrupt lawmen who snatched at her sleeves and skirts and hair, cursing her with bared teeth. Children who held up their mutilations before her, gear-smashed fingers and wheel-cut limbs and hoof-kicked faces, wishing she'd done more for them, and the woman from Cabin Creek holding the bloodied wreck of her husband's head in her lap, shrieking like something not quite human.

She tried to hide beneath the covers, but the visions were still there.

She saw her boys in the deep folds of the hills, marching along the creeks and ridges, breaking like a red tide at the foot of the mountain. Mother swelled her lungs and yelled to them, but her voice carried no sound. It was just smoke. She screamed and screamed and it was all just smoke.

The morning the fever broke, she ignored the warm compresses and pineapple juice on her breakfast tray and began dictating telegrams, rifling off messages to governors and tycoons, bureaucrats and senators, shooting long-range missives onto the desks of friends and enemies. Offers of help, pleas for assistance, requests for meetings. She'd bring her spirit to bear on those who'd watch the battle from afar, men in clean suits and high offices who'd influence the outcome as sure as pieces on a chessboard.

Now the heat rose fuming from the blacktopped streets, as if they'd been sloshed with buckets of kerosene. As if she could light a match and turn this whole white city into a mile-high cathedral of fire, the smoke curling thousands of feet heavenward, seen for hundreds of miles in the surrounding country. Seen from the top of Blair Mountain, perhaps, bearing away the ashes of every double-talking, two-faced politician in the whole damned city.

Sometimes she wished she could.

Now she stood before the ornate facade of the State, War, and Navy Building, a 566-room behemoth Mark Twain had famously called "the ugliest building in America." She chuckled at that. Every square inch of the place was crowded with ornamental cornices, porticoes, colonnades, pediments, and other architectural extravagances. It looked more like the palace of some inbred French emperor with powdered cheeks and a three-pound miniature poodle than the rightful home of the war offices of the United States of America.

She cocked her head beneath her bonnet, eyeing the sun. High and hot, rising toward its noon zenith. The President's deadline was noon tomorrow—a line drawn in the sand and thrown out of hired aeroplanes, peppering the hills. An ultimatum.

The sun hung boiling over the building, making ants of sweat crawl down her skin, and Mother couldn't help but think of Smilin' Sid standing before the stone facade of that West Virginia courthouse one month ago. She wondered if he'd sensed his death was near, the men waiting in the shadows of the courthouse, crouched like gargoyles in the alcoves. He could stand toe-to-toe with any thug, but what was flesh against stone? Against these buildings of white granite, like chiseled mountaintops or carved icebergs, big enough to tear ragged the steel ribs of the *Titanic* or call down whole heavens of fire, reducing nations to heaps of rubble.

In the Old Country, people had whispered of the wee folk of the woods— *aes sídhe*—fairies who lived in stone rings and underground forts, little hills and hollow hawthorn trees, their power ranging just beyond the sight of humankind, carried through winds and music, wreaking havoc if they were not appeased.

These stone buildings did something similar, she thought—connected as they were through a vast network of letters and telegrams and telephone wires, all part of a common bedrock. As if they were but the visible outcroppings, finely tooled and faceted, of an invisible power that ranged beneath the land.

State and law, money and influence. Empires of men who took their certainties from boardrooms and telephone lines, campaign donors and typewritten reports. Men who rarely saw the inside of a factory or mill or mine. Who'd never worked their hands bloody or lungs black, yet could wield incredible power over those who did.

Someone had to bring that world to them, make them know it existed.

Someone had to raise Hell on them.

Mother hitched her handbag higher against her side. Her breath was short, her joints still pained, but it was her heart that hurt her most. Broken. That was the thing, the crux of her condition. It felt like someone had stuck her hand flat on a table, palm down, and hit it with a hammer as hard as they could, three or four times, wrecking the insides for good, smashing the bones and knuckles so they'd never heal right, then stuck that broken thing in her chest and called it her heart.

Strange thing about broken hearts, though—they kept working. She'd keep fighting for her boys, no matter how many disowned her. Her love, like any good mother's, was not conditional.

Mother, wearing her old black battle-bonnet and frilled dress, squinted a last time at the noon sun, then hiked her skirts and stepped beneath the vast shadow of the granite edifice, climbing the stone steps to face the Secretary of War.

CHAPTER SIXTY-ONE

FRANK, CROCKETT, AND A small crowd of miners stood around the object sticking up out of the creek shallows. A length of iron gas pipe two feet long and six inches wide, with hexagonal caps screwed onto either end and a plunger sticking out the top. It had landed upside down in the soft bed of Crooked Creek, right between a pair of women washing out bloody dressings to reuse on men wounded at the front. Just stuck there in the mud, undetonated.

A bomb.

Dusk was coming down, the shadows seeping longer from the trees. The creek water eddied and spun around the strange object. The eyes of the men were wide, as if they looked upon some crude sword set in stone.

Who would dare to pull it?

Frank looked at Crockett. The big Devil Dog was still worked up after his duel with the biplane. Apple-cheeked, panting through open jaws. He'd only gotten off a quick burst as the flying machine roared over the spur, but he seemed changed. The bombing had done something to him. A madness was in him now. A fury. Not the deep and hidden coals, smoldering, which Frank had known for so long. No, Crock's fury was bright and wild; he was on fire, ready to burn down the world.

"Y'all git back," he said, stepping down into the creek.

Frank snatched his arm. "Step off it, Crock. No reason to go down there."

Crockett's nostrils flared. His gaze moved slowly to Frank's hand on his arm. Wormy blue veins were crawling out of the man's temples; red-burst capillaries blazed beneath his eyes. His language seemed stranger and older, said singsong: "I'd ask ye kindly to unhand me."

They had to be the two strongest men on the mountain.

"Or what, Crock?"

"I won't ask ye again."

A cruel little blade appeared in the man's hand, hooked like an eagle's beak. Drawn from some secret pocket on his person, kept near to hand for such occasions. Frank felt the sudden softness of his belly, his jellied insides and dark skin—said to be equal under God and law but too often trespassed with the blades and bullets of paler men.

Still, his grip remained. "Drop my guts if you want, Crock. But it won't put them bombs back in the air, nor leave enough of me to help you shoot your way to the other side of the mountain, now will it?" He nodded toward Blair.

Crockett's eyes went to the bomb sticking up out of the creek. His voice dropped. "The boys is liable to call it quits after this. To run on home."

Frank shook his head. "I got no home, Crock. My wife's dead, the company took my house. My granny knows I ain't coming back. I do, I got nothing but a noose waiting on me, prison cell if I'm lucky. How 'bout you?"

Crockett twitched his nose. "Naught for me, neither."

"Then you and me, Crock, we ain't going home, no matter what the rest of these boys do." He held out his hand. "Are we?"

The bearded man breathed. The olden script on his chest relaxed slightly. He took Frank's hand. "Never go home."

"Never go home," said Frank.

Crockett looked back to the bomb. "What about that? Cain't just leave it there for some poor son-bitch to stub his toe on it."

He'd hardly said it when a small, square-jawed man came leaping down the far embankment in a rumpled coat and tie. Bill Blizzard. Without a word to any of them, he took off his boots, peeled off his socks, rolled up his trouser legs, and hiked out into the creek. All around, the miners who'd crept close to witness the confrontation between the pair of big miners were scurrying back, climbing up out of the creek and crouching behind trees and boulders, near as they dared, ready to duck and cover.

Frank and Crock hustled behind a boulder and peeked around the side. Blizzard didn't seem to notice. He looked at the iron pipe bomb from one angle, then another, rolling up the sleeves of his coat, muttering to himself. "Wee buns. Nothing to it. Go on, then."

As they watched, the small man grabbed the iron plunger with both hands and heaved the bomb right out of the muck, staggering backward slightly with the effort. He held it there mud-chunked and dripping like a fish he'd caught,

a prize catfish noodled out of some deep hole in the bank. "Would ye look at that, boys."

Crockett cupped his hands to his mouth, hollering for all to hear. "Let's give it back to Don Chafin arseways!"

The men at Crooked Creek roared.

CHAPTER SIXTY-TWO

THE SECRETARY OF WAR'S reception room was a massive chamber of rich mahogany and ornate chandeliers. Winged griffins shouldered the heavy fireplace mantel and a vibrant fresco adorned the milk-colored ceiling: Mars, god of war, seminude beneath his plumed helmet, holding the reins of two rampant warhorses. The flags of various military branches hung diagonal from the walls, tipped with martial spades and spear points. Beneath them, a slick-haired clerk sat behind an oaken Federalist desk the size of a baby buffalo.

Mother had been waiting the better part of an hour for her appointment with the Secretary. She looked at her reflection in the mirror over the grand fireplace, then at the portrait of George Washington hanging on the textured wall behind the clerk's desk. The revolutionist general was adorned in full military regalia, a small mountain of navy wool and buff lapels and gilt buttons. Fringed gold epaulettes adorned his shoulders; the white waterfall of a ruffled shirt crashed down his chest. The old cherry-tree killer, who could not tell a lie.

Mother clucked. "Somebody must've chopped down a whole forest to decorate this room."

The clerk folded his hands across his desk, interlacing his fingers. "The rooms of the Secretary of War have more wood than any other office suite in the building. Mahogany, maple, black walnut. The wainscoting is cherry."

"How appropriate," said Mother. "Tell me, sir, what do you think of the trouble in West Virginia?"

The clerk had a small, sharp nose; it twitched slightly at the question. He took his fountain pen from the brass holder on his desk. "I *think* that is beyond my purview, Mrs. Jones. I am not hired for my opinions."

Mother Jones approached his desk, wading wide-legged over the parquet floor, her swollen feet straining her pumps. The hard rasp of her stiff-starched

dress audible in the grand room. She paused at the very edge of the giant desk—a cannonball of a woman, her shadow splashing across the man's desk blotter.

"But surely you do have them, son. Opinions?"

The clerk paused in the scratching of his pen and cocked his head, as if he'd heard something in the silence of the chamber she had not. Perhaps one of the fae folk had whispered in his ear.

"The Secretary will see you now."

"YOU MIGHT AS WELL try to sweep up the Atlantic Ocean with a broom," quoted the Secretary of War, reading from the intelligence report on his desk. His office was even more opulent than the reception room, a vast chamber of polished battle regalia, walls of gleaming swords and oiled rifles. He frowned, lacing his fingers. "This is from one of our sources on the ground, Mrs. Jones, asked whether he thought the Union leadership could dissuade these miners from further violence."

Ocean with a broom. Mother felt a hot sting in her breast, remembering how her boys had marched past her, sure as a king tide. Still, she had more than a pinch of pride in them—they'd called her bluff, they had. Her phony telegram. And they were rising up now, as she'd always preached they would. The only problem with rising up was getting cut back to ground—especially when the man with the reaping blade thought you weren't but a bunch of weeds.

Mother leaned forward in the overstuffed leather chair. "And what source on the ground would that be, Mr. Secretary, pray tell?"

"I'm not at liberty to say."

"A source on the side of the miners, or the coal companies?"

"On the side of the United States of America, Mrs. Jones."

"Ah," said Mother, patting the chair arms, slick with polish. "And have you been down to West Virginia lately, Mr. Secretary? To coal country?"

"I have not."

"If you had, Mr. Secretary, you'd know the United States of America isn't the same to everybody. No, sir. Folks down there, on both sides, they're fighting for their country. *Their* America. Their vision of who she is and what she'll be. Same's this country did sixty years ago when it rent itself in two. Same's it did not a hundred years before that, when it broke the thumb of the

Crown and folks from all over the world wanted to come here, to this place where such a thing was possible."

The Secretary nodded. "That's exactly why we have to stamp out this revolt as quickly as we can. We have several million unemployed in this nation, Mrs. Jones. If this Appalachian uprising were to catch fire and spread beyond the state's borders, we could find ourselves with an insurrection beyond our means to contain."

Mother leaned forward, gripping the brass knobs of the chair arms. She'd found herself in such armchairs many a time, in the high offices of judges and governors and magnates. Old white men, all of them. But if there were one good thing about being nearly a century old, it was that all these old men hiding behind their desks weren't but schoolboys compared with her.

"I assure you, Mr. Secretary, that everything in West Virginia will turn out all right without the nation's armed forces being sent."

The man folded his arms across his desk. His thin white jowls were cleanly shaved, his gray mustache small and trim. His navy tie was knotted hard against his plump throat. "You're fond of calling these men *your boys,* are you not?"

"I am, sir."

"And did you not try to persuade *your boys* to lay down their rifles some few days ago, before this violence began?"

"Aye, I did."

"Tell me, Mrs. Jones, what was the end result?"

Mother felt that sting again—a hard little jag in the heaving of her heart, as if the man had delivered his question at the end of a barb. She gritted her teeth. "I was unsuccessful then, I was. I don't approve of their course of action. But they had to make themselves heard, Mr. Secretary. And they have done."

The man's face darkened. "This is a civilized republic, Mrs. Jones. Armed rebellion is not how our citizens are heard."

Mother glanced at the portraits on the office walls, heroes of the American Revolution scowling in their powdered wigs and high coat collars—men who'd thrown off the yoke of the most powerful king in the world. "Our forefathers hanging here on your walls, Mr. Secretary, they might beg to differ."

"Those men were fighting against tyranny."

Mother leaned forward again in her chair, making it groan. The old ire was rising in her chest now, the thunder. "Tyranny, Mr. Secretary? I wonder what you might call a system in which a skilled labor force the size of a small nation are made to work in conditions more dangerous than armed service in the Great War, are paid not in legal tender but company scrip, housed not in personal homes but company camps, where they and their families are given zero compensation for job-related injury or death, and any drive for better wages or safer conditions is back-broken by a private army of company spies and hired gun thugs who regularly throw families out into the cold and beat fathers with brass knuckles, who have fired machine guns into tent colonies and done cold-blooded murder in broad daylight on the front steps of an American courthouse—*just last month*. If not tyranny, what would you call such a system, Mr. Secretary? Certainly you wouldn't call it *American*."

"Miners are not slaves. They are not forced to work in the coalfields. It is a choice."

"A choice, aye. To work or starve. You've said it yourself, Mr. Secretary, there are several million fewer jobs in this country than working men. Join or die."

The Secretary's cheeks reddened. He folded his hands across his desk. His fingernails were trim and square, gouged clean. "Regardless, Mrs. Jones, my job is to preserve peace. If this Redneck army does not stand down by the President's deadline tomorrow, we will have no choice but to send in the United States Army to put them down."

Mother sniffed. "I have it on good authority that bombs have already fallen on West Virginia. American civilians, bombed by American warplanes, on American soil. Surely a first for the republic. What do you make of that?"

"Those were not our warplanes, Mrs. Jones. Not yet. But they may be soon. You say your boys wanted to be heard. I say it's time they start to *listen*. If not to you, Mother, then to Uncle Sam."

CHAPTER SIXTY-THREE

MUSA MOVED WEST THROUGH the dusking forest, following a rocky creek. The sun lay low on the ridges, lancing red through the treetops. The shadows were long around him, jagged as claws, and darkness was welling up out of the ground, setting nighthawks and long-eared bats to flight. In old times, the hour when the panthers and wolves would be coming awake, stretching, making ready to hunt. The hour when he felt most at ease, hidden in the falling cloak of night.

He had no map and didn't know the name of this creek, but he knew by the slope of the terrain that it must feed down into the Guyandotte River. He never gave much credence to map names, knowing most every wet lick and bust of rock big enough for a name had carried one older than what was on the map. Names from the people before his, the people before even them. If you were close enough to a thing, it didn't even need a name. A scent could be a name. The particular crook of a river. The name and the thing could be one and the same.

Musa stopped. Voices were carrying along the creek, skipping down the rocks. He bent slightly, slowing, slinking from shadow to shadow.

He kept thinking of his father back at the camp. His sweet *baba* covered in blood, his eyeglasses smeared dirty. His fingernails grimy. His black mustache flecked with ash and dust. He felt protective of the man at times. He knew his father was a very good doctor, but he sometimes lost himself in what he was doing, in his work, forgetting the world around him. Musa did not.

He wanted to stay at the camp, but his father needed him now. His family. He would get them out of harm's way, and Aidee's family, too.

Aidee. Adelaide O'Donovan. Already she was a world to him, the scent of blackberries and stinging sweat. The arch of a scar-nicked eyebrow, one bright green eye boring into his. She was the creek behind her family's back pasture, where they dipped and splashed. The goose pimples that reared up on his skin when her breath touched him.

Musa paused beneath an old bone-white sycamore, listening. The east side of the tree felt cool against his cheek. He could hear the bull-throated frogs bellowing along the creek and the surging thrum of the katydids and cicada, like one giant rattlesnake. Voices, too, tumbling out of the dusk. He crept closer, crouching in a pawpaw patch, listening. He raised his head. Through the gray twilight, a small group of men clustered around an iron pipe set carefully on a rock. They scratched their chins and regarded the curious object.

"Wish we had an airy-plane of our own," said one. "See how they like one of these coming down in they laps."

Another man, small and square-jawed in a ragged coat and tie, shook his head. "Aye, but the newspapers would have a fit. If we dropped a bomb, they'd have the Army here in half a minute."

"What then, Blizz? Haul it back to the camp?"

The small man shook his head. "We'd not want it around that many folk."

Musa, listening, slowly twisted a pawpaw from a branch above his head. The green fruit was just right, tender between his fingers, the skin black-speckled. He drew his bowie knife, Toothpick, inch by inch.

"Well, we can't leave it here for a body just to trip over and get blowed up to Kingdom Come."

Musa halved the pawpaw on the blade of his knife and squeezed the flesh into his mouth, pale and slightly sweet, tucking the toxic seeds into the corner of his mouth for safekeeping. Beneath him, the small man thumbed his chin. "Reckon we ought to get it out the battle zone, across the Guy-n-dotty somewhere. Stash it somewhere safe. Maybe a farmer's barn or old mine. Somewhere secret, nobody can tamper with it. Might come a time we need it."

The men around him nodded. It seemed like the best idea.

The small man rubbed his hands together. "Well, who's volunteering?"

No one spoke. They scratched their chins and tugged their earlobes and took note of their boots.

Musa stepped out of the patch above them with a pawpaw in one hand, Toothpick in the other. His possibles bag was slung over his shoulder.

He spat out the seeds. "I'm heading thataway."

CHAPTER SIXTY-FOUR

MISS BEULAH SAT IN the holler dark, rocking in her chair. The pale canvas tents of the colony glowed faintly beneath her, lantern-lit from within—so much prettier than they looked in the daytime. And quiet. A barking dog, a banged cookpot, a woman hissing at her children. No menfolk, not hardly. Most of them were either locked up in jail or gone off to the march, and the troopers and Baldwins and vigilantes with them—everyone gone to fight.

A lonesomeness had come to sit with her. Her feet had swelled and nobody to drain them, no Doctor Moo, and she knew her grandboy might not come back. Not ever. Not after what he'd done. Throwing down on those troopers the day of the raid. She didn't fault him for it—not after how those police had done him in McDowell. He'd be crazy to let them take him again. But the law wasn't like to forget what he'd done. No, sir. He was a marked man now, an outlaw. He'd have to live on the run, ever listening for the cry of bloodhounds on his trail, like those last old bears and wolves and panthers they chased out of these hills, running them to ground. A fugitive. A man with no earthly home.

The thought tore at her chest. He might come back to visit her now and again under cover of darkness, coming like a shadow out of the woods and vanishing before daybreak. A ghost, same as rest of her family.

She touched the heels of her hands to her eyes, breathed.

Yes, the lonesomeness had found her tonight, curled up like a cannonball on her bony chest. She'd learned long ago that turmoils of the heart did pass, and no matter whether it took hours or days or weeks or years or decades, there was comfort in knowing they would. There was another side of the mountain, a sunnier side, and the long dark tunnel of pain and unknowing would lead to light. But she was so old now she might not have time enough for the pain to pass, not here in this world, and there was only the hope of the Kingdom to come, the eternal reward. Sweet Jesus who could tend any wound, kissing it full of sweet and healing blood, and the dancing ancestors, welcoming her home.

She closed her eyes and thought of her spirit slipping the ancient birdcage of her breast, wriggling between her ribs and spreading wings of pale fire, rising like a sweet bird out of this coal-dark holler and wheeling high above the land, turning circles with delight, and sweeping still higher, past the clouds and climbing up there with the stars, any one of which might be the bright Kingdom itself, sparkling up there among the lesser heavens. There she would go.

Home.

She heard a skitter of stones and opened her eyes, her heart skipping at the thought of Frank returning home, slipping out of the darkness. Instead, a pair of eyes stared at her over the rocky edge of the creek, round and wide and full of molasses. A pair of tufty black ears.

A dog.

Most of the camp strays had no manners, none. They came nosing into any business they could, acting sweet one second and snatching scraps the next. She'd hollered them off enough they no longer messed around her porch. Knew better. But this one seemed different. A gentler spirit about him.

"Hidy, stranger," she said, holding out a hand. "Ain't seen you round these parts before."

The black dog looked one way, another. Unsure. He had a wild, slightly bewildered look, wispy hair curling from his eyebrows and chin.

Miss Beulah leaned forward in her rocker. "You fretting them other camp hounds? Fuck 'em, baby. Don't none of them mess with Miss B."

The dog rose up slowly out of the creek. His body was arched like a racing hound's but with dark, sheeplike hair. Most dogs would come and sniff her fingers, try to lick off whatever they could of her last meal. This one didn't. This dog lowered his head, moved past her outstretched hand, and pressed his head to her chest, as if to comfort or be comforted. His hair seemed too fine for these hills, more smoke than fur. Miss Beulah gently scratched him behind the ears.

"Hello, sweet boy," she said.

CHAPTER SIXTY-FIVE

DOC MOO SAT BLOODIED on the schoolhouse stoop in the hour before dawn, his hands shaking as he tried to tie a length of twine around the temples of his eyeglasses. They kept slipping down from his brow, sliding on the greasy sheen of sweat and grime that covered his skin. He hadn't washed, hadn't hardly slept or eaten. He no longer knew what day it was.

He'd been working nonstop. Gunshots, shrapnel, broken limbs. They'd set up a triage station beneath a canvas fly in front of the schoolhouse, routing lesser cases to one of the nurses or veteran corpsmen. The gravely wounded came to Muhanna's desk. His fingernails were grouted with dark-dried blood, and though he'd stitched up fifty men or more with his forceps and needle holder, he couldn't seem to get these knots for his glasses right. He was getting irritated and stopped a moment to gather himself.

He breathed. In, deep, out, deep.

He looked up at Blair. At least the predawn hour had brought a rare quietude. The sky was lightening, no sun yet. The mountain a deep, dark blue.

He couldn't get Musa out of his mind. The boy had to be safer out on the trails and roads than here, where bombs were falling and bullets flying—didn't he? And the boy's mission was no contrivance. If the violence spread, Moo wanted his family out of its path. All of Matewan. He'd grown up hearing of the atrocities of civil war, not just here in America but in his own homeland.

When the Maronite peasantry overthrew the Druze feudal lords, there was massacre, outrage, and pillage on both sides. As always. His father had rarely given details in the stories he told of his time in the war, in the fighting around Mount Lebanon and the Beqaa Valley, where ancient Roman columns stood like dead trees, fire-scorched and bullet-pocked. But Moo came to learn what was unsaid could be as powerful, more powerful, than what was stated outright. The power of negative space. The way it forced one to imagine the unspeakable. His father telling of a Maronite militia returning to their home village to discover a Druze cavalry unit had visited while they were away—and several of the women and children had gone mute, never to speak again.

Homes could be rebuilt, possessions replaced, but certain traumas never healed. He worried the violence could spread from this pocket of coal country to the towns, the cities. Shops burning and glass in the streets. Mothers wailing, keening over sons and daughters killed fighting or running or just walking in the wrong neighborhood at the wrong hour. Atrocity and massacre, irregular factions matching blood with blood, as if the Old Testament mathematics of eye for eye might one day work out. As if they ever had.

And Moo had taken a side now. There were those who might want to punish him however they could, to strike deep behind the lines. To hurt his family.

FIRST LIGHT CAME TRICKLING along the ridges, touching the tops of the trees. They forded a shallow part of the Guyandotte River where the stones were smooth beneath Musa's bare feet. He'd led his ward all night, staying well ahead of the miner who carried the bomb high on his shoulder like a giant hammer—a device that might blow him into the treetops if he tripped and dropped it.

They'd kept their distance, communicating via bird calls and flashes from Musa's flint striker—when to stop, move, or hide. Several times in the night, Musa signaled for them to halt along game trails or creekbanks while armed men passed through the darkness. Once a buck with velvety antlers stepped out of the woods and bent his head to drink from the creek, his hide silver beneath the moon.

The water of the Guyandotte was cool and dark around Musa's waist, untouched by the impending sun. Downriver, he could just make out the N&W trestle bridge, which Blizzard had instructed them to avoid, as it would be guarded. When Musa reached the far bank, he squatted on a flat rock and watched the dark figure come wading across the river, wide-legged, hugging the iron bomb to his chest for extra security. The man rose up out of the shallows with the water streaming off him, spilling out of his overalls.

He stopped twenty paces short of Musa's perch. "You supposed to be keepin' your distance, young mister, case this baby goes boom."

Musa halved a pawpaw on his knife blade and held it up. "Thought you might've worked up an appetite."

"Thank you, but I'd rather keep my belly empty till the job's done."

"Fair enough." Musa hopped down from the rock and looked east, judging the time. "If Mr. Blizzard was right about this old mine, we ought to be there before the sun clears yon ridgeline. Come on."

Soon Musa found the old narrow-gauge rails that Blizzard had described, where mules once pulled squeaking coal carts in the days before tipples and conveyors. The tracks were overgrown; Musa could tell nobody had come this way for weeks.

At the top, he found the mouth of a boarded-up mine amid rusting hulks of ancient machinery. An old steam donkey with a bullet-pocked boiler, mine cars with rust-seized wheels. He found an iron kingbolt in the bed of a double-axle cart and pried open the boards. A breath of cold musty air, like the mountain exhaling.

He stepped back a safe distance as the miner came forward, lighting an old oil-wick cap lamp before ducking into the mine. Despite himself, Musa crept forward to watch him descend into the darkness, the oil flame burning over his head like the little painted tongues of holy fire atop the porcelain saints in the shadowy corners of Father Rossi's church. It lit square after square of frame timbering, licking down the great throat of the mountain. Then gone.

Musa waited at the edge of the drift mouth, peeking now and again into the darkness. Three minutes, five. He'd started worrying when the man finally reappeared, smiling now, teeth flashing, shoulders swaying under his little lamp flame. He slipped out from between the pried boards and began hammering them back into place with the kingbolt.

"There's a burden I'm happy to lay down. They said it wasn't like to blow on its own, but they weren't the ones had to carry it half the damn night." He turned and held out his hand to Musa. Up close, in the growing light, he looked familiar. "Thank you for your help tonight, little man. Very brave of you. I'm Frank, by the way."

Musa's mouth fell open as he took the man's hand. "Wait, are you *Big* Frank, Miss Beulah's grandson?"

"That's right." The big man squinted one eye. "Now I see it. You Doctor Moo's boy, ain't you? Musa. The one was running supplies around the schoolhouse. Your daddy know you out here?"

Musa nodded. "Yes, sir. After they dropped the bomb, Papa sent me on a mission to get our people out harm's way case the fighting reaches that far. Told me to get Miss Beulah, too, and anybody else I could from Lick Creek. That's where I'm headed." He paused. "You want to come?"

The big man gritted his teeth and looked back toward Blair. The morning sun was breaking across the land, striking the misty slopes. Already they could hear the shooting starting up again. "I'd like to, Mr. Musa, but I gave my word I wasn't going home, not till the job was done. We got to break through the Gap today, make it to the other side of that mountain."

Musa nodded and unslung his possibles bag. "Miss Beulah made me this."

"She's a wonder with needle and thread, ain't she?"

"You ought to take it with you."

Frank took a knee beside Musa, crossing his arms on one thigh. They were about the same height now. Musa could see the scarred terrain of the man's shoulders and forearms, like a war had been fought on his skin. Tiny toy soldiers with artillery and flamethrowers.

"You keep that bag, Mr. Musa. Every good scout needs his possibles close by. I'm glad to know Mama-B will be in good hands. After last night, I couldn't wish no better scout for her. If I see your daddy again, I'll tell him to be proud."

Musa nodded. "I'll tell Miss Beulah the same thing, Mr. Frank."

Big Frank squeezed Musa's shoulder. Tears in his eyes now, as if he were seeing the boy from a distance, from the far side of some ravine he'd crossed and couldn't go back. "Tell her I love her, too. Can you do that?"

Musa straightened. "Yes, sir."

The big man squeezed his shoulder again, then unknotted the bandanna around his neck. "I want you to have this here neckerchief of mine. You earned it. You can tell folks back home you were a real Redneck."

Musa stood very straight as the man looped the bandanna around his neck, knotting it fast. He looked back toward Blair Mountain; Musa could see his chest rising and falling. "I never been one for church, but I remember this one verse about the mustard seed."

Musa nodded. He'd to memorize it for Sunday school. "If you had faith the size of this mustard seed, you could say to this mountain, 'Move from here to there.' And it would move."

"That's the one," said Frank. "The very one. Mama-B, she used to say it was the size of a man's faith that mattered most, not his arms nor back. No arms in the world can move mountains, no matter how much coal they can shovel. Now I know how right she was." He looked back at Musa and held out his hand. "Faith."

Musa shook his hand. "Faith."

Then the big man was up and gone, jogging back down the old tracks, hurrying to cross the river before the rising sun caught him out.

CHAPTER SIXTY-SIX

HIGH ON THE DEFENSE line, the reporter lowered his field glasses. "You think anything can stop them, Major Gaujot?"

Bad Tony said nothing, belting more rounds from his machine gun.

All through the night, Blair Mountain had erupted with jagged planes of light, antic figures scurrying before the stuttering illuminations of gunfire. Behind their bulwarks, the defenders became shadow-haunted, firing at any trace of movement, man or beast or ghost. With dawn, their fears were realized. The misty ridges began cracking with the rifles of shooters who'd crept close in the night.

More bombs fell that morning, rocking the ridges to their bedrock, and still the miners kept coming. It seemed the bombs had only stoked their fury, redoubled their drive. Again and again, the reporter watched them marshal their numbers in the trees or along the ridges, then burst into another charge, the defenders' guns tearing into their ranks each time.

They heard the schoolhouse below the mountain had been turned into an infirmary, the bloody wrecks of men laid out on the plank floors, tended by wives and daughters in makeshift nurse's caps.

"I don't understand it," said the reporter. "They keep coming straight into the guns, like they aren't even afraid."

Bad Tony fired a burst into the trees, then tilted his jaw toward the newsman, keeping one eye aimed through the iron latch of the leaf sight. "They're afraid, all right. Sweating like whores in church, they are. Asses puckered tight as granny's jam jar. It's just they're more afraid of where they come from than where they might be going."

"Don't you think that adds meaning to their cause?"

"Means more of them are going to die for it."

A runner came scampering up to their position. "Message from Sheriff

Chafin," he said. "A constable's sister wired from Virginia, said a whole squadron of Army bombers lifted off from Langley Field this morning, headed west and loaded for bear."

"And?"

"And the Baldwin-Felts got multiple sources confirming the bombers still headed our way, following the James River across Virginia. Could be in case the Rednecks don't stand down come noon."

Bad Tony sniffed, traversing the gun. "Ain't but rumors till they get here. I seen them Army fliers dive for the ground at the first spit of rain."

"What you want me to do, sir?"

Tony scratched his chin. "Go tell it on down the line. True or not, it'll keep the men's spirits up."

"Yes, sir."

The newspaper reporter rose slightly to look down the defense line. Baldwins, constables, troopers, and militiamen were firing down into the narrow gap in the mountains. Every shot from the miners seemed to trigger a hundred in return. Thousands of spent casings lay piled in the trenches. A blizzard of brass. He thumbed the point of his pencil and checked his watch. Ten o'clock. Two hours.

"You think the President's ultimatum will stop them?"

Tony cocked his eye at the sun. "It don't, they'll be needing hip-waders in that schoolhouse."

DOC MOO LOOKED OUT the window to see a line of prisoners coming down off the mountain. Men in khaki shirts and white armbands, hangdog and ragged, shambling down the road with their hands bound and a rope running the length of them. A skinny, red-faced miner in overlarge overalls was driving them along, poking at them with his rifle, shouting and harrying them like a sheepdog.

"Hie, hie, you sons of bitches, keep it moving."

He sat them down against the wall of the schoolhouse, swinging his rifle back and forth across their faces. "Just you sons of bitches try it. Just one of ye try it."

Doc Moo finished dressing the wound of the miner on the table, cleaned his hands, and ventured outside to check on the new prisoners. Their guard had sat them on the unshaded side of the schoolhouse. They had their faces buried in their arms. Their balding pates were sunburned, their khaki shirts and trousers drenched dark with sweat. Moo fetched a bucket of water for them to drink.

"Whoa, whoa, whoa," said the miner, holding his rifle crossways to block his path. "Where you think you're going, Doc?"

"These men are badly dehydrated, in need of water so they don't stroke out. Now if you'll excuse me."

The red-faced man stepped in front of him. "No, Doc, I don't reckon I will. These sons of bitches here are lucky we don't line 'em up and blow their brains to the wall. The sun wants to kill them, it ain't no fault of ours."

"Actually, it would be very much our fault. Now kindly step aside and let me administer aid to these men. I see some of them have wounds that need tending. If they infect, they could lose digits, limbs, or worse."

"Oh, you mean like this." The miner held up his left hand, wiggling the stumps of three fingers. "Blowed off at the Island Creek Number Nine." He pointed his rifle at one of the prisoners. "I offered to do office work, but Mr. Simms here, the mine super, he given me the boot, put me and mine out our house without a red cent. So excuse me if I don't give a good Goddamn if his pecker itself turns black and falls off. Hail, I might take a mind to blow it off my own self."

His breath smelled like kerosene, and he was swaying slightly in his boots.

Moo nodded. "I'm sorry that happened to you, Mister . . . ?"

"Buddy. You can just call me Buddy."

"I'm sorry that happened to you, Buddy, but I'm in charge of this aid station, and I won't have men dying on my watch, prisoners or not." He started again, still holding the bucket, and the guard sidestepped to block him, leveling his rifle at Moo's belly. "Don't make me, Doc. I'll put your fucking guts in the wind."

Moo stared at the muzzle of the rifle. The sun hung high and hot, ticking toward noon. He wanted to be afraid, to feel his veins run cold and his legs carry him safely back inside, but the old blood was rising instead. He'd had his hands in the hot guts of too many screaming, frightened boys over the past two days. This likker-breathed son of a bitch, so quick to send a bullet ripping through the glorious organs and tissues of a fellow human being. Moo wanted to rip the rifle from his hands and beat out his brains with it.

He closed his eyes and tried to count to ten like Buddeea told him, but other words came rolling off his tongue, strange to him, said as if in a dream.

"My name is Doctor Domit Ibrahim Muhanna of Mingo County, West Virginia. I was born in the village of Hadath al-Jebbeh, in the mountains of Lebanon, where the Muhanna ancestry can be traced in an unbroken line to the twelfth century. I speak six languages, am the father of three daughters and one son born in this country, and I was a personal friend of Sid Hatfield. If you kill me, you kill every man, woman, and child I will save between now and the time of my death, including your own comrades in the days to come. Now step aside, or one of my men will be forced to make you."

"One of your men, huh?"

The crack of a hammer. The miner looked up to see a patient hanging from one of the blown-out schoolhouse windows, a big revolver leveled. "Let him pass, *Buddy*."

"You gonna shoot me if I don't?"

"I believe we got six witnesses here would say you done shot your own self." He nodded down at the prisoners lined up against the wall beneath him.

"Seven." Another patient came limping around the back of the schoolhouse, carrying a double-barreled shotgun. "You leave the doctor to do the doctoring, and hie yourself back on up the mountain. Put that rifle-gun to better use."

"Who's gonna guard the prisoners?"

"I am."

"Look at you. What if they run?"

"They ain't outrunning two barrels of buckshot, and neither are you. Now go on. It's the mean sons of bitches like you we need up on Blair, not down here."

The skinny miner seemed to see the truth of that. He huffed and spat at Doc Moo's feet, then turned and started back up the mountain, walking wide-kneed, arms out, like he had something heavy hanging between his legs. Moo watched him go, trying to calm his breathing, waiting for his fury to subside.

Above him, the sun had nearly reached its noon zenith. The President's deadline. Moo wondered whether the Rednecks would come down off the mountain and *retire peaceably to their abodes,* as the leaflets commanded. Or would that be like trying to put blood back into a wound?

CHAPTER SIXTY-SEVEN

FRANK AND CROCK BATTLED their way uphill, slogging up a muddy creek. Their boots scraped on moss-slick stones and their elbows were bloodied, their knees capped with mud. It was too steep for the carrying pole, so they took turns hauling the canvas-wrapped Gatling gun on their shoulders or against their chests, fighting every step of the way, foot after foot, inch after inch. A string of miners followed them with the tripod, magazines, and ammunition boxes.

At times, Frank could see little for the sweat burning his eyes. All he saw was Crock's giant, muddy rump hovering over him, the man's haunches quivering with exertion. Frank's lungs felt like fiery wings inside his chest, and he thought again and again of the Guyandotte he'd crossed that morning—how dark and green and cool. He'd drunk mightily from the river and now it was pouring out of his skin.

He wondered how Crock was still going. The man was ox-strong but fleshy, like he'd never passed up a plate of fatback or funnel cake. Heat rash had broken out beneath his armpits and he was red-cheeked as Santa Claus in those tin Coca-Cola signs.

"Hey, Crock, anybody ever tell you you look like a likker-crazed Saint Nick? You come down from the North Pole to hand out hot lumps of lead to the naughty, that it?"

Crock paused and set his back against a tree, his boots propped on the wet roots squirming down the creekbank. He was cradling the canvas-wrapped parcel in his arms like a hundred-pound baby, the TEUFELSHUND tattoo heaving up and down on his hairy chest. He grinned. "Know what my daddy used to tell me?"

Frank shook his head. "What?"

"Daddy, he used to say, 'Son, in this world, a ugly man's got to be double tough compared to a handsome one. But you, my boy, you best be bullet-proof.'"

They broke out laughing, cackling on and on like madmen, tears streaming down their cheeks. Frank fell forward on his hands, laughing so hard he could barely breathe, his body aching with the effort, while Crock was sneezing and snorting, the big gun bouncing against his belly. Below them, the others looked wide-eyed at one another.

Frank was glad to know if he were going crazy, he wasn't going alone.

When he and Crock had recovered, they continued climbing, reaching a little flat spot on the creek where they found a likker still. The copper pot and spiral worm were well-built, not the cruder work of the blockaders around Lick Creek.

"Likely one of the Czar's," said Crock.

Sheriff Chafin was rumored to run a thriving whiskey trade out of Logan County, a well-financed operation.

"You jealous, Crock?"

The big mountaineer had made it clear that loading coal wasn't his only vocation. He huffed. "Shit, t'ain't but popskull compared to my doublings." He set down the gun and fished his flask out of his bib pocket and sucked off a pull, hissing fumes through his dark teeth. He held out the flask to Frank. "Go on, get ye a slug of that."

Frank looked at the proffered flask, the spigot still wet. He couldn't in his life remember a white man offering him a drink from the same bottle or cup. They might work together in the mines, live on the same streets in the company towns, but certain lines stayed firm. He wasn't much of a drinking man, but it would be a grave insult to refuse.

He took the glass flask and had a pull. A white-hot meteor roared down his throat, a blazing fist. His own breath scorched his nose hairs coming up. "Got damn, Crock. You trying to kill me?"

Crock sniggered. "That there's my Jumpin' Jehoshaphat run. It'll drive ye car, straighten ye pecker, and burn ye neighbor's house down, all in the same night." He grinned like a proud father.

Almost noon when they finished setting up their shooting emplacement, pulling stones from the creek and mortaring them with mud. They mounted the Gatling gun on its tripod, loaded it with a fresh magazine, and swiveled it toward the enemy trenches two hundred feet below.

Their work had paid off—they'd flanked the defenders' front line of trenches. They could now shoot nearly sideways along the enemy lines. It didn't look like there was any spot along this spur flat enough to erect such a position, but Crock had seen something in the creek that told him there was a stilling site up there—enough flat ground to set up the gun.

He squinted down the barrels and elbowed Frank. "Now we'll see how yon sons of bitches like a little something we call enfiladin' fire."

CHAPTER SIXTY-EIGHT

THE DEFENDERS EYED THEIR watches. Almost noon. Minute hands crept toward the President's deadline. Seconds ticked. The sun hung close and hot, sucking the sweat from their skin. An eerie lull surrounded them, only the katydids thrumming, the tinny whines of gun-pummeled eardrums.

Maybe they gone home already.

The hell they have.

Dead if they don't.

At noon on the mark, when the hands of every watch upon the parapets took aim at the sun, a single cow horn blew from the green darkness of the mountainside, low and wailsome, like the herald of some barbarian horde.

The mountain erupted.

A GATLING GUN RAKED the front line of trenches at Crooked Creek Gap, firing from a high and wicked spur where no one expected such a weapon. The fusillade turned men out of their positions or kept them nailed in place, clinging to cover.

Bad Tony and the reporter weren't there. During the lull, Tony had moved them to a bunker of mossy fieldstones hidden inside a large rhododendron thicket, a cloud of pinkish white blooms. Just before noon, someone had brought Bad Tony a long single-shot rifle, an enormous gun with a rabbit-ear hammer and long brass telescopic sight. It lay on its canvas scabbard next to the machine gun. The reporter didn't know arms, but the rifle looked like something designed to kill bison or elephants or Ford motorcars.

Beneath them, men were pouring out of their trenches, retreating, many of them limping or bleeding, dragging friends or comrades. Others had wedged themselves into tight nooks or log barricades, hunkering low, rising now and again to return fire. No one had reckoned on the miners hauling a heavy gun up to such a high vantage.

The reporter looked at Bad Tony, who lay hunched behind his Browning machine gun, breathing through his nose. He didn't look surprised, nor had he fired a single round.

"What are you waiting for?"

Tony ignored him. He was squinting down the sights, chewing the inside of his lip, gently stroking the spot where the stray splinter had impaled his cheek. A bloody little scab. The reporter looked to the boys farther back in their crude bunker, sitting ready with cartridge belts and ammunition boxes. They shrugged.

The reporter looked back to the trenches. It was a rout. The men in the forward lines were too exposed. A whistle blew and they poured out of their trenches en masse, heading for secondary emplacements they'd dug during the night, ducking and scrambling as they went, their canteens and ammo pouches and field glasses flying wild on leather slings as a great banshee's wail rose from the trees behind them.

A swarm of Rednecks broke from cover, charging up the draw in bandolier-slung overalls and chore jackets and mismatched uniforms. They overran the newly abandoned trenches with hardly a shot, rearing back to howl and trill, crazed with victory. The reporter couldn't believe how close they were, close enough to throw a rock.

Then he realized why Tony had waited.

"GOT-DAMMIT!" YELLED CROCK. "THEY got a MG hid up in that slick!"

Star-shaped flashes racketed from the muzzle of the hidden gun, shivering the blossoms of the thicket, sending rounds straight into the miners in the trench. Several men went down in a flash, their blood puffed pink in the sunlight.

Crock elevated the gun on the enemy position but the barrels spun empty. Frank was still waiting on another magazine from the ammo boys, who were hurriedly reloading the hundred-round brass clips from the boxes in their laps, feeding in the cartridges by hand. Crock looked at Frank and then to the boys behind him. He reached out and snatched a magazine from one of their fists.

"How many?"

"Not fifty."

"Better than nothing."

Crock rose up to his full height to jam the clip into the top of the gun—
normally Frank's job. Down across the field, the machine gun had ceased firing, as if finished with the miners who lay dead or squirming in the long belly
of the trench. There came a single high crack, different from the others, and
a red slash exploded beneath the big man's jaw, spewing hot across Frank's
face. Then he was on the ground with Crock, trying to hold back the blood
spurting from the ragged side of his neck.

It was going everywhere, bright and slick, pumping between his fingers,
scattering like fire ants. Like trying to hold back a spring, a river. Crock
reached up and grabbed hold of the back of Frank's neck and pulled him close,
trying to speak over the blood bubbling at the corners of his mouth.

"What is it, Crock? Tell me, brother. Tell me."

The big Marine coughed and choked, trying to get something out, but it
was all blood and sputum. He squeezed Frank close, palming the back of his
head, driving them forehead to forehead. His words foamed red on his lips.

He died with a jolt, as if his spirit had cracked free of his skin.

Frank rammed his head into the man's chest and roared.

"DAVY CROCKETT," SAID BAD Tony. He slipped the long buffalo rifle
back into its canvas scabbard. "There's a name don't none of them deserve."

The reporter looked down at the bloodied, smoking trench. He wondered
how many corpses were being carried down the back sides of these ridges,
spread out in schoolyards or field tents. How many body parts gathered up
from bomb craters, piled into ponchos or sleeping blankets. Across the mountain, across miles of battle lines, he could hear the gunfire still going strong.
Hundreds of rounds per minute. Thousands per hour. Tens of thousands.

He looked at Tony. "You think this is the Second Civil War?"

Bad Tony looked up at the crackling sky, as if watching for the rumored
bombers to arrive, their vast wings clouding the sun.

"If it ain't, it's putting on one hell of a show."

CHAPTER SIXTY-NINE

FRANK AND THE OTHERS knelt over Crockett. He'd died so fast. So much blood. It was everywhere, all over the dirt and stones and weeds. All over Frank's hands and arms and chest, still hot. His face. He wiped his mouth with the back of his hand and tasted it, red-metallic on his lips.

His muscles quaked over his bones. His veins felt full of blasting powder. He wanted to jump down the face of the spur and bolt across the field and smash through that machine-gun bunker like a human ram, killing every man inside. He wanted to show them what hands that worked a coalface twelve hours per day could do, how he could rip their shoulders from their sockets and crush their throats like soup cans, twist their skulls from their necks and stomp their noses flat. He was every inch more man than them, and yet that was just what they wanted from him. Such a display. So they could shoot him dead in that field, a train of gunfire driven straight through his heart.

The others looked ashen, their lips colorless. Like men coming down with a sickness. Hot fear splintering through their veins, running amok. One of them shook his head. "I never thought it would be Crock. Him out of everyone."

Neither had Frank. But he knew Crock would've scoffed at that notion. *The fuck it won't.* Frank looked at the others. Their blanched faces and huddled shoulders. The spirit flying out of them. The fight. If Crockett could be killed, they thought, anyone could. That idea could spread like a contagion through the ranks.

Frank shook his head. He couldn't let that be Crock's legacy.

He said it straight at first, without song: "Davy Crockett's spirit has arisen from the grave." He looked to the men around him, nodding the words into them, putting them to the tune, meeting each man's eyes until his voice joined in . . .

Davy Crockett has arisen from the grave,
Devil Dog is he in an army of the brave,
Davy Crockett has arisen from the grave,
And he's got him a Gatling gun!

As they sang, Frank took the only paper he had in his pocket—one of the Presidential leaflets—and unfolded it on his knee, turning it over to the blank side. He found the nub of a weigh pencil buried among the pocket lint and tin scrip and jammed it into a cartridge case to write with.

When he finished, he refolded the leaflet and slipped it into the bib pocket of Crockett's overalls, leaving one corner dog-eared over the hem—a message to ride down with the body. Around him now, the hillside was taking up the song.

Glory, glory, hallelujah! Glory, glory, hallelujah!
Glory, glory, hallelujah! The Rednecks are march-ing on!

One of the ammo boys handed Frank a fresh magazine. One hundred rounds. Staying low, Frank reached up and fit the clip into the receiver. The sun was getting low, the hills turning gold.

He began to crank the firing handle of the gun.

CHAPTER SEVENTY

MISS BEULAH CHUCKLED AS she felt the pink sandpaper of the dog's tongue. The great hound had remained by her side since his appearance last night, though a can of red salmon from her prized stash of relief truck delights hadn't hurt, nor a bite of lard-soaked bread from her supper.

As a girl, she'd given names to every half-wild dog, cat, and raccoon running around the fields and barns, but she'd never had one of her own. In the coal camps, it was hard enough to fill the bellies of her own family. She'd heard talk of feeding bones and table scraps to dogs, but she'd never had any such leftovers. The dishes were licked clean and the bones went to broth or stew. Many a finger was cut on the lip of a soup can, scouring for one last taste. Not to mention those suck-egg Baldwins were always itching to get their pistols out, and it wasn't rare to see somebody's pet shot down in the street.

But this boy here, she couldn't help but smile as she scratched his chin and behind his ears. She missed having somebody to spoil. Her husband had allowed her to dote on him when she could, to scratch his scalp with her nails or surprise him with an unexpected can of peaches or plums from the company store no matter how steep the price. But Frank never trucked with that kind of thing. Said he couldn't even taste the sweetness—the company gouge was too bitter on his tongue.

Miss Beulah always knew such a man mightn't be suited for happiness in this world. But then the world wasn't like to change without people who'd rather die than buckle. That's where the damn Baldwins came in, happy to oblige.

The wiry-haired hound put his chin on the arm of her chair, looking up at her with puffy eyebrows. She knew some dogs to give a sweet face when they wanted something, only to steal away the moment they got their morsel. But this boy here didn't act that way. He was giving out sweet eyes all the time, unconditional.

"We got to name you, I reckon." She took an old piece of coal scrip from her pocket, rubbing it under her thumb. "What name you want?"

The dog perked his ears at the question mark in her voice. It was dusk and the sun was low, coppering the high trees of the ridge. The hound turned his head, hearing something in the distance. A great chestnut tree hovered on the hillside over his head, the branches sun-flamed like a thick set of antlers.

"Moose," said Miss Beulah. "That's your name. I never known one till you." She set the old piece of scrip on the arm of her rocker, pocket-worn blank, and began to scratch at one side with her knitting needle.

As the shadows grew longer, sprawling across the camp, Moose seemed to get nervier, cocking his tufted ears here or there, hearing things she could not. She wondered how far gunshots could carry for a hound. Whether he could hear the guns of Blair Mountain like distant thunder. Wouldn't surprise her. Back in 1864, when Sherman swept through the land in a storm of fire, people knew he was coming long before the news reached them. The birds had flown, the hogs dug deeper wallows, and the dogs crawled up farther beneath the cabins each night.

She scratched Moose between his ears. "It's okay, sweet boy. They a long way off yet. We got plenty a time."

She believed that, too. It wasn't just jawing. Ask her two days ago, and she'd have said the reaper-man was knocking his blade against her door. But she didn't want Moose to worry about such things. He had the look of a creature kicked and harried every minute from his mama's belly, yet gentle besides. His ears jumped again and she decided he needed a song, something pretty for his ears, such as she had to give. She cleared her throat and decided to sing him the song of her own name—the song her own mother had loved so much.

> Down in Babylon, on that old field,
> He saw that chariot wheel,
> Well, not so p'ticular bout that chariot wheel,
> He just want to know how the chariot feel,
> Way down yonder on Jordan shore,
> Angels say that time will be no mo,
> Well, some come crippled, and some come lame,
> All come hoppin' in my Jesus' name,
> Well, got me a home in Beulah Land,

Not goin' to stop until I reach that land,
I'm a-gon meet my mother in Beulah Land . . .

It had been years since she'd sung that song, and it seemed just the time to raise it again. Finished, she leaned back in her rocker, feeling the welcome weight of the dog's head in her lap. It was full dark now and she felt tired, her eyes heavy, but that was okay. She had somebody here to wake her if need be. She could rest.

CHAPTER SEVENTY-ONE

THE BRIGADIER GENERAL ROSE from his desk and removed his reading glasses. It was after midnight. His joints popped and crackled like cold sapwood beneath his pajamas. He walked to the window and clasped his hands behind his back, standing before the pale specter of his own reflection. A bald man, his mustaches broad and pale, faintly cavalier.

He sighed through his teeth. The reports on his desk were clear. Over a million rounds fired. Bombs dropped on American soil. Americans fighting Americans in trench warfare. An unknown death toll, rising by the hour. And, at noon, like ten thousand gunfighters in a Hollywood Western, the miners had stared down the Presidential ultimatum hanging over their heads like the sun itself and never blinked, shooting right through the deadline.

He had no choice.

The general breathed in, readying himself. Soon he would wire the War Department to request the deployment of the United States Army to West Virginia. He'd have the state governor roused from bed to tell him the news. The man had been begging Uncle Sam to intervene, to snuff the insurrection burning at the feet of his state, blistering the toes of his biggest campaign donors—the coal operators.

The general's assessment would not be kind. Already, he was turning the words over in his mind, assembling them like the boxcars of a troop train:

> *It is believed that the withdrawal of the invaders . . . would have been satisfactorily accomplished . . . but for the ill-advised and ill-timed advance movement of State constabulary on the night of August 27, resulting in bloodshed.*

Now he must reassert law and order in a failed state. Already, it seemed, he could feel the distant rumble of mobilization tickling the soles of his feet. The thud of infantry boots and iron-shod hooves, the wheels of howitzers and gun carriages, the sizzling roar of bombers, as if their manifold reverberations traveled long miles through the earth, seismic, rising up through his heels, swelling him with power. His chest. His word. Soon, with an utterance, he could command violence of biblical proportions, as if anointed with the powers of a god.

He looked at his swagger stick, a stubby billy club hanging from the brass knob of the wardrobe, dangling by its leather wrist lanyard. Already, the small wooden cudgel seemed to shiver slightly, newly weighted, as if it might snap free of its anchorage and plunge through the floorboards, impaling itself in the concrete floor of the basement. The kind of cudgel Uncle Sam might carry in his left hand, unseen in the recruitment posters, ready to cast a shadow of threat across the land.

THE BUGLER STRODE THROUGH the predawn darkness, his heels striking crisply across the parade ground. He stood straight as a ramrod beside the flagpole and lifted the polished kink of brass to his lips, as if for a kiss. His lungs swelled beneath his uniform blouse. In this moment, at this hour, he was not one man but many, dawn-dark ghosts divided across forts and camps on every side of West Virginia, sounding the simultaneous call of reveille beneath their campaign hats, the unsung lyrics tumbling into the ear canals of still-sleeping men, invading their dreams.

> *You've got to get up*
> *You've got to get up*
> *You've got to get up this morning*
> *You've got to get up*
> *You've got to get up*
> *Get up with the bugler's call . . .*

The men of elite infantry regiments in four states rolled out of their bunks. Their bare feet slapped the floor; their dog tags jingled from their throats. Their orders had come through.

"Hear that, boys? We're going to the Mountain State!"

The trains were already loaded, waiting. Soon, the black iron engines would cough great gouts of coal-smoke from their stacks, their steel driving wheels rolling the first few inches, stretching the mile-long chains of cars coupler to coupler, clanking, straining, gaining momentum, and then the locomotives would be under way, chuffing out of their stations, the troops waving their caps to well-wishers and sweethearts. Soon, the great war trains would be steaming toward West Virginia from every cardinal point of the compass, like crosshairs converging on Blair Mountain.

CHAPTER SEVENTY-TWO

MOTHER JONES CLUTCHED HER chest. The floor swayed beneath her as she clanged the telephone back onto its cradle. The planks swooned with the walls, blood lurched in her brain. The call had awoken her—a Union official, delivering the news. The War Department had ordered the United States Army to West Virginia. Not guards or reservists, but crack infantry units.

"War."

She whispered the word, staggering backward from the telephone, clasping her breast with both hands now. "War." She felt a terrible wound there, like she'd been hit with a sledge. A grave blow. The hardest she'd felt since '67, when the yellow jack struck down her little ones, when Memphis was a city of the dead and she dressed each of her children for burial and her husband, too. That wound, never healed—she felt it blow wide open, sending her reeling.

"My babes. My babes."

Mother's heart faltered. The whole bedchamber had gone dizzy around her, swimming in dim lamplight. The windows were shuttered and she felt trapped, not just in the room but inside the cage of her own bones, her own failing flesh. She was clawing at her breast. The pain there unutterable, a lead slug or driven pike. Worse. She'd forgotten you could hurt this bad. She couldn't breathe. Fear, that little snake she'd kept at bay so long, kept lockered and starved, came speeding through her veins, coiling around her ribs, squeezing the very air from her chest, and oh Christ oh Mary she couldn't breathe.

Mother wanted to make it to the window. To cast open the shutters. To see the black trees and blue streets and white buildings of the capital city, moon-pale in the darkness. They still held such promise, she believed. The prospect of justice on earth. Every man, woman, and child respected, equal in the eyes of the law. The freest state in the history of the world.

She was dying. She wanted to see it all a last time. That dream.

Mother stumbled again and grabbed the bedpost. The window was too far. Her hands were tingling, her fingers numb. Her spirit straining against her bones, her heart trying to hammer its way out of her, to burst through the wound in her chest. Oh Christ oh Mary it hurt.

Is this what it felt like for Sid?

Her hands were curling up like an old crone's, cramping and seizing. Her feet were leaden, dead in her slippers, her knees giving way, buckling beneath her. She was sliding down the bedpost, grasping it like a lover. Saliva ran from the corner of her mouth, hanging from her chin. She'd been struck down, she had, sure as an assassin's bullet.

God damn them all. King Coal and the Baldwins and the rest. They wanted the Army, they did. They wanted the cudgel to come down. The hammer. They want the Union to be crushed, buried, never to rise again, no matter how many broken bodies it took.

The walls were shrinking around her, turning dark at the edges. There was not enough air in the room, the house, the world. She couldn't breathe. She tried to call for help. Her friends downstairs. No sound from her throat, no croak. No breath in her lungs. Her voice had betrayed her, her hands and her feet. Her heart was broken, split like a stone.

Mother lay retching, gasping, clutching her breast. Her temple pressed to the ground. The boards were racing away from her. She could see an opening in the floor, ragged at the edges, trembling like the surface of a well. A portal, hailing her into the long night where her babes slept, her husband. She could almost see the other side, the shadowlands beyond the pale.

She'd thought it was fear stealing her breath, twisting her own ribs around her heart. But here, at the brink, Mother realized she was not afraid to slip the flesh, to walk in those dark and nameless hills. If there be thugs in those lands, she'd fight them, too. The demons and the haints would flee before her. The Devil would know her name.

No, her fear was not for herself, but for those she left behind. Those who still needed her, her words and spirit. Mother closed her eyes. She couldn't go. Not yet. She must cast her voice across the land once more. She must make herself heard. Perhaps now, with the veil so thin, they might hear her, her voice bridging the expanse. They might listen.

Mother creaked open her iron jaw. She spoke the very name of her heart.

"My boys. My boys."

CHAPTER SEVENTY-THREE

STILL DARK WHEN MUSA slipped out of the trees above Lick Creek, looking down at the strikers' encampment pitched along the banks of the rocky branch. The smell of cold woodsmoke drifted through the air, a bluish sting in his nose; early dew shone on the grass. Little movement around the place. The leaves shivered around him. A sense of impending storm.

Since splitting with Big Frank at the mouth of the old mine, he'd covered the better part of thirty miles, keeping to the creeks and game trails whenever he could, stopping only to refill his canteen or pick some sustenance to keep him going. Puffballs, blackberries, or dandelions he ate blossoms and all, chewing as he went.

When he started to get tired, he thought of Aidee. She was a jolt in his bloodstream, wings for his spirit. He'd think back to the first time he met her. The little creek that divided his family's property from hers. She was sitting cross-legged on a flat rock in the middle of the raveling current with a flurry of dragonflies around her, flashing in the shaft of sunlight, almost metallic, like some kind of whirlwind. She seemed in a world of her own, bent over a book.

Musa had happened upon her during a hike for gooseberries.

She didn't look up from her book. "I see you looking."

Musa jumped. He never got caught out like this, by anyone, ever. He felt like a startled deer. "I didn't mean to spy. I just now come up on you."

She turned a page. "I know."

Musa came a little closer, standing barefoot in the stream. He didn't want to spook her. She seemed some kind of magical fairy or sprite. Her skin luminous.

"What are you reading?"

She looked up, turning the book so he could see the spine: THE JUNGLE BOOK by RUDYARD KIPLING.

"One of my sisters has that on her shelf," said Musa. "Do you like it?"

"I do."

"Do you think I'd like it, too?"

She looked him up, down. Her big, spring-green eyes seemed to take in every part of him. His outfit of cutoff overalls and bare feet, belt-knife and tatty plug hat. She seemed to smile at the corners of her eyes, and then her mouth gave in, too. "I got a feeling you might. But I'd have to know you better, to make sure."

Musa squatted on a rock across from her. "What do you want to know?"

MUSA CAME DOWN THROUGH the grass with the dew wetting his trousers and the sky a vast dark ocean, the holler sides steep and black as canyon walls. In the night, he thought he'd heard singing on the wind, an old hymn or ballad flying with the bats and nightjars. Just the ghost of a song. Then gone.

Miss Beulah's tent was high at the back of the camp, a little distant from the others. As if she had some kind of special status. An elder. He could see her in the rocker in front of her tent, chin in hand. Up early. Probably she couldn't sleep.

As he neared, he saw an animal curled up at the old woman's feet. As if it felt his gaze, the animal rose and turned toward him. Musa froze in midstep. He thought he'd seen a wolf—a creature of myth, not seen in these parts for years. A miracle. Then he blinked and realized it was not a wolf but a large dog, slim and leggy, arched like a racing hound, with wild smoky hair that blended well with the surrounding dark, as if kin to the night.

A wolfhound.

Musa was watching the dog so closely he didn't notice anything amiss until he was at the edge of the light thrown from Miss Beulah's lantern. A trembling pool. And he saw the old woman seemed still, even for someone sleeping. Too still.

He squeezed the strap of his possibles bag with both hands and focused on her chest, the sharp washboard of her breastbone where it showed above her rough cotton shift. He saw no movement, no rise and fall of breath. He needed to get closer, to check her pulse. Musa looked at the dog. Great dark eyes behind a long snout, whiskers sprung wiry from his chin. The animal sat back on his haunches, allowing him.

Musa nodded. "Thank you, buddy." He came forward, knelt down, and placed two fingers against the old woman's neck as his father had taught him. Her skin was cold to the touch. No pulse.

She was gone.

She'd died with her chin in one hand, looking down at the dog at her feet. Musa pulled his fingers from her neck and gripped them in his opposite hand, squeezing as if to comfort them.

Gone. Tears sprang up in his eyes. The dog shifted slightly on his front paws, a worried look on his face. Musa looked at him. "She's gone, buddy. Though I reckon you already knew. I'm sorry."

The hound took a step forward, lowered his eyes, and pushed the crown of his head into Musa's chest. Held it there. Skull to sternum, as if the bony architectures of head and chest were made for each other. Musa looked down in disbelief at the animal now attached to him. Then he held the dog and began to cry.

After a minute, he lifted the dog's head. "Just a minute, bud. Something I got to do."

He rose, cupped his hand to Miss Beulah's ear, and whispered the words he'd promised he would. Then he pulled off the red bandanna and put it gently over her head. A piece of Mr. Frank to stay with her. When he was done, he rose to alert the rest of the camp. Then he would start for home, the hound following with him.

A storm was coming, and he had to get everyone across the river.

CHAPTER SEVENTY-FOUR

DOC MOO STOOD BEHIND the schoolhouse, relieving himself on a tree likely to wither and die after this battle given how many miners had watered it. As he was buttoning his fly, he heard a gritty swish of clothing and a man appeared out of the dawn darkness of the woods, a small man in shambled hat and coat and trousers, a knotted tie tucked into his shirt. His jaw was wide and square like a prizefighter's, though he'd make one of the lighter weight classes, flyweight or bantam. Wiry and quick, with outsized fists.

He shot out his hand. "Bill Blizzard, United Mine Workers."

Doc Moo knew the name. A district leader who seemed to be in some kind of command. He shook the man's hand. "Doctor Domit Muhanna."

Blizzard nodded. "I want to thank you for your work here, Doc. Word's got out. The boys up on the line, they're thankful to know we got somebody down here who ain't some damned sawbones. Not like the company doctors they're used to."

"I've done my best."

"It's known and appreciated. I'd like to say your work is done here, Doc, I sure would, but it's doubtful. Word is, Washington's deployed federal troops. They're heading our way even now, trains and bombers."

"What happens when they get here?"

Blizzard shook his head. "I don't rightly know, Doc. Depends on their orders, that and the mood of our boys. One thing I do know, it's like to be hell on the mountain today. So I wanted to ask it direct, can you stay another day?"

Moo nodded. "As long as I'm needed."

"Thank you, Doctor. Means the world to the boys up the line to know you're down here. It'll keep their spirits up."

"I'll do my best."

Blizzard nodded and looked up the mountain. "Our sources tell us the defenders are running low on ammo. Today's the last, best chance for our boys to bust through and teach Chafin, the Baldwins, and the coal operators a lesson before Uncle Sam arrives. Last chance to make all this blood mean something."

Doc Moo looked down at his hands, the dark-dried creases of his palms. *Inshallah*, he thought. "With God's will."

Blizzard nodded. "Amen, Doc. A-fooking-men." He thrust his hands into his coat pockets. "Well, I better get on down the line, keep on spreading the word."

"When will the troops arrive?" asked Doc Moo.

Blizzard looked to the sky. It was beginning to pale. "Word is, a storm forced the bombers down somewhere in Virginia yesterday. I imagine they'll be in the air soon's the weather clears. Now the troop trains, Doc, the troop trains . . ." Blizzard's voice trailed off and he squinted an eye in the direction of the Guyandotte River. "We'll see if them troop trains don't get themselves delayed somehow."

FRANK CROUCHED ON A ridge beside the Bad Seven, deep inside enemy lines. They'd been fox-walking all through the night, rolling their weight slowly onto the balls of their feet, gently compressing sticks and leaves, making as little sound as possible. They paused here, gathering their breath, then descended into the trees, following Bonney into the lower darknesses of the Guyandotte River.

The Hellfighter had appeared at Frank's position just before dusk. He looked different from when Frank had last seen him. His eyes lurked inside deep hollows and his cheeks were sunken, his face skull-like, as if part of him had died alongside his brother. He carried a bolt-action rifle with a telescopic sight. Green rags and vines draped from the barrel and hung from his overalls.

He had five men with him, three of the original Bad Seven—the Poles and one Provenzano—and two new men. One old, one young. A father and son.

"Got us a little assignment," he told Frank. "You up for night-walking?"

"Where to?"

"Hell, most likely."

"Here I thought we were there already."

Bonney grinned. "Gonna seal off the gate so the devils are stuck inside with us."

Before setting off, the Hellfighter made each man turn out his pockets to ensure they had nothing metallic to jingle, no scrip or keys or loose cartridges. He had them double-knot their bootlaces high and tight above their ankles, nothing to trip or snag, and he smeared a paste of shoe polish and burnt cork ash across their overalls in tigerlike stripes, mottling their silhouettes against the surrounding night.

Bonney walked point, leading them through the darkness, while Frank was second in line, armed with an ancient double-barreled shotgun they'd furnished him. Then came a long-boned teenaged miner, already a veteran of the coalfields. He was unarmed, toting a canvas haversack on his back like a schoolboy, his hands hanging from the thin shoulder straps. The contents were carefully wrapped in bandannas so as not to rattle.

Behind the boy walked his father, a Black man in his fifties, his temples and sideburns gray-worn beneath his rumpled miner's cap. He walked back-bent, stooped from decades in the mines, carrying an ancient leather mailbag cradled against his chest, as if a babe slept beneath the brass buckles and broad flap.

His name was Boom. Frank had heard the stories but never met him. In his thirties, he'd blown a charge in a mine that collapsed the wall of an old chamber, releasing a great pocket of blackdamp. These days miners had canaries to alert them to the lethal gas, the birds carried in glass revival cages in which they could be resurrected again and again by the simple twist of an oxygen valve.

But Boom had no such bird to alert him. He went unconscious and couldn't be revived until twenty minutes later, laid flat beneath the sun outside the mine. Wherever his soul went while he was out, it returned with a newfound knowledge of explosives. An artistry. Such was the story told. They said he could eye a length of fuse down to the millisecond, more exacting than any stopwatch, and blast a twenty-room mansion into the granite belly of a mountain, complete with flushing toilets.

The Da Vinci of Dynamite, they called him. *The Beethoven of Boom.*

Inside his mailbag, cradled carefully, were bundled sticks of dynamite, resting in a bed of sawdust and wood shavings. The explosives, purloined from a company store, had been sitting on the shelf too long. The nitroglycerine had begun leaching from the sawdust sorbent, sweating through the heavy paper wrappers. Liquid nitro, highly unstable. Now and again, Boom hummed or crooned over the leather bag, as if singing lullabies to a sleeping child.

Bonney led them lower, lower, creeping through the night, their bootheels seeking purchase on dewy roots and rocks. Now and again, in the distance, they heard eruptions of gunfire, each shot echoing ridge to ridge, fading, like shadow battles of the one being fought.

The Guyandotte River roved through the darkness, winding toward Logan. Soon they were kneeling on its shoals, concealed in a bed of reeds, looking up at the skeletal trellis of the Norfolk & Western bridge—the one the troop trains and company reinforcements would cross.

Bonney crouched next to Frank, scanning the trestle through the long scope. The rifle was an old Swiss Vetterli from the previous century, a military rifle that fired powerful black-powder cartridges—a gun storied to take down bear at range.

Bonney looked back over his shoulder. "What you think, Boom?"

The old dynamiter spread his hands across the broad flap of the mailbag and looked to the sky over the bridge, as if envisioning a work of art. "High as heaven, baby. Gonna tickle the angels' feet."

Soon they were watching Boom's son scale the stone piers of the bridge, the mailbag strapped across his back. The boy was barefoot, his fingers and toes seeking ridges and crevices in the mortared stone. The green river fumbled against the piers beneath him, gurgling and foaming. Long before it had a name, the Guyandotte had sawed a channel for itself through the bedrock of these mountains. Given enough time, Frank knew, it might cut the very legs from beneath this bridge, lapping the stone piers into distant sands, dropping the rusted skeleton of the trellis into the riverbed.

They couldn't wait that long.

Dawn was breaking, raking through the cloud cover. Within half an hour, the rising sun would touch the far ridgeline and come crashing down the slope, hounding the last shreds of night from the hills—no more darkness to hide them.

Frank looked back at Boom. The old dynamiter's eyes were raised to his boy, his gnarled fingers interlaced. The boy had ascended into the eaves of the span and sat hunched there amid the underpinnings. Bonney raised the long rifle again and squinted through the scope, scanning the bridge and riverbanks for sentries or traffic. Then back to the boy. He did it in a certain pattern, in certain intervals, precise as a pocket watch.

The boy lifted the bundled charge of dynamite from the leather satchel slowly, carefully, holding it apart from his body. His father, known all through the coalfields for his cool nerve, was breathing audibly now.

"Know who it was invented dynamite?"

Frank raised an eyebrow. "Who?"

"Alfred Nobel," whispered the old man. "Same one founded the Nobel Peace Prize. Ain't that some shit."

The boy was standing now, lifting the dynamite into the shadowy recesses above his head, nestling it among the braces and beams. He pulled out a roll of twine and fastened the charge in place, then climbed up through the cross-beams, emerging onto the tracks. Here he knelt and lifted a can of kerosene from the bag and began dousing the rail ties.

If the blast didn't destroy the bridge, the fire would.

The kerosene fumed around the boy. The sun had touched the top of the ridge and come filtering down the slope, a slow avalanche of light. Frank wiped his forehead. The very dawn seemed dangerous, as if it could ignite the bridge with the boy still up there, trapped in flames.

Finally, he ducked through the trestle and squatted on the end of a cross-beam high over the deepest part of the river, fishing in his bib pocket for a cigarette, a rollup twisted thin and tight from a scrap of newsprint. He lit it and inhaled.

Somewhere, across the vast miles of this land, the great war trains were under way, thundering through tunnels and hollers, swinging along rivers and ridgelines, hooting and shrieking through small stations at speed, steaming, smoking, ripping up flurries of leaves and dust in their wake. Frank could almost hear them, the warlike pounding of their pistons.

The boy blew a long plume of smoke, then turned and touched the cigarette to the kerosene-soaked ties. Strakes of flame leapt from the tracks above the charge. Boom's boy turned and leapt from the bridge, bare heels close together, hands crossed over chest, the empty mailbag fluttering from his back like a failed parachute. He smacked the river feet-first, disappearing for one moment, two. Then surfaced, his dark head bobbing toward them, his arms grappling with the current, pulling him toward shore.

Frank pulled the boy from the shallows as the first faint threads of smoke rose into the lower strata of sunlight, black and distinct, unraveling like blood in water. Bonney squeezed the boy's shoulder, then turned to Boom and the others. "Y'all head back now before it gets light. Me and Frank got this."

When they were gone, Bonney handed Frank a leather tube. "Gift from one of our less lucky friends. Eyes out for sentries."

Inside was a spyglass, the name of the maker inscribed on the side: UTZSCHNEIDER UND FRAUNHOFER, MÜNCHEN. Someone's souvenir from the trenches, taken from a fallen German artillery spotter or infantry officer. Frank propped the heavy end of the spyglass on his fingertips and looked through the eyepiece. The world jumped closer, an amplified sphere. He began making long sweeps along the foot of the span, the tracks, the riverbanks, looking for anything out of place.

Songbirds were coming to life, trilling and whistling as the sunlight caught them in the trees. Doves cooed. A red cardinal swung from tree to tree, following his dun-colored mate. The flames seemed to be rustling along the tracks, as if having trouble coming awake. Since they had no long fuse or plunger, they had to wait for the fire to ignite the charge.

Frank was sweeping the far riverbank when something caught his eye. He worked the focus. A man. Reclined at the base of a tree, dressed in khaki shirt and trousers, hat pulled over his eyes. Asleep. A driblet of saliva hung at the corner of his mouth. A rifle stood propped beside him, a white armband around his shirtsleeve.

Frank touched Bonney's elbow, pointed across the river. "Sentry, eleven o'clock. Neath that big sycamore."

The other man nodded, looking through the rifle scope. "Got him."

Frank squinted back into his own eyepiece. The sun was crawling down the jigsaw bark of the sycamore's trunk, inch by inch, creeping toward the top of the man's head. The early flies were aloft, swirling, their bodies glowing in the slashed bars of sunlight. Sun or flies or smoke—any second something would jerk him awake.

Bonney moved the Vetterli's forestock to the top of a log, steadying the barrel. Frank knew his crosshairs must be dancing over the sentry's chest, light as a daddy longlegs. No chance of missing from this range. Like hammering a rail spike into the man's heart. A sleeping man. An American.

Frank licked his lips. "I don't know. Don't feel right to me."

"They kilt Lacey."

"That one didn't."

"I don't do it, he could still douse the fire in time."

Frank nodded. Troops, ammunition, and reinforcements could come rolling across this bridge today, all but sealing the miners' defeat. All this blood for nothing. Frank looked down at his hands, the scabbed slash in one palm. No answer came to him.

He closed his hand and looked at Bonney. "Maybe there ain't no right answer."

"Maybe not."

"Ain't but one thing to ask then."

"What?"

"What would make our mamas most proud?"

"Never had one," said Bonney. "What about you?"

CHAPTER SEVENTY-FIVE

MOTHER JONES AWOKE IN bed, the glow of dawn in the room. Shadowy figures hovered at her bedside, murmuring. She couldn't decipher their words. Voices like a purling stream, a language of water and stone. She didn't know where she was, if this bed were in Heaven or Hell or Washington, D.C.

She'd been doing what the church might call good works for the large part of her life, but she'd raised a lot of hell, too. She'd spoken against *sky pilots*—priests in the pockets of King Coal and Big Steel—and she'd harbored a secret belief that God was a woman. *Creation something born, not erected.* Surely the sky pilots would consign her to Hell for that.

She just breathed, floating like an airship amid the white clouds of cotton bedding. Didn't move, didn't open her eyes more than a nick. It almost seemed she could stay here, just like this, in this thin slice of another world. No ghosts touched her here, no body pains. No hard wrenching of the heart, as if someone were adjusting the meat of her with a knife.

But she'd never been one for rest, stasis. For years, she'd had little home but the kindness of friends and comrades, miners' shacks and haylofts and her own shoes. She wasn't going to spend the Hereafter in bed, if that's where she was. The Long Home. No, if this were Heaven, she had questions for the Almighty, she did. And if this were Hell or Washington, she had tails to twist.

Slowly the voices began to take shape, the words becoming discernible, shifting into a language she knew. She could hear Emma and Terence Powderly—her friends and hosts. And a learned man, too. A physician. Discussing her health.

Eyes still slit, Mother sniffed loudly. "Am I dying, Doc?"

The bedside figures jumped, throwing their hands to their chests. Emma leaned down and touched her head. "Mother, you're awake!"

"Just resting my eyes, darling. So, Doctor?"

The doctor was tall and long-jawed, dressed in a dark suit and tie, a stethoscope looped around his neck. "It seems you've had a nervous episode, Mrs. Jones. No evidence of stroke or heart attack. I've been talking to Mr. and Mrs. Powderly here, and I believe it may be a symptom of nervous exhaustion, *neurasthenia*. What some are calling 'Americanitis.' An increasingly common condition."

"Americanitis?"

"Think of your body as a machine, Mrs. Jones. It has a finite amount of nervous energy, which it replenishes through rest, recreation, and fellowship. Working too hard, for too long, in too stressful of an environment overtaxes the body's nervous system. Body pain, dyspepsia, morbid fears, and fatigue can result, as well as acute episodes which resemble heart attack or stroke, but are not dangerous. Nerve attacks."

The doctor turned to Emma and Terence, as if they were her parents. "I've seen the affliction in one in thirty of my patients. We believe rapid modernization is exacerbating the condition here in America. Our bodies are simply not designed for such overstimulation. It's plaguing men and women of station and standing. Generals, surgeons, executive officers. Overworked. For a woman like Mrs. Jones, it's incredible it took so long to develop."

Mother twitched her nose. "You should go down to West Virginia, Doctor. I'd like to see what the company bosses thought about an outbreak of *Americanitis* in miners working seventy hours a week in the hole. I'd like to make a world where the bosses would give one ounce of a good Goddamn."

"I understand, Mrs. Jones, but you need to rest if you want to keep fighting for that world." He touched her shoulder. "Or you won't live to see it."

"I ain't in it for my health, Doctor. But I know you're probably right." Mother laid her hand on the doctor's arm. "I'll rest for a spell, it's about time, and what else do I need, Doctor. Perhaps company?" She patted the man's bony hand. Cold as bone. No wedding band.

He removed it. "Rest is most important."

"*Bedrest*," said Mother.

The doctor glanced toward the door. "Yes, yes. Any rest." He looked at the Powderlys. "I'll have a full prescription delivered this afternoon." He looked at his watch. "I had better be on my way. Appointments."

He packed up his medicine bag and stood by the door, looking back over his shoulder. "I'll come by tomorrow to check on you, Mrs. Jones."

Terence walked the man out and Emma turned in her collared dress and set her elbows on the bed, her chin in her hands. "You are *bad*, Mother."

Mother winked at her friend and set her hand on her arm. "I'm just getting started, Emma. I need to send a telegram."

HIS NAME WAS BOYDEN Sparkes, traveling correspondent for the *New York Tribune*. He came dashing down the steps of his office, his travel satchel and typewriter strapped across his chest like a set of crossed bandoliers. He paid the newsboy on the corner a half-dollar to borrow his bicycle. Soon he was mashing through the early streets of Cincinnati, crouched on the squeaking springs of the seat, ringing the brass handlebar bell to alert shuffling pedestrians and street sweepers of the clanging steel skeleton beneath him, outfitted with wicker basket and carbide headlamp and wide gullwing handlebars.

He was headed for the nearest rail station, where he had to catch a train already rumbling out of town on the B&O tracks.

Sparkes had made his name as a correspondent during the Great War, following the American Expeditionary Force across the Western Front. He'd served as an eyewitness to the ravages of trench warfare, where the modern age of tanks and planes and artillery guns met tactics little evolved from medieval times, and there were more dead men than poppies in France. Since then, he'd been covering politics, baseball, and other topics for the large Eastern papers.

In his pocket was an express telegram delivered by courier that morning:

TROOPS DEPLOYED TO WV STOP COULD BE SECOND CIVIL WAR STOP YOU SHOULD BE THERE STOP CATCH FIRST TRAIN YOU CAN STOP TELL IT LIKE IT IS STOP MOTHER JONES

Sparkes knew the 19th Infantry Regiment out of Camp Sherman, just east, would be the first unit to reach the battle zone, and he had to be aboard their train.

The dawn sun was shining directly in his face, filling the streets with light as he weaved in and out of crosswalk traffic and clattering motorcars, the great chains and sprockets and wood-hooped wheels of the bicycle squeaking and clunking beneath him.

His breath was spuming from his mouth, his luggage banging at his hips. He felt like one of those French or Belgian cyclists from the 1919 Tour de

France, men just out of the trenches who'd pedaled the battle-shredded roads, dodging bomb craters and unexploded artillery shells, drinking brandy from their bidons and dripping liquid cocaine into their eyes for speed.

The low roof of the station came into view, silhouetted against the rising sun. The long iron slug of the train was already rolling, heading out of town. He cranked harder on the pedals, his vision narrowing down to a tunnel. He leapt off the bike at the edge of the tracks and handed it off to another newsboy, and then he was running for the tail end of the train, the red caboose gaining speed, moving away from him. He was running in his ankle boots and flopping bags, feeling the gravel of tobacco smoke in his lungs.

A grizzled trainman stood on the rear platform, holding a cob pipe against the chest of his coveralls. He squinted an eye down at the frantic creature beneath him, the knees pistoning beneath the corduroy trousers, the black necktie flying behind him like an airman's scarf. The trainman leaned an elbow on the rail, casual, like they might discuss Babe Ruth or the weather report. "Who are ye, son?"

Sparkes roared between breaths. "Boyden Sparkes! *New York Tribune!*"

The trainman narrowed his eyes like an old sea captain, stepped lower on the platform, and clasped Sparkes's hand, hauling him up onto the caboose. Sparkes collapsed in a pile of tweed, sweat, and baggage straps, blowing like a death-driven horse.

The trainman toked on his pipe. "You're that famous war correspondent, ain't you?"

"Don't know about famous."

The man reached into an inside pocket of his coveralls and handed Sparkes a battered brass trench flask. "You best tell the truth what's happening down there in West Virginia. I don't want to wish I given you the boot stead of a nip of my special apple brandy."

Sparkes unscrewed the cap and lifted the flask to the trainman. "The truth," he said, taking quite a large slug for seven o'clock in the morning.

CHAPTER SEVENTY-SIX

BAD TONY LOOKED WEST. A column of smoke was rising from the Guyandotte River. The railroad trestle. He looked back to his ammo runner, speaking through his teeth. "How many rounds left, did you say?"

The boy wiped his forehead with the back of his sleeve. "Ain't but ten belts left for the Browning, sir. I thought we had more in the other truck. We're running low on cartridges for the high-powers, too."

Tony growled. "We had north of fifty thousand rounds yesterday."

"It's been a whole hurricane of shooting, sir. Some of the boys, they're ankle-deep in brass. It's filling up their trenches and boots, coming out their dang ears."

Above the foxhole, the incessant splinter and crack of the sky, the air sizzling with crisscrossing rounds. The fire was as thick as anything Tony had experienced overseas. He pointed to the column of smoke. "See that smoke, that's the bridge over the Guyandotte River going up. They're trying to burn it to cut us off from reinforcements or resupply."

"You think the Army's going to get here in time?"

"Not if they have to swim the fucking river."

"What are we gonna do?"

Tony touched the bloody spot on his cheek where the splinter had gone through. He stroked the wound lightly, thinking. Then looked at the runner. "Run down and call the sheriff, tell him to turn that little air force of his into a supply line. I don't know what them little puddle-jumpers will carry, but whatever they can. Tell him it's highest priority. Do it yourself and keep it quiet."

"Yes, sir." The boy looked doe-eyed down the defense line, where constables and militiamen were shooting their rifles as fast as they could work the bolts and levers. "Shouldn't we tell the men to start conserving ammo?"

Tony shook his head. "Hell, no. They'll panic, thinking the line won't hold. We'll get overrun."

"You think they'd bolt if they knew?"

"They're civilians, most of them, so we can't shoot 'em if they do."

FRANK AND BONNEY WATCHED the bridge sentry scrambling up the soft slope of the riverbank, fighting for purchase, grabbing fistfuls of dirt and muddy roots. He was dragging a three-gallon milk tin behind him, the bright water of the Guyandotte sloshing from the bomb-shaped vessel. A one-man bucket brigade. His rifle was slung across his back, his boots and trousers mud-caked. Above him flames were crackling on the bridge, sending a pale haze of smoke into the sky, a ghostly watchtower.

The man had awoken with a start, clutching his chest as if shot. A dream. Certainly he hadn't seen the two men lying just across the river, sniper and spotter. Hadn't seen the shooter remove his finger from the trigger and retract his barrel into the reeds. A man who'd heeded the whispered words of the friend beside him.

Mama-B, she'd say to do the hard thing. Seems to me, giving him a chance is harder than pulling a trigger.

They could see he was a plain townsman, dressed in the rumpled khaki and white armband of the local vigilance committee. Probably he had his own office in town, his name painted in gold on the pebbled glass door. An attorney or insurance man. A cut-glass whiskey decanter on the sideboard, a set of snifters, a small nickel-plated derringer in his desk drawer.

For years, the troubles of the mines had remained at a remove for such men, grumbling along the edges of the county—a threat the Czar kept at bay, walling off the county with his army of deputies and secret agents. No Mother Joneses, no Sid Hatfields, no agitators or organizers. Now that once-distant reality had punctured the ramparts, threatening to thunder down their streets.

The Czar was said to stand sweaty and overwrought in his makeshift headquarters, telephones held to both ears, his bowtie wilted at his throat. Meanwhile, the townsmen had risen to defend hearth and home, donning armbands and ankle boots—men who wore glossy belts and loafers to work, cuff links and tie pins and class rings. Men who believed that beneath their starched shirts and soft bellies, they retained the same strength and prowess as their forebears, who'd cut their lives bloody from these hillsides and survived, sending their descendants down into the towns. Now they'd been given a chance to prove themselves, to show they still carried that same mettle in their bones.

Frank watched the man drag the heavy tin onto the smoldering bridge. It was excruciating to witness; he was making headway against the flames. The ties and timbers hadn't caught fire like they'd expected—perhaps the heaviness of the morning dew.

"Maybe I should just wing him," whispered Bonney.

"Could you do that?"

"With this thing?" Bonney nodded to the giant Swiss rifle. "Like to lop a whole limb off his trunk. It's black powder, too. Not smokeless. Now the sun's up, one shot will give away our position."

Frank looked to the hills above them, crawling with patrols. They were deep in enemy territory. He looked to the spot where the dynamite charge lay hidden beneath the tracks. Any second, a speck of glowing cinder or drip of burning kerosene could touch the leached nitroglycerine and detonate the charge. The tracks would erupt, their wooden ties and iron rails flailing heavenward, a cloud of debris rising over the river. The sentry would be hurled like a ragdoll through the air, his name cast into every newspaper in the country.

"See if you can't just scare him off," said Frank.

"They'll see us."

"We got to try."

Bonney set his eye into the scope, leading his target slightly. The man on the bridge looked wretched, dragging the heavy milk tin banging down the tracks, water sloshing out with every step. Wretched but determined.

Bonney fired. The gun bucked, sending forth a great plume of powder-smoke as the slug sparked off the iron girders. The man kept going. One shot among a cacophony of others. He was lost in his own agony, driving himself to the edge of infarction. They watched him reach the core bloom of the fire, where the heat had to be rising through his bootsoles, blistering the balls of his feet. This dentist or druggist or insurance man. He roared over the pain, heaved the milk tin high to his shoulder, and turned it upside down.

A thick hawser of water poured straight into the heart of the fire. Pale blooms of vapor boiled outward, breaking around his knees. His hat was wafted from his head, tumbling off through the steam and smoke, and Frank could almost see his face roasted red.

The fire guttered beneath the stream of water, the outer tongues of flame canting this way and that, as if trying to escape. They began winking out, one after the next, snuffed into coils of smoke. Soon the milk tin rested empty on the man's shoulder, big as the spent brass of a field gun, and the embers fumed at his feet, all but extinguished.

He began stamping out spot fires. He was nearly dancing, his hobnail boots pounding a lively jig, when he froze on his tiptoes, staring straight down between his legs.

"Shit," said Bonney. "He just saw the charge."

It would be just visible between the ties, a waxen bundle that could've blown him tap-dancing into oblivion, sprinkled down on the Guyandotte like a butcher's special. That still could. The man set his fists on his hips and bowed back on his tiptoes, raising his voice to the sky. They couldn't hear him from this distance, but they could see the thick worms of his neck veins standing out, the spit flying from his upraised mouth.

"He's cursing hell out of us," said Bonney, tapping his finger along the trigger guard. "No idea we could put a bullet through his head anytime we want to."

Frank nodded. "Must be how God feels sometimes."

Bonney grit his teeth. "All the time."

CHAPTER SEVENTY-SEVEN

MUSA STEPPED FROM THE trees, looking at the square white house across the field. The O'Donovans' place. He'd already been home to alert his mother and sisters, slipping through the back door at first light and rousing them as gently as he could, telling them of their father's wishes—to head to the Kentucky side of the river until the danger passed.

"And who is this?" his mother had asked, pointing a whole hand at the giant wolfhound that had followed him into the house, long nails tapping on the wood floors.

"This here is Moose." Musa had found the name scratched onto a piece of ancient coal scrip strung from the dog's neck on a thin length of twine. He looked at the big hound. "He was Miss Beulah's."

His mother's eyes softened. "Was?"

Musa nodded. "Yes'm. I went to see her on my way here." He paused, breathed, and touched the dog between the ears. "She's passed, Mama."

His mother held a hand to her mouth, then took Musa into her arms. She said nothing, just held him, cupping the back of his head.

Now, while she and his sisters readied the mule and cart, Musa had come to alert the O'Donovans. He'd never been up to Aidee's actual house before— they always found each other in the woods, along the creek or atop one of the lookouts.

Her father had been a king hogman, a raiser of prize red Durocs, and Musa had never felt comfortable around him. He seemed to appraise the people around him with a hard-squinted eye, studious of their grooming and muscling, coloration and poundage. A man who never let his neighbors forget how long his family had been on the land, how deep their blood ran through these hills. Though he'd died last spring, his spirit seemed to hang about the homeplace.

Now Musa had to march in there and hello the house. Hiking thirty miles in a day was scarce bother to him, but this last hundred yards was harder than all the rest put together. Moose looked up at him, waiting. Musa squatted down beside the dog and scratched the back of his neck, then wrapped his hand in the strap of his possibles bag.

"Faith," he said, then rose and set off toward the house.

Aidee herself answered the door. He saw her green eyes first, which seemed to glow bodiless within the dark interior of the house—bright as whole worlds—and then the rest of her came into view, pale and lithe, her feet bare. Her eyes and mouth were wide, as if she'd still grow into them, and though they were both undersize for their age, she was half a head taller than he was, her body slim and angular, draped with a frayed gingham dressing gown.

"Musa," she said. Her eyes were bright, her cheeks flush behind the cracked door. He couldn't tell if she was excited or worried to see him—maybe both.

"I'm sorry to call out the blue," he said. "But I got an important message for your mama."

"Is everything okay?"

He nodded. "Daddy and I been up at Blair. He's afraid this Redneck war could come this way, wants us to hightail it across the Tug till it dies down."

"He doesn't think we'll be safe here?"

"They dropped bombs already, Aidee. From aeroplanes. They say there's more coming—" A claw caught his throat. Hot sparks behind his eyes. He looked down and coughed into his fist.

"Is your daddy still up there?"

Musa nodded. He didn't feel he could speak. That swell in his throat.

Behind him, he could hear the world coming alive, blackbirds and robins sporting in the trees. Moose stood just shy of the porch steps, where Musa had asked him to heel. He thought of his father back at the schoolhouse, covered in sweat and blood. His throat again.

"Why don't you come inside," said Aidee.

Musa rocked from one bare foot to the other. "Ain't washed."

Aidee reached out and took his hand, leading him into the house. "May I have that note for Mama?"

Musa handed it to her, the paper creased neatly beneath his mother's index finger.

"I'll take it up to her and be right back, okay?"

Musa nodded again. Aidee set her bare foot on the first step of the staircase, then turned, walked back to him, put both hands on his cheeks, and kissed him on the mouth, hard and long and sweet, and it was the first time ever. Then she was gone, up into the mote-swirling dimness of the stairs, her bare feet flashing as she went.

His heart was a crazy thing in his chest.

CHAPTER SEVENTY-EIGHT

FRANK AND BONNEY WERE still watching the bridge sentry, the great plume of powder-smoke rolling downstream from Bonney's rifle, when a sand-bagged handcar appeared on the tracks above them. The muzzle of a machine gun swiveled their way.

"Run!"

Automatic fire tore into the reeds. They scrambled up the bank, turning just long enough to see a squad of khaki-clad men leaping down from the car to give chase. The two miners clawed their way through a tangle of heavy brush as rounds caromed through the willows. They gained a little trail along the river and began to run. Frank thought their pursuers would give up once they'd set their quarry to flight. They didn't. They were scampering from tree to tree now, hooting and firing, as if flushing animals through the woods.

He followed Bonney up a rocky creek that crossed the trail, staying low, the pair of them slipping and scrambling, fighting to get a lead on their pursuers. They came out on a steep, woody ridgeline and began running along the edge, pushing hard, zigzagging in and out of the trees. Frank looked over his shoulder again.

He never saw what tripped him. Before he knew it, he was plunging down the steep face of the ridge, down through briars and slicks, sliding and somersaulting, trying to cover his head so a rock or tree trunk couldn't bash his skull. Finally he lay still, curled up in a stony creekbed that fed the river. He could hear the men passing on the ridgeline above him, still chasing Bonney.

"I think we winged him, boys. Let's go, he can't run forever!"

By the time Frank climbed back to the trail, the sun had shifted in the sky and the men were long gone. He'd lost the shotgun in the fall and so tread carefully in the pursuers' wake, one hand on the revolver strapped across his chest, afraid at every bend of finding Bonney shot-riddled or swinging from a tree. An hour later, he lost their trail amid a rocky branch. Hard to believe any pack of townsmen could catch Bonney in the woods, but if they'd wounded him . . .

By noon, he'd made his way back to the friendly lines at Crooked Creek Gap, hoping to find Bonney and the rest. Instead, he found himself holed up in a shallow trench, pinned beneath a relentless hail of fire. The others told him it had been this way all day—they'd hardly gained an inch of ground. They had no news of Bonney or the others.

In the late afternoon, he heard the whistle of an inbound train. The sound hit him like a nail in the chest, an iron spike. That train would roll over the bridge they'd failed to blow and come hissing to a stop on the far side of Blair Mountain, where a line of motorcars would already be waiting, engines running. In less than an hour, the defense line would have enough ammunition to stave off Armageddon.

Frank looked up through the trees, fighting the urge to scream. He'd lost everyone. Evie, Lacey, Crock—all dead. He didn't know where Bonney or the rest of the Bad Seven were, if they'd even made it out alive. Didn't know when he'd see Mama-B again, if ever he would.

Tears scalded his cheeks, fat and hot. Around him, men were preparing for another charge. Loading magazines and checking chambers, kissing saints' medallions and crossing themselves, muttering prayers of protection. Making ready to go over the top. Men with rocklike hands and crinkled faces and outsized forearms.

He didn't know any of the men in the trench with him, their names. But he knew they were proud of who they were and the work they did. The work of hard men in deep places. They knew, if not today, they could die in slate falls or rock bursts or blasting accidents, by gun thugs or firedamp or coughing up black blood long before their hair turned white. They had to face those destinies morning and night. They lived with them, slept with them, dreamed them.

A sudden warmth in Frank's chest, explosive, a vast ache for these men. Some young, some old, their faces seamed with grit. He wanted to grab up the boy next to him, to hug him close to his chest, to say he was proud to stand with him. But a trench whistle had sounded down the line and the men were already rising out of their trenches and scrambling over the top, out of his reach, into the fire.

CHAPTER SEVENTY-NINE

DOC MOO BENT OVER the shrapnel-pocked thigh of a miner, forceps raised, about to go in. The man had been hit two days ago. Bomb blast. His friend said he'd been too scared to come at first, afraid he'd be charged for visiting the doctor. He didn't want the company to dock his pay.

The wound had begun to pucker and Doc Moo was concerned of gangrene setting in. They had no anesthesia and the man was writhing white-bellied beneath him, eyes glued to the forceps, whispering prayers in Polish. Moo nodded to the nurse, who set a stretched leather belt between the man's teeth. At the touch of the forceps, the man bucked and roared through the leather bit. Doc Moo felt the stainless steel tips touch something hard, foreign. He prodded the area, feeling for the best way in, the man juddering beneath him as if shocked.

It didn't help to focus on a patient's suffering, so Moo had learned to tune out the screams and pleas. Push them to the periphery. Like someone who lived next to train tracks, who could sleep while the house threatened to shake right off its pilings. Still, it was a relief when the man passed out, his body falling limp. His tortured spirit gone to another place, at least for a time.

A story had been circulated during the Great War that God would give you no more pain than you could bear, that you'd pass out before it became too much. Doc Moo knew that wasn't strictly true but he could imagine what comfort it might give. That simply believing such a thing might make it true.

He got hold of a shell fragment and began to work it from the wound. People thought of butchery as crude work, even brutal, but it was so much neater in fact. No screams, no fear of death or dismemberment. Smooth, practiced cuts on flesh far beyond feeling. Not so with surgery. He dropped the fragment into a porcelain bowl at his elbow and began to prod the next wound in the man's cratered thigh.

The nurse touched his arm. She was the same square-jawed miner's wife who'd served with the Red Cross in the War—a blood-soaked godsend. She pointed to the dish.

Moo retrieved the bomb fragment and held it higher to the light, rotating it in the forceps. Beneath the blood and tissue, the fine threads of a machine screw.

The nurse swallowed. "Christ, I never seen that in a bomb. They wouldn't load it with those, would they?"

A shiver ran up Moo's spine. "I don't know." He tapped the dish. "Let's not throw this away. Someone ought to see this."

"Yes, Doctor."

Over the next hour, he pulled fragments of nuts, bolts, screws, and nail heads from the man's pockmarked thigh. Hardware intended for construction and assembly, for the shelter and so-called progress of mankind, turned to the violent disassembly of the human body. Moo began to feel unwell as he worked, weak. His blood running thin. His faith. Each fléchette chipping at some utter part of his spirit. Nicking and scoring his insides. Whittling his bones.

He was cleaning the last of the wounds when the floorboards began to thrum beneath their feet. Soon the bomb fragments were rattling in the dish. He and the nurse looked at each other.

"Cover!"

Moo threw a canvas sheet over the man's exposed wounds as dust shook down from the rafters and aero engines roared overhead, loud as whirlwinds. It seemed the schoolhouse roof would be ripped shrieking from the joists. They looked through the blown-out windows to see a flight of Army fighter-bombers crossing the camp in echelon, Liberty planes with V-12 engines and forty-foot wingspans, each bristling with machine guns. The warplanes peeled away in formation, the starry roundels flashing on the undersides of their wings.

One of the wounded men turned from the sill. "Eighty-eighth Aero Squadron out of Langley, Virginia." He sniffed. "Telling us they're here."

Doc Moo set his hands on the desk and closed his eyes. He wanted to pray but the words wouldn't come. So his prayer was just a vision. A shield of light cast over the mountain, sheltering the men upon its slopes, on both sides, and he down at the bottom, inside this very schoolhouse, small but tireless, with iron bones and chainmail nerves. A man who could wade blood for days. He prayed to be that man. To remain so, for however long he must.

Come dusk, the dead and wounded were brought down in throngs, carried on men's shoulders or makeshift litters, some wrapped in blankets or coats. So many it seemed the mountain itself was bleeding.

CHAPTER EIGHTY

BOYDEN SPARKES OF THE *New York Tribune* rode aboard the first troop train into West Virginia. There was no press car, so he rode among the soldiers themselves, most of them dozing in the rocking dimness of the unlit passenger coaches, saving their strength. Sometime after midnight, the engine slid into a small station on the outskirts of the battle zone. A lone sergeant stepped down onto the darkened platform and did an about-face, one arm behind his back.

"Faaall out!"

The infantrymen jolted awake, accustomed to such abrupt wakeups. They donned their packs, secured their rifles, and marched down from the coaches to line up on the platform. There they stood rigid as statues, chins tucked to Adam's apples. Not a single yawn. Meanwhile, small crews scurried here and there, setting up supply and communications posts.

Sparkes walked over to a group of young officers standing around a map on a barrel. He'd just introduced himself when a man in a shambled suit came striding up the tracks toward them, his feet crunching in the railbed. His suit hung tattered from his shoulders, his tie ragged. He looked like he'd been sleeping rough for days, fully clothed, if he'd slept at all. Still, he came striding through the ranks of enlisted men with an air of command, aiming straight for the ring of officers.

He held out his hand. "Bill Blizzard. President, Subdistrict Two, United Mine Workers of America."

The officers' mouths fell open. Sparkes had heard talk of the man on the train. His dossier had made quite the splash. The typed words of one military intelligence source: READY TO FIGHT AT THE DROP OF A HAT. NO HAT NECESSARY. They suspected he'd become the miners' field commander.

The ranking officer, a captain, leaned toward him. "Mr. Blizzard, is it true you're the general of the Redneck army?"

Blizzard scratched his grizzled chin. "Army?" He looked theatrically at the ridges around them, black as ramparts against the upper night. "What army?" He grinned.

The officers tensed, perhaps sensing the little bars of rank pinned on their collars, gold and silver, twinkling beneath the station lamps. After all, snipers could be hidden in the black woods beyond the lights. During the American Revolution, frontiersmen armed with Kentucky rifles had perched in the tops of just such trees and shot British officers from their horses, throwing Redcoat lines into disarray.

Blizzard looked here and there, eyeing the high ridgelines on either side of the tracks, as if seeing things they could not. He twitched his nose. "Me, a general? No, sir. Far from. But I reckon a good many of the boys in the hills will listen to me, such as I am."

"And how many are they, Mr. Blizzard, would you guess?"

Blizzard scratched his chin again. "Well, now, sir, I wouldn't like to hazard a guess on that figure. Hell, a lot of boys come out the hills already. Gunshot, mind ye. Or bombed out by one of them hired planes. But there's a good many boys still up there, too." He squinted one eye at the officers, not quite a wink, then spotted Sparkes, who stood out in his civilian garb of tweed jacket and black tie. "And who might you be?"

"Boyden Sparkes, sir." He held out his hand. "*New York Tribune*."

"Sparkes?" The man's hand was dry and hard, callused like stone. "Sparkes," he said again, shaking a little longer. "You that famous war correspondent?"

"I don't know about famous."

The captain stepped in, holding up his hand. "If I may, Mr. Blizzard, here's the question. Will your men come down peacefully from the hills, or won't they?"

Blizzard winked at Sparkes, then turned back to the captain. "Well, like I told ye, Cap'n, it's a good many come down peaceful already. Brought down on litters, they were, their souls fled to the Long Home. Several many this afternoon, in actual fact. Hell, one of the boys was a decorated Marine Corps man. Kilt him a hundred Germans at the Battle of Belleau Wood, they say. A by-God war hero. He was shot down yesterday fighting a bunch of coal company thugs and assassins like them that gunned down Smilin' Sid not a month ago. Shame to the shields they wear, them that have them. Most got no legal authority at all."

The small man looked up at the dark sky beyond the station lights. "They was up in them hired planes earlier. You can see the bomb craters for your own selves. Look like pockets of evil, bad spots in the earth. One landed smack between a couple ladies doing their wash in a crickbed. A dud, thank God. Can you imagine if it blew? Hell, there wouldn't be no turning back from that, no sirree."

Blizzard looked back at them, one face to the next. He tugged straight the crumpled sleeves of his shambled coat. "You want to know if the boys are like to come down peaceful, do ye? I don't speak for them. Every man up there will have to decide that for himself. But I'll tell you they got no quarrel with the United States Army. Lot of the boys served in your very ranks, overseas. Over There. Lot of them decorated, too, like the one I told you about. Some are wearing their uniforms even now. Your uniform." He nodded to the men's fatigues. "They don't want a fight with you. They just want a fair shake. Can you give them that?"

The commanding officer glanced to his lieutenants. "To the best of our abilities, Mr. Blizzard."

Blizzard looked slightly sideways at them, grinding his teeth. "All right, Cap'n. You give me a squad of soldiers to take up the line, to show our boys you're the real thing, not some rumor or ruse, and I believe I can have them off that mountain come daylight. The lion's share, at least."

The captain nodded and turned to one of his lieutenants, telling him to form a detail to accompany Blizzard to the line. The subordinate saluted and turned on his heel. The captain looked back to Blizzard. "Are you armed, Mr. Blizzard?"

Blizzard shrugged. "Ain't totin' but a short gun."

"A short gun?"

A lieutenant leaned to the captain's ear. "I believe he means a pistol, sir."

The captain held out his palm. "Let's see it."

Blizzard froze, lock-jawed, staring at the officer's hand. Sparkes could see a battle erupting inside the man's skull. Lightning forking, gears grinding. Finally he sniffed and reached into one of his coat pockets, slowly, eyeing the guards in the darkness, their unbuttoned holsters. He produced a small snub nose revolver butt-first from the pocket.

The captain took the gun, turned it over in his hand, and handed it to his lieutenant. "Permit?"

Blizzard sniffed again, puckering his mouth tight. He cocked his hip and produced a lumpy wallet, peeling apart a ham sandwich of sodden cards and papers and notes to find a dog-eared pistol permit.

The captain took a step back to hold the document beneath the light of a station lamp, looking down his nose like a train conductor or traffic police-man. Satisfied, he handed back the permit, then motioned for his lieutenant to return the sidearm to its owner.

Blizzard looked around the ring of faces. "Let me ask ye something, Cap'n. You mean to let our boys keep their firearms only if they got a permit, that right?"

"That's the law, Mr. Blizzard."

"And the men on the other side of that there mountain. All them Baldwin thugs and corrupt lawmen and law-and-order vigilantes. They'll keep theirs?"

"If they have legal permits, yes."

"Which Sheriff Don Chafin of Logan County can issue them. The Czar."

"If that's within his powers, then yes."

A spark in Blizzard's eyes, like burning fuse. "You do see the problem with that, don't ye, Captain?"

The captain spread his hands. "It's the law."

The fuses glowed brighter in Blizzard's eyes. "I should of knowed. Only King Coal's men end up with guns. You think that's a minor detail in this scenario, but it ain't. No, sir. Not in the least. The second you and your men leave this place, we'll be powerless. Unarmed. They'll know we can't fight back. They'll shoot the best of us dead in the streets, same as they done Sid. Same as they'd do our own sweet mothers if they stepped in front of a county courthouse with evidence in their mouths. You and your men will be long gone, back at your camps and forts, training day and night to defend the great liberties of this country, the ones inalienable and endowed to all, and we'll be dying right here on American soil, again and again, gunned down like we ain't got the same rights as everyone else. It's the same as always, my friend. It ain't a damn thing changed."

The captain held out his hands again. "It's the law."

Blizzard's eyes were glowing now, like a man fired with likker or religion. The officers seemed to lean back and turn their heads slightly, as if he might detonate. He looked past them to the infantrymen on every side, hard-faced beneath their tin-pan helmets, and then to the dark hills around them, full of

CHAPTER EIGHTY-ONE

"IT'S THE SAME DAMN story as always, Blizz," said Big Frank. "Don't you see that?"

Blizzard looked down at his boots, rubbing his chin. Hundreds of shadows had gathered along the rocky banks of Crooked Creek, shifting in the darkness, whispering among themselves. Their heads nodding.

Law only serves them that's in power.

Ain't no different than always.

Our boys died for nothing.

Blizzard shook his head. He'd been all across Blair Mountain in the night, hiking from unit to unit, speaking in trenches and foxholes, telling the men it was time to stand down, to go home. The U.S. Army had arrived. Their fight was with King Coal, he told them, not Uncle Sam. With thugs and corrupt lawmen, not American soldiers. They'd put up one hell of a fight, and then some. But they couldn't fight the United States military. Most of the miners agreed, and word spread through the night. Time to pack up, to come down the mountain, to head home.

But Big Frank and the other miners at Crooked Creek Gap had been in the bloodiest fighting of the battle. Men had died before their eyes. Friends. They couldn't go easy.

"I don't like it, neither," said Blizzard. "But this ain't the state militia or [gua]rds. I saw them, boys. War train a mile long if it was an inch, and that's [just] the first. This is the United States Army, dressed in the same uniform some [of yo]u are wearing now, and they've come with howitzers, motor-sickles, and [machi]ne guns. It will be a damn massacre, and won't a single American outside [the coa]l camps of this state give a good Goddamn about it either, about any one [of us g]own to hell or our starving children left behind, because it ain't the gun [thug o]r company bloodhounds or vigilantes no more. It's the United States unseen men. A single wink or word or snap of his fingers and it seemed those ridges could explode.

He looked to the officers. "I'll see what I can do."

With a crack of cinder, Blizzard turned on his heel and strode back into the darkness, alone. He walked stiff-backed, mindful of his steps, like a man holding a live grenade.

One of the lieutenants looked at the captain. "Should we have let that man walk free, sir?"

b

w

gua

just

of yo

mach

the co

of us b

thugs o

TAYLOR B

Army. You know who it was on that train I met? The 19th Infantry Regiment. The Rock of Chickamauga. Hard of the hard, ready to shoot and bayonet whatever they're pointed at. And there's at least two more regiments on the way."

Another voice from the darkness. "What about Crockett and all the rest kilt up here? Thirty-some, they say, just here, just today. We go home now, what the hell did they die for?"

Blizzard squinted, his eyes moon-specked. "They died for a cause they believed in. If we go on, we kill that cause, and their memories, too. They died for their children, and their children's children. For solidarity, and a better future. For us. If we go up against the U.S. Army, there won't be no future. We will kill that cause, bury it dead in the ground beneath a sea of blood. Crock and the rest? They won't be heroes no more. They'll be called criminals, insurgents. Murderers. Not only dead, but dishonored. Their names sullied. And we'll be the cause of it, us here on this creek, sure as we spat on their graves."

The men were nodding now, hearing him.

"We go gentle, and we might just show this country we ain't in it for the blood. No, sir, we're good Americans standing up for the freedoms taken from us. The rights this country promises. The liberties. The same ones thousands before us died for. And there's a chance our stories will be heard. The cause won't be killed alongside them that died for it."

The men nodded, whispering to one another.

We can't let this be the end.

Let's bury them with honor.

Solidarity forever. Let the cause roll on.

One of the men hugged his rifle close. "What about our guns? We supposed to give them all over to the Army? The second they leave, we won't be but lambs for the slaughter. The Baldwins will kill us for sport."

Blizzard cracked his knuckles and winked. "Now, about that."

THE MINERS WERE DISPERSING, taking up their packs, talking of how they'd get home. What roads or paths or hopped trains. Frank stepped up to Blizzard and took his arm, lowering his voice. "They're like to string somebody up for all this, Blizz. Maybe you."

Blizzard ground his teeth and cocked his head. Veins popped out of his neck. "They can try."

"See they don't."

"And you? You going home?"

Frank sniffed and looked up the creek. Dark, rock-ridden banks and canted trees. The glint of water over stone. A hundred different shades in the night, shifting like ghosts. He shook his head. "Home? No, Blizz. Not like this. This is surrender. Only home I got's on the other side of that mountain."

Blizzard reached for his arm, but Frank was already gone, vanishing into the trees. He was headed toward the double knuckle of Blair Mountain. A great fist in the night, still clenched.

BOYDEN SPARKES WATCHED THE dawn ridges pass through his window. They'd left a rear guard at the outlying station and headed deeper into the battle zone. Now the troop train was pushing through the early mists that hung heavy in the hollers and along the ridgelines, shrouding the world against the impending sun. Inside the passenger coaches, the soldiers were dozing again in their seats, their snores filling the cabin.

Sparkes had hardly slept. He was filled with the sharp air of the front, his pencil whittled sharp, ready to scratch down the story of the place, as if tracing out its heartbeat on ticker tape. He'd been watching the ridges, the early light sectoring down their faces, catching the miners' shanties perched high in the mists, clinging reckless to what looked like vertical hillsides gouged bare of trees. Some were shuffled together in ranks, their hovel roofs protruding like shelves of giant fungi or a poorer version of Mrs. Winchester's house. Many were hollow-looking, their windows dark.

He was glad he'd received the telegram from Mother Jones. His own sources had been slow to keep him apprised of the situation here, as if they hoped he'd miss the train, pass on the story. Not a direct attempt at suppression, but he had enough experience to sense the words not said, calls not made, telegrams not sent.

Now Sparkes eased up from his seat and stepped carefully down the aisle, careful not to bump any of the men awake. He felt like a headmaster letting them sleep a few more minutes. In 1916, he'd been mustered into the 1st Illinois Cavalry when Pancho Villa was raiding along the Mexican border. The U.S. Army had called up the state guards to support the American expeditionary force plunging deep into Mexico, pursuing the bandoliered revolutionary general. But the men on this train were a different breed, not guardsmen but crack infantry, many with experience overseas.

Rumor was, Sergeant Samuel Woodfill was on this train, the most deco-rated soldier of the Great War, a man who'd charged three German machine-gun emplacements during a battle in the Meuse, advancing through thick fog and mustard gas, fighting hand-to-hand despite his gassed lungs. Woodfill had been discharged as a captain after the war and reenlisted as a sergeant—and he might well be on this train, headed to Blair Mountain.

Sparkes reached the back of the car, lit a cigarette, and slipped outside, closing the door softly behind him. Leaning on the railing of the gangway, he watched the mist-laden hillsides shuttle past, blue in the dawn, pocked here or there with the paling antlers of blighted chestnut trees. Forest giants, can-kered and dying, as if they'd sucked up some poison through their roots, coal or gunpowder or hate. Sparkes had seen them dying all through their range, but they seemed sadder here, where some had grown the size of castle towers.

The early light, pale and watery, seeped farther down the hillsides, catch-ing on roads tangled with cut telegraph lines, the wires lying about in cursive scrolls. As they rolled closer to the front, Sparkes began to see traffic out there, dark shapes trundling down the roads, lumbering through the mists. Men and wagons and flivvers, rattletrap automobiles that lurched and jounced through the ruts.

Everyone was heading out of the battle zone, it seemed—an exodus of men in rumpled denim overalls, their bandannas hanging soiled from their necks like dried gouts of blood. A whole river of them, flowing opposite the slow chug of the train. Many of them walked with their arms crossed high against their chests, thumbs sticking up, or with fists thrust low in their hip pockets, shoulders slumped.

None of them, saw Sparkes, was carrying a gun. Not one.

He squinted an eye out there, aiming his mind on the point, then turned and opened the door of the next coach down the line. Here, the soldiers were waking, yawning, palming the sleep from their eyes. Sparkes walked down that aisle and then another and another, each coach full of stirring men, as if he were the one tickling them awake, feathering their noses with his passage. Finally he arrived at the caboose, where a sentry checked his press badge and granted him entry. Sparkes passed through a cabin of adjutants, nodding hel-los, and stepped out onto the rear platform of the train.

To his surprise, Blizzard was standing there among a group of young of-ficers in breeches and Sam Browne belts. The man looked like he'd been all across the mountain in the night. His jacket hung from his shoulders like an organic thing, draped with moss and leaves, and Sparkes could smell him. Soil and smoke, wet stone and rimed sweat. He must have swung up onto the caboose in the last hour, returning from his trip to the front lines.

Blizzard was watching the roads, a store-bought cigarette pinched between his fingers, surely proffered by one of the young lieutenants. There was a heavy silence on the little balcony, every man watching the emigration in the mist.

Sparkes licked his lips. "They're not armed, are they? Where are their rifles?"

The officers stiffened—hadn't they noticed?

Blizzard turned from the rail and sucked hard on the cigarette, crackling it down to a nub before pinching it hot from his lips. "Guns is hid. High up in the hills, where we can find them when need be. Stump holes, tree hollows, buried in slickers beside old Indian trails. Need ye a century to find them all."

He mashed the cigarette butt beneath his thumb, a sprinkle of ash. "We ain't about to get gunned down in the street once you boys is gone."

The officers looked at one another, said nothing. What could they do? Out on the roads, the men drifted through the mist, a trail of smoke-blue ghosts in the dawn.

CHAPTER EIGHTY-TWO

FRANK PRESSED UPWARD AGAINST the current of retreating miners. They were coming down off the mountain in droves. Frank paid them no mind as he worked his way up the steep trails, over the muddy roots and dead leaves. He hoped to find some diehards up on top of Blair, men who hadn't given up the fight.

A lot of the men seemed happy the troops had arrived, as if they'd scored some victory. They thought the soldiers would be on their side, would help ensure they got fair treatment. Frank knew that wasn't but a castle in the sky. He knew how it worked. The Army officers would do what they were ordered to do, and those orders would come down from Washington, where coal money had put plenty of men in positions of power and influence—and favors were expected in return.

Frank no longer felt angry, just dazed. He could barely remember the last time he'd slept, ate, or not been afraid. His arms and chest were crusted with blood and clay and dirt. His thighs burned, his hip smarted. Old wounds felt new. His whole body felt like it was coming apart at the seams, put through a decade of abuse in just a few days.

Still, he didn't know what to do but to keep on going. He couldn't go home. Couldn't surrender. He'd promised Crock that much. He kept thinking of the big man struggling for his last breaths, drowning in his own blood, trying to tell Frank something before he was gone. What? That question might haunt him the rest of his days.

An ache rose again in his chest. He didn't try to stop it. He let it come this time, rising all the way up into his throat. A hum, powerful enough to vibrate his teeth. He thought it would bust through his mouth, becoming a wail, but instead the sound found a rhythm, a tune. He sang no words, but they were just beneath the surface, there against the backs of his teeth.

Mine eyes have seen the glory of the coming of the Lord,
He is trampling out the vintage where the grapes of wrath are
*   stored . . .*

The same melody that passed like a soul through so many songs, jumping from one hymn to the next, animating the stories they told. From the "Battle Hymn of the Republic" to "John Brown's Body," from the Union anthem to the bawdy ballad of Davy Crockett they'd made up on the mountain. The same tune, one and all. The lines and verses of the various songs hummed in his mind, melding into words his own.

Mine eyes have seen the rising of the army of the mines,
We are trampling out the trenches where the King of Coal abides,
We have loosed the fateful lightning of ten thousand strengthened
* minds,*
The Rednecks are march-ing on!

The song came louder from his lungs, still without words, his throat swelling, booming out the melody. The sun was breaking over the mountain. Between bars, he could hear the crack of gunfire still sounding from the mountaintop.

THE TROOP TRAIN CAME chuffing into the small station at Sharples, five miles short of Blair Mountain. Sparkes leaned over the rail of the caboose. The place bustled with miners come down from the front lines, men hollow-eyed with ragged scrapes of beard. Bib overalls, red kerchiefs, woolen bedrolls. Every age of man, every color, pimpled boys and gray grandfathers walking side by side.

Sparkes watched a clutch of miners on the platform, Black men with rumpled short-brim caps cocked bold over their eyes. An enlisted man hung out of a coach window, clanging his helmet against the side to get their attention. His regulation crewcut gleamed, his hair parted as with a razor.

"Well, hidy there," he said.

Sparkes wasn't from Appalachia, but anyone could tell the corporal didn't have the accent for the words he spoke. He was having a jape. "How many boys is it kilt up thar on Blair?" he continued.

Up thar.

The miners had a slight rake in their shoulders, saw Sparkes. Their arms hung long and loose, slightly bent—a muscular slouch, like boxers in street clothes. Their leader was dark-eyed and wiry, with the tattoo of a coiled snake on his upper arm, set against a heraldic crest. Mark of the 369th Infantry, Sparkes knew. The Harlem Hellfighters.

One of the other miners spoke up. An older Black man. "They been haulin' the dead out these mountains day and night. Three hundred niney-seven kilt."

The corporal looked back at the other soldiers in the car. "Ye-all heard that? This old boy here must be their adding machine!"

Laughter rang through the troop compartment. The corporal looked back out the window, glee-faced, ready to poke more fun, but the small squad was already gone. Sparkes had watched their leader make a small jerk of his head and they'd melted away in the throng, quick as deer in a wood. The corporal stared dumbly from his window, mouth agape.

The orders came through to detrain. Sparkes grabbed his leather grip and portable typewriter, swinging one over each shoulder, and stepped down from the coach. On the platform, he saw Blizzard going from knot to knot of men, wearing his fermenting coat and wild stubble, talking up close to their ears.

"You think he's the *generalissimo* of this lot, like they say?"

Sparkes turned to find a woman with short curly hair and tortoise-rim glasses, dressed in canvas trousers and heavy boots, a leather satchel strapped over one shoulder. Her eyes were bright with intelligence. She stuck out her hand. "Mildred Morris, International News Service."

"Ah, I know your byline," said Sparkes, shaking her hand. "A pleasure." He turned to look back at Blizzard, who was still working the platform like he had a dynamo for a heart. "He's a force of nature, whatever he is. Reminds me of a stick of lit TNT, rushing around before he blows."

"I reckon we all run short of fuse one day."

"Indeed."

"I hear they're still fighting up on Blair," she said. "You want to hire a car, see if we can get up there?"

THE ROAD WAS MONSTROUS, a rutted track that might've been hacked from the mountainside with ax and dynamite. They were wedged in the rear seat of an open-topped Ford tourabout, knee to knee, their luggage strapped willy-nilly to the bent fenders and running boards. The driver was a local electrician named Ball; his wife rode shotgun, a baby clutched to her breast. The car lurched and bucked, battling every foot of road. Jolting, squeaking, hissing. The engine fumed and bubbled, threatening to overheat, and Ball rammed the car through rocky streams with gritted teeth, as if driving a mule to its death.

"Say you write for a New York City paper?"

"*New York Tribune,*" confirmed Sparkes.

Ball looked over his shoulder, not even watching the road. The baby was fast asleep, rolling back and forth in the saddle of its mother's breasts.

"Well, is it true what they say?" he asked.

"What's that?"

"Y'all got alley-gators size of submarines down there in ye sewers?"

The man grinned at them from the front seat, punching the gas, smashing the car through another rock-strewn torrent of creek water. As with Blizzard, it was tough to tell whether the man was toying with them or not.

Mildred bent toward the man, grinning. "Submarines, hell. We got gators so big they could eat U-boats whole."

Ball smiled broadly. Maybe New York people weren't so bad after all.

Now Mildred leaned toward Sparkes and lowered her voice, a conspiratorial whisper. "Says a lot you're here, you know."

"How's that?"

"The nation's foremost war correspondent, in West Virginia? I read all your dispatches from the Western Front. Never thought you'd be reporting from a battle on American soil."

Sparkes shook his head. "Me, neither, Miss Morris. Never in my life. But I felt some pressure to stay home, to keep quiet on this one, which always makes me want to come. What about you?"

Mildred gripped the back of the front seat as the car jolted over a rock. "A woman can't afford to sit on her feet in this world, can she? Plus, I got an express telegram from Mother Jones saying I ought to be here."

Sparkes smiled, thinking of the telegram still folded up in his own coat pocket. That wily old hell-raiser. He wondered how many other correspondents had received such a telegram.

Higher on Blair Mountain, the slope steepened, pitching up the nose of the car until it seemed like they were on a Coney Island roller coaster, ticking toward the first drop. Sparkes was almost relieved when the car stuck in a gluey suck of mud, rocking helplessly on its axles, and they had no choice but to dismount and continue on foot.

Sparkes and Mildred each paid Ball a dollar for the ride.

"Watch out for them gators," he said, folding the bills into his bib pocket.

Soon they were climbing, panting, crawling nearly on all fours, their hands groping for slick trunks and slimy stones, seeking purchase. The air cool and moist, as if they were climbing into the clouds.

They rounded a switchback and happened upon a brawny Black man in overalls, shirtless beneath the denim straps. He had a revolver strapped across his chest on a leather belt, a rifle cradled in one arm. His bare shoulders glistened with sweat, scratches, scars.

He held out his hand. "Name's Frank."

The feel of the man's hand startled Sparkes. Fingertips like living stone, the whole palm callused with ten thousand hours of swinging pickaxes or coal sledges. Sparkes had shaken the hands of four-star generals and war heroes, Babe Ruth and the President of the United States. Theirs seemed the hands of children compared.

"Where you people headed?" asked the big miner.

"Blair Mountain."

"This *is* Blair. They nearly blown the top off it."

"Where is the top?" asked Sparkes.

The big miner looked over his shoulder. "You sure you want to go? Fighting ain't stopped up there."

Sparkes and Mildred looked at each other. "We're sure."

SOON THEY WERE CLAWING toward the crest of the mountain, their breath roaring hot-fired through their teeth. The mist had begun to move around them, weaving and swirling, as if made from very fine thread. The sky was ghost-gray through the trees, iron-smelling, promising rain. They were toiling to match the pace of the big miner who swaggered before them, limping slightly, his shoulders rolling as he walked, his boots stomping their way up the steep trail.

He stepped over a fallen tree and looked back at them, waving his hand. "Keep on talking. Mountain's crawling with guns. Best you don't sneak up on somebody unannounced."

The correspondents nodded. When the big miner turned back around,

Sparkes cocked his head toward Mildred, keeping his eyes on the trail. "I can hardly breathe. Let alone speak."

"Amen," she said. "Our man Ball might say we need to quit taking so many big-city elevators."

Sparkes nodded. "Way the world's going, they might just build them into these mountains."

"Or cut their tops down to size," said Mildred.

"Or that."

Soon, any pretense of speech was gone. They were scrabbling toward what looked to be a crest, a steely light rifling down through trees. Sparkes had traveled through the Argonne Forest, a dark realm where every wet black tree still held bullets from the Great War, and he'd ridden through the pale moon-scape of the Mexican mountains, where men had been ground into dust for eons. The thrill of cresting the mountain rose in his belly, tinny in his blood. He pushed himself harder, faster. The thud of his heart in his ears, the crack of guns. He forgot his pain, the acid crackling in his thighs, the hot ash in his lungs. He was approaching the story, the one he'd come to write. He could sense it just ahead, waiting for him.

They passed through a last dark arcade of trees, light-shot, the ground mossy underfoot. The big miner seemed to disappear before them, thinning out, vanishing into the wall of light, and then they were there themselves, high on the mountain, flushed with glowing mist, ready to witness the sight.

The ground beneath them detonated, smashed open with gunfire, and Sparkes felt the rounds penetrate him, white bolts of fire streaking through his flesh.

CHAPTER EIGHTY-THREE

"FRIENDS!" THEY SCREAMED, HUGGING the earth. "We're un-armed!"

The firing stopped. A voice called down from a trench near the summit. "Hands up!"

Sparkes opened his eyes. His face was smashed down in the dirt. The ground shredded around him, bullet-pocked, the mist swirling. His vision was blurred, his head rocked—it felt like he'd been clubbed. He lifted a hand to the side of his head. A wet furrow in his scalp. His fingers returned bloodied, trembling, covered in shreds of skin and hair.

"I'm shot."

"*Don't touch it.*" Mildred's voice. She came belly-crawling toward him like an infantryman and took his wrist, holding his hand aside so she could inspect the wound. "Only grazed you, thank God. Though you might have to part your hair differently from now on."

Another cry from atop the slope: "Hands up or we start shooting again!"

They lifted their hands slowly from the brush, struggling to their feet. Sparkes felt a squishy sensation in his right boot and looked down. From the knee down, his trouser leg was sopped with blood. No pain yet.

He looked around. Among them were two miners who'd fallen in as they climbed, acting as escorts. Everyone daze-eyed, their hands raised in strange wonderment, as if they'd risen unexpectedly from the grave.

"I'm shot," said Sparkes. "Anyone else?"

One of the miners raised his hand slightly higher. His other hand palmed his hip. Sparkes didn't see the big miner who'd been leading them up the slope.

"Where's the one named Frank?"

No answer. He could be hiding in the tall grass or bushes. He could be dead.

Sparkes looked at the hip-shot man. "Can you walk?"

"With high-powers throwed down on me, reckon I could jump bobwire."

Sparkes looked at the rifles bristling from the trench above them. "You're in luck then, my friend."

They started up the hill. Mildred looped his arm over her shoulder, holding his wrist with one hand and grabbing the back of his belt with the other, while the second miner helped his injured comrade. Together they hobbled their way up the slope, breathing together, fast and loud. The sky was turning a darker gray, lowering, crouched heavily over the summit. The air was going cold, the sun masked in cloud. An Army bomber crawled across the sky, following the ridgeline.

At the top, they found a squad of state police lying in a fortified trench, each man squinting down the long barrel of a military rifle. Behind them, stitched across the summit, were bulwarks and slit trenches and machine-gun nests. The trees were strung with telephone wires and cartridge belts, canteens and jackets and neckties.

Their small party stood awkwardly in front of the troopers, slightly to the side. Sparkes touched his hand to his chest. "I'm Boyden Sparkes, on assignment for the *New York Tribune,* and these are my comrades, Miss Mildred Morris of—"

A belt of gunfire erupted from the trench, ripping just past them. When it ended, they stood clinging to one another. One of the troopers raised his head from his rifle, watching the shattered leaves flutter down from the shot-up trees, as if reading signs in them.

"You get one?" asked another trooper.

"Ain't for sure. Thought I saw a big'in." He cocked his chin back to Sparkes, keeping his eyes downrange. "Who'd you say you were?"

"I'm Boyden Sparkes, on assignment—"

"Listen, I don't care if you're the Great Bambino. On that side of this line, you're a Redneck."

"Isn't there a challenge you're supposed to give, a password?"

"Oh, you didn't hear it?" The trooper grinned and patted his gun. "Sounds like a Springfield rifle."

The troopers took them into custody, marching them at gunpoint just behind the defense line. They saw trenches full of the spent brass, powder-blacked and misshapen, along with soda bottles, mason jars, tobacco boxes. Magazines and lunch pails, headache powders and used matchsticks. The troopers led them to a telephone box pegged to a tree. The wires ran down the back side of the mountain, zigzagging through the woods. The lead trooper cranked the magneto and set the receiver to his ear, his elbow cocked high and sharp. "Send up the paddy wagon, just caught us another party of Reds up here on the line."

He squinted an eye at the voice on the end of the call, as if it might help him hear better. "Say what? Oh, yes, they're still alive."

The paddy wagon was a commandeered grocery truck. When it came rolling up behind the trench, they were loaded into the slat-sided bed, their wrists locked into iron manacles with chains secured to a ring in the floor.

The troopers were watching the truck pull away, seeing off their prizes, when Sparkes glimpsed a shadow rise from the tall grass behind them, sprinting back down the slope they'd just climbed. The man was hunched for speed, making for the cover of the trees, for some kind of freedom. Frank. He vanished into the woods just as the rifles cracked behind him.

CHAPTER EIGHTY-FOUR

DOC MOO STOOD IN the back of a wagon, helping load the dead from beneath the shade tree. The sky was low and close, thunderous, dark as the face of a hammer. Dead men lay all about him, staring up from the bed of the conveyance. He was covered in their blood, patched and slashed and speckled with it, as if he'd been the one to kill them.

For some of them, he knew, he would grapple with just that fear, their faces coming back to him unbidden. Men who'd teetered on the verge between worlds, bleeding out, lips blue, and he couldn't save them. Perhaps he should've clamped a different artery. Perhaps he should've administered another round of chest compressions. Or perhaps he should've given up sooner and moved on to the next patient, saving lives farther down the line.

Perhaps, perhaps, perhaps—that word, he knew, could drive a person right out of their head. His own father, who'd seen so much blood and death in their homeland's civil war, had worked himself down to the very bone. Moo sometimes wondered if the old man had been punishing himself somehow, grinding such questions down into the bed of the earth he plowed. Such memories.

As for himself, he'd done what he thought was best, over and again, operating on each successive body brought into the makeshift surgery. He'd worked until he saw strange colored orbs floating in his vision and heard spirits whistling outside the schoolhouse windows, staying awake on chewed handfuls of coffee beans and whispered repetitions of the catechism in English, Latin, Arabic. His nerves, once like woven iron, had been strung out into thin strands of wire, linked together with Hail Marys and Our Fathers and Worlds Without End.

Doc Moo set down the corpse in his arms and looked up at the dark sky. Any moment, a wire of lightning could descend like a finger of God and strike him down beside the men in this truck. He squinted up at all that angry darkness and made the sign of his faith against his chest, sending up a small prayer.

Father God, please grant safe passage to these souls, especially
those whose bodies I couldn't save. As for myself, I ask only for
the safety of my family. With me, do as you will.

He lowered his head and went back to work, hefting bodies into the bed, finding places for them to lie. He hadn't seen all of these men. Those brought down dead from the mountain had been taken straight to the shade tree, not the schoolhouse, and he still feared he could uncover Frank or Bonney or even little Musa, God forbid, caught in a crossfire or ambush. He had no way of knowing if the boy had made it safely home until he could find a working telephone.

Though most of the miners had come down off the mountain, Blair Mountain still sizzled and cracked with sporadic gunfire. It seemed the battle could erupt again at any second, the slightest spark from detonation. As if there were not coal buried in the belly of that mountain but gunpowder or dynamite. The heavens rumbled with threat, pulsing, while military planes droned beneath the iron clouds.

The next body was heavier than the rest. A bear of a man, bearded and hairy-shouldered, his thick white neck blown ragged. It took six of them to lift him into the wagon, heaving and straining, spitting through their teeth.

"Law," said one. "How'd he haul hisself up that mountain?"

"Hush your mouth," said another, crouching down beside the man as they laid him into the bed. Gently, he swiped the mess of dried blood and dirt from the man's bare chest, as if revealing the name on an old gravestone. "You know who this is?"

"Who?"

"Look it."

The other miner bent down, squinting at the tattoo inked across the man's chest. "It ain't even English."

The two men looked up at Doc Moo. "Say, Doc, you don't happen to know what this word means?"

Moo removed his glasses and cleaned them on his shirt, then bent to look, his hands braced on his knees. "I believe it's German. Means Devil Dog."

The miners' eyes widened. "This here is Davy Crockett, the Gatling gunner!"

"No," said the other. "That was just some song they made up on the mountain. Not somebody real."

The two miners leaned over the dead man. Their mouths open and eyes wide, as if looking upon some beast of myth, a brute thought to exist only in tales and ballads. A paper stuck out from the man's bib pocket, bearing a large, bloody thumbprint. One of the miners gently pulled it out.

His jaw fell open. "Doctor Moo?" He held up the bloodied paper. "It's for you."

Moo cocked his head and took the note. Indeed, his name was penciled on the outside. Slowly he unfolded the letter, written on the blank side of a leaflet.

DEAR DOCTOR MOO,
I DON'T KNOW I'LL MAKE IT OFF THIS MOUNTAIN ALIVE.
PLEASE TELL MAMA-B I LOVE HER. TELL HER I HOPE TO SEE
HER ON THE OTHER SIDE OF THE MOUNTAIN ONE DAY.

YOU ARE A GOOD MAN, DOC. SO IS YOUR BOY. BE PROUD. IF
SOMETHING HAPPENS TO ME, HE KNOWS WHERE THE DUD
BOMB IS HID. LAST I SEEN HE WAS SAFE ON THE FAR SIDE
OF THE RIVER.

—BIG FRANK

Tears rammed into the backs of Doc Moo's eyes. They came burning down his cheeks. He fell to his knees in the bed of the wagon and held the note to his chest and let it come, he let it all come crashing out.

CHAPTER EIGHTY-FIVE

THE RAIN BROKE LOOSE in a roar, a violent barrage come slapping down on the streets of Logan. Storm drains boiled, gutters foamed. Sparkes and Mildred rode with their backs against the buckboard slats of the paddy wagon, watching the town assemble itself from the storm.

Another war train had just pulled into the station and soldiers were hurrying through the city streets in slickers. Officers rode in motorcycle sidecars; sentries erected barricades. On Stratton Street, a commander in a long trench coat waved his swagger stick like a conductor, lining up two columns of infantry between the lunch counters and shoe shops and pool halls. On a cross street, a mule passed with its head down in the harness, pulling an artillery gun.

They were taken to the Aracoma Hotel, headquarters of the Logan defenders. The lobby had been transformed into a mess hall, and the hallways and anterooms were lined with rifles. Sparkes and the others were shuffled into a hotel suite that smelled rank, thick with sweat and whiskey and cigar smoke. A colonel of the state guard had his forehead on his desk, his tie hanging rumpled between his knees. He was snoring, his hand lying inside an open desk drawer. Probably a bottle there, empty. A pair of deputies dozed in armchairs behind him, their ashtrays heaped, their pistols spilling out of their coat lapels, while officers and staff came and went from an adjoining room, faces glazed with sweat and fatigue.

The infamous Sheriff Chafin sat perched on an oversized couch. The man they called the Czar. On a coffee table before him sat a whole bank of telephones—models of every size and description, some ringing, some not, their wires strung helter-skelter across the floor, into other rooms and hallways. He was shouting back and forth between a pair of receivers, his cheeks pouched red.

"How many rounds, you say? Thirty-three left? Christ, man, you're cutting it close. Another supply train's just arrived. Yes, they're loading the trucks now, the ammo will be there in fifteen minutes." He turned to the other receiver. "Yes, the Army's just arrived, they'll be taking over the defense line. Yes, I'll see they head to your sector first." He looked up. His eyes had purple creases beneath them, as if he'd been punched. He gestured with one of the phones. "Deputy, these people are bleeding on the floor, please. *Deputy*." A deputy roused himself and spread a towel for them to stand on.

Finally the sheriff hung up and checked their press credentials and identification. "What about these two?" He jutted his chin toward the two miners.

"In our employ," lied Sparkes. "Our hired guides."

The sheriff raised his eyebrows. "You got receipts to prove it?"

Sparkes opened his mouth, caught out.

Chafin smiled. "Naw, I'm just jerking your chain, Mr. Sparkes. You and Miss Morris here are free to go. Why don't y'all go get yourselves a warm meal downstairs. My deputies here will make sure you have clean rooms to rest up and write your stories. We'll send a doctor around, too, get those scrapes bandaged up."

Mildred stepped forward. "*Scrapes*, Sheriff? These men were shot by *state police*."

Before Chafin could reply, the coffee table leapt alive with ringing telephones. Three, four, five at once. The high sheriff floated his hand over the rattling machines, pouching his lip with his tongue. One of them looked like a TNT detonator, a wooden box with the receiver jingling atop its brass stand like a plunger. He snapped the receiver from its cradle, clapped his palm over the mouthpiece, and cut his purpled eyes at them.

"Y'all just remember who your friends are, huh?"

With that, they were escorted from the room.

SPARKES SAT HUNCHED OVER the typewriter in his skivvies, his wounds bandaged, his socked feet hooked in the spindles of a ladderback hotel chair. The spring-loaded keys punched their letters hard and neat across the page, forming long trains of sentences, the carriage return ringing as he reached the edge of each line. He was writing the story of his trip into coal country, into the heart of industrial violence in America.

He wrote of riding on the very first troop train into the battle zone, the cars loaded with a vanguard of handpicked infantrymen, the engine pushing three empty flatcars like barges in case of explosives or ax-felled trees or other barricades. He wrote of barefoot women and children perched high on cabin stoops, strange-faced and gaunt, watching the train pass through the dawn, raising their hands to the soldiers, and Blizzard riding on the rear platform of the caboose, watching a miner return to his family, the wife dressed in calico, the children clutching their pappy on the porch of their little house beside the tracks.

Sparkes was deep in the piece when someone hammered at his hotel door. "One moment."

He slipped into his trousers, cinching his belt as he limped toward the door. "It's Mildred."

"Coming." Sparkes turned the knob.

"Goddamn censors!" she said, marching into his room. Her face was knotted, her cheeks fired red. A bull-faced state trooper followed her into the room. He had his spine bowed back, his thumbs hooked in his gun belt.

Sparkes hadn't invited the man into the room. "Excuse me?"

The trooper shrugged, setting one hand on the butt of his revolver. "I go where she goes, buddy." He tapped his toes on the floor. "Orders is orders."

Mildred crossed her arms, flexing her muscles. "They want our stories checked by censors. I protested, and look what they gave me." She cocked her head at the slouching trooper. "A chaperone. And not just outside my door. He's been ordered to follow me into my room." The man was twice her size, built like a bullmastiff.

She lowered her voice. "I've taken to writing my piece in the lobby."

Sparkes looked at the trooper. "You must be joking."

The man shrugged again. *Orders.*

"I care more about the censors," said Mildred. "That's a clear breach of the First Amendment, and no one around here seems to give one inch of a God-damn about it."

Sparkes looked at the trooper. "Whose orders are these?"

"Come down through a colonel of the state guard."

Sparkes thought of the drunk officer in the sheriff's office, the one dozing at his desk. He shook his head. "The United States Army is in charge here now," he said. "*Federal* troops, not state. And certainly not Sheriff Chafin."

The trooper squinted out the window, his elbow cocked high from his hip.

He tapped his fingers on the butt of his gun. "Well, buddy, I hear the U.S. Army, they done set their headquarters up there in Madison. That's a town on the *other* side of Blair Mountain. We're still in charge of keeping order here."

Sparkes looked at Mildred. "Who's the censor?"

BAD TONY GAUJOT HELD the typewritten pages between his large, flat thumbs. Sparkes watched his eyes flit across the sentences, jumping from phrase to phrase, sometimes back again, rereading. His eyes were clear, sharp, hard. He'd won the Congressional Medal of Honor, knew Sparkes, as had his older brother—the only such pair in American history. He'd spent the battle on the Logan defense line, running a machine gun. His uniform blouse was draped from a coat hanger, his sleeves rolled, the muddy tattoo of a heart on his forearm.

"Cut this," he said, setting the paper on the table, striking a sentence with his thumbnail, hard enough to leave a crease: ~~Gaunt-faced women, barefooted and expressionless watched the troops pass. Some of them waved halfheartedly.~~

"No sob stuff for these Rednecks," he said.

He went on cutting and deleting, killing more lines, turning images into ghosts. People who once existed in the story were cut out. They disappeared between the lines, into the margins, like they'd never been.

Sparkes ground his teeth. He'd followed the American Expeditionary Force across Europe in the Great War, working on the bloody edge of the campaign, and never faced such a knife. The man before him seemed so sure of himself, so certain of his rightness. "No patriotic stuff from these people," he said, cutting another line.

"You seem pretty cavalier about this, Major. You're cutting awfully close with the United States Constitution right now, don't you think?"

Bad Tony raised one eye at him. "All that time on the front lines, writing your stories, and you ain't learned how it works yet. *'Tis the victor who writes the history—*"

"*And counts the dead.* Yes, I know the quote."

The old battler nodded, as if they'd come to some agreement, then cut another line from the story.

CHAPTER EIGHTY-SIX

MUSA STOOD HIGH ON the Kentucky side of the Tug Fork, watching the storm pulse over the hills on the West Virginia side of the river. He couldn't see all the way to Blair Mountain, but he knew the thunderclouds must be there, too, pummeling the place.

They'd crossed the Tug earlier that afternoon. He and Aidee, their families, and Miss Beulah. Her body. The old woman was laid out in a pale shroud in the back of the cart, trailed by a flock of mourners from the Lick Creek colony and a single dark wolfhound.

Musa was glad to have everyone safe on this side of the river, but they'd had no word from his father yet. No one knew if more bombs had been dropped on the mountain or the schoolhouse overrun. If his father were alive, wounded, imprisoned. Telephone lines remained cut, roads blocked. A state of civil war.

They were staying with family friends here on the Kentucky side of the river, but the crowded rooms were too much for Musa. He had to get out. He and Moose had come out to the cemetery near the house, a steep green lawn of stone monuments where it seemed a single false step could send you sliding down the slope, toward a long drop into the green river below.

Musa had found the grave of Sid Hatfield. The ground was still unsettled here. A raw place in the earth. Later, a great tombstone might be erected, a monument with his face or deeds etched in stone. For now, only a modest head-stone shouldered from the ground, adorned with sodden flowers and tassels.

A light rain fell slanted over the graves, beading in the wiry hair of Moose's coat. Musa knelt beside the dog, ruffing his neck. What had happened here, what was still happening beneath that coming storm—it seemed resounding, a hammer's blow to the very bell of the state, the nation, the world. Musa could feel it in his bare feet. Like history rumbling. But already he wondered how the outside world would hear it, if at all. For here was a land of steep slopes and dark hollers, heavy mists and deep mines—so many places to hide, to bury the truth.

"Not if I can help it," he told Moose, thinking of the bomb he and Big Frank had hidden.

Still, he felt a darkness closing in, the stony faces of tombstones and the dead moldering in the ground beneath them, their spirits unsung. A storm crushing the sky, flattening it close over his head. The rain coming ever closer, moving like a wall, falling harder every second.

Then a voice lifted from the edge of the graveyard.

"Musa!"

He turned to see Aidee there. She leaned rain-slick over the iron stakes of the fence, waving to him. Her face shone like a silver bell.

"Musa, look who's here!"

A hooded figure stepped to the fence beside her, clad in a dark oilskin slicker, his face shrouded from the rain. Musa rose and hurried toward them through the gusting wet, his possibles bag thumping against his ribs and the wolfhound running at his side. Then the figure removed his hood, smiling despite the storm, and Musa's heart nearly leapt from his chest.

"Papa!"

AUTHOR'S NOTE

NO SOONER HAD THE miners surrendered than the state charged more than one thousand of them with treason, insurrection, and murder. Bill Blizzard went to trial first. In a strange twist of fate, he would be tried in the same small-town courthouse where John Brown had been found guilty on similar charges for his famous raid on Harpers Ferry in 1859—that ill-fated attempt to spark an antislavery rebellion across the American South.

Old Man Brown had ridden to the gallows atop his own coffin, drawn by a pair of white horses, and left his final words scrawled on a scrap of paper for his jailer: *I John Brown am now quite <u>certain</u> that the sins of this <u>guilty land</u> will never be purged <u>away</u>, but with Blood*.

In Blizzard's case, the state prosecutor recused himself, calling the trial a farce, and the coal operators' own attorneys stepped in to lead the prosecution. Yes, the hired guns of the Coal Operators Association would try a man for treason against the state and bill that state more than $100,000 for the privilege—such was the law in that time and place.

Blizzard was acquitted after the defense unveiled their secret weapon, an unexploded bomb dropped on the marchers. It was dismantled on the courtroom floor to reveal a cruel payload of intended shrapnel: fifteen nuts, seven bolts, a ratchet wheel, and a bucket's worth of nails, screws, and irregular metal fragments meant to liquify human flesh. The miners cheered the verdict, carrying Blizzard through the same streets that led John Brown to the gallows, but such victories were few.

The Battle of Blair Mountain was quickly forgotten, the story cribbed, its soul cut out. The largest battle on American soil since the Civil War, buried. A million rounds fired, unheard. The coal operators hired one of the nation's foremost evangelists to preach against the Union miners, Billy Sunday, who called them "human lice," while industry-funded politicians and newspapermen denounced them in the press. Soon, few outside of Appalachia had even heard of Blair Mountain.

Mother Jones's heartbreak nearly killed her. Her rheumatism flared up, vicious as a fiend, and over the intervening years, the black-dog blues came to sink their teeth into her heart again and again. Still, she lived until 1930, passing away just months after her one hundredth birthday celebration (though some sources say she was but ninety-three).

In 1933, newly elected President Franklin D. Roosevelt signed the National Industrial Recovery Act into law, which guaranteed the right of American workers to join labor unions of their choosing. It was part of his famous New Deal legislation, aimed to bring the United States out of the Great Depression.

Though Mother Jones didn't live to see this victory, Bill Blizzard was one of the first UMW leaders sent back into the Tug Valley, where he drove from town to town in an old Ford jalopy, announcing the news on a loudspeaker. He was welcomed as a hero, given gasoline and biscuits and more names on his rosters than he'd ever dreamed. The Tug Valley was organized.

The battle lost on Blair Mountain had been won in Washington. Thug rule in Appalachia was a dead beast walking, doomed. And yet the thunder of the battle can still be heard today. If you stand still and listen, truly listen, you can hear it echoing in our streets and valleys, here and abroad.

If this book were a body, it would be a skeleton of historical fact fleshed with imagination (fiction). I have endeavored to remain true to the historical record wherever I could—and many of the most pointed, telling, and outrageous scenarios are grounded in witness testimony, newspaper accounts, court transcripts, or the work of historians. That said, many of those very accounts are puzzling, factually problematic, or downright contradictory. I believe it's the fictioneer's work to cast the light of imagination into such shadowy spaces, to bring them alive, and this I have endeavored to do.

Doctor Domit Muhanna is inspired by my own great-grandfather, Doctor Domit Simon Sphire, a farmer's son who emigrated to the United States from Mount Lebanon in 1889, at the age of fourteen, alone but for a priest as chaperone. He graduated from the University of Kentucky School of Medicine, eloped with Buddeea Muhanna of Deir al-Ahmar, and became a well-respected physician and medical examiner in rural Kentucky. My maternal grandmother, Amelia Sphire Smart, was the fourth of six children, five daughters and one son—the "baby," Mosa. My great-grandfather and I share the same birthday, and I've always felt a special connection with him because of that—especially because my grandmother liked to remind me of the fact.

Big Frank Hugham is inspired by two men: Dan "Few Clothes Johnson" Chain, a prominent labor organizer with fists like "picnic hams," who was a member of the Dirty Eleven commando force during the Paint Creek Mine War of 1912, and Frank Ingham, a veteran Mingo miner and UMWA member who was beaten, jailed, and evicted on multiple occasions for his Union membership and sympathies. Ingham's wrongful arrest and attempted murder in Welch runs particularly close to the scenes portrayed in the book.

I am heavily indebted to my friend and freelance editor, Jason Frye—a native son of Logan County, West Virginia—for his stories, encouragement, and sharp-eyed editing—and also to the directors of the West Virginia Mine Wars Museum for providing invaluable recommendations during my journeys to the historical sites described in this book—some of which remained at risk of mountaintop removal mining.

I've included a bibliography to recognize the most enlightening and helpful books that accompanied me on this journey, and more information on the "Second Battle of Blair Mountain" to protect and preserve this historic battlefield.

I am grateful to all of the authors who've delved into this subject, and most of all, to all those who've stood up to the injustice they saw in their world—often to their own ruin.

Today, I like to imagine Mother Jones at her one hundredth birthday celebration, standing at the top of the stairs, ready to descend among her friends and guests—many of whom she knew she'd be seeing for the final time. I see her holding the balustrade in her gnarled hand and closing her eyes, praying that these stories would find new breath in years to come, rising among those who need to hear them most.

THE TERM "REDNECK"

To quote the West Virginia Mine Wars Museum: "Although the term 'redneck' predates the Mine Wars era, this period is often understood as the birth of the term as slang in America. It was originally used in the popular media to denigrate an Appalachian working class uprising as backward, uneducated, and dangerous, and the stereotype and negative use of the term persists today."

ACKNOWLEDGMENTS

TO AJ, WHO MAKES my heart go boom, thank you for your love and faith, especially during the darker moments of my journey with this book.

To my mom and my sister, who are always ready to lend a listening ear or keen eye. I'm damn lucky to have such a tight-knit family.

To my old man. Thank you for the man you were, for what you taught me before you left, and for your words and whispers that remain with me, showing me the way.

To Jason Frye, who is my confidante, collaborator, freelance editor, and most of all, my friend. I'm so damn grateful we found each other in the old office/insane asylum. This one is for you.

To my editor, George Witte, for the many years of support, wisdom, direction, care, guidance, and mentorship. I think our relationship is rare in publishing these days, and I'm incredibly grateful for it.

To Jess Zimmerman and my entire team at St. Martin's. You bring my work to light, and I'm so damn appreciative for everything you do. You rock.

To my agent, Julie Stevenson, for your wise insights and strong encouragement, for believing in and fighting for my work. I'm so happy to have you in my corner.

To Shaun Slifer, Kenzie New-Walker, and everyone at the West Virginia Mine Wars Museum, whose direct, hands-on work underpins much of this story—thank you for welcoming this book with such open arms. Everyone please go visit them in Matewan!

To St. Martin's art director Jonathan Bush, who created this incredible cover—it felt like a rare bit of destiny to learn that you also designed the museum's journal, *In These Hills*.

To Leena Dbouk, who was kind enough to help me with Arabic language and dialect questions. "There are those who give with joy, and that joy is their reward." —Khalil Gibran

To Ann Teaff, for all of her research into the family history, both at home and in Lebanon.

To the good people at *The Bitter Southerner*, who published the short story that inspired this book. You sing the song for a better South, and I'm proud to lift my voice with yours.

To all the booksellers across the country who put my work in the hands of readers. Getting to know y'all has been the unexpected treasure of this journey.

To my friends at Starland Yard, PERC, and Foxy, who help me stay well-caffeinated and hydrated while I work. Your daily smiles mean more to me than you know.

Last of all, to Heilan, Pumpkin, and Archer—my furry office mates, research assistants, and fellow nap-takers. May your water bowls always be full, and the squirrels just beyond your reach.

QUOTE CITATIONS

An inexhaustive list of sources for real quotes or significant phrases from contemporary publications, eyewitness testimony, or the work of historians. I believe some of these words are that much more powerful in light of the fact that they were gleaned from the historical record.

Page 10: "one hundred [more] men to hell": Shogan, 106; testimony of Toney Webb, transcripts of Sid Hatfield's murder trial

Page 40: "down the road apiece": *New Republic*, Sept. 21, 1921, 87

Page 89: the "better people" of Mingo County: Savage, loc. 1176; *NYT*, May 19–20, 1921

Page 137: "We have gathered here today . . . even the heavens weep": Mooney, 89; Shogan, 161

Page 150: "I request that you abandon your cause . . . from the state of West Virginia": Gorn, 272

Page 183: "Whereas, the governor of the State of West Virginia": Proclamation 1606, Warren G. Harding

Page 217: "ocean with a broom": West Virginia Coal Fields Senate Hearing, 972

Page 244: "It is believed that the withdrawal of the invaders . . . bloodshed": Shogan, 200; *NYT*, Sept. 3, 1921

Page 287: "their adding machine": Savage, loc. 2628; *NY Tribune*, Sept. 4, 1921

Page 300: "Gaunt-faced women . . . half-heartedly": Savage, loc. 2723; *Roanoke Times*, Sept. 9, 1921

Page 300: "No sob stuff": Savage, loc. 2724; *Roanoke Times*, Sept. 9, 1921

Page 303: "human lice": Shogan, 218; *New York Journal*, April 15, 1922

BIBLIOGRAPHY

When Miners March, William C. Blizzard, PM Press, 2010

Gun Thugs, Rednecks, and Radicals, David Alan Corbin, PM Press, 2011

Mother Jones: The Most Dangerous Woman in America, Elliot J. Gorn, Hill and Wang, 2001

Mixed Up in the Coal Camp: Interethnic, Family, and Community Exchanges in Matewan During the West Virginia Mine Wars, 1900–1922, Lela Dawn Gourley, Old Dominion University, 2019

The Devil Is Here in These Hills: West Virginia's Coal Miners and Their Battle for Freedom, James Green, Atlantic Monthly Press, 2015

Autobiography of Mother Jones, Mary Harris Jones, Dover Publications, 2004

The Speeches and Writings of Mother Jones, Mary Harris Jones, University of Pittsburgh Press, 1988

The Road to Blair Mountain: Saving a Mine Wars Battlefield from King Coal, Charles B. Keeney, West Virginia University Press, 2021

Struggle in the Coal Fields: The Autobiography of Fred Mooney, Fred Mooney, West Virginia University Library, 1967

They Say in Harlan County: An Oral History, Alessandro Portelli, Oxford University Press, 2011

Thunder in the Mountains: The West Virginia Mine War, 1920–21, Lon Savage, University of Pittsburgh Press, 1990

The Battle of Blair Mountain: The Story of America's Largest Labor Uprising, Robert Shogan, Basic Books, 2004

African American Workers and the Appalachian Coal Industry, Joe William Trotter Jr., West Virginia University Press, 2022